I0670374

DELPHI

THE ICHOR SERIES
BOOK THREE

TRISH D. W.

Delphi

Copyright © 2023 by Trish D.W

Editing by Anne Dehler

Cover Design by Fantastical Ink

Interior Design by Brady Moller

trishdw.com

ISBN: 979-8-9866431-3-7

TRIGGER WARNING

This story contains mature topics that may trigger some readers, and can be inappropriate for a younger audience. These triggers include: discussions about mental health (i.e. grief, depression, PTSD), self-harm ideations, gore, conversations about pregnant women and children's deaths, and adultery.

Dedicated To: My high school Latin teacher. Thank you for teaching me about the gods' complexities. Your lessons were one of the many pieces of this story's puzzle.

THE PROPHECY

On the eighty-eighth night of the
eighty-eighth year
When crimson shifts to gold,
A prophecy will unfold.
From the ashes of time,
Eight figures will rise.

Eight, the sacred number of immortality,
Seals the destiny of a seer and a savior,
A heart and a hammer,
A singer and a seeker,
And a hero and a huntress.

A river of black will cease to exist,
Unless the one with sight sees through the mist.
A world of hatred and oaths will prevail,
Unless the oracle can see the truth and can
derail.

The ultimate fate is decided when the heart
*   twice fails,*
And from the savior, a terrible scream will wail.
The sound will echo forevermore,
And from the scream, spawns a war.

Hatred and Sight,
Oh, how they will fight.
The winner is untold,
But one thing is known.

Whichever side has the hammer which swings,
The hero who knows he must bleed,
The muse who no longer sings,
The seer, who sees the future with great speed,
The huntress who clips the monster's life strings,
The heart whose life will cede.
The savior with death she brings,
The seeker with life he leads,
Will be gifted the role of eternal queens or kings.

The world will crumble like Pompeii,
But the seeker will guide fallen friends away.
To safety, the seeker will find the ashes he will
*   revive.*
The world will be unlike any other and will eter-
*   nally thrive.*

Unless the hatred wins,
Then the seeker and the seer, the hero and the
*   hammer will surely die.*

PROLOGUE

SAFFRON

It has been eighty-eight years since I ended the second Titanomachy War, and became a goddess of deliverance, bones, and humanity. In those years, I have watched both incredible and devastating occurrences.

The first year as a goddess was a blur of climbing achievements, where I aided in stabilizing a world in ruins for five hundred years. I stood beside Hattie, Diam, Zig, and millions of humans, and we rebuilt the world torn down by the gods. The prisons around the world were decimated, leaving behind only rubble. Where death tainted our world, we created life as jobs, buildings, houses, and stability grew like seeds in the ground.

In the second year as a goddess, I officiated Diam's and Hattie's marriage. Zig couldn't stop crying as he sat in the pews beside Hermes. He wailed into Hermes's arms as Diam promised to always love Hattie a little more than the day before, and Hattie promised him a blossoming life together.

In my third and fourth year, I made two life-altering decisions.

One, I created a building for the gods when they visited earth. Each floor was designated to honor a different Olympian. The top floor was mine. From sunrise to sunset, I worked in this building with Hattie as my assistant, and I devised solutions to the world's problems. Poverty-stricken towns did not suffer for long. Diseases found quick cures. Justice was swiftly exacted.

Second, I started a relationship with Hermes. We went on dates, which were nothing like the fruit, and they were incredible. As Hermes and I discovered who we were together, without the barriers of prophecies and lies, Hattie's belly was swollen with two babies. Both were born back-to-back. Diam and she named their first daughter Panda. Their second daughter was Tulip, like the deceased Panda's favorite flowers.

Within ten years as a goddess, Hattie and Diam had three children—Panda, Tulip, and Jakob—and I was married to Hermes. Zig dated a woman named Darcy, and Zig would come over to Hermes and my house every Thursday night for dinner and gossip. When Hattie could get away from the house, she joined Zig and me. The world was booming with business and hope, and I was happy. Peace, once an unreachable dream, was in the palm of my hand.

The first decade as a goddess was my favorite.

I cherished those ten years. Even when Diam's hair speckled with gray, and Zig could only drink two glasses of wine because his doctor was concerned about his heart. Mostly, I ignored the pain Hattie felt in her knees and the wrinkles that formed on her forehead. I chose obliviousness to the signs that my friends were growing older, while I stayed vibrant and young, because I was so happy.

Then, fifteen years after I became a goddess, I found Zig dead in his home.

He was sprawled on his living room rug. His eyes were open but stared at nothing. Hermes stood over Zig's body, and he gave me the saddest expression while shaking his head and telling me the truth I didn't want to hear. My friend, who I laughed with and loved too much for words, was gone. He wouldn't smile again or tell me a ridiculous joke. He was dead.

I ignored my husband, not wanting to believe it. Instead, I stared at Zig's corpse and his hand, which rested on top of his heart. I'm an all-powerful goddess, and no matter how many times Hermes told me I couldn't save Zig, I wanted to try. I put his head on my lap, and I tried to force his heart to beat again. To exist a little while longer.

I failed Zig.

There was nothing I could do as Hermes whisked Zig's soul to the Underworld. I waited for Hattie and Diam with Zig's body, and I didn't cry until the funeral because I was fearful of my tears. Because I knew, as Zig's corpse lowered to the ground, that he was only the first in a long line of deaths I didn't want to face.

That day was the moment I lost a little of my happiness, like a jar spilled over. Zig took over Charon's long-vacated position as ferryman in the Underworld, but he was still dead. Gone prematurely from a world he barely got to live. Zig didn't get to propose to Darcy like he planned. All because his heart was too big and beat too fast.

Six years later, Panda died in a car accident.

She was only seventeen years old.

Ten years after Panda's death, Diam's doctor found a tumor on his colon. Apollo continued to come down from Mt. Olympus. He healed Diam's tumors each time they appeared, but Diam continued to get slower. Winced a lot more. Walked with a cane.

Tulip and Jakob had families of their own, and they visited us less. Hattie's hair turned completely white, with none of the familiar inky streaks. Her face fell with wrinkles. Our nights filled with laughter and wine turned into mid-afternoon tea. Jakob moved halfway across the world to a country in the Eastern hemisphere, and Tulip had one daughter of her own with her husband.

Diam died at seventy years old, which was barely a blink of an eye for me. He collapsed onto the floor and never stood back up. Thanatos told me Diam had a brain aneurysm on the same day he was supposed to die from colon cancer. The same cancer Apollo kept healing.

"That's the thing with death," Thanatos said to me that night when I cried for my friend. "It's unavoidable. You can be the most powerful immortal in existence, but you cannot stop death when it wants a soul. There was nothing you could've done, Saffron."

But I didn't believe him.

And that jar of happiness tilted again, spilling out some of what lay inside.

Hattie was getting old, and at eighty-one, she moved in with Hermes and me. She was ninety years old when we found out that Tulip's husband died of a stroke, and Tulip now raised her teenage daughter on her own. But on the day of the funeral, Hattie asked Tulip where her husband was. Almost all my happiness tipped over because we were at his funeral.

4

She couldn't remember.

Apollo told me Hattie had dementia, and I stopped everything in my life to help my friend. Aphrodite and Hermes took over the duties at Olympus Industries. Hermes and I had brought Tulip and her daughter, Jasmine, to live with us. Hermes raised Jasmine with Tulip while I nursed Hattie's failing body and mind day-by-day.

My husband and I stopped talking during this time. We lived two separate lives, but neither of us cared. He had his time with Jasmine and Tulip, raising the young girl like she was the daughter he always wanted to have with me. I had my waning minutes with Hattie. We should've cared that we didn't want to spend time with each other, but we didn't. I wanted my friendship, and he wanted a semblance of family.

Hattie died at ninety-eight years old, and seven days later, Tulip died from a heart attack.

Hermes and I had Jasmine, who was rosy-cheeked and pregnant, but all my happiness tipped over. The jar was emptied. After decades as a goddess, I realized I hated my immortality because I had to watch everybody I love die. I wish I could die, too.

I stopped smiling after Hattie died, which was twenty years ago.

A switch turned off in my head when Hattie left the world of the living, and I changed. When Jasmine started abusing drugs, I didn't notice until she left her five-year-old daughter, Jamila, on my doorstep and never returned. Hermes and I raised Jamila, and while there was love when I became her mother, I never smiled.

For twenty years, I have not smiled.

Not even once.

I stare out the window in my office at Olympus Industries, and I gaze at the world I created with my friends who died so long ago. Buildings are tall enough to reach Mt. Olympus, and from where I stand, I can see family-owned businesses flourishing and schools letting kids out for the day. The world we created from the debris of servitude is glorious, but I cannot be happy at the sight any longer. I should've died already; I wish I had died already.

Three knocks turn my attention away from the ever-changing world.

Jamila stands in the doorway, looking so much like Hattie that sometimes the sight of her hurts. Jamila's skin is darker than Hattie's, a dark shade of brown identical to her biological parents. Her hair is a beautiful curly mane of black and brown ringlets, contradicting Hattie's pin straight, inky locks. Yet Jamila's face is so much like Hattie's. Round cheeks, narrowed eyes, and a sneaky grin.

"Hi, Mom," Jamila says.

"Is it time for our lunch break already?" I ask Jamila, who is more than just my adopted daughter; she's my assistant, too.

Just like Hattie was when this building first opened.

"Sadly, no. You have a visitor."

"What kind of visitor?" I ask quizzically. "No other god is in the building."

"There's one god in the building," Jamila says, amending my previous statement.

"Who?"

Jamila doesn't need to answer my question because I can hear the goddess's heels exuberantly clicking against the floor. I glare at Jamila, who holds her hands up in mocked innocence. Aphrodite's hot pink heeled stilettos come into view before her consistently changing form pushes past Jamila. She strolls into my office, ignoring the annoyance Jamila and I share in our narrowed scowl.

Staring at Aphrodite is like a rotating disc of people. Every second, she transforms into a gorgeous new person. No face is identical to one another. They all vary in color, sizes, and nuances.

"Stick to one look, Aphrodite," I state. "You're giving me a headache."

"I see you're just as grumpy as you were the last time I was here."

Aphrodite listens, though.

She settles on her newest favorite form, one she adopted a few months ago. Endlessly long legs, smooth olive complexion, and down-turned brown eyes partially covered by thick black bangs. This form has the poutiest lips possible. Her thin-bridged button nose has a pink septum piercing, and her left arm is covered in tattoos of flower petals. Pink roses and red anemone brandish her flesh as two symbolic flowers wrap around her forearm and wrists like inked jewelry.

Aphrodite calls this form her *modern look*.

She grins at me. "I have delightful news."

"I doubt it." My attention shifts from Aphrodite to Jamila, who shrinks in the doorway. "Do you want to go to the gyro place down the street and pick us up some lunch?"

Jamila runs out of the room before Aphrodite can spare her another glance. Since childhood, Jamila has feared Aphrodite. She can face the gods of death and fear, but in the company of love, Jamila flees. Perhaps it is because Jamila is a rare beauty, and she fears the love Aphrodite could give her. Or, it is a secret I do not know about my daughter that incites this hesitance in Aphrodite's company.

The moment the door closes behind Jamila, Aphrodite rushes towards me. She slams two perfectly manicured hands down on my desk. The pink glitter shines under my desk lamp, and she leans in until we are face-to-face.

I frown. "I can smell your coffee-breath. Take a few steps back."

"You're no fun." Aphrodite pouts, but listens. She takes two steps back as if remembering why she's in my office, and her grin returns. "I found her," she announces.

"Found who?"

"Apollo's soulmate. I do not know how we missed her. She lives here in our city."

The words suck the air out of my lungs.

Two days after Hattie's funeral, Aphrodite gifted me a distraction the best way she knows how. Aphrodite enlisted my help to find Apollo's soulmate because she thought it would give me joy. She didn't need my help; I knew that then and I know this now. Aphrodite wanted me to get out of bed and to be giddy again. Love gives Aphrodite happiness, and she thought it'd give me some happiness too.

But my jar was empty when Hattie died, and no amount of searching for my friend's soulmate was going to change this indisputable fact.

Still, I helped Aphrodite.

Twenty years ago, Aphrodite was convinced that Apollo's soulmate would be alive right now. After eons of heartache and death, Apollo deserved his great love. His third love, who was created for him just as he was created for them. For the past twenty years, we hunted for Apollo's soulmate. Met with men and women who we thought could be Apollo's future, but we failed each time. We've scoured the world, ventured across countries and oceans, but we've never found them.

Five times, we've hunted the world for Apollo's third love and haven't found them.

How did Aphrodite find her after so many years?

This isn't the question I ask aloud, though; instead, I inquire. "Is she good for him? He needs somebody who is good."

"Don't you know, Saffron?" Aphrodite says with a blend of giddiness and mischievousness. "All the best romances have a bit of chaos."

ONE

HERMES

As the clock tower in the Underworld chimed midnight, starting a new year, a woman with hair like wheat emerged from the River Lethe. She was no older than twenty when she died. She swam through the River Lethe for thousands of years and forgot her former life. Until the clock chimed a new year. Then, this tiny woman rose with fear widening her doe-shaped eyes.

And from her lips, she screamed.

The river's water lapped at her waist, and a shapeless, gray tunic clung to her shivering flesh. She was dead, a wanderer in a river of forgetfulness, but she stared at me like she was about to die for the first time. Fear laid bare on her face as she screamed and screamed and screamed the same haunting words.

"It's time!"

"It's time!"

"It's time!"

January first is supposed to be a day of excitement, the beginning of a new year, but as I stood between Hypnos and Thanatos, I only felt dread. We moved towards the woman, who bellowed these two words. When one of us, Hypnos, touched her shoulder, she silenced.

The woman no longer spoke in screams.

Instead, she told me a prophecy.

It was a prophecy about the eighty-eighth year after Saffron became a goddess. Of hatred and an oracle fighting a gruesome battle. Of death and an eternal queen. The woman's voice trembled with each word she uttered to Hypnos, but once she finished her story, her eyes wandered away from him. His hand still touched her shoulder, but her gaze locked on something else.

Someone else.

Fearfully, the wheat-haired woman whispered. "It's time."

We followed her gaze and found Styx.

Half her body was above her river, elbows rested calmly on the riverbank. With her chin nestled in her palms, the face of true evil stared back at me. The wheat-haired female screamed again in the company of Styx, the source of her terror. She yanked her shoulder out of Hypnos's grasp and willingly swam back into the River Lethe. Hiding in oblivion, rather than facing Styx.

Styx smiled at me.

I have lived for eons, yet nothing has terrified me more than Styx's elation, or the words that followed that eerie smile. "Tell your wife I'd like to see her as soon as possible." She hummed at Thanatos. "Happy New Year, Death. You and I are going to become well acquainted this year."

She slithered back into her river, but I knew as the clock

chimed midnight that Styx would not hide in her river for long.

Eighty days ago, the new year began. The eighty-eighth year since Saffron became a goddess. In eight days, a war surrounding Styx will begin unless Saffron stays away from the Underworld. Unless we find the oracle first and stop the prophecy from ever beginning.

I will not pretend I've been a great husband. I am a god riddled with errors, but I will protect Saffron. From today until my very last, I will do everything in my power to ensure Saffron never enters the Underworld until this year is over. That she never sees Styx on the eighty-eighth day of the eighty-eighth year and unknowingly starts a war that will end with an eternal crown on Styx's head.

Eighty days ago, the new year began, and Hecate suggested secrecy. She advised us all to hide the truth, to protect Saffron from sacrificing herself to Styx's plans. All the gods and goddesses in the Underworld agreed. Zig agreed, too. Hades, Persephone, Thanatos, Hypnos, Hecate, and I will stop Styx before anybody else discovers the prophecy. We will ensure Styx does not steal the throne Zeus sits on. For eighty days, we hunted down anybody who could be on Styx's side. At the sake of my marriage, I've lied to Saffron every day for eighty days for her protection.

But I fear, as the day of the prophecy inches closer, that all our efforts will be for naught.

That Styx is twenty steps ahead, readying her head for the crown.

TWO

HARTIKA "HART" SOMMERS

There is no spontaneity in dating your high school sweetheart, much less wearing his ring on your finger. In a world where humans are free to roam wherever they desire, I have entombed myself in a mediocre life of predictability and depravity. I have placed myself in a custom-made prison, where I hold the key but do not escape.

For as long as I can remember, all I've ever wanted in life is paradoxical to a normal one; or worse, a predictable one. Since I was a child, sitting on my father's lap as he spun stories of the past, I've wanted adventure. To be the next person to slay a creature like a Nemean Lion, or to be the bride of a brooding god from the Underworld. I wanted a life that surpassed the mundane ordinance of my current predicament.

And yet, instead of venturing out of the small town that birthed me, I keep myself imprisoned.

When I was fourteen years old, I met my fiancé in our science class. He was a little cocky, but he was cute, and he made me laugh. Other than my family, Lowell Black was the only person in my life I loved. We were best friends in middle school, and when he asked me out freshman year of high school, the answer was an easy yes.

He sealed my fate with his confidence and his eyes, which were the richest shade of brown with one black freckle in the left iris. I let him tighten the cuffs of my restraints after my family died when I was seventeen years old and moved in with him. My prison was secured when he asked me to marry him on my eighteenth birthday, and I said yes because I was too afraid to lose the only person left in my life.

Even though I knew he was cheating on me with at least two women, I said yes because I loved his dependability and friendship more than the possibility of love.

Six years ago, I let him kill the adventurous side of me the moment he slid the engagement ring on my finger. I allowed him to subdue me. He never told me to, but because of our engagement, I turned down an art job on the other side of the country. I let him turn me into an unhappy housekeeper in our apartment, which nobody entered. My dream job was to paint, but all I painted was my face with too much makeup and a convincing lie. I wore a smile that masked the unhappiness, dragging down my aspirations for the continuance of life.

Every morning for the past six years, I repeat my daily cycle.

Each morning as I brush my teeth, I ponder leaving Lowell, but dash down the thought as soon as it enters my mind. I could find the man I love, but I accept that appreciating Lowell's company is good enough. Those two words, *good enough*, echo in my head each morning as a mantra to stay with Lowell.

Instead of slaying a monster, I take a shower. Rather than drawing for the elite on the other side of town, I spend almost two hours turning my face into a work of art only Lowell sees. Then, instead of living the life I yearn for, I clean the apartment in a dress Lowell likes; today, the dress is yellow and adorned in daisies.

Around three every afternoon, I spend hours slaving upon the stove to create a magnificent dinner. I cook and hope he gifts me with a rare smile and genuine appreciation, but that never happens. When Lowell walks through the apartment door at six at night, he kisses my cheek before taking a seat at the dining table. I ignore the scent of another woman's perfume on his collar.

I listen to him talk about his day as I nibble on the food I spent hours cooking, and I try not to cry as I realize how pathetic my life has become. Dinners are always the time of day when sorrowfulness threatens to strangle me because Lowell is on autopilot around me. My mantra of *good enough* is the smallest whisper during dinner time, today and every day.

Lowell doesn't notice my sadness. He never notices my melancholy state, or he ignores it. I'm not sure which. He continues to talk about his day, never wondering why I do not respond. He explains what he and his secretary did at work, as if I do not know he is cheating on me with her. And his hair stylist, our next-door neighbor, and whoever he finds at the bar he frequents every Friday night.

I do not talk at dinner, but he does not care. Nowadays, I barely speak. My world is quieted because my thoughts are always too loud. Lowell doesn't attempt substantial conversation, not today or any other day.

He is perfectly content with me being a shell of a woman. A robot, who will play the part of the stereotypical wife. A beautiful mute, who will remain closed-lipped about his extracurricular activities. I am most perfect when I smile, force myself to say I love him instead of the truth, and hear him lie back to me.

"Do you want help with the dishes?" He asks, just like he asks every day.

"Sure," I respond.

I wash the dishes, pass them to him, and he dries them and places them in the cupboard. Our routine is seamless, but it's empty of genuine passion. We do not talk when we do the dishes, not like we used to as children growing up. I glance at him every few seconds, and he smiles at me every so often, but that's it. No conversations, no happiness in each other's company; we are nothing.

My solace is once he goes into his bedroom, promising me a wedding that neither of us really wants, and I go to my separate room.

We have been together since we were in middle school, and yet our bedrooms have always been juxtaposed. There is never temptation to venture into the other room. Except for the once-a-month trip Lowell takes to my bedroom. The endeavor lasts less than fifteen rushed minutes. We are together out of mutual obligation, and we prefer separate bedrooms.

Once I am away from Lowell, I take pounds of makeup off my face. It is after the façade falls off that I become who

I really am. The woman who Lowell snuffed out with convincing words and charming smiles. The woman I let Lowell hide because he is safer than being alone. Because he is safer than venturing out into the adventurously dangerous unknown.

Tonight, I grab my favorite pen and paper, which I hide underneath my bed, and I draw the perfect face.

I've never seen this man before, but I draw him every single night when I am free of my adulterous fiancé and my facades. Once I am free, my mind always goes towards this man. He isn't real, but my hands draw this exquisite creature like he is right in front of me. My hands design him with finite detail.

His hair is a mixture of curly and wavy, and although the texture is thick, his tresses only trickle down to his forehead. When I draw his hair, most of the locks are pushed back by gel, but this time there is something different in his mannerism.

Something animalistic.

Loose tendrils of sun kissed blonde hair fall onto his forehead, ending right above his eyebrows, and this unhinged aspect of him is entrancing. Although I am only using a black pen, I can see the color of his hair, eyes, skin, and thin lips as if he is right in front of me. Like he is modeling for me.

His eyebrows are only a shade or two darker than his hair, more of a dirty blonde than the brightness of his tresses, and they are thin. Normally, men's eyebrows are bushy like Lowell's, but this mysterious man has thin and defined eyebrows. Almost as if he is created to perfection.

His eyes are always squinted, and yet, somehow, I can still see the vibrancy of his irises. They are a sharp blue, like the clearest sky on a magnificent day. There is always an unfamiliar emotion in his eyes whenever I draw him. Some days, he is smiling with a crinkle in his eyes. Other days, there's a frown with a faraway expression on his face. Happy, sad, and neutral are the primary emotions I see on his face, but this time, there is a feral desire possessing him.

I can always tell the emotions brewing in those hypnotic blue eyes, but this time, I only see lust.

His lips are different today as well. They are normally either spread into a full grin or in a frown. His thin, yet tempting, lips are pulled into a smirk on both sides. They barely tilt upward, but that reaction shows his dimples and all the sinful ideas going on in his blonde head.

He hasn't shaved.

Normally, this mysterious man has a clean-shaven face, but today is different. Today, he has little stubbles of dirty blonde hair across his button chin and above his lips. While I like his clean-cut look, I can't help but stop drawing him as I fall into a deep, entranced spell at the sight of him with facial hair.

I fell prey to Lowell's smile many years ago, but this fictitious man has more magnitude than Lowell ever will.

When I delve into those enigmatic blue eyes, I want to find Lady Hecate and beg the witch goddess to bring this drawing to life. I'd give away my soul to have this fictitious man become my everything. Although he is a figment of my imagination, my body sizzles with the possibilities for him and me. If he could somehow be real.

"If only, if only," I croon. I tear the piece of paper out of my drawing pad and place another drawing of my fictional man in my side table drawer. Setting him upon the stacked pile of similar drawings hidden in my side desk drawer. "Until I see you again."

As my eyes flutter shut and I prepare for another predictable day, I see the man with golden tresses, and the sun in his blue eyes, staring back at me behind closed lids. Because of him, I genuinely smile for the first time today.

And then my day begins all over again.

THREE

SAFFRON

A s punishment for killing nightmares himself, I am plagued with restless slumber.

The rare moments when sleep captures me, terror emerges. I dream of ravens drenched in gilded blood, Hattie's dark eyes dimming with death, Zig's lifeless hand over his failing heart, and an empty glass chalice. The glass was once full, brimming with red and gold liquid, but the contents spilled out, staining the table the chalice sits upon.

These images flash through my mind, like a slideshow played on repeat. Sometimes, they change. I'll see Eros's arrow as it pierces Willow's flesh instead of Zig's hand on his chest; other times, it'll be the sight of Diam's body in a casket replacing the chalice. The raven and Hattie are stagnant, but the others are interchangeable. Terrifying images no amount of time can ebb away.

But the noise stays the same. Three clocks tick at different intervals. Soft crashes of river water fighting to touch the shore. Clatters of a wedding ring leaving my husband's finger and reaching the unforgiving ground. They accompany the images, forever tainting the sanctity of my slumber with grim reminders of my past and future.

There is no longer bliss in my sleep, only strife awaits me on the other side.

This morning, I wake with the moon's beam shining through the parted curtains. The sun's gilded presence won't arrive for hours, long after the desire to sleep is gone. I reach out for the right side of the bed, just as I do each fitful night, but it's too cold. Hermes should be here, but instead of feeling the warmth of his chest, my fingers graze the crumpled paper. Instead of his snores filling the room, I'm left choking on silence.

Instead of my husband, there's a gold, five-hundred-dollar Monopoly bill.

My disappointment echoes in the quiet.

Thirty or forty years ago, at the start of our fall, Hermes and I developed a quick form of communication when he must suddenly leave. Each color bill signifies his location. Pink means he's at Olympus Industries. Yellow means he's running messages all around the world. Green is the Underworld. White is when he is visiting his son, Hermaphroditus. Blue is when he's out with friends, which in the beginning always meant Dionysus. Last, gold is for Mt. Olympus.

I'd bet my immortality he is not on Mt. Olympus, despite the gold Monopoly bill between my fingers. But I do not search for him. I am not Hera, scouring the world for her husband, who doesn't want to be with her. No, I'm too tired to be like Hera, Hebe, or Hephaestus, searching for the person who lied in their marital vows.

Instead, I get up from bed and prepare for my day.

I slide on a white cotton robe and trudge down the flight of stairs towards my kitchen. Despite the Monopoly bill, I hold fragile hope I'll see my husband at the staircase, untying his winged sandals with a hurried need to join me in our bed. To wrap his arms around me and kiss me on the top of my head. Or I'll hear a door open, and he'll emerge. Hope should've died decades ago, alongside my friends, but it lingers like a disease I can't fight off.

By the time I reach the kitchen, Hermes is nowhere in sight.

He doesn't walk through the door when I make coffee, or when I wish for anything to diffuse the silence in the room. Hermes isn't here, and standing behind the gray kitchen island with my cup of coffee warming my palms, I ache for somebody to fill this void. In a house too quiet, the name I whisper echoes.

"Iris," I say.

A second passes, then an archway of colors bleeds from the ceiling onto the alabaster floor. Iris's rainbow manifests, but she is not within the greens and blues. When the magic diminishes, Hypnos and Thanatos stand on the other side of the island.

Hypnos's gray garb blends into the countertop and chromatic colors of the kitchen, but his twin brother, Thanatos, starkly exists in onyx. The lighter shades of my home are fogged by his obsidian presence.

"Good morning, Saffron." Thanatos's voice is the calm of raging storms.

"It's not morning yet," Hypnos says, glowering at his brother with fatigued disdain. "It's one thirty in the morning. I'm the god of sleep, who doesn't get any rest."

The twins mirror each other in appearances, but their personalities are rivals. Thanatos is calamity, while Hypnos is raucous destruction. They wear the same dark hair, shortly cropped to their scalp on the sides and longer in the middle. Both brothers are the same height, same build, but otherwise opposite. One has eyes dark as death, but the other wears the same silver eyes as his other brother.

As my storyteller.

Hypnos speaks to me but doesn't look in my direction. Eighty-eight years have transpired since I killed his son, Morpheus. Since I murdered his brother, Epiales. But it hasn't lessened our grief. I cannot look at Hypnos without seeing Epiales within his silver eyes and multitude of scars. In return, Hypnos cannot see me without reliving his son's murder by my hands.

There was once a time when Hypnos and I were friends. When Hypnos flirted with me, desired me, and teased me endlessly. Those moments died with Epiales and Morpheus, leaving behind only ashes scattered in the wind. I see Hypnos almost every day, but we are worse than strangers. We are ghosts in each other's eyes, ones we desperately try to ignore.

"Please tell me you have made enough coffee for me," Hypnos says.

But he doesn't wait for my answer.

He walks towards the coffee maker behind me, while my focus remains on Thanatos. He knows what I am going to ask him, but he still waits for the words. Maybe he is afflicted with the same futile hope as me. Perhaps he hopes I won't say the same sentence I've uttered every night for the past few months.

Hope is pointless.

"I want to go to the Underworld," I say this at the same time Hypnos groans. "Thank the gods there's coffee."

Thanatos sighs, dejection reaching his partially hooded face. "You know I can't take you to the Underworld."

"Why not?" I ask. "I want to see them."

Thanatos never asks who I want to see because the list is immense. I yearn for Zig's optimism, Diam's dry humor, and Hattie's comfort. I want to see Atalanta and Achilles again, who were once my guards, when I was a princess in the Underworld. My parents, Persephone and Hades, come to visit my house once a week, but I cannot go to them. A place that was once my home has been barred from me, and nobody will tell me why.

Thanatos stays silent.

I hate the silence.

"I could walk down myself," I say.

"Cerberus and your parents will block the gates," Thanatos answers.

"I'll kill you."

He shakes his head. "No, you won't. You have the power to, but not the black heart to go through with it."

I flinch at his words as my tears build.

"I hate you."

The words crack like glass. Thanatos has heard the lie so many times he doesn't react. For over three months, I have been forbidden from entering the Underworld. Secrets lay on my loved ones' tongues, never leaving, no matter how many times I ask for the truth. I'm banned from visiting the dead because something worse waits for me. A formidable, mysterious danger nobody will divulge. Even though I am the most powerful deity in the world, everybody still treats me like the same child who needed protection in the prisons.

"Just tell me why. Why can't I go to the Underworld? Why can't I see them?"

Thanatos bows his head, his face completely concealed by the shadows of his hood. "I'm sorry, Saffron."

The room is so quiet, except for Hypnos slurping his coffee. "You'll be allowed back when it's safe," Hypnos says from where he stands behind me.

"You both keep saying that."

"Go rest," Thanatos murmurs, voice too delicate. "It's not healthy to sleep as little as you do."

I close my eyes, where my nightmares always wait, and I whisper. "Get out of my house if you will not help me."

I wait ten seconds, and when I open my eyes again, they're both gone.

"I HAVE WONDERFUL NEWS!"

Aphrodite bursts into my office without warning. She's in the physical form of a tall, leggy blonde woman. She slams her manicured nails on my desk and grins from ear-to-ear.

Unamused, I take a sip of my fourth cup of coffee. "You're loud today."

"And you're unsurprisingly crabby," Aphrodite retorts.

I frown. "What is your exciting news?"

Instead of telling me, she shows me. She rounds the corner of my desk and takes both of my hands in hers, pulling me up to my feet. She guides me to my window, which overlooks the entire city, then points down at the building's entrance.

"What am I supposed to be looking at?"

Argus's car sits in front of the building, and he strolls inside as the valet peels away with his car. But it's the girl in a sundress, who trips behind him, who garners my attention. From this angle, all I can make out is a pale pink dress and long, curly black hair reaching her waist. I do not need to see more, though. Based on Aphrodite's excitement, I know exactly what her news is.

"That's Apollo's third love."

Aphrodite surprises me. She wraps her arms around me from behind, hugging me as she squeals. "Apollo's soulmate has arrived!"

FOUR

LAMB

I spin the apple stem around the pad of my thumb and pointer finger, twisting until it breaks. The mute sound is an echo across the grassy fields and high-risen trees. Only then, once the untouched apple is scathed, do I speak to the silenced wind.

"Happy sunrise, Willow."

I rest my head against the tree. Lifeless, sandy hair drops past my waist and skims the fall leaves underneath me. The sunrise is beautiful today. Willow would love it. The colors creep up from the endless trees, bursting with ever-changing leaves. It's like the sunrise begs to blend in with the fall colors, the oranges of the sky matching the foliage.

But I cannot bring myself to find comfort in the beauty; instead, my arms scatter with bumps. The air is warm despite the time of year, but I am chilled to the bone. Frigid, like we are riding through the woods in January cold.

"Something bad is about to happen, Willow," I whisper to my best friend.

She cannot hear me from her eternal home in Elysium Fields, but she's the only one I can admit my fears to. If I tell Sika, Dýnami, or Akita, fear will follow them around every corner. Cause them to find shapes in the shadows. As the rest of the huntresses slumber, their snores and mumbles filling the air, I stare at the sunrise. I peer at the array of pale colors glistening the sky like Willow's face is in the sunset. Like her presence forms the clouds and her smile makes the sun a little brighter.

"Nymphs have been disappearing. Diseases are returning and killing towns at quickened rates." I sigh. "We're searching for the nymphs right now, but I have a feeling we will not find *just the nymphs*. Something is coming for us all, Willow, and nobody else feels its frightening presence but me."

I lift the apple, but when I bite into it, there is an absence of flavor. It's like I'm eating dirt, swallowing it down like glass. The burst of juices on my tongue burns the sensitive buds, making me loathe my favorite breakfast treat.

"Maybe I think life has been too calm for too long and I'm manifesting darkness. Maybe I've grown senile in my old age, and I no longer find enjoyment in the calmness. There's been no monsters to slay, no runaway prisoners to track down. There's been peace, even when nymphs are missing and diseases are emerging. Maybe I miss the chaos, but I think it's more than that. I think the greatest danger this world has ever seen is creeping out of its hiding spot, and it's coming right towards us."

I take another bite, but soon after, the apple falls from

my fingertips. It rolls across the fallen leaves, the crisp green of the fruit contrasting with the yellow and oranges of the wild. The apple lies face down on the ground a few feet away from my crossed ankles, and if I look closely enough, I swear it's rotting from the bottom.

I wonder how much longer it'll take for the rot to reach the top, destroying everything at its core.

"I hope I'm wrong, Willow, but if I'm not." My whispered admission intermingles with Dýnami's snores and Artemis's soft, sleep-induced murmurs. "Then I fear more huntresses will die; I fear I will join you in Elysium Fields sooner than planned."

The other huntresses, now thirty of us, lay scattered around the burned out firepit. Both old and new huntresses, some with scarification marks but most without, obliviously sleep away the day before. They wear content expressions on their faces, while I could not sleep for more than an hour since we started our hunt for the missing nymphs.

Since I felt a female cackling at my back, waiting to plunge the knife.

Another breeze caresses my neck, sliding my hair off my shoulder. The warm air smells of vanilla, like the soap I once loved. The same soap Willow always stole from me, and I can no longer wear without remembering what I've lost. I must be going mad with old age because I truly think she is here in front of me. Her scent brushes across me and confirms my deadliest suspicions.

Danger is coming.

And none of us are ready for her wicked touch.

FIVE

HART SOMMERS

My eyes obediently open to the chime of my alarm clock, and with one hit, I scramble out of bed.

Just like every morning, I prepare myself for when Lowell wakes up for work. I go to the bathroom and make sure my naturally bushy eyebrows are plucked, defined, and appropriate for his eyes. I am an artist, and while I do not have the luxury of a painting career, I use my face as a canvas to create a masterpiece. My lids are speckled in gold and brown, bringing out my irises' natural hue, while my eyeliner is thick and sharp at the ends.

I dab brown lipstick upon my full, petal-shaped lips to match the eyeshadow, and I place fake eyelashes on top of my naturally full set. Lowell compliments me whenever I wear fake eyelashes, and while I hate searching for his validation, I can't stop myself. My face transforms as I pick up my primer, concealer, bronze, blush, and contour. For two hours, I perfect my face until I look airbrushed.

Unrecognizable.

I stare at myself in the reflection as I pull my hair out of the intricate braids I wove the day before. I barely watch the long, thick black tendrils fall to my waist in perfect curls. My eyes do not look away from my face covered in makeup. While it looks beautiful, and I look as perfect as possible, I hate the sight in front of me. She's a farce, the woman staring back at me in the mirror's reflection. A woman I scarcely recognize.

"It's good enough," I whisper as tears build up in my eyes. "It's good enough."

I wait until the tears subside, but never fall, and I continue my routine.

Today, I choose a pale pink sundress with straps tied together in a bow. Then, I go to the kitchen. By the time he is awake, French Toast with sliced bananas and strawberries are at his usual spot at the dining table, and he greets me with a small peck on the cheek. No electric pulses course through my veins. The kiss is reticent of a stranger rather than my fiancé.

"Good morning, babe," Lowell says as he walks towards his breakfast plate.

I say nothing, but he doesn't notice. He never notices. Instead, he eats his French toast in silence while I sip my black coffee across the table from him.

"Hey, H?" He says.

I look at those dark eyes, the ones I once fawned over, and I am bored. So terribly bored. "Yeah?" I respond.

It's the first word I have said in almost four days.

"I'm going to be home a little late today," Lowell responds. "Some work meeting or whatever. Don't worry about dinner, kay?"

Right.

I nod my head, and he nonchalantly returns to his breakfast, but we both know the truth in his words. His weekly *work meeting* with his hair stylist is tonight. The same hair stylist who left her earring in his coat pocket one day for me to find. I think she thought I would leave him when I found the earring, but she doesn't know me very well. She isn't the first, or the last, mistress I will discover.

Eventually, he leaves for work, and I continue my chores for the day. I hand-clean his dish and begin the same repetitive cycle of events that is my tedious life.

But then the phone rings.

The phone never rings. There are only two people that have the number—Lowell and his receptionist—and neither of them calls. I stare down at the phone as an unfamiliar number blinks on the screen, and I do not hesitate. Even if it is just a man calling to scam me, then at least it is something different.

I answer on the second ring.

"Hello?" I hate how hoarse my voice sounds, representative of how rare I speak, but the person on the other line doesn't notice. Or doesn't care to mention it.

Instead, the sultry male voice coos. "Good morning. Is this Hart Sommers?"

"Yes, it is," I say, with obvious confusion. "Who is this?"

"Hart Sommers," this deep voice on the other end tastes my name upon his tongue before he purrs. "This is Adonis from Olympus Industries. How are you this morning?"

I do not respond.

Instead, I laugh.

A ridiculous laugh escapes my lips for the first time in what could be months. Holy gods, I don't think I've laughed in over a year. Tears spring to my eyes from just how much I am laughing at the man on the other end of the phone, but he is eerily silent. He waits until my laughing subsides, and he is still patient until I find the ability to speak once again.

"Lowell isn't really a prankster, so who put you up to this? Was it one of his mistresses, huh? Was it Sally, or maybe Melody? Which one was it, *Adonis*?" I sneer at the last name with the greatest hint of sarcasm. "Maybe Cleo grew a funny bone overnight."

Adonis sighs. "Miss Sommers, I assure you, this is no practical joke. I am calling on the behalf of Lady Aphrodite. She heard about your artwork through Ílios Art Institute, who once offered you a job six years ago. Unless you are not the Hart Sommers I am searching for."

I am deathly silent as the most ridiculous, and naïve, part of me believes his words as truth. My art teacher in high school placed one of my paintings in her art show downtown, near the end of my senior year. The head of Ílios Art Institute purchased my art piece. He offered me a job on the spot.

Two weeks later, Lowell proposed, and I chose the safe path.

"I, um, turned down a job there six years ago," I respond, my voice wobbly.

Adonis hums on the other end. "The head of the Institute, Byron Fairchild, still has your art piece on display. Lady Aphrodite saw your painting when she was at Mr. Fairchild's household, and she was impressed with your work. She would like you to come down to Olympus Industries for a commissioned job."

I have been a mute for so long, I cannot find my next words. There is a long pause of silence between us, and I do not know how to break the quiet. I almost drop the phone a few times as sweat forms on the palms of my hands. Because of how erratically my heart beats against my chest, I swear I am having a heart attack.

"Miss Sommers?" Adonis finally inquires.

"A commissioned job? For an Olympian?"

"That is what I said," he says with light humor in his tone.

"But the job, the one Lady Aphrodite wants to offer me. You know, the commissioned one-"

Before I can put my foot in my mouth more than I already have, Adonis interrupts me. "You want to know the job's description?" he guesses.

I nod, only to remember he can't see me nodding, and I gulp out. "Yeah."

"Lady Aphrodite believes many gods are long overdue for new portraits. She would like to commission you to paint a select handful of gods and goddesses. If you accept the position, Lady Aphrodite will pay you twenty thousand per god."

I drop my phone.

"Oh, gods." I fall to the floor. On my hands and knees, I grab the phone with both hands and press it against my cheek. "You're really serious?"

"There is a car stationed outside your apartment building as we speak. If you accept her offer, then you'll enter the car in the next thirty minutes. The choice is entirely your own, Miss Sommers, but once the car is gone, so is Lady Aphrodite's offer."

I am still quiet when Adonis hangs up the phone, but once the call ends, I drop my phone to the ground again in disbelief. I do not have the strength to get up from my knees, much less the ability to breathe properly. Clutching my chest, I lay on the kitchen floor and force my airway to function.

I force myself to see this as the greatest gift. Making myself believe my scattered, yet optimistic, thoughts as truth. A truth that does not frighten me but leaves me excited for a new opportunity. Until the reality of intertwining my destiny with the gods exhilarates me.

My eyes flutter towards my bedroom. The door is ajar, and just barely, I can make out my bedside table. Inside the mahogany drawer are the sketches of the fictitious man, who has been my sole excitement in this tedious world. Now, I am given a chance to let my childhood dreams come alive. Rather than fantasies, I can create masterpieces for the *gods*.

I no longer hesitate.

I am done hesitating.

Amidst my crazed racing, I haphazardly shove all my recent drawings into my old portfolio binder, yank on a pair of worn-down tennis shoes, and run out of the house. I do not bother locking the apartment door behind me as I race down the stairs and throw open the front doors. My mind has no time to ponder how unusual I look, wearing a full face of makeup, a sundress, and ten-year-old tennis shoes splattered in paint and holes. All I can think of is the car outside my apartment building, leading me towards a life of adventure and art.

I half expect there to be no car.

A large, insecure part of me expects Lowell to be leaning against the tree outside of our building, sporting an enormous smile upon his face. I want there to be an adventure, but I picture Lowell laughing at his prank so loudly that leaves fall from the nearby tree. To watch as my hope is severed like a limb from my body.

But I see the car.

Lowell and I are not poor, but we do not live in the best part of our small town. Every inhabitant of this apartment complex either rides the bus or owns a rundown car. The car in front of me stands out with its luxuriousness. It's black, sleek, and expensive. All the windows are darkly tinted, where I cannot see the driver, but I advance towards the car with a flutter in my chest.

I am scared, yes, but more than that, there is excitement. Perhaps this is the day I finally get the life I have always dreamed of. Where I can escape the dull ordinance of my imprisoned life. A shackle I foolishly chose years ago. Today, I hope to reverse the mistakes of my younger self.

I slide into the passenger seat of the car, and when I turn to face the driver, at least a hundred different pairs of eyes stare back. His eyes blink at different times, but all of them are a dark shade of brown. His tan complexion is excessively decorated in a hundred eyes, which narrow at the sight of me.

He asks in a deep, vibrato voice. "Are you ready to go to Olympus Industries, Miss Sommers?"

"I am."

Argus, the one-hundred eyed giant, drives away from my apartment building and takes me towards my destiny within Olympus Industries.

SIX

HART SOMMERS

Except for the grocery store, I haven't left the house in three months. I sit in the back seat, the leather squeaking with the nervous tick of my hip, and I laugh. The sound is ridiculous and devoid of genuine amusement. A hyena yelping is more graceful than the noise leaving my lips, but I cannot stop myself from laughing.

About a dozen eyes on the back of Argus's neck look at me, narrowing in confused judgement.

"Sorry, I'm just really nervous," I play with my feather-shaped necklace, fidgeting with the worn-down jewelry. "It's not every day I get a call from Adonis asking me to see a goddess for a job interview. The most exciting part of my life includes drawing an imaginary blonde guy, and while that is fun, it's nothing compared to this. Well, it's *not nothing* but-"

"You're rambling again," he grunts before pulling into Olympus Industries.

There are coffee shops, restaurants, banks, and other businesses surrounding the massive building. These establishments add wealth to this street, but nothing compares to the excellence of this golden institution. The bricks, doused in the color of the gods' blood, soar as high as the clouds. Some people say the elevator within Olympus Industries leads straight towards Mt. Olympus, because not a single person can see where the tower meets the sky.

I've driven by the building a few times, but I am still in awe. Argus drives us towards the revolving doors, where earth nymphs wait as valets. Once Argus peels himself out of his seat, I scramble out of mine, hurrying so I don't lose my guide.

Argus keeps a few of his eyes on me, to make sure that I am following, but he doesn't walk with me. He is ten feet ahead of me as we venture into Olympus Industries. Once I step through the revolving doors and into the illustrious building, I gawk at everything.

I admire the statues of the Olympians, standing at over twenty feet tall beside each door, elevator, and window. The ceiling is gold, splattered with red paint in honor of Saffron, the demi-goddess who changed the world. But the most impressive aspect of the building are the Grecian paintings on the walls in between the alabaster columns. They tell the story of the epic fight between Kronos's army and the Olympians.

One painting eloquently shows Saffron levitating in the air above the Labyrinth. Ares, Hermes, Hephaestus, and Hecate stand in a circle around Circe's bones. Huntresses are illustrated with arrows flying across the maze towards Typhon, the father of monsters. I stare at the artwork with a rapt fascination.

Another art piece is of the first Titanomachy war, which took place eons ago. Long before Saffron existed. Zeus stands powerfully beside his siblings, lightning bolt raised against Kronos and the other titans. The dual paintings are directly beside each other, giving the spotlight to the two greatest godly heroes from the two deadliest wars.

Zeus and Saffron.

The strongest god and goddess.

Argus grunts, bringing my attention back to him. In a surprisingly calm tone, he says. "Lady Aphrodite and Lady Saffron will come down and retrieve you shortly. Do not leave the lobby." Argus doesn't need to say *or else*, but it's laced in the order. "Welcome to Olympus Industries."

The one-hundred eyed giant strolls out the revolving doors, but he doesn't leave. He stands guard outside of the building, his hand tightly gripping the sledgehammer fastened in the sheath around his belt. At least a dozen eyes are still on me, waiting for the moment I may misbehave.

I let out an audible gulp of fear.

I am still facing Argus as I walk backwards into the depths of the lobby. My clumsy feet disobey my desire to remain poised in a room of elegance. I tumble backwards. Argus's eyes shine with humor at my expense, and I open my mouth to let out a soundless scream. I never reach the ground and experience the grunt of pain and embarrassment.

Warm hands catch me.

With this touch, electricity captures my body, igniting my veins and enlivening me. They feel like the first true breath after decades of suffocating. Lowell has touched me before, but my body has never reacted to him. Not like this.

I have never had goosebumps the way I do now. I've never felt like I could be addicted to touch. Not until now.

The stranger helps me to my feet, and as soon as I'm oriented, I turn around to look at the man whose touch left me wanton for more. Immediately, I am absorbed in all too familiar blue, slightly squinted eyes. I see the sandy hair that is both curly and wavy, the tresses that I've drawn countless nights. I stare at the upturned nose that I have always had difficulties drawing perfectly.

"Oh my gods, it's you," I gasp.

I feel sick to my stomach. Worse, I'm scared. Terrified. Am I going crazy? Has the excitement from today left me hallucinating, or is this a sick trick a god has played on me? My imaginary man, who I've drawn every night for years, is right in front of me.

Although there is electricity with his touch, far too much to be normal, I rip myself out of his embrace. I shuffle backwards until I hit the wall behind me. My imaginary muse smiles at my reaction. It's the same gigantic grin I have admired in my drawings, which always steals my breath away and leaves me wishing he were real.

He takes a step forward. Then another. Each step he takes closer to me makes me flinch. Fear brews inside of me, and it must be clear on my face, but he continues to advance towards me. In long, languid steps, he breaks the distance between us. Steals every breath from my lungs. His hand lays upon the column nearest him. He leans forward, his face a few inches from mine.

"What is your name?"

His voice is liquid nectar, more so than even Adonis's, and that electricity returns with a vengeance. My entire body is on fire because of his question. He's my imagination, but at this moment, he feels actualized. I belong in a mental institution because when I look at him and melt under his voice; I think he's real. Not a figment of my creation, but a living male.

My eyes dart around the lobby of the building, expecting to see people gawking at me as if I have lost my sanity, but nobody is looking. A few people glance at him, nodding at him with unspoken greetings. My imaginary muse. People in this room look at him like he's real.

"Most people get excited when they meet a god for the first time," my imaginary man speaks again. "But you look terrified of me."

"You're a god?" My question comes out as a squeak.

Oh gods, I'm going to pee my pants.

"Prove there's a brain with that beauty and guess which god I am, μέλι."

I have spent months stenciling his face, memorizing every detail and curve. I've imagined vivid fantasies as I gaze into these sharp, sky-blue eyes. Finally, they are in front of me and just as tantalizing as they were in my drawings. His blonde hair I've imagined running my hands through a thousand times tempts me, but who he is beneath the beauty?

The gods no longer wear tunics everywhere they go, but their style is revered around the world. Not even the greatest celebrities in the world compare to the excellence of the gods in both appearance and fashion. Or, well, everything. Nobody compares to the gods.

He is in a black suit adorned with gold embroidery. Gilded snakes are designed around the cufflinks, the hems, and even his jacket pocket, where a handkerchief sits. It is black, just like the suit, but the handkerchief has a design of a golden sun in the middle. The symbol stands out against the black material, confirming he is real and he is a god.

"You're Apollo," I say these two words with hope I'm wrong.

Because if I have been drawing a god I never saw before, I have more to fear than my sanity. I hope he is my imagination and that I'm going crazy. I stare at the golden-haired man in front of me, waiting for him to laugh and say he isn't a god. That he isn't Apollo, god of prophecies and song.

However, when he smiles, my frown worsens.

"I am." There is a prolonged silence as I fight too many thoughts in my head. His smile falters, concern flickers across his face. "Have I done something wrong? You look like you are going to stab me."

"This was a bad idea." The words come out with my fear. Slipping out from under his arm, I stumble back a step. "I'm sorry, but I have to go."

I turn around, ready to run out of Olympus Industries, but then he touches me. Destroys my body with emotions I should not have for a god. I swirl back to him, invigorated by a face created with perfection.

"Μέλι, have I done something wrong? I didn't mean to frighten you." Concern laces his tone, forehead scrunched.

"You scare me," I whisper.

"Why?" He asks. "What have I done? Please, tell me so I won't make the same mistake twice."

His thumb slides across my forearm, the pad gliding up a blue vein on my deeply tanned skin, and the world disappears. Darkness takes control, and I am no longer in Olympus Industries. My mind zooms to the future, where he and I exist.

In this future, I see two baby girls, one with his golden blonde hair and one with my brown locks. One girl with the blonde hair has the same electric blue eyes and upturned nose as him. Meanwhile, the other girl is a replica of me. Not as tan, but everything else reflects my appearance. My lips, my cheeks, and my wide-eyed expression.

With my eyes closed, I see Apollo holding both girls, one nestled in each arm, and he is crying. But he is also smiling. He sobs in this dream as he stares at the children that I know are our daughters. The two perfect demi-gods we created with love and a promise of forever.

Apollo rips his hand off my forearm, and the future fizzles away.

The darkness ebbs away, and Apollo stares at me with a slack jaw. His face now mirrors the fear I have on mine, intermingled with disbelief. I take a step back, one hand wrapped around my forearm as he once held. We cannot speak, not yet, but we can't look away from one another, either. A future is mapped out in front of our eyes, transforming strangers into something more.

"Who are you?" Apollo asks.

But two goddesses walk towards us, stopping me from answering his question.

SEVEN

HART SOMMERS

Two goddesses, one of love and the other of bones, capture the sun's gaze. Their radiance steals the room's focus. Every person in the lobby, humans and low-level gods alike, is transfixed by the two females. Men and women stare at Aphrodite's endless legs and Saffron's prominent hips with a mixture of desire, awe, and envy. Even Argus, from his station outside of the door, has dozens of eyes hypnotically fixated on the women. Apollo is splendorous, but he does not capture eyes like Aphrodite and Saffron, the two most beautiful deities.

The lover and the savior.

Aphrodite is the taller goddess out of the two, with a short black bob surrounding her heart-shaped face. Bangs cover her forehead, longer strands slides down the expanse of her cheeks. She struts towards Apollo and me as if the floor is her runway. Amusement paints her full, indigo lips.

Aphrodite is radiating, but nobody is more captivating than the hero of humans. The goddess who I've idealized since I was a little girl hoping for more in my world. She is power. That is the best way to describe Saffron, who stands beside Aphrodite with the world heavy on her shoulders.

She is beautiful, with high risen cheekbones and a round face complimenting a full-figured, bottom-heavy physique. Yet, there is more to Saffron than her attractiveness. She is more than a pretty face. She is strength. Power clings to her flesh like a coat of armor. Aphrodite flaunts her pleasant appearance, but Saffron unintentionally steals the show of life.

"Apollo, darling!" Aphrodite's heels tap the surrounding floor until she comes to a complete stop beside Apollo. They're both the same height when she's in her heels, and Aphrodite easily lays her head on Apollo's shoulder and wraps an arm around his. That's when she focuses on me, her beauty like a cold slap on the face. "Who's your friend?"

"I-" Apollo stops, brows furrowing as realization dawns on him. "I don't know yet."

Is that disappointment on his face?

"Well?" Aphrodite inquires, solely focused on me. "Who are you?" She tilts her head, her bangs falling with the movement.

My throat is sand because Saffron, the goddess of bones, is standing right next to me. Her shoulder is a breath away from mine. Meanwhile, Apollo and Aphrodite are a foot in front of me, staring at me like I am someone important. Like this one, lowly human's name matters. My hands uncontrollably shake, and my palms sweat. No matter how many times I wipe them on my sundress, more moisture builds.

After too long of a silence, I find my voice. "I'm Hart

Sommers, and I am here for an interview with you, Lady Aphrodite."

Aphrodite glances at Saffron, a hidden secret on her smirk. Apollo follows the movement, brows furrowing more. Slowly, his eyes wander back to me. Those stunning blue eyes capturing mine and reminding me of the future we saw together. His gaze holds the question he asked me earlier; the one question I couldn't answer.

Who are you?

"How wonderful!" Aphrodite exclaims, her excitement pulling me away from Apollo and back to where she stands beside him.

Her head is no longer on his shoulder. Excitement laces her voice, and she removes her arm from Apollo's as she moves towards me. In three quick strides, her heels tapping, tapping, tapping nearer, Aphrodite has my clammy hands in hers. She squeezes them, her perfect French tipped nails a stark contract against my tanned hands.

"Gerald from Ílios Art Museum was certainly right about your beauty, Miss Sommers. You are so adorable." She spins her head back to look at Apollo and asks. "Isn't she the cutest?"

"Exquisite, indeed."

My cheeks burn upon the compliments, but I can't look up from Aphrodite and my intertwined hands. Even as eyes burn where I stand, I centralize on Aphrodite's nails, not sure if I want to blend into obscurity or bask in their attention.

"You're freaking her out," Saffron breaks the momentary silence. "Knock it off, Aphrodite."

Aphrodite takes one hand out of mine, flippantly excusing Saffron. "You're so overdramatic, Saffy."

She frowns. "Don't call me Saffy."

Apollo, silent since his compliment, stares at me. His question repetitions in my mind, asking me again and again who I am. He knows my name, but that's not his question. His eyes plead for a reason behind the moment we shared, the daughters cradled in his arms, but I have no answer. I cannot think about him, much less look at him, without wondering how I saw what I saw. Pondering who I really am.

"Where are we going for the interview, Lady Aphrodite?" I ask, ending Saffron and Aphrodite's bickering and distancing myself from a fate I'm fearful of.

Of the man I fear.

"Follow me!" Aphrodite uses her free hand to pull me away from Apollo and Saffron.

The farther we move away from him, the more intensely I feel his stare at the back of my head. The louder I hear his question, and wonder the same thing. Aphrodite leads me into the elevator, pressing level five.

As the doors close, I spare a glance at him. The man, who I once thought was a figment of my imagination, but now I know, is something more grand. Saffron is no longer in the lobby. It's just Apollo, and he's focused on me. His mouth is slackened in shock, and I can hear that damning question like it's being screamed into my ear.

Who are you?

Just as the doors ding shut, I mouth, *I don't know.*

EIGHT

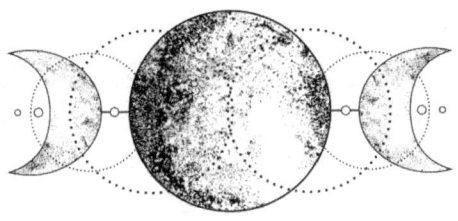

HECATE

J ust as prophesied, on the eighty-eighth year after
Saffron became a goddess, I found the oracle. The
first living oracle in two thousand years has been
born, waiting for destiny to pluck her from her
mundane life. She was difficult to find, but today I finally
found one key to Styx's reign.

I am one step closer to having my soulmate, Mastiff,
back. To see his crooked smile, hear his scratchy voice
calling to me, and to feel his lips against mine. I am a
villain. Each act I make in Styx's name is traitorous to
everybody else I love, but I do not regret my actions. I am a
villain for Mastiff because the world didn't let me have him
when I was good.

The benevolent gods fail because they put duty before
happiness, and I am done being kind for the sake of others.
I am a villain because I deserve my happiness over anybody
else's.

That's why I walk down into the Underworld on the

eighty-eighth year, after Saffron became a goddess. The year the prophecy begins. The year of death as the worst of all wars begins. I pet one of Cerberus's heads as he obliviously lets me go through the gates of the Underworld, and I stride towards beginning this bloodied battle. With my chin tilted high, I cloak myself in invisibility the moment Cerberus's heads are no longer geared in my direction.

Zig, the new ferryman, does not see me as I step a foot into the River Styx. An icy shiver encompasses my ankles, and every instinctual part of me wants to flee from her deadly clutches, but I push past the fear and descend further. I let the frigid water lap around my waist, claim my shoulders, and steal my breath.

The dead swim around me, moaning in agony because of a fruitless afterlife. Somewhere in the dark waters, Mastiff is waiting for me to save him. I lower myself deeper into the abyss until Styx emerges from her underwater kingdom.

Each time I see Styx, I find her more frightening than the time before. Her beauty interweaves with poison, but she prefers the terror. Styx floats in front of me in a gown, clinging to her lithe frame like blackened cobwebs. Her short, stringy dark hair sticks to her cheeks and curls around her striking jawline. A single index finger reaches towards me, the tip blackened like her soul, and it takes every molecule of bravery not to flinch away from my future queen.

Styx tucks a piece of my onyx hair behind my ear, her touch as cold as death. Despite myself, I shiver and avert my gaze away.

"Do you have news for me, witch?" Styx's voice is equally ethereal and monstrous, a hymn and a curse.

With that one touch, Styx brings oxygen back into my lungs, but my head remains bowed. "I found the Oracle, Lady Styx." My voice is a whisper, but it speaks my excitement.

"For nearly two thousand years, I have waited for those words. Since the last oracle spoke of my destiny, I have waited for Saffron's birth. Itched for her transition to deity. Starved for the eighty-eighth year to arrive. Now, my time has come." Styx's voice is always monotone, but today, there is a lilt of anticipation.

I lift my head and find the coldest, darkest eyes glinting with pride. For my eons' long existence, nothing has terrified me more than Styx's happiness.

"My ascension towards the crown is a long, treacherous road. It's finally here. Victory, however, cannot be achieved until she is dead. My success will only come with the oracle's demise, so I ask you, witch, why isn't she with you?"

This is the question I feared. A few weeks ago, I narrowed down my search to two women. One, a blonde agoraphobic woman named Meara Anderson; the other, a demure housewife named Hartika Sommers. I sent one goddess out to spy on Meara, while two goddesses poised as Hartika's fiancé's lovers to gather information. One is Lowell's hair stylist, the other his work assistant.

Nemesis heard enough from Hartika's fiancé, Lowell, to confirm our suspicions. We plotted her execution, but on the day I went to her apartment to bring her to the Underworld, I found Argus driving away with her. If I had gone one day earlier, Hartika would be here in Styx's clutches, but I was too late. I followed Argus, and he led her towards the one building I cannot enter without suspicions.

Olympus Industries.

Right into the gods' clutches.

"Argus took her before I had the chance," I admit.

There is silence.

I did not use to mind the quiet, but in Styx's company, silence means she's thinking devious thoughts. There isn't a molecule of kindness within Styx. She epitomizes her titles as the personification of hatred. Her thoughts are polluted with malice. I became a villain because of circumstances, but Styx has always been a monster, hiding her truth with a pretty face and miles of deadly river water.

Finally, Styx says. "How many living family members does she have? It'll be easy enough to draw her out with a dismembered hand or two."

Magic flares in my open palm and an image forms in the smoke. Styx watches the live video of Hartika's fiancé, Lowell, laughing with Nemesis inside a hair salon. The oblivious human doesn't realize he is in the company of evil. That his life teeters towards an early finish.

"Lowell Black, her fiancé." I explain. "He is the only person, according to Nemesis, who has spoken to Hartika in years. If we want her away from the gods, he is how we can leverage her."

"Was Saffron at Olympus Industries when the oracle was taken there?" Styx asks.

"Yes, your majesty, she was."

When Styx smiles, a part of me wilts, like she syphons the scattered remains of my happiness. If I had the strength, I'd stumble backwards, but I am in a river of her domain and I am helpless. Styx is so close to where I stand. I can see every emotion flickering in those dark, soulless eyes. Brutality and pure evil thrums within them, and I chose her. To be by her side, fighting her battles, for a glimpse of what I want most.

I am no better than the woman ruefully smiling back at me.

"Hermes and the others won't let her come down to the Underworld, especially if they know she is the oracle. But perhaps we can use this insipid boy to trick the oracle. To get her to bring herself and our savior down to my depths."

"How do you propose to do that?" I ask.

"Do you doubt my intelligence?" Styx asks immediately.

"No, of course not."

"Then trust in my plan without further elaboration. Let the others know the Olympians' demises will be soon. The plan will begin, and gold blood will shower the sky like raindrops."

The world has underestimated Styx for eons. Because she is within a river, they've forgotten her strength. The power within her is a volcano, patiently waiting for the right moment to erupt and destroy the most beings in her molten rage. Styx might be in a river, but it's by her own choice.

She is a patient killer who is ready to strike.

I fear her because I know her power, and never in my life have I forgotten the depths of her deviousness. Zeus and many other Olympians underestimate Styx, but that will be their greatest downfall. I hate myself for who I have become, but I know I chose the right side. The wise side. Styx is about to let herself out of her cage, and the other gods won't forget about her.

Never again.

I bow before my queen. "As you wish."

Before I swim to the top, Styx says. "And Hecate?"

"Yes?"

I turn around to face her once more, and that barely there smile of pure hatred is painted on her face like a radiant tragedy. "Send Nemesis down to me."

I swim away, mentally apologizing to everybody who will die in the warpath to Styx's throne. But as my head breaks through the river water, I also whisper one promise to my Mastiff.

"I will see you soon."

NINE

SAFFRON

I sit in my office, elbows resting on my desk as words of the world's growing destruction bleed through the pages. Mass casualties I am responsible for fixing.

Since I created Olympus Industries, Zeus has delegated every job on Earth to me. He wears the crown and sits on the throne, but I work in my office on every job that is meant for him. He is the king, and he pulls my strings to do his bidding. In the beginning of my time as a goddess, I loved the role Zeus gave me. However, in the recent months, the continuous problems arising are too heavy for me to carry on my own.

I loathe Zeus for giving me this responsibility alone, as much as I hate my existence.

The human's savior, what a joke.

Jamila's timid three knocks tap against my closed office door, and I know what waits for me on the other side. While Aphrodite is interviewing Apollo's soulmate, I have actual work to complete. The world's strife builds, and Zeus has left me to carry the burden.

"Bring them in," I say to Jamila.

A few seconds later, four immortals walk into my office.

Apollo enters first, his sun-kissed hair disheveled and his eyes not focusing on anything in particular. Hart's presence unnerved him, and without a word, he takes his usual seat to the right of my desk. Normally, he has a joke on his lips, but not today.

Behind him, Artemis walks into the room. She glances warily at her twin brother, but she doesn't vocalize her concerns. Instead, she nods at me, I nod back, and she sits in the chair closest to Apollo.

Next is Asopus, a prominent river god. When he storms into the room, he glowers at me with seething hatred. This glare worsens each week when his missing daughters are not found. While Zeus is king, Asopus blames me for their disappearance. As if I am the direct result of their absence in their rivers. Like I am their abductor.

He takes the seat farthest from me, like my proximity sickens him.

Last, Hera enters the room. When I first held a meeting amongst the gods, Hera insisted on an invitation. She hates me, the most powerful product of her husband's infidelity, but she arrives at these optional meetings every Tuesday at noon. Out of all the gods, I am cursed with Hera's continuous arrival. She interjects nothing of importance. No, Hera arrives every Tuesday to listen to the world's problems and blame me for their existence.

As usual, she sits in the brown-and-blue seat directly across from my desk. Her lips, always painted a deep shade of purple, are curled in a cruel combination of abhorrence and amusement.

"Anybody else?" I ask Jamila, who stands in the opened doorway with her hand still around the doorknob.

She knows the words I weave in between my question. Every week, I plead with Zeus and Hermes to show up. Zeus needs to hear how dire the situations on Earth have developed; he needs to help. Meanwhile, I want my husband here for moral support. Hera doesn't strike me with a sword, but her words hold lethality. As the weeks of unsuccessfully helping the world, Hera's insults bleed me out more than I wish.

Sympathy flickers over Jamila's young, rounded face. "Nobody else," she responds.

Hermes used to always come to these meetings, to be the one standing in my corner, but that changed a long time ago. We've been so distant for so many years that I cannot pinpoint when we stopped being a team. I wear the role of his wife like a sash of honor, but that sash is littered with holes. No longer taken care of when harsh winds hit it.

I still hope he'll walk through those doors with his half-cocked smirk and a twinkle in his green eyes, but it's a fickle dream. Hermes doesn't show up for me anymore.

"Let's begin then," I say. I force my words to strip away my emotions. The hurt I feel at his absence. The reminder that I am no longer the same woman he married.

Jamila leaves, closing the door behind her, and I focus on Apollo.

"What's your report on the Nosoi?" I ask him.

In South America, the Nosoi are spreading a deadly disease that's killing humans at astounding rates.

The Nosoi are personified spirits of plague, sickness,

and disease as shadowy black birds. They have not been an issue since the Bubonic Plague, disappearing with the dangerous disease. But recently, they have come back. Growing at rates nobody can understand, much less defeat. The few times gods have gone down to these countries and destroyed the birds, they multiply the next day. The Nosoi are claiming hundreds of thousands of lives. They emerged the first week of January, and as we near the end of March, they're still roaming the world and infecting defenseless humans.

Apollo doesn't respond, eyes staring out the window behind my head. Teeth gnawing at his bottom lip.

"Po?" I ask again, using his nickname.

Artemis elbows her brother in the ribs, spurring him out of his thoughts. "I'm sorry, what?"

"I want your report on the Nosoi," I repeat.

"Right, the Nosoi," Apollo rummages his hand through his hair. A shaky sigh leaves his lips, then he says. "Asclepius, Paean, our apprentices, and I have been in South America all week. We are healing the diseased as fast as we can, but the mortality rate keeps growing because we can't find whoever is bringing the Nosoi there. I've never seen them hide as well as they are now, or multiplying as quickly as they are. As more humans are growing ill, Asclepius, Paean, and I do not have the time to kill the Nosoi because we're trying to save the dying."

There's a pregnant pause as my eyes move towards the pictures that brutally decorate my desk. Dozens of pictures detail the gruesome disease the Nosoi have created in South America. The citizens' skin starts off with one black mark on their forearm. It almost looks like the symbol of a river, but within twenty-four hours, the black marks grow across their flesh. The black spots are the first signs of decomposition. Followed by their skin slipping off their bones and tongues falling from the victim's mouths. Within a week, their eyes bleed black, and brittle bones turn to ash.

I look at a picture of a pregnant woman; her blackened hand resting on top of her swollen belly. Blood and sores seep from every pore, and her mouth is open in a scream no longer heard. My stomach curdles with disgust, and as I mentally whisper an apology to this woman, Apollo speaks again.

"We need more help, Saf. The entire continent could die if we can't get some more immortals down there."

I focus on Hera, but before I can ask, the queen shakes her head.

"Zeus gave *you* the job of protecting humans," Hera sneers. "He won't send anymore gods down to do your job. Why aren't you down there with Apollo, Paean, Asclepius, and the surplus of humans? Hunting down these tiny birds?" The condescension in her voice is clear to everybody in the room. "You are supposed to be all-powerful."

Asopus smiles with amusement.

Apollo, however, glares at Hera. "She has enough on her plate here. While Aphrodite floats around at galas, Zeus seduces his way through every male and female in the world." Hera flinches at that, but Apollo continues. "And Dionysus drinks himself into oblivion every night. You expect Saffron to handle everything, but she can't. She's playing her part in helping, but the other gods are not. Hestia could-"

"The answer is no," Hera interrupts. Her dark gaze zeroes on me. "Go yourself, *Savior*."

Each time I try to leave my city to help Apollo, Paean,

and Asclepius, Hermes stops me and brings me home. If not him, then Hades or Persephone. Once, Thanatos grabbed me. I'm a prisoner in my own town, never allowed to venture outside its gilded gates.

Hermes and I argue about his incessant need to protect me, and each time I ask why I am unallowed to go anywhere, he lies to me. When I ask him about his motives, Hermes reminds me he is the god of trickery. The longest I've ever remained in South America was five minutes before Hermes found me and dragged me home.

But Hera doesn't need to know this.

"I'll see if Hermes will join you," I tell Apollo, but we both already know the answer. "And if not him, perhaps Hecate will."

Apollo nods his head.

"Now, what about my daughters?" Asopus snarls the question, glaring back-and-forth between Artemis and me. "What are you two doing to find my daughters?"

All around the world, river nymphs are going missing. Without them, rivers are becoming inhospitable and the creatures within them are dying at monumental rates. Asopus is performing the jobs of all his missing daughters, leaving him unable to search for them.

Two and a half months ago, when they first started disappearing, Zeus let me send Artemis and her huntresses on a search. Still, none of the nymphs have been found. Iris has joined their hunt, but without Zeus allowing more gods to help the world's problems, the nymphs remain missing.

Artemis begins. "My huntresses and I have checked every square inch of the world, at the sake of their physical and mental health. We've traveled across the seas with Poseidon's help, and we've hunted for them on every acre of land. We will continue to search, but we've scoured the entire world and haven't found them."

"And let me guess," Hera says to me with a sneer. "You haven't gone to help them, either?"

Asopus answers for me. "No, she hasn't." His hatred bubbles out of him, steaming the air.

I ignore their comments. Just like my efforts in South America, I'm stopped each time I try to join Artemis and her huntresses. It seems like the only times I see my husband are when I try to help the world and he stops me, putting me back in our home. The only words we share are through screamed declarations of anger.

"Nymphs aren't humans," I say to Hera, a line I've practiced over the past eleven weeks. "So, will Zeus allow more gods to join Artemis and her hunt?"

"Iris joined a few weeks ago," Hera says. "Two goddesses and a dozen huntresses should've already found them. Their incompetence shouldn't be rewarded with further help."

"You're more than happy to join us, Stepmother," Artemis snarls, eyes narrowing in displeasure. "There's always an empty spot on the forest ground for you to sleep beside us."

Hera ignores Artemis, just as she does every week.

"What else is going on?" Hera asks me, already knowing the answer. "I've heard there's a murderer around here, killing mothers and their children. You are too frightened to leave your town to help the nymphs or the humans in South America, yet you still cannot save the humans in your own town. Countless mothers have been murdered alongside their toddlers, and you have done nothing about it."

On January first, I received a phone call from the human

police department informing me of a gruesome murder. A young mother was viciously tortured and killed. Her toddler laid dead beside her. Since that day, I have received a phone call every single evening from the police captain. Every day, a young mother and her child are killed. The women are always in their twenties, and their children are always between the ages of one-to-ten years old.

Thanatos won't let me into the Underworld, nobody will, but he interviewed every woman who was murdered. Each of them gave the same description. A creature sheathed in shadows comes to them, knife slitting their throats before they can let out a scream. The children provide the same description. Nobody can tell me if their assailant is male or female, human or godly.

"The police and I are-" I begin.

"Not doing a thing." Asopus interrupts.

"She's doing her best," Apollo snaps at Asopus.

Hera's laugh is cruel. "Your one-sided crush on a married woman is pathetic, Apollo. It's blinded you from the truth."

Apollo recoils from the comment as if her words slapped him across the cheek.

"And what truth is that?" I snap at her.

I shouldn't have said anything. Hera doesn't matter to me. She isn't a goddess I love or care for, and I should've kept my mouth shut. Instead, I stoked the fires of hatred within her. Hera gifts me a barbed smile before telling me her version of the truth.

"The truth is," Hera says, her voice deceivingly sweetened. "You were prophesied to be a creation of greatness. The most powerful child of Zeus's, but the prophecy got it wrong.

You are nothing but a disappointment, who should've been killed when you still bled red. We lost our chance to end your life, and it's a mistake I remind Zeus of every single day."

Hera stands up, leaving without another word. Asopus glares at me once more, then follows behind Hera. The door slams behind him. The two framed pictures from my wedding day shake from their post on the wall. Just like everything else in my life, the two pictures symbolizing Hermes and my elation are ready to collapse.

"I can get Ares to join us," Artemis says, her voice quieter than its usually boisterous octave. Her words pull me out of my reverie. "He'll bring Phobos and Deimos with him, too."

Ares hasn't left Mt. Olympus since the day I became a goddess. Except for the few times I have gone to the land of the gods, then Ares is conveniently not there. For eighty-eight years, I haven't seen the god of war, but my heart still skips a beat at the mention of him. The smallest spark of electricity hits my fingertips when his name leaves Artemis's lips. I hate the feeling his name gives, even after all these years.

My eyes level on a picture of my wedding day with Hermes. Without looking away from the framed past, I respond to Artemis. "Perfect, thank you. Is there anything I can do to help? Do you need any further supplies?"

"We're fine, Saffron," Artemis responds, her voice tinged with sympathy.

"The Nosoi," Apollo begins.

I speak before he can continue. "I didn't want to say it while Hera was here, but Hestia, Psyche, and Demeter have arrived in South America. They'll take over your duties healing the sick and tracking the Nosoi while I need you here."

"Why am I needed here?" He asks.

Because your soulmate is here, I want to say.

Instead, I respond with a partial truth. "I need your help with the murders. The list of people I trust keeps getting smaller, and I need you here. Humans are in an uprising over the murders, and if I do not find who is the killer soon, then I fear riots are the least of our issues."

While I am the goddess of humanity, many other immortals do not care about the fickle lives of humans and their deaths. Apollo, however, does. He knows the humans will turn on the gods, and while many forget the power of human prayers, I do not. Without the humans believing we can protect them, they'll stop praying to us. Eventually, we'll all disappear from existence.

Right now, that idea doesn't sound too dreadful.

"I'm starving," Artemis says, deviating the conversation away from the darkness of the world. "Do you guys want to grab some lunch? I've been living off squirrel meat for the past two and a half months, and I'm craving anything else."

Apollo smiles.

I do not.

"Let's do it," Apollo says.

"I can't. Maybe next week." My lie echoes in the now-quiet room.

"Next time," Apollo says, the words hollowed out.

Artemis says nothing, but she nods her head. They leave my office, and a few minutes later, Hart Sommers enters the room with a cart full of art supplies. I say nothing as she wheels the cart inside my office, sets up her easel, places an empty piece of paper on top of the stand, and nervously glances in my direction. Her teeth nervously bite into her bubblegum pink lips.

"I got the job," Hart says with a slight waver in her tone.

"I see that."

A lapse of silence hits the room.

Hart clears her throat and says. "I'm told that you're my first client. That I should draw you. I'll admit, I'm a little nervous. So, I think I'm going to make my first sketch on paper just in case I mess up. Then I'll move it onto a real canvas sometime this week. I really don't want to mess up but-"

She continues rambling.

I lean back in my chair, assessing the human woman in front of me. Her long hair is pulled up into a messy bun, rosiness dotting her tanned cheeks, and hope for a better future lives in her wide gaze. She is everything I used to be. A happy, oblivious human. We look nothing alike, Hart and me, but I see my past self in her.

Gods, I miss who I once was.

"Then let's begin," I say.

I try to smile, but I'm far too tired and so I only stare forward, hoping for a few hours of rest from a world I no longer enjoy.

TEN

HERMES

S ince Styx's tyranny against the world began, every newly deceased soul I've retrieved screamed in agony. My second home has been the southern region of the world, where the Nosoi birds have infected humans with a fatal disease.

These souls scream when I come for them. Their minds eternally burn from the unbearable pain that terminated their lives. I move to grab their arms of mist, but they pull away with phantom pain from their mortal life. The sores from the Nosoi diseases pepper the victims' skin. Dastardly, blackish gray spots erode their veins, tearing apart muscle and bone until nothing else is left behind.

Humans' hearts cannot withstand the agony of decomposing while alive. The Fates do not plan these deaths in South America. Their life strings are not clipped by Atropos; instead, their thread of life disintegrates. Their souls turn to ash like their souls have been dead for centuries.

Since the prophecy came to light in the Underworld,

there's been a shift in the atmosphere. The icy feel of Styx's eyes watching everything is ever-present. I once loved the Underworld, but it is now tainted by the goddess of hatred. She has unleashed diseases designed to ravage parts of the world. Ordered murders of innocent children and mothers within a five-mile radius of Saffron's office. Abducted river nymphs from their homes. She is a monster, cloaked in intelligence and obscurity.

Her existence has darkened the Underworld.

I deliver the screaming, thrashing souls from South America to the entrance of the Underworld. Hades waits with a hand on one of Cerberus's heads. The loyal, three-headed dog looks to the sore-littered souls and whimpers, nestling himself closer to Hades's side. Neither Hades nor I force falsities.

"We are doing what is morally right in the long run, even if it seems unpleasant now."

"She thinks I'm cheating on her." My words are acid on my tongue, but I admit the truth. "I'm never home anymore, constantly avoiding her because our lies stack too high. When I'm not avoiding her, I'm running around this world, plucking souls taken too soon from the mortal realm. Styx is killing at a faster rate than I've seen since the two great world wars. I do not have time for her, and when I do, I still avoid her. Spending all my time in the Underworld with my former lover, instead of staying beside my wife."

Hecate and I have been working closely since Styx's prophecy unfurled. Almost my entire day is spent with Hecate. We scour the world together, searching for the Nosoi that disease the world, and hunting for Styx's traitors lurking in broad daylight. Sometimes, Hecate assists me with all the souls I must collect. So, the few times I talk to my wife, and she asks me about my day, Hecate's name is always on my tongue. The goddess who I once loved as much as I love Saffron.

I know what Saffron thinks. She believes I'm bedding Hecate again, but I cannot admit the truth of my fidelity without confessing the convincing lies I've kept away from her. Hecate tells me to inflame my wife's suspicions. She suggests I admit to an affair with Hecate because then Saffron will stop trying to come down to the Underworld. At the cost of my marriage, I can save her from Styx with a carefully threaded lie.

Hades pets Cerberus's head, murmuring. "What would you prefer, Hermes? Her thinking you're cheating on her or her discovering what Styx has in store for her? Would you rather suffer a few months of discomfort in your marriage, or would you prefer Styx's plans to come to fruition? We both know the details of that prophecy, and there's no pleasant outcome for Saffron."

One specific part of the prophecy plays in my head, reminding me why every lie is well told.

And from the savior, a terrible scream will wail. The sound will echo forevermore.

If the war begins, then Saffron suffers. It's an irrefutable fact, one that drives all my decisions. Hades and I stand at the gates of the Underworld with over a hundred newly dead souls behind me. Almost all are victims of Styx's games.

"I'll leave you to it," I say, bowing to Hades.

My wings lift me to the Underworld's ceiling. I am ready to leave when I see her. A goddess draped in a gray, shapeless tunic. Her dark, wet hair clings to her olive complexion. She is not meant to be in the Underworld, yet I see her rise from the River Styx wearing mischief like a crown. Oizys, goddess of misery, glides from the River Styx. She announces herself as a traitor to the Olympians as the river's dark water drips off her.

I rush towards her, rage and desperation quickening my wings.

Before she registers my arrival, my hands grab her biceps, and I pull her towards me. We soar through the air, her screams notifying everyone in the Underworld of her treachery. My movements are as fast as lightning. I slam her back into the wall nearest Tartarus.

Thanatos, the guard of Tartarus, jumps back as I crack the wall behind her. Oizys gasps, her head bouncing off the wall. It is the only movement she makes. After the sound of her skull cracking against the wall ebbs, she remains eerily still with my hand wrapped tight around her throat. My other hand grabs both her wrists, pinning them above her head. Thanatos stands behind me, not asking questions. He watches the interaction with mild confusion.

A dribble of gold blood trickles from the corner of her lips as she wildly grins. "This is a fun position we're in, Hermes, but what would Saffron say?"

My hand around her throat tightens. "What were you doing leaving Styx's domain?"

"You know exactly what I was doing."

"Why?" Thanatos growls. I do not mistake the shock of betrayal in his voice. It makes the one word he croaks out sound guttural. More of a growl than a spoken word.

The danger lurking within Styx's uprising is that gods and goddesses, who we've trusted for eons, are discarding the masks. They reveal their true intentions. Admitting their greedy desire for more power than Zeus's reign provides.

Kronos evenly divided the world between gods and titans, but Styx is far worse. She weasels herself in between the gods, titans, and personified daemons. While Zeus and the gods loyal to him have been believing Styx's containment in the River Styx, she has slithered through our ranks. Whispered promises into other's ears before any of us knew she was a viper, sinking her fangs into our bloodstream.

Nobody is trusted now.

And Thanatos is learning that fact right now.

"I'm the goddess of misery," Oizys says. My nails dig into her flesh, and as I cut skin, gilded ichor slides down her tanned, elongated neck. She purrs. "And it's about time the rest of the world lives in misery with me."

Thanatos takes a few retreating steps, nodding his readiness at me. Neither one of us hesitates. He opens the gates to Tartarus. I pull her tighter to my chest, spinning our bodies so her back faces Tartarus's eternal imprisonment. She stares at me, without an inkling of fear for her eternal fate; instead, she keeps that wild, untamed smile. I take a step towards Tartarus, my hand tightening around her throat.

"I'm one of dozens who fight with the true queen," Oizys says, her voice lilts with mania. "And I'm one of the weakest of the lot. My power is a small kernel of what Styx has collected over the eons."

We stand on the edge of Tartarus, her heels dangling off. With my grip on her throat, I lean her body backwards, and she grasps my forearm with both her hands. Oizys does not fear Tartarus, but she holds on and stops herself from falling into the prison's merciless grasp. But not out of terror. Pure determination intermingles with her insanity. She grabs me, keeping herself in my line of vision, because she has more to tell me.

I fear her words more than she fears Tartarus.

"You've only known about the prophecy for eighty days, but she's known for two thousand years. Patiently waiting until your wife appeared in this world and became the goddess she was destined to become. Eighty days of defensive fighting means nothing. Not compared to the centuries Styx has spent preparing her offensive strikes."

Faster than I expect, Oizys uses her grip on my forearm to hoist herself until her face is right in front of mine. Her lips crash against mine, tasting nothing like my wife's. I shove her away, realizing a moment too late that I let go of the enemy. Oizys cackles, her manic smile twitching at the corners, and lets go of my forearm. Willingly, she falls into the obsidian depths of Tartarus.

The whole way down, Oizys laughs.

Thanatos closes, then locks the gate behind Oizys. We hear the moment her body smacks against the ground because the laughter is gone. There is only silence in the prisons within the Underworld, but my mind screams at me. Warning me of imminent danger. Telling me that everything I've done to stop this war from coming to fruition is merely an instrument furthering Styx's fight for the throne.

Hades runs into the room, followed by Cerberus and Hecate. "What in the gods happened?" He asks, looking between Thanatos and me.

For the first time in a long time, my answer is truthful.

"I do not know."

ELEVEN

HART SOMMERS

My father's favorite immortal was Saffron, goddess of deliverance, bones, and humanity.

Now, here I am, standing a few feet in front of her.

I should be excited, asking her all the questions my dad always wanted to know, but a wave of sadness crashes into me. Seeing her is a painful reminder that he's gone. It's been ten years, but the dull ache of his death continues to linger. My grief varies in its pain, but in Saffron's presence, it's sharper than it's been in years. I've seen sculptures of her in museums. Witnessed murals decorate brick buildings around town. As I look at her now, I am reminded of the little framed drawing my father kept in the living room of her.

Saffron is in front of me, but all I see is myself rewinding to the past.

To my dad.

"I like Lady Athena best," Mom said, then immediately

looked at my father. She had a small smile on her face, knowing she'd incite his rant about Lady Saffron.

As always, it worked.

"Olympus, no!" Father exclaimed. He moved towards my mother, fingers grasping her chin as he tilted her face to his. "If you weren't so beautiful, I'd divorce you right now for that statement."

Mom's smile widened, not believing his bluff. Undoubtedly, Mom heard this preposterous threat a dozen times a day, and each time Dad proclaimed this falsity, he placed a kiss on Mom's lips. This time was no exception. I turned away, and my brother made a barfing noise as our parents kissed.

As soon as they pulled away, my father sat on the armchair of the loveseat Mom rested on, and he looked at Suraj and me. "Lady Athena is a wise and powerful goddess, but she is not the greatest in this household. We are free people, rather than slaves, because of one immortal. If not for Lady Saffron, our savior, who knows what our world would look like with Kronos reigning over Mt. Olympus?"

He told me the story of Saffron and the last Titanomachy War almost every Saturday night during our game night. Mother would smile proudly at her husband, who she fell in love with when she was only twelve years old. Decades later, she still stared at her husband as if he held everything wonderful in the palm of his hands.

"Rupert," Mom teasingly said. "Haven't Hartika and Suraj heard this story one too many times? Let's tell them the tale of Atalanta's race or Paris's judgment."

We all knew Dad's answer before it left his lips.

"Eesha Sommers, the nerve of you!" Father exclaimed, humor lacing his voice as he declared. "These kids cannot hear enough about the grace of our savior! Did Atalanta race to our *freedom? Did Paris make the judgement that freed our ancestors from their shackles? No, Lady Saffron did."*

"I want to hear about Lady Saffron again," I smiled at my father, who was the moon and the stars in my eyes, and he looked at me with the same ardent affection.

"What about you, S. J?" Dad asked my younger brother, Suraj. "Are you ready for the tale?"

He pouted. "I want to hear about Lord Hephaestus's traps."

Lord Hephaestus had always been Suraj's favorite god, mainly because they both share a significant limp in their step. But my father shook his head. "We may talk about that mighty god after the greatest Olympian's story is told."

As we ate dinner together, Father rambled on about the mighty Lady Saffron. He told us about how she spent eighteen years in a jail cell ruled over by Lady Hecate, Lord Phobos, and Lord Deimos. She was almost killed by Lord Ares after he won her in the arena, but Lord Hermes dashingly saved the day and captured his future wife for himself.

There, they discovered her two different colored blood. One was the red crimson blood that spilled from our veins, but the other one was the color of the gods- ichor. Kronos knew of Lady Saffron's powers and tried to manipulate her to stray from the gods, but she wasn't convinced by the powerful Titan.

She fought with the Olympians, even when Kronos was winning the war.

"She could've done the safe thing and joined Kronos. He was winning the war and had entombed most immortals in the Dagger of Chains." Dad gripped his pasta-filled fork tightly. He leaned near me and whispered. "But she fought for us. Choosing the harder path and dying for our freedom. She is the reason we have a nightly dinner together as a family. We are not divided across the world. Our skin is not blemished with scarification *marks, and she is who we thank for every meal we eat." Father pointed an index finger at Mom and Suraj, wiggling the digit between the two. "That is why she is more important than Lord Hephaestus and Lady Athena, because she chose us."*

He wrapped his arm around my shoulders and kissed the top of my head. He and I were agreed. Lady Saffron was the greatest goddess in the world. But a part of me liked her so much because my dad was enamored by her actions. I wanted to be just like my dad, down to the gold-feathered necklace he wore around his neck.

"That is why," Dad declared. "If I ever meet her, I will kiss the feet that walked towards righteousness for our people."

"It's been almost a hundred years, Dad," Suraj said in a whiney cadence. "What if she's changed?"

"Don't worry about how she's changed, boy, think about what she did. I don't care if she would decapitate me on sight. I would still remember what she did for us. Without her, I could not be with your mother. You two wouldn't be under the same roof as me, and my death would've been many decades before now."

A few years later, he died in a car accident.

Still loving the goddess who stands before me.

TWELVE

HART SOMMERS

For the past hour, I have bathed in the silence of Lady Saffron's company. She remains still, the perfect model for any artist, but there's a lifelessness to her I didn't expect. While her beauty is almost suffocatingly present, there's no gleam to her. A pretty canvas with no depth inside, as if her soul was plucked from her body.

In the room's muteness, fog clouds the air in my mind. Phantom hands slide across my skin, land underneath my palms and guide my drawing pencil. This apparition is another part of me, an extension of myself that only emerges in spontaneous sparks. It is a sensation I get every time I have drawn Apollo while in my bedroom's quiet solitude. I embrace the feeling of another soul slipping into mine.

When the fog takes over, I create my greatest art. At times, it is frightening. The creations I make are not always real. They are variations of a future that does not yet exist. I can still see the present in front of me, but the veiled fog lets me see with another pair of eyes into a different world. I believe I have gone insane, but I welcome the madness as it gifts me artistic brilliance.

Even in the fog of my mind, I am all too aware of Saffron's appearance. Mom always joked that Dad liked Saffron so much because he found her equally powerful and beautiful. I do not blame Dad for his infatuation. She was side-by-side with Aphrodite, but Saffron stands out even in the goddess of love's company.

I am twenty-six years old, almost eighty years younger than Saffron, but the latter appears younger. Her appearance has both sharpened features, like high-risen cheekbones and a pointed jaw; however, she remains overtly feminine with rounded eyes, heart-shaped lips, and plump cheeks. The ghost of a dimple hides behind her frown, waiting to reveal itself.

I wonder, as I draw the outline of her firm frown, how much more radiant this drawing would be if she smiled. I could draw those deeply indented dimples, find the light that sparks her dark brown eyes.

She is flawless.

"You're beautiful," I murmur softly to myself.

I glance up at her, gauging her reaction. For a moment, I think Saffron is going to smile. The right corner of her mouth twitches, but her frown is victorious against the fight for happiness. If possible, her already dark eyes fall into an abyss of sadness, turning nearly black in front of me.

"As are you, Hart," she solemnly remarks.

"You were my father's favorite goddess." The laugh that escapes my lips is tinged with mournfulness. "If only he could see me now, standing a few feet away from you, drawing you and talking to you."

"Were?" Saffron asks, noting the past tense I used.

"Ten years ago, he and my family died in a car accident."

"I'm terribly sorry for your loss," Saffron says, her words no louder than a whisper.

"Life has to keep going, even after death."

She doesn't respond to me, her disagreement louder than any scream.

We are silent again, my last words echoing in the office, and I resume drawing her. I let the fog and those phantom hands take me away, and for a moment, I forget who I am drawing. My hands furiously draw. I outline Saffron's pear-shaped body and stencil flower petals and bones around her opened palms. She is right in front of me, but I am no longer in the room with her. I am thrown into the scene I create upon my once-empty canvas. I let the story of Saffron and her powers whisk me away from the tense silence between us.

The moment the fog leaves my mind, the phantom hands slip out of mine. I have finished my drawing of her. The pencil slips from my hand, clattering without a sound onto the carpeted floor. Saffron and I lock eyes. My grip on the canvas is unsteady. It's been almost ten years since I have shown another person my artwork, and I have never given a piece of my art to a goddess.

Twice, I nearly drop the canvas, but it lands in Saffron's awaiting hands unscathed.

She turns the canvas towards her, and I watch as anxiety quickens my heartbeat. My hands are suddenly clammy, and I rub them against my dress, eyes flickering between Saffron and my sweat-stained outfit. Saffron's mouth drops open, and where there was once sadness in her eyes, it's replaced with undiluted fear.

She drops the canvas on her desk, eyes swimming with tears as she stares at me. "What did you draw?" Saffron asks, voice whispered and wobbly.

"I drew you," I say, but I'm laced with uncertainty.

"How did you draw him?"

She doesn't need air to breathe, but she is breathless. She does not look away from the drawing in her grasp, even when her arms tremble. My artwork captures her every thought, blinding her to the disbelief I wear heavily on my face.

"Him, who?"

We both stare down at the canvas at the same time. It sits there, taunting us, from atop of the desk. I thought I drew Saffron, standing regally in a purple tunic gown with bones and flower petals surrounding her open palms. The image in front of me is only a fraction of my truth. Saffron is only one of the two immortals drawn on the canvas.

Saffron is standing tall and proud with a crown made of bones upon her head of braided chestnut locks. Beside her is a man I have never seen before, but I know isn't human. Just like Saffron, he is cloaked in power that is only designed for the immortals. He stands half a foot taller than her, with a mane of curly, black locks and smooth, olive skin. His large hand is placed upon her shoulder. He is staring at her proudly, with love pooling his silver eyes, and she has her hands raised up in the air.

Hands coated in blood.

Although there is no color in my drawing, I know both red and golden blood coats her hands. I know everything about this piece of art, like I was there when the events unfurled. If they have unfurled yet.

Saffron and the mysterious male stand in an empty field, only accompanied by an erupting volcano and fallen corpses. She wears a crown of bones, but they lie around her, too. Scattering around her feet like ants. Levitating above her head like raindrops that have not fallen. Blood splatters her beautiful face, both gold and red, and a single tear rolls down her left cheek. The mysterious god looks at her with pride, but she cries at the murders she's inflicted upon this battlefield.

"Holy gods," I gasp, stumbling away from Saffron, who still hasn't looked away from the canvas. "I have to go."

I trip on the leg of the chair closest to me, falling to the ground. Only then does Saffron look at me. Tears well up in her eyes, mouth gaping with disbelief. She tries to speak, but I scramble to my feet before I can hear a single word.

I run.

Fast.

Jamila, Saffron's assistant, jolts to her feet. Quizzically, she looks at me, focusing on the fear painted on my face. "Are you alright?" She asks.

I shake my head, running and stumbling towards the emergency exit. The elevator will take too long, but when my hand wraps around the door leading to the stairs, Saffron's office door opens. She stands there, clutching the canvas in one hand, and I know she has questions I do not have answers for. Or worse, answers I fear admitting aloud.

I run down the stairs.

"Hart, wait!"

I don't wait.

THIRTEEN

LAMB

"I never thought the day would come." Dýnami's dramatic sigh can be heard for miles. She throws her mostly eaten squirrel on a stick onto the ground and grumbles. "I am sick of eating squirrel meat."

Sika picks up the squirrel on the stick, brushing off the leaves and dirt, and chimes with a barely hidden smile. "Fine, I'll eat yours, too."

Sika has barely eaten her squirrel when she picks up Dýnami's, bringing it closer to her mouth. Before she can take a bite, to nobody's surprise, Dýnami reaches forward and rips the squirrel on a stick out of her hands.

"On second thought," Dýnami chimes. In two hearty bites, Dýnami finishes her squirrel. She glances at Sika, who has only eaten a bite out of her squirrel, and asks. "Are you going to finish that?"

Sika passes her barely eaten squirrel to Dýnami, and her girlfriend happily munches on the food. Akita, who sits on the other side of Dýnami, stares with disgust. The expression on her slim face worsens when Dýnami talks again with the squirrel's legs dangling out of her mouth.

"I'm pretending it is some Rocky Road ice cream," she announces mid-chew.

"Why must I tell you every day to eat with your mouth closed?" Akita asks with a groan.

Roxie, a new huntress of only a few months, attempts to hide her amusement by placing a hand over her mouth.

"I'm sorry, I didn't quite hear you." Dýnami says, leaning towards Akita with her mouth wide open. I'm fortunate that I'm on the other side of Sika, unable to see the chewed-up squirrel in Dýnami's mouth. "What did you want me to do?"

Akita shoves Dýnami's shoulder, and the latter huntress falls on her back with laughter. As she laughs, she continues lying on her back without a care in the world. Dýnami takes another bite out of her squirrel. Akita, seeing this, rolls her eyes.

"You are like a dog," Akita mutters.

"Funny you say that, since you are the one named after a dog," Shikari chimes. She nods her head at Akita's scarification mark, an akita dog, on her left forearm. The dark scarification striking against her pale, almost alabaster, skin.

"What's wrong with being named after a dog?" Another huntress, Hound, angrily asks. Her knuckles, already bloodied and scabbed over, whitened underneath her clenched fists.

Shikari's laughter is almost as loud as Hound's boots smacking the ground. She jolts to her feet and is ready for another fight. Hound's temper is as quick as fire to a candle's wick, and Shikari stokes the flames with expertise.

Akita watches the argument she began with pride, taking the first bite of her breakfast as the show begins.

Shikari stands, accepting Hound's invitation for a fight as she pulls her long, onyx hair into a lazy ponytail.

Vee, a new huntress who joined us five months ago, snorts beside me. "Don't they ever get sick of bickering?" She asks me.

Her voice is a whisper beneath Hound and Shikari's fight. Cheers erupt from the other huntresses. The others, who have quickly picked sides in the fight, scream their opponent of choice's name. Vee and I slip away into a conversation away from the argument, venturing further into the woods. We lean against two twin trees about twenty feet away, so we are close enough to witness the mayhem but far enough away to hear each other talk.

"We are all more sisters than friends, and sisters bicker as easily as they breathe. I would say you'll get used to it, but." I nod my head toward Frigate, one of the eldest huntresses. "Frigate is almost three hundred years old, and she still gets a headache from all the arguments."

Sure enough, three minutes into the fight, Frigate stands to her feet. She's a petite woman, barely over five feet tall, but she is well regaled in the group of huntresses. Other than me, Frigate is the oldest huntress, and that garners her respect amongst the rest of the women. She walks in between Shikari and Hound, catching Hound's burly fist mid-punch.

Frigate's narrow eyes glower at Hound. "I am about two seconds away from impaling myself with my own arrow if you continue this nonsense." Using her grip on Hound's fist, she pushes her back to her seat on the floor, then glares at Shikari. "Sit down, you wily child." Shikari obeys, then

Frigate glares at Akita and Dýnami. "And you two, if you must argue about proper etiquette every morning, for the love of Olympus, stop sitting next to each other."

Frigate sits down, tiny body physically trembling with annoyance.

The rest listen to Frigate, but Akita looks to me, lips pursed like she ate a full lemon. "Are you going to let her talk to us like that? She treated me like a child!"

Frigate rolls her eyes.

I bite into my squirrel, amused. While Artemis is away attending a meeting at Olympus Industries, I am left in charge of the huntresses. Sika amusedly calls me Mother Hunt, and unfortunately, the title has spread to all sixteen huntresses.

I wait until I swallow my bite of squirrel before responding. "Yes, I am."

Dýnami lets out a loud snort. A piece of squirrel meat is stuck in between her gaped front teeth, which becomes more prevalent as she yells out. "Happy breakfast, sisters!"

Akita grumbles, but the conversations between the huntresses resumes. Within five minutes, Hound and Shikari are sitting next to each other, laughing at one another's jokes. Chiding comments are interwoven with a few singing huntresses and many half-eaten grilled squir-rels on a stick.

"How does it feel?" Vee asks, eating her breakfast beside me.

"How does what feel?"

"To be the oldest huntress. To be Artemis's second-in-command."

The squirrel's meat turns to ash on my tongue. There are moments when I forget Willow isn't dead and I am not the eldest here. I force myself to misremember that I am surrounded by huntresses at least a hundred years younger than me. Sometimes, I imagine my initial huntresses are alive with me, just gone hunting in the woods. It's been decades since I lost Willow, but Vee's question opens the scabbed wound of her death.

I look to the sky, where the sun blazes down on us, and I truthfully respond. "Terrible."

Vee wants to ask more questions. She is always curious, but she never has a chance to ask. In a ray of rainbows, Artemis has returned to our camp. As the archway of colors dissipates, I expect to see only Artemis and Iris, but three men accompany them. Huntresses, who were previously laughing, assume a fighting stance. Arrows rest on their bowstrings, ready to impale the male gods if needed.

I stand in the middle of my huntresses, my breakfast long discarded, with one hand raised in the air. If my hand falls, then their arrows will fly across the room; however, if I close my hand into a fist, they will lower their weapons. Artemis looks at her huntresses with pride that warms away her frigid sadness. Beside her stands Ares.

I close my fist, disarming the huntresses behind me.

"Morning, girls," One of Ares's sons, Phobos, says with a meek wave.

He lingers on one huntress with unmistakable intrigue. When I follow his line of vision, Vee is glaring at him, her finger threateningly grazing an arrowhead. Murder is written on her gaze, daring him to stare at her a second longer. Wisely, Phobos looks away, clearing his throat.

"You couldn't find any goddesses to ride with us?" Sika asks, glancing disapprovingly at Ares and his sons.

Artemis smirks. "Athena and Nike were busy, so I had to settle."

Ares looks down at his sister, eyes narrowing. "Way to make a god feel welcome," he says, voice thick with sarcasm.

Artemis ignores him, focusing on us. "The longer we go without finding the nymphs, the higher chances a war will arise between the gods. Around a dozen nymphs have gone missing. The numbers slowly rise each week we go without discovering where they were taken, and it has the other gods on edge. We need to split up into teams, and we will meet at this spot every Friday to check-in."

"What?" Hound asks. "You want me to work with a male?"

"Silence," I say, glaring back at Hound. Anger rolls off the quick-tempered woman, but she obeys. Turning to face Artemis again, I ask. "What will the teams look like?"

"That depends," she answers, gaze drifting to the huntresses behind me. "Anybody who does not feel comfortable working with a male, step forward and I will ensure you are in either Iris's or my hunting team."

Hound steps forward, along with Gigiana and Shikari. A delayed second behind the others, Frigate hesitantly steps forward. Huntresses do not live as long as Frigate and I without averting away from announcing weaknesses. I've always known about Frigate's past, every gnarly bit, but it's a story she keeps locked away. To Frigate, her past is a weakness, and as she stands in this group, her chin stays raised and she refuses to look anybody in the eye.

"You'll join my hunt," Iris tells the four huntresses, then her multi-colored eyes flutter upwards, finding Artemis.

Her dark skin blushes the many colors of the rainbows as she flirtatiously says. "Try not to miss me too much, Artie."

Artemis, forever oblivious to her charm on women, confusedly responds. "I don't miss people unless they're dead. Did you anger Saffron?"

Iris was smiling, but after Artemis's tasteless response, that smile falters. "Right," Iris quips. She clears her throat. "Until I see you again, then."

Iris and the three huntresses disappear within her rainbows, transporting away from their campsite. As the rainbows dissipate, the four women gone, but a gift is left for Artemis. Two pink cypress flowers lay on Artemis's open palm, one fully bloomed and the other hiding. Ares looks down at the flowers, then back at Artemis's gilded blushed cheeks, and he smiles.

I think it's the first time I've ever seen the god of war smile.

Artemis drags a finger across the pink petals, transfixed on the present. Maybe she isn't as oblivious as I once thought. Perhaps I am the oblivious one because I just now realize the crush is not one sided. Artemis stares at them, like it is the first time she's seen flowers. She smiles as if Iris invented cypresses.

The silence is loud.

Clearing her throat, Artemis says. "Right, let's separate everybody else into search parties."

Artemis assigns me to her search party, alongside Akita and our two newer huntresses, Daphne and Kerria. From morning until sunset, we ride west towards the Mediterranean Sea. Artemis believes the nymphs could be on an island near the sea, where many islands have been forgotten over the centuries. We travel on our horses until Akita's stomach growls louder than any bear in the woods.

Only then do we find shelter for the night. The five of us sit around the campfire, eating the leftovers from Artemis's early lunch with Apollo that day. Eventually, Kerria, Akita, and Daphne fall asleep with bellies full of food other than squirrels, and it's just Artemis and me.

"How did they behave while I was gone?" Artemis asks as she places another twig onto the fire.

"Just as you'd expect."

"How many people did Hound fight?"

I smile. "Just Shikari this time, but if Frigate didn't step in, then I think Dýnami and Sika were going to join in."

We sit in blissful quiet afterwards, letting the crackling wood of the fire placate us. Artemis pulls the two flowers out of her pocket. A soft smile grows on her lips as she traces the petals.

"You two are pretty cute, you know," I interject.

"Your horse is trying to eat tree bark," Artemis quips. Sure enough, when I look over at my newest horse, Gemma, she has her mouth wrapped around the trunk of the tree.

"That might be the dumbest horse I've ever had." We both laugh, but I steer the conversation back to her and Iris. "Don't pretend you didn't hear what I said."

"Maybe I didn't," Artemis says, playing dumb. "Your very soft-spoken."

"Careful, Artemis. You're showing your age."

Artemis glares at me, but there's playfulness in the action. "I've heard Zeus smite humans for less offensive comments."

"How would you survive without me in your old age?" I

tease. "I'm your best friend. You'd be far too helpless without me."

"A goddess, helpless?" Artemis laughs. "You've gone senile over the years."

"Willow would be happy for you," I say, suddenly somber. "If that is what's stopping you from anything with Iris."

Her smile falters, and the flowers slip from her fingertips. Both the bloomed and timid cypresses cascade down to the grass, the movement too slow to be picked up in time. I almost regret my words, but instead of apologizing, I continue. After almost six hundred years with Artemis, they are words she needs to hear.

"I know you loved Willow, and neither one of you said a word. You both had five hundred years, and fear stopped you both from speaking the truth. How happy do you think the two of you would've been before her death if you had those moments together? If you knew how much she loved you, and how much you loved her before she went to the Underworld. Think how-"

"Lamb, enough."

I don't stop.

"Ever since we started looking for the nymphs, I've had this terrible feeling in my gut that our worst war is on the horizon. Don't keep your emotions inside when you don't know when your day is your last. You both may be goddesses, but we've seen gods die, and you deserve love rather than regrets. And we both know you regret not telling Willow, even if you're still too scared to admit it."

Artemis is quiet for a while after that. Almost five minutes pass before, too quiet, she says. "I ask all my huntresses to make an oath against romances because I, too, have made that same oath."

"No, we made an oath against men. Not romance. Otherwise, you would've punished Sika and Dýnami for their recently evolved relationship." I place a hand on Artemis's, and after a hesitant second, she holds my hand back. I can barely decipher the color of her eyes in the dark night in the woods, but I feel her stare as I say. "Iris is very much female, and you very much deserve romance."

There's more we both want to say.

Secrets destined to unfurl.

But the Fates have woven us another path.

As the other huntresses sleep beside the campfire, Artemis and I jump to our feet. My hand is around my arrows, waiting to place them on my bowstring. Standing in between two willow trees is Sinope, the first nymph stolen from her river.

She is as ethereal as I remember, in a billowing grayish blue gown. Her hair moves as part of a river, constantly streaming down the expanse of her back. Sinope and her sisters have always looked like apparitions to me, not fully present. Tonight, underneath the soft moon's beams, Sinope looks more ghost than nymph. She sways in between the trees, arms stretching out for us.

"Sinope?" Artemis takes an eager step forward, eyes overly assessing the nymph several feet away. "Is that really you?"

"Artemis, I'm not sure-" I begin.

"Save me," Sinope interrupts, but her whispery voice sends shivers down my spine. It is her voice, but it isn't, either. There is an undertone of wrongness about it. "I'm so scared, Artemis."

Before I can stop her, warn her of the ominous feeling that we're moving towards danger, Artemis rushes after Sinope. She speeds towards the two willow trees, and I have no choice but to run after Artemis. I feel the trap, jaws wide open and ready to clamp down on us.

Yet, I still rush after Artemis.

FOURTEEN

HART SOMMERS

A s I race down the stairs, I wait for the sound of a second pair of feet chasing after me. My haggard breaths intermingle with the humid, barely air-conditioned stairs. I wait to hear Saffron's voice screaming my name. My lungs restrict, my legs burn, and I fly down several floors, but I never slow. I dreadfully expect the cold caress of her magic pulling at my bones. Paralyzing me. Killing me for knowing what I should not.

Yet, each time I sharply turn ahead, only the empty staircase stares back.

With both hands, I push open the door and barrel into Olympus Industries' lobby. Saffron is not waiting for me with an army, weapons pointing in my direction, steel winking at me under the florescent lights. The building's exit, which is guarded by Argus, is only fifty feet away. The people exiting and entering the building are oblivious to the erratic way my heart slams against my chest. My mind conjures the worst images of my execution, my blood staining the polished floor.

It takes every fiber of self-control to walk, not run, towards the door.

Every few steps, I nervously glance at Argus, waiting for the bored expression on his face to transform into enraged determination. At any moment, he will receive a call from Saffron, and I will die. I keep the thoughts on repeat in my head as I escape Olympus Industries.

This morning, this building elicited hesitant excitement. How can only a few hours shift my views so drastically?

Olympus Industries brings out a terrifying side of me I am not ready to discover. It is a monster in my reflection, and I do not want to look into that mirror. I stumble over my feet a few times, but other than an unamused eye roll from some of Argus's eyes, he allows me to leave without a second thought.

On a typical day, I have time to appreciate the sunset and the way the sun partially hides behind skyscrapers. It's one of my favorite parts of the day. The way the dark purples and pinks play off the buildings' windows, shimmering like glitter upon the road.

It is radiant.

Today, however, I stare at the sun and am reminded of Apollo. The god I have been drawing in my bedroom for years. The male, who transported me to a vision of the future where he and I have twin daughters together. I see the sun, but all I think about are his golden, curly locks. I wonder how soft they must feel now that I know they're real and not a figment of my overactive imagination.

Instead of finding beauty within the sunset, I see the

way the dark purples and pinks bounce off Saffron's office window. She stands there, holding the canvas I drew of her. On that cursed canvas, there's a man I've never seen before drawn beside her. The goddess of bones stares down at me from her window. Although her office is on the highest floor, I swear I can see sadness brimming her round face. I am witness to the confusion in her wrinkled brows because of questions she didn't get the chance to ask before I ran away.

Cabs zoom passed where I stand in front of Olympus Industries, but it will take too long to hail one. I need to leave. Now. If I stay much longer, then I'm unsure if I will run back in or if Saffron will change her mind about letting me go. The longer I stand here, staring at her office window, there's a higher chance she will change her mind and hunt me down.

I'm exhausted, both physically and mentally, but I still run away from Olympus Industries. My apartment is miles away, but each time I think about slowing down, I see a blur of Saffron and Apollo's faces. Their mutually shocked expressions mold together, their lips forming the same question I cannot avoid.

What are you?

My legs burn, begging for reprieve. I use their pain as a distraction from the question I fear the answer to. I do not want to know what I am, and why I create an otherworldly story when my drawing pencil meets a canvas. When I round the corner and see my apartment, run-down and suffocatingly mundane, I've never felt happier to return to my normalcy.

I thought I wanted excitement in my life. A deviation from predictable existence. I change my mind. Sliding my key into my apartment door lock, I decide I want to hide in this apartment. I want to stay in this cycle of boredom and never come out again.

I swing open my apartment door, welcoming its normalcy.

But the Fates have paved my path in another direction.

The Fates are cruel. They adhere to my request for freedom from a life of ordinance. They deliver a wicked story for me, one where I can see the past and future when nobody else can.

As soon as I take the first step into my apartment, the temperature drops by twenty degrees. When I exhale, a plume of cold air filters out. I should turn around, run from the harrowing feeling that my home has changed, too. I don't. Instead, I take two steps and close the door behind me.

Lowell shouldn't be home for another few hours, yet I say his name with great hesitance. "Lowell?" I take another two steps, then ask. "Lowell, are you home?"

These five words are more than I've spoken to Lowell all week, but regardless of our dilapidated relationship, he's my safety net. When I fall, I always know he's there to catch me. The rest of the world changes too fast, but he's always there. He may not be a fiancé who loves me the way a future husband should, but he's dependable. A friend more than a lover.

And as I advance towards his room, I fear I am losing him too.

"Lowell?" Again, I say his name as I walk through the apartment.

The temperature drops another twenty, maybe thirty, degrees. I'm wearing a sundress. The material is too thin for cold temperatures. Goosebumps scatter up my arms. I rub my hands along my biceps, trying to bring warmth. There's nothing but iciness and a sick sense of dread.

Something is wrong, and when I turn to face Lowell's closed bedroom door, I have a sinking suspicion that I'll find the source of the coldness and fear inside.

The doorknob burns my hand with its icy touch. I drop it with a hiss. When I look down, my open palm is covered in crystallized snowflakes. The level of frigidity in my apartment is not humanely possible. An immortal stands on the other side of this door, and for a moment, I want to be a coward. To flee what awaits me.

That's when I hear him.

Lowell's voice is diluted, and I cannot decipher his words, but I recognize the fear in his muffled screams. I wrap my hand around the doorknob again. Coldness seeps into my skin and freezes my blood, but I open the door. Only a few seconds ago, I determined I would run away from the gods and the part of me they enliven.

Yet, here I am, walking into undeniable danger.

My eyes quickly land on Lowell. He sits in one of our chairs they dragged in from our tiny dining room. His entire body is coiled in ropes. Blood blooms on his forehead, the crimson shade bright on his dark complexion. His eyes are wide with fear and they brim with tears. He shakes, trying to pull the ropes off his body, when he sees me. His muffled screams grow louder, but with duct tape over his lips, I cannot understand a word he is saying.

Two women stand on either side of Lowell, and I recognize them both.

One, with rich brown skin and braided hair white like snow. This is his assistant, one of the many women he's been cheating on me with. Before, she hid her icy powers behind stylish gloves and an excessive amount of makeup. Now, I realize too late that she is not human. She no longer disguises her otherworldly characteristics. Like her frost-bitten fingers. But I should have known before today. For no human could be as beautiful as her. She has high-arched, white eyebrows, full lips, and dark skin devoid of any blemishes.

His hairstylist, who I should have known isn't human, stands on his other side. Her eyes, a dark shade of hazel, speak a story of malice and vengeance. She is barely contained rage that is bottled into a petite, plump body.

The white-haired goddess palms a knife that resembles an icicle. It is pressed against the side of his neck. The shorter goddesses, with a knife already stained red at the top with blood, lazily drags her weapon down his arm.

It's the latter who speaks first, her voice harsh yet ethereal. "We have much to discuss, little oracle."

FIFTEEN

SAFFRON

It has been eighty-eight years since I've seen his face, one I've mourned and yearned to glimpse one more time. By Zeus's command, Epiales's memory was ostracized by the rest of the gods. His statues were decimated and paintings were ripped to shreds. When he died, so did his image in my head. I stopped remembering the vibrancy of his silver eyes. The way his tight, dark curls would brush across the top of his eyes. And that gods forsaken smile that would lock up my body.

I do not know how, but Hart gives me a chance to see Epiales again. Standing beside me in this portrait of doom and bloodshed. Although it's just a sketch without color or meticulous detail, I can see him in vivid shades of silver, gold, and ivory. He's as real in this drawing as he was almost a hundred years ago, and tears roll down my cheeks as I trace his outline.

Gods, I've missed him.

This ache in my chest has lessened over the decades, or

perhaps I feared my own emotions. I pushed down the anguish over his death caused by my hands. I busied myself with Hermes, my friends, and building Olympus Industries. No one else, except Hypnos and Thanatos, mourned Epiales. None of us can vocalize our sadness because it is a damnable offense to mourn the loss of a traitor.

I have had no choice.

I ignored my sadness.

Every few seconds, teardrops land on Hart's drawing. My tears dilute the war scene around us, a war I've never seen in person, but each tear avoids tarnishing Epiales. I blind myself with the sight of Epiales that I ignore the rest of the image and the warning it gives. Only when the volcano blurs from weeping do I realize the macabre nature of this canvas.

Only now, as I see the depravity and murder around our bodies.

In the eighteen years that Epiales and I were intertwined, I had only seen him wear fear so blatantly upon his face once. This painting is the second time. He is frightful of what he and I are about to become, and that is when I finally focus on his hand upon my shoulder and, subsequently, me.

I wear a crown of bones upon my wavy brown locks, and there is fresh blood smeared on the bones. A mixture of red and gold blood slides from the bones onto my face, careening down my cheek like tears. I know I am a killer in this drawing, and all the fallen bodies circling around Epiales and me are my victims. Anyone who looks upon this drawing would label me a monster, a killer of both humans and gods, but I see the truth.

Defeat weighs heavily on my face. I kill others in this

image, but I lost the real war. While I may be the executioner, somebody much more powerful plays the strings that are tied around my wrists.

If a person glimpses at this drawing, Epiales and I appear monstrous. The nightmare and his god-killer. We are the terror parents warn their children against. The villains instead of the heroes.

His hand is on my shoulder as I cause this bloodshed. There is a small smile pulling at his lips that gives the impression that he is proud of who I am. That he wants me to be a killer of the world. He dons an outfit fit for a ruler as well, yet I see his truth in his eyes, and I am drowning in the waves of his fear.

This artwork is fictitious because Epiales is dead and I am not a mindless killer, but my spine ices over with trepidation. I stare at us surrounded by brutal carnage. A mass execution we are responsible for, even if it is against our volition. While I know he is dead and I am not defeated, I have this terrible ache in my stomach that this image could become a reality.

The office door swings open, giving me only a second to react. Quickly, I place the drawing on my lap and throw a coat over my thighs as a blanket. Aphrodite, Eros, and Dionysus stroll through the room, but they're looking at each other as Dionysus cracks a joke involving a grape seed and a cyclops. With waning time, I wipe away the tear stains lining my cheeks.

By the time they all face me, ear-splitting grins on their faces, I place the mask of indifference back on my face. Aphrodite glances between the unused easel, the scattered drawing pencils, then glares at me with narrowed eyes.

"Why did you scare off Apollo's mate? What did you

do?" Two perfectly manicured hands rest on her hips. Although there's a crease in between her thin, slightly arched eyebrows, I cannot take Aphrodite's rage seriously. I do not respond to her, and after a few tense seconds of silence, Aphrodite sighs and says. "Per usual, dear friend, I must fix your mistakes."

"Name one other time you've fixed a mistake of mine," I retort.

"Anyway!" Aphrodite strolls towards the two chairs opposite my desk; Dionysus takes the other seat; Eros, however, leans against the wall closest to the door with one knee propped up. Slapping her hands theatrically on the top of her thighs, she pulls my focus back to her just as she announces. "We're going to have a ball."

Dionysus shares Aphrodite's excitement; meanwhile. I ask Eros, the only sane god in this room. "Is she serious?"

"There was once a time when you enjoyed symposiums," he responds in his calm, consistently sensuous tone.

"And it's the perfect occasion to bring Apollo and Hart together," Aphrodite adds. "Both will be invited, and since nobody would say no to the wedding anniversary of two gods, they'll both accept. I'll personally beautify Hart, and then BAM!" Aphrodite claps, and when her hands part, her grin is all-encompassing. "Their love story will begin."

Amid this drawing burning a hole in my lap, I almost forgot why Hart came to Olympus Industries. She is Apollo's soulmate, his third great love, who he is prophesied to love forever. She is not simply the woman who gave me a glimpse of a future that should not exist within a drawing. Hartika Sommers is destined for Apollo.

I nod my head, processing a fifth of her words as I

murmur. "Sounds like a good idea. What day? I'll clear my calendar."

I should tell them about the drawing, which is neither fictitious nor from the past, but from some distorted future. Yet, for reasons I cannot fully comprehend, I remain silent. I let the other gods laugh amongst themselves, oblivious to the war of conflict in my mind.

Dionysus breaks through my reverie as he says. "We're aiming for March twenty-ninth. Of course, we'll have to speak with Zeus and garner his approval for Hermes to take that day off, but I think we will convince him." Dionysus sneaks a glance at Aphrodite, who reminds the room she is the goddess of love with a seductive smirk.

"I'll make sure Zeus gives Hermes the day off." Aphrodite winks at Dionysus.

I catch Eros in the back, not hiding his disgust at his mother's tactics. He rolls his eyes, arms crossed over his chest. "Why am I even here for this?" He asks in a grumble.

My husband's name on Dionysus's lips stops me from focusing on anything they're saying. I hear Hermes's name, but all I can think about are the nights when his side of the bed is cold. I curse myself by thinking of the arguments he flees from before they can be resolved. Hermes's name fills the air, tainting my thoughts with the growing fear that he is cheating on me. That his love for me fizzles more each day.

That he stopped loving me when I stopped being the naïve girl who loved strawberries and dreamed of a world full of hope.

"The event for the ball is your and Hermes's eighty-fifth anniversary," Dionysus responds. "Of course Hermes needs to be there."

I didn't realize until now that our eighty-fifth anniversary was coming up.

When was the last time he and I celebrated our marriage? Twelve years ago? Maybe twenty-five? More importantly, when was the last time we were grateful for our holy union? When was the last time I glanced at my husband, the second man I've ever loved, and was truly happy? When was the last time he looked at me with the same ardent affection as he had all those years ago in the gazebo? Since a became a goddess, has he ever loved me the same way he loved the human side?

"Right," I say, yet the word cracks and splinters. Neither Aphrodite nor Dionysus realize, but Eros does. He focuses on me as I swallow a plate of glass and say as composed as possible. "That sounds like a great idea. I'm sure it'll be an unforgettable anniversary."

"Now, I must ask again, where is our little painter?" Aphrodite asks, and if I did not know who she was referring to, she motions towards Hart's forgotten supplies. "How did you scare her?"

The words are lodged in my throat. Even the lies I wish to spew remain stuck, inescapable from the anxiety drowning me. Hart scared me, not the other way around. The drawing and the secrets they tell are daunting. If Hart didn't rush out of the room with fear widening her eyes, it would've been me who fled the room. Me, who ran from a human girl with skills far from mundane.

"Fine, be secretive," Aphrodite announces. She stands to her feet, brushing off the invisible debris on her pink pencil skirt, and says. "I'll swing by her house and insist she return tomorrow. Toodles!"

She waves goodbye to us, then disappears in a plume of pale pink smoke.

"I better get going too," Dionysus stands from his seat. "Orgies cannot host themselves."

He leaves in a web of grapes, vines, and plum-colored shadows.

Eros glances at me from where he stands against the wall, then softly, he asks. "Is everything alright, Saffron?"

"Perfect," I lie, eyes never wavering from his. "Never better."

The left corner of his lip tilts upwards. "Your lying hasn't improved over the century."

"I'm not lying."

"When you're done lying and need somebody to talk to, call me. I've been told I'm a great listener."

Eros opens the office door, and the moment it closes with a soft clink behind him, I pull the drawing from my lap. Epiales's face haunts me with its cruel combination of beauty and mayhem.

But for just a moment, I let his face bleed through my vision until all I see is him.

SIXTEEN

HART SOMMERS

"Who are you?" The words come out more assured than I thought possible. I glance between the two powerful, frightening deities, and the assertiveness I held when I asked the first question dissipates. I stutter. "Did." I clear my throat, unable to ask the entire question on the first attempt. I try again. "Did Lady Saffron send you?"

It's the goddess of ice who speaks, full lips curving into a cruel grin. "I am Khione, goddess of snow, and no, little oracle, Saffron didn't send us."

"Somebody much more powerful than the god-killer sent us," the shorter goddess says.

The words still my heart. For who could be more powerful than Saffron? She is the prophesied child of Metis and Zeus, designed to be the most lethal of all deities. Saffron can kill gods when nobody else can, yet they say another is stronger than her. Who?

In the back of my mind, where rationality burns

through my fear. I remember the drawing I made of Saffron earlier today. The goddess is drenched in blood, her hands guiding death towards her in a wave of bones and anguish. Her face is forlorn and her helpless pierces through the artwork.

"You're frightening her, Nemesis," Khione says.

Her tone is teasing. Playful, even.

Lowell whimpers in between them, body trembling. Khione's blade knicks his flesh, and a stream of red blood careens down his throat. It drips onto the ground, staining the cheap beige carpet with the first sign of the gods' malice.

"What do you want with us?" I ask.

By the synchronized, growing smiles on both their lips, I wish I could retract my words.

Khione still holds the knife to Lowell's flesh, but faster than I expect, Nemesis's hand wraps around my jaw. Nails dig into skin as she pulls my face down. I am so close to her, our foreheads collide together, that I can taste the acrimony on her breath. The odor is worse than decomposing flesh or singed hair. She smells like she is rotting from the inside out, desperate to bring others down with her to the depths of her anguish.

"There are many things I want, little oracle."

Her thumb slides across my flesh, and every inch of me crawls with disgust. Her touch is like a thousand spiders littering my flesh, and it takes every morsel of self-control not to wiggle away. I do not understand why Lowell is having an affair with her. While she is gorgeous in an otherworldly fashion, her touch feels too much like death. Like the tart taste of misery.

Nemesis watches me fight off the urge to distance

myself from her, and she responds by clenching her hand tighter against my face. If she applies any more pressure, my bones will break.

"I want to be more than just a goddess of evil deeds and divine retribution," Nemesis continues as she drags the sharp nail of her thumb across the curve of my jawline. "I want to be revered." She smiles as she adds. "Feared and respected. I am solely known for punishing Narcissus for committing hubris, but what else is there to my legacy? Nothing, little oracle. I want to make the world and its humans suffer, but I'm slowly being forgotten. What I want is to bathe this world in my hatefulness, but Zeus won't let me."

"But *she* will," Khione gleefully adds.

Nemesis's nail knicks my skin, the pain sharp and poignant. I stumble away from her, my hand clamping my cheek that is dribbling with blood. The red liquid slides down Nemesis's thumb, and she looks at me unblinkingly as she puts her digit in her mouth and sucks the blood. My stomach rolls with disgust, and if Lowell didn't need my help, I would run from this room.

"What I want," Nemesis says as she pulls her thumb out of her mouth with a pronounced *pop*. "Is to change this world to fit my interests, and you are one small step in helping me achieve what I want."

Today, my world has changed. Tilted on its axis, spun around a thousand times, and morphed into a reality I do not recognize. I've ridden in a car with Argus. Met Apollo when I thought his face was a fictitious imagination. Foresaw a future for Saffron that bathes her in human and godly blood. Before today, I thought myself wholly human, inexplicably ordinary. Yet, as two goddesses stand before me, needing my help for a war creeping out of the shadows, I know I am not completely normal.

Although I try to make my voice as strong as possible, it wobbles with trepidation, as I say to Khione. "Let Lowell go."

"What do you know about curses, little oracle?" Khione asks.

Nemesis strides back to Lowell. As soon as Nemesis's blade is pressed against his throat, Khione moves towards me, hips swaying with each step. Her dress is overtly extravagant, crystalline snowflakes cinching her waist and creating a floor length halter gown. There's a small train on the gown made entirely of ice.

Somehow in a tight-fitted dress, Khione produces a rolled-up contract, tied with a simple black ribbon. A gold S is stamped over the black ribbon, securing the two fabrics together. I shouldn't know what the S stands for. Neither Khione nor Nemesis have said her name, but I know. Just as I knew Apollo's face, down to each minute detail, years before I met him. Just as I knew too much before being told.

"You are Styx's puppets," I say, eyeing the golden "S" on the scroll.

"In eight days' time, Lowell will die," Khione says.

She ignores my comment, but her silence confirms the truth. Styx is creating an uprising.

Lowell whimpers from his chair, rope distorting the sobs fighting to escape his lips, but I hear him say. "H." His nickname for me since we were children sounds devastating in these circumstances.

"Unless," Khione says.

She extends the scroll, and I accept it.

I break the golden "S" sealing the scroll, pull the ribbon

off, and reveal Styx's commands. As I read the letter, my heart shatters with each carefully written word. Hopelessness grips my throat, stealing away my breath slowly and torturously.

Khione knows I am reading Styx's contract, but she cliff notes it. Her voice is as cold as the ice she commands. "There is one way to save Lowell Black's life. On the eighty-eighth day of this year, you will bring Saffron to the Underworld. If you deliver the goddess of bones to the true queen, then you will save your fiancé's life."

Nemesis uses her free hand to grab the rope in Lowell's mouth. As soon as she tugs down the rope, Lowell's screams fill the room. His howls threaten to shatter the windows and glass lampshades.

"H, please!" Snot rolls down his nose, dropping on his upper lip as he begs. "Don't let me die!"

Beneath his screams, and my heart that loudly beats like a drum against my chest, Khione speaks in a calm, low voice. "You must sign at the bottom if you agree to save your fiancé's life for Saffron."

Saffron is the world's savior, the hero of mankind.

She has saved millions, maybe billions, of human lives throughout the course of her existence. Songs are sung in her honor. Statues are chiseled to her perfection. But I am supposed to lead her into Styx's clutches. The goddess who gave humanity their freedom is the same goddess they demand I steal. They demand the loss of her freedom.

Without Saffron, many will suffer.

But Lowell is all I have left in this world.

When my family died, he took me in. He convinced his parents to shelter me in their home, and when we both reached adulthood, Lowell provided me with this apartment. He is far from perfect, but he is the only semblance of family I have left. When everybody else around me died, Lowell helped me to my shaky feet.

As I sobbed into his arms on the night I identified their bodies, Lowell promised he'd never leave my side. It's why we're still in this loveless engagement. Despite his adultery, overconfidence, and lack of communication, Lowell Black is true to his word. He has never left me. We are not in love; we are far from it, but he's the only family I have in this world. My family roams through the Underworld, but Lowell is here and alive.

He provided for me when I needed it most, and this is when I can repay that debt.

Unless I choose Saffron over him. That's the real question.

Do I keep Saffron safe? Millions depend on her. She is the savior of humanity, but she is not my family. Lowell is. So, do I choose her, or do I save Lowell's life? My family and only friend, who has been there in my most desperate times. Will I be selfless and save Saffron, or will my selfishness guide me towards Lowell's safety? I do not love him the way I should. I love him the way I loved my brother, and the way I think I'd love a best friend if I had anybody else in my life.

Tears stream down my cheeks as I make my decision. "Give me a pen."

While Lowell sighs in relief, I can hear my father's disappointment ringing in my ears, as if he were here.

"Open your palm," Khione says.

I obey. A small tornado of ice and snow materializes in the palm of my hand, and when it dissipates, a white pen sits there.

I move towards the wall nearest me, placing the contract against the wall and the tip of the pen on the dotted line. My hand moves, ready to form an H, when my vision blurs and a fog suddenly obstructs my senses. Phantom hands guide my body, turning my head towards where Nemesis stands with a knife against Lowell's throat.

"Before I sign, you should know something, Lady Nemesis."

The voice that leaves my lips is both mine, but not mine. The phantom hands are on my body, and they slide into my skin. Another version of myself, one not fully human, takes control. Seizes my body and speaks words I do not fully understand because they are not of the past or the present.

They speak of the future.

"When the Savior's hands drip with ichor and bones make a crown on her head, it is because of you. It is your blood that will stain her hands first. Your bones that will first make the crown for the queen of humans. The bones in your arms will be pulled out first, then she will take your kneecaps and elbows. Tears will spill from your pretty, green eyes, Lady Nemesis, and you will beg for mercy. It will not come, that mercy you will plead for. The goddess of humanity will take, and take, and take until you are nothing. In that last moment of your life, you will wish you heeded my warning. Wish you returned your fealty to King Zeus. Just as all who follow the personification of hatred, you will crumble like Pompeii."

My laugh is vicious, like the two goddesses before me, and they have every reason to fear the sound.

"All who follow Styx will crumble like Pompeii."

The words echo throughout the room as if a thousand

versions of myself hover together. A dozen pieces of myself stand as faceless apparitions in this room, and they whisper the same sentence at different intervals. Khione stumbles away from me, dark eyes widening with fear. Nemesis's hand on her blade trembles, then drops onto the floor. Even Lowell pales in his chair, fearing me almost as much as he fears the two goddesses cursing him.

The fog dissipates, and all that remains is the promise behind them.

I sign the dotted line, then drop the pen and paper. Before they touch the ground, Khione and Nemesis disappear in a tornado of ice with the completed contract. The very contract which makes me a traitor to the goddess who saved humanity so long ago.

My movement is dazed, but I kneel in front of the chair Lowell is tied to, trembling as I remove the ropes around his body. He is speaking to me, thanking me for saving his life and apologizing for all the affairs over the years. I can barely hear him, his words thousands of miles away.

Instead, the drums of war beat against my eardrums.

The screams of billions, who beg for mercy but receive mercilessness in return. Cackles from malicious lips, who rejuvenate themselves to the strife of others. I cannot see the faces of those who suffer, but I can feel the kiss of the blades that end their lives. I can hear the screams they let out that both screech with fear and echo with the daunting realization that they will not be saved. Clinking swords and helpless whimpers through until I can feel blood sliding down my ears and joining Lowell's blood on the cheap beige carpet.

By saving Lowell's life and signing that dotted line, I started a war I'm not sure the good side will win.

SEVENTEEN

LAMB

I run with Artemis, weaving between trees and leaping over moss-covered rocks, but the entire time, I know we should stop. Sinope is not here, and on the slight chance she is, she is leading us towards a trap. Her voice is too willowy, not nasally like it normally is. It's Sinope's face, her almost translucent body we saw, but this isn't her.

"Artemis, stop!"

But she is on a path, refusing to see anything else but a solution.

"I need to run faster," Artemis says, her breath shallow and desperate. "I need to find them."

"Artemis, this is a trap!"

She veers right, following Sinope's retreating form, and I follow. I try to run faster than Artemis, so I can wrap my arms around her and throw her to the ground. To stop her from landing in the trap perfectly designed for her. But I'm not quicker than a goddess of the wild. I am only a human, trying to win a race against an immortal.

"Artemis, please!"

"I need to find them." She endlessly repeats these five words. Sometimes, they are soft mutters under her breath. Other times, she screams it until the surrounding trees shake with fright.

Faintly, I can hear three pairs of feet behind us, as the other huntresses cannot catch up. My lungs scream, begging for reprieve, as I try to keep pace. I cannot lose Artemis, and it is the only mantra I focus on as I push my body to its limit.

Willowy leaves dangle from bent tree branches. They conceal a piece of the world, and the moment Artemis's hands grab onto the branches and part them, I know this is it. Our trap lays wait for us behind the leaves.

I may not be an oracle. I cannot see the future, but I sense our imprisonment behind these curtains. Danger awaits, but I choose to join Artemis wherever she goes. I push through that same curtain of tree branches. My mind tells me to turn around, but I ignore my rationality. Screaming one last command to the huntresses behind me, I attempt to prevent the others from the same fate as us.

"It's a trap!" I bellow. "Don't follow! Find Saffron and tell her!"

As soon as I step through the curtain, the world around me transforms.

Suddenly, I am no longer in the depths of the forest with my huntresses, but my feet smack onto a sandy ground, surrounded by miles of water. I am five hundred and ninety years old, and I have scoured this world with Artemis and the huntresses a hundred times over. Yet, I look upon the white sandy shore, where lemon and kiwis hang from tree branches, and I do not recognize this island.

But I recognize the two hundred water nymphs weeping in their confinements.

They're curling their bodies into fetal positions inside bronzed cages. All of them shiver despite the island's warm weather. Their wrists and ankles are tied in ropes, their heads hanging low in saddened shame. Within these cages, Sinope sits, crying alongside her sisters. She does not wear the same gown as the version of Sinope we followed here, but she is in the tattered outfit from the day of her abduction.

Just as I feared, Sinope didn't lead us here.

Someone much worse did.

Above me, in a cloudless sky, there's a closing portal. The very portal Artemis and I fell into. It is a swirling mass of emerald mist. Resembling a moss-covered cloud, the portal shrinks in front of my eyes. Our freedom slips away as the portal disappears. When it is the size of a peanut and my hope has been slashed to the bone, an arrow flies through the opening.

I recognize Artemis's signature arrow. The dark arrowhead contrasts with the white note impaled at the tip. The arrow slips through the portal a heartbeat before it disappears. That tiny white piece of parchment restores my faith in surviving our captivity.

Artemis sighs as she lowers her bow. "You were right," she solemnly says. "She trapped us."

"Sinope didn't trap us," I say while motioning towards the caged nymph.

"Not her," Artemis says.

"Then who?" I ask.

Artemis no longer looks at me. She stares at a figure several feet away. I follow her gaze, landing on the false

Sinope. She stands there with a smirk on her face, and then she transforms. Green smoke curls around her body, shedding Sinope's features and revealing our true captor.

She no longer has Sinope's shoulder-length black hair; instead, her hair becomes curly. It lightens several shades, too, until it is as golden as the sun. Sinope's frame is extended by three, maybe four, inches. More weight is added on her breasts and stomach. Sinope's nose, mouth, and forehead morph into another goddess's features.

Last, Sinope's dark brown eyes become purple, and Artemis sneers. "Calypso."

Calypso is a few inches shy of six feet, standing in a teal gown draping over her body. For eons, she's been the sole occupant of Ogygia, a mystical island nobody can find unless she allows you entrance. Pure evil has taken siege over Atlas's daughter, and all hope of freedom dwindles into nothingness.

"Hello Artemis," almost as a second thought, she glances at me. "And what is your name?"

"Lamb."

She looks me over, unapprovingly. "A fitting name for such a docile little thing." She opens her arms out, showcasing her world. It is a beautiful prison, but a prison all the same. "Welcome, Artemis." Again, as a second thought, she adds. "And the little lamb."

The same shade of green smoke as the portal slithers across the white sand like snakes. I move my hand back, reaching for an arrow, but my weapons are gone. The snake latches onto my ankles, and as the smokey creature encircles my leg, it leaves behind chains. My freedom is stolen from my grasp by magic I cannot fight against.

The moment the chains immobilize us, the green swirls

of magic manifest a cage identical to the ones imprisoning the nymphs. The ceiling of the cage grazes the top of my head, and the walls touch my elbow and knees. There is just enough room to exist, and not an inch more.

"Don't worry," Calypso says to Artemis. "You'll be freed in eight days."

"Why eight days?"

"Because the Savior must do what she does best." Calypso grins. "She must save your lives at the expense of her own."

She walks away, teal gown swishing in the sand.

The moment she is out of earshot, Artemis whispers. "Did you recognize the magic's color?"

There are few witch goddesses, especially after the last war, but each one has a specific hue of green magic. With their vast power comes a color identifier. The shade of moss is signature to only one witch. I nod my head, unable to say the words out loud.

Artemis, however, has no hesitance.

"Whoever Calypso works for, Hecate is on their side."

"Who is it?" I ask, nearly fearing the answer. "Who planned all this?"

We both know Calypso is too dim-witted, and Hecate is not a leader. Merely a follower. So, who is the master of all this treachery? Who is trying to incite a new war? Artemis is silent, and that is answer enough.

She doesn't know, but she's terrified of whoever it is.

EIGHTEEN

HERMES

I do not know when I stopped seeing my house with Saffron as home. But today, I sit on the dock overlooking the River Styx beside Zig, and I realize the Underworld is my home. I belong amongst the gods who rule over the dead, but I should find this sense of belonging in the mansion I share with my wife.

Zig passes me a bottle of wine, and my lips move to say the words *I need to go home*. However, I wordlessly take the bottle. Instead of saying *I need to go see my wife*, I drink the wine.

"Have you seen her today?" I ask, motioning my head towards the River Styx.

We tempt the Fates, sitting so casually on the dock overlooking Styx's watery domain. Our feet do not dangle over the railing, waiting for clawed hands to wrap around our ankles, but we are testing our safety all-the-same.

I pass the bottle of wine back to Zig, and just before he

places the drink to his lips, he answers. "Once. She wished me a good morning."

He drinks as I ask. "Anything else?"

"Why must you ask questions you already know the answer to? It makes drinking with you quite boring."

Still, he passes me back the drink, continuing our daily routine.

Throughout my marriage to Saffron, her friends transitioned into our friends. Zig has been at the other end of my laughter for decades, but when I try to find the words to explain my relationship struggles with Saffron, my lips falter. There is so much I wish to say, but I drink and pass the bottle back to him. I suffer in the silence until the dry, red wine slides down my throat again.

"I got a clue about the Nosoi today," Zig says.

For months, I have been twenty steps behind Styx's plans. No matter how quick I am, how well I can trick, she continues to elude me. She's a meticulous, calculated villain of brains and apathy. In her company I am lesser.

Unless I can keep Saffron out of the Underworld for the next eight days.

"One of the newest souls you brought in was lucid," Zig explains. He wears a smile on his face, but it is as tentative as his words. His voice is laced in uncertainty because, just like me, Zig feels defeated by Styx's continuous success. "She said she saw a goddess materializing new Nosoi. A hood covered most of her face, but the human confirmed the killer's gender."

Suddenly, I sit up. "That narrows down the suspects by half."

"And she saw long, black hair," Zig says.

The wine is long forgotten as I face my friend. Zig opens

his mouth, ready to elaborate, when pink, heart-shaped mist materializes in between us.

Aphrodite, her appearance constantly shifting, emerges in a silk pink dress. She holds the bottle of wine that sat where she appeared, reading the label before frowning. "Truly, boys, you must get better taste in wine. Merlot is out of style."

Zig, almost offended, stands up, rips the wine bottle out of her hand, and plops back down on his seat at the dock. He nurses the wine bottle, cradling it like one would a child. Aphrodite's attention has already shifted onto me. Her face continues to change, but her smile is widespread in every form. Her eyes change shape and color, but they all peruse the expanse of my body before meeting my gaze with a wink.

"Well hello, former lover. Aren't you looking particularly forlorn today? It's not a cute look." Aphrodite purrs all her words like a cat, attempting to seduce her mouse into compliance before she pounces.

I frown, unamused. "What are you doing in the Underworld, Aphrodite? You hate it down here."

"That I do." Aphrodite humphs as she glances around the dark, cavernous walls and wrinkles her ever-changing nose at the gray and black rivers. "It's dreadful, but you are here more often than in our world of color, so I had no choice."

"Why did you have no choice?"

"Because I have delightful news for you."

"Doubtful."

"You can be quite hurtful, Hermie."

"Perhaps my words are barbed because you insist on calling me Hermie," I retort.

"You didn't mind that nickname when we were lovers."

"Yes, I did." I remark. "But I was less-than honest at the time."

"Rude," she quips.

The whole time, Zig cradles the bottle of wine, eyes darting back-and-forth between Aphrodite and me with unabashed amusement.

"Why are you here?" I ask again, more irritable this time.

"I convinced Zeus to give you a day off." Aphrodite's grin is manic, displaying all her pride in achieving the impossible.

My frown becomes more pronounced. "A day off?" I ask, incredulously. "You know I am the god of trickery, right? Pranks do not work on me."

"It's not a prank, you crabby male. I had a pleasant talk with Zeus, and he generously agreed to-"

Before she can finish her sentence, I snort.

Her eyes narrow. "What's so funny?"

"After a nice talk?" I ask, sarcasm and amusement weaving together.

Her smile dissipates. "Fine, I seduced him. Why does it matter how I got him to agree? You should thank me, Hermie."

"Why did you want him to have a day off so badly?" Zig asks before drinking the bottle using both hands.

"Because Dionysus is throwing a ball on March twenty-ninth. It will be a celebration of you and Saffron's eighty-fifth wedding anniversary. We have the entire night planned out, down to the Hors d'oeuvres-"

Aphrodite rambles on about the anniversary party she and Dionysus are hosting in Saffron and my honor. They will find any excuse to have a party, and my wife and I are this event's reasoning. We are the lucky guests of honor, even if it is a role we did not ask for. Typically, I'd laugh off this invitation and tell her I'd attend so she'd leave, but the party's date stuns me silent. March twenty-ninth is the eighty-eighth day of the year.

The day Styx's war will begin.

I lock eyes with Zig. Aphrodite paces between us, partially obscuring our view from each other, but the fear in our expressions remains the same. Aphrodite is oblivious, but Zig and I hear the moment Styx's head pops out of the river. She, too, listens to Aphrodite's plans to hold a ball on the same night Styx is destined to start a battle for Mt. Olympus.

This ball is the perfect location for Styx to announce her war. When everybody's inhibitions are lowered and drinks incapacitate stronger deities like Poseidon and Dionysus. I turn my head towards Styx, and her abysmal gaze pierces through my heart like a javelin. She is poison, seeping into my veins and promising a cruel demise.

The bare scope of her shoulders is visible from above the water, but the rest of the body is submerged in her dark waters. Her short, black hair clings to her face, curling around the harsh cut of her jaw. She is bathed in the darkness of her river, but on the same night as this cursed ball, she will rise.

As if she can read my mind, the tiniest smile pulls on the left corner of her mouth.

"Hermes!" a shrill voice screams.

I whip my head towards Aphrodite, where she stands with her hands pressed to her hips and a scowl on her lips. "What?" I ask, almost dazed.

"Were you even listening to me?"

"I can't wait for the ball, it sounds wonderful," I lie through my teeth.

Her grin returns tenfold. "Wonderful!" She exclaims. "Now, I'm off to convince an adorable human painter to find true love. Toodles."

Aphrodite leaves as she arrived, in a puff of pink, heart-shaped mist.

The moment she is gone, Styx's eerily monotone voice chills the air. "A ball sounds exhilarating."

Zig and I turn to face her, threats clawing up my throat, but she's already gone. Back inside her watery abyss, scheming her way to the throne.

"Saffron can't go to that ball," I whisper with certainty.

Zig, however, asks warily. "How can she not attend a ball that's in honor of her marriage?"

If there is no marriage to celebrate.

I do not respond to him, not while Styx can hear me. "I got to go," I say instead.

My winged sandals whisk me away from the Under-world. Zig still sits cross-legged on the river's edge. I fly through the world until I land on the front porch of my mansion with Saffron. Only then, when my hand is reaching for the doorknob, do I answer Zig's question.

"I must break my wife's heart."

I open the door and enter my home for the last time.

NINETEEN

HART SOMMERS

I t's not until night, when Lowell has finally dozed off after many tears, apologies, and glasses of neat gin. Finally, I am alone.

I seclude myself in my bedroom, where I am not continually reminded of Nemesis and Khione. While in my small, pale-yellow room, I can pretend, for a few precious hours, that my life has not tilted on its axis. When I am in my room, I have not met and frightened the goddess of humanity. Did not make a deal with Styx to betray the goddess of humanity.

My life is normal within this room, or as normal as it can be. I curl up in my bed and gaze at a drawing I made of Apollo before I ever knew what he looked like.

My drawing pad is open, and I flip to the last page I created. I cannot pull my gaze away from him. He stares at me from the other end of the drawing, as if he has come alive, and reaches out to brush a piece of hair from my forehead, tucking it behind my ear. This is merely a drawing, never enlivened with colors, but I can taste sunshine on my tongue as his scent encompasses me.

He's not here, yet he's here at the same time. This is only a piece of artwork, but now that I know he isn't a figment of my imagination. His callous fingers graze my exposed collarbone, his lips explore the expanse of my neck, and his leg brushes against mine in the most sensuous promise. I move to close the drawing pad. Electricity scours up the length of my body and settles in the pit of my stomach. I cannot bring myself to look away.

Then the doorbell rings.

I flinch, dropping the drawing pad.

A part of me screams to run, but I do not. Slowly, I rise from my bed, grabbing the first item that can be used as a weapon. A partially eaten chocolate bar. It can hurt nothing larger than a fly, but I clutch it with both hands like it is a mighty sword.

With each step I take out of my bedroom, through the living room, and towards the front door, I am disturbingly quiet. Only the tips of my toes land on the hardwood floor. I mirror my movements from the spy movies that Lowell forces me to watch. The normally irritable, old apartment ground does not squeak or moan underneath my steps, and for a moment, I believe I am stealthy. Able to be undetected by the person on the other side of that door.

"I can hear you," a sing-song voice chimes from the other side of the door. "Please open the door, Harty. Your balding neighbor keeps staring at me, and I do not believe his heavy breathing results from poor health."

My mind is scattered in a thousand different directions, and I take too long to process whose voice slips through my apartment. I fear the worst, believing Khione or Nemesis have returned. Or that Saffron has finally tracked me down to ask me about the art piece.

Or, the worst outcome, it's Styx. I've never met the goddess who reigns over the main river in the Underworld, but her name alone sends chills down my spine. While Thanatos is the personification of death, Styx's name incurs an unnatural sensation through me. This one syllable makes my body feel like I am burning alive within the heart of a volcano.

But that voice, so unnaturally sensuous, pulls me out of my fear. "Lady Aphrodite?" I ask.

I swing open the door, and while her physical form differs, I immediately recognize her as Lady Aphrodite, goddess of beauty and love.

She stands before me in the same pale pink outfit, but her skin is currently the darkest shade of brown. Her once shaggy, shoulder-length hair is sheared closer to her scalp but remains onyx hued. This version of Aphrodite has wide eyes that overtake half her face, and her cheeks are the color of rose petals. She's achingly gorgeous in a way only Aphrodite can be.

"May I come in?" She asks.

Then, she glances back at my neighbor across the street. As she said, Yazdan leans on his closed apartment door, wheezing at her. Yazdan is a sixty-eight-year-old man, who smokes enough hookah to fill the entire apartment floor in the scent of mangoes and tobacco. But she's right. He is not breathing heavily solely because of his damaged lungs. Yazdan is harmless, but in the unbeknownst company of a goddess, he is a staring, sweating mess.

"Go inside, Yazdan, or I'll tell your wife about this," I say.

In three hobbled steps, Yazdan goes back inside.

Shouldering past me, her heeled shoes stomp through my tiled kitchen floor, and glides through my living room. She lays out across my couch. Resting her head on one armchair, she dangles her feet off the other. We've only met today, but Aphrodite acquaints herself in my home like she's been here a thousand times before.

Hesitantly, I close my apartment door and walk into the living room after her.

"I must apologize for today," Aphrodite begins. She materializes a champagne glass filled to the brim with a pink, bubbly drink. "I do not know what Saffron did to frighten you off, but I apologize for leaving you with her. Over the past few decades, she has been far too moody. I should've kept you all to myself, or dropped you off with a friendlier god."

The image I created for Saffron this morning burns through my mind. I see the bloodshed, the bones, and her lover in brutal strokes all over again. My throat is like shards of glass, each breath painful to take.

Somehow, I find my words. "Lady Saffron was very kind."

Aphrodite crinkles her nose. "Sure she was. Saffron is as kind nowadays as a prickly cactus."

Suddenly, she sits up on my couch, and instead of the beverage, her right hand holds an envelope. I do not know where the glass went, but she does not give me time to ponder long. An envelope with my name extends in my direction.

"To apologize and stop you from quitting your job, I want to formally invite you to a ball at Dionysus's house. It's a rare achievement to be a human invited to join the ranks of the gods at one of our events, especially one thrown by Dionysus."

Aphrodite wiggles the envelope towards me. She impatiently waits for me to pluck the invitation from her hands and readily accept. Each time I blink, I see Khione and Nemesis with that damned contract. I hear their threats like they are gusts of wind in the room. The threat of Styx looms over me, a shadow I cannot avoid.

"Lady Aphrodite, I-"

"Just Aphrodite, darling."

"I'm flattered that you invited me, but-"

"Harty." Again, Aphrodite interrupts me. Her smile is gone, but the invitation is still extended towards me. "Please tell me you are not about to reject my offer. As quaint as this little abode is, do you want your entire life to slip by while you stay here?"

Aphrodite stands up to her feet, towering over me at a staggering six feet tall. She strides towards me as if she knows my entire life story. Understands and sympathizes with me. She takes both my hands and places the envelope on top of them.

Dark eyes stare down at me as she says. "I must admit, before I hired you, I watched you for a few days. And darling, I am in the business of love, and I did not design your match with Lowell Black. Neither did my son, Eros. He is temporary, a fleeting thought, but the true love I know you deserve is out there. I may not know what it is like to be in love, but I know how to create love for others. Hart Sommers, I have made you one of the happiest love stories, if only you'll reach out and take it."

"You do not know love for yourself?"

"I know what false love is," she answers solemnly. "I

know that love is like a candle. For some, the candle burns forever, but others watch the candle's fire disappear, but stay in a lightless relationship because it's familiar. Safe, even. I know how it feels to stay in a marriage without love because it's safe. But you do not deserve safe. Apollo doesn't either. Open that apartment door, leave, and embrace the gift of true devotion that is presented to you."

"Apollo?"

Aphrodite squeezes my hand. "Tell me you will attend this ball. That you'll leave these safe, lightless apartment walls and explore what you deserve."

She does not wait for my answer. In a plume of heart-shaped smoke, Aphrodite is gone, but she leaves behind the invitation. She leaves behind my chance to see Apollo.

"H?" a groggy voice calls out, followed by his bedroom door opening and his feet shuffling towards me. "What are you doing standing in the middle of the living room?"

His hands move to both sides of my waist to pull me against his chest, but I shuffle away. I turn around. Lowell stands a foot away with confusion and fatigue splattered on his face. He is only in a pair of boxers, his hair disheveled, and a stream of dried saliva sticks to the corner of his mouth.

"What's wrong?" He asks, still oblivious to the invitation in my hand.

"Nothing," I say, but stop. Shaking my head, I correct myself. "Actually, a lot is wrong. I got to go."

Fog dusts over my vision as I grab my purse, slip on a pair of sandals, and move to the apartment door. Lowell follows behind me, and he might be talking, but I cannot hear him.

The same familiar sensation I get when I draw settles

over me like mist atop a river after a day of rain. Although I cannot see or hear Apollo, it's him I see sitting in an art room in his house. Through an apparition of myself, far from my tiny home with Lowell, I can see a vision of Apollo. His heavy sighs and the clink of ice between his drink steal all my focus, and I know I need to be with him right now. The fog possessing me repeats Aphrodite's words on an endless loop.

Explore what you deserve, the voices in my head whisper.

"I got to go. Don't follow," I say to Lowell, but I do not wait for his response.

I open the door, and although I've never been there before, I run out of my apartment and towards Apollo's house.

TWENTY

SAFFRON

"Are you ready to go?"

Argus's gruff voice pulls my gaze towards him, but many of his eyes wander to the pictures scattered beneath my trembling hands. Crime scenes of murdered mothers. The autopsy photos of the victims of the Nosoi disease in South America. They cover every square inch of my desk. Hundreds of unsolved deaths lay here. They remind me of my failures because I cannot find the answer to the questions they all ask.

Who is responsible for my death?

"I should stay a little while longer," I murmur, eyes returning to the pictures.

As soon as the words leave my lips, the grandfather clock right outside my door chimes a melancholy tune. The sound echoes through the quieted building, silencing my words.

"It's midnight," Argus says, his voice holding a softer tone than before. "You should get some rest."

I stop my next words. Yet my mind is filled with questions I want to scream to the skies. What am I going home to? An array of emptiness awaits me in a home too large for one person. When I am at my place, I am reminded of the past. Why should I go home? All I see there are days when Hermes and I were happy. Of days when Hattie was still alive. Why should I go home when all that place brings me is sorrow?

"Are we the only two left in the building?" I ask, deflecting his statement.

He nods. "I sent Jamila home about two hours ago, and everybody else left before sunset." Argus hesitantly steps inside, but beneath his mighty feet, the ground quakes with his movement. "Let me take you home, Saffron."

I do not remember when Argus and I became friends, or when he started waiting every night to walk me out and drive me home, but it's become my favorite part of the day. Because of Argus—always because of Argus—I stand up from my desk and walk out of the building. He walks a few steps behind me as I leave the office, but he always opens the stair doors for me, followed by the front doors of Olympus Industries.

We talk a little, but we revel in the quiet. He allows me a moment of peace in the calamitous world I live in. There are no expectations when I am in Argus's company. I am not the Savior, weighed down by the world's presumptions of me, and he is not a guard burdened to always protect. We are simply Saffron and Argus, driving through town, and enjoying the view.

But all tranquility has an expiration date.

Before my gated house, dozens of men and women stand in rueful protest. They hold signs that say SAVIOR OR

DOOMER? Or YOU ARE NOT OUR SAVIOR ANYMORE. Argus drives up to the gate, and as he rolls down the window to punch in the gate code, the protestors' screams reach my ears and slice my heart.

"Why haven't you stopped the killings?!"

They scream, their voices are out of sync, yet they hit their mark. Family members of the murder victims bang on the car windows. They bellow their rage at me because I cannot find their loved one's killer.

One man, looming over six and a half feet tall, is here every day. Gareth French, the father and husband of the first victims, stands in front of the car as the gate swings open. In his hands are a bouquet of bluebell flowers painted red like blood. Every night, I stare at Gareth French through the tinted windows, and he glowers in my direction before throwing the red painted bluebells towards me.

"Would you like me to dispose of the humans?" Argus asks as he rolls up his window. He asks this question every night, and I always respond the same.

I shake my head and whisper. "No, Argus, they deserve to hate me."

Gareth and the other protestors move, as Argus drives through the opened gate, and up the driveway towards my mansion. There is one light beckoning me home to the right of the front door, but otherwise, it's a tomb. Only the dead reside here, in the dark place I once lovingly called home.

Argus gets out of the car, then a moment later, opens the passenger seat and extends his hand. On his cracked, dry lips is a forced smile I've grown to appreciate across the decades. It's the only spot on his body where there are no eyes, and while the expression is forced, he has a beautiful smile.

I accept Argus's hand and let him pull me out of my car. The protestors scream from their place behind the gate, spewing hatred for my inability to solve the murders. Some, bellowing their belief that I am the killer. I am no longer their Savior. I could not save their families. To them, I am a failure.

Argus squeezes my hand before letting go, and together we walk in silence towards the entrance. "Thank you, Argus."

He opens my front door and escorts me into my home. "You do not have to thank me for caring."

"Do you want to come inside for a cup of nectar?" I ask, but even as the words leave my lips, I am certain of his answer.

He shakes his head. "Not tonight. The protestors have grown louder. I would feel a lot safer standing outside your door, so nobody gets past these gates and causes you harm."

"You do not have to be my guard tonight," I say.

"I know." That small, forced smile returns. "But as your friend, this is what I'd like to do."

"I'll bring nectar out to you," I promise.

As I walk through the front door, Argus whispers. "Have a good night's rest."

He shuts the door behind me.

My footsteps echo in the empty room, the soft clicks of my shoes bounce off the bare walls. There was once a time when the walls were covered with photographs. Images of Hattie and me smiling, arms around each other's shoulders. Hermes and I when I first explored Mt. Olympus. Zig, Diam, Hattie, and me, posing in front of the newly finished

Olympus Industries. My fondest moments once graced these walls, but I took them all down a few years ago.

Death stared at me from all angles.

Now, pale white walls are all that is left.

I step into the kitchen, ready to make a cup of nectar for Argus, when I come to a sudden halt. A face I haven't seen in almost two weeks stares back at me, green eyes dim under the single kitchen light. Hesitantly, I walk inside.

"Hermes," I whisper my husband's name with undeniable shock. "Hi."

The saddest smile a person can wear peels over his lips. "Hi," he says back.

TWENTY-ONE

SAFFRON

I move towards the fridge, but with each step I take, I imagine him disappearing. For his image to be a mirage that evaporates once I'm hydrated. I pull out a pitcher of nectar, and the gold liquid shimmers despite the dark room. I turn around to face Hermes again, and he is still here. He leans against the kitchen island, arms crossed over his chest.

"Do you want a glass?" I ask. "I was making one for Argus, but-"

"Saffron." He says my name like an ancient tragedy, as if I am already gone from his life and he mourns our past together. "We need to talk."

I know what he wants to talk about, but I cannot handle another jab right now. I can still hear the protestors screaming their rage. Still see that red-painted bouquet of bluebells being thrown. Hera's words from earlier today bounce off the empty walls while Hart's drawing burns a hole in my jacket pocket. Today has drained me of any form of strength, and for this conversation, I need to be strong.

Yet, I am too weak.

I feign obliviousness. "What about?"

I grab three glasses from the cabinet and line them side-by-side. As I lift the pitcher of nectar, Hermes's voice shatters my resolve. "We cannot have a ball in honor of our wedding anniversary."

My back is to him as I pour the first cup. Despite my upbringing in the prisons, I am an intelligent woman. It took many years to learn how to read or write. I spent almost three decades beside my tutor, Daedalus, in the Underworld. Five days a week, three hours a day, he taught me how to process the words that tilt and sway on the pages. Then, when I became proficient in all areas, he began teaching me multiple languages. Philosophies and inventions. Mathematics of the highest calibers and variations of scientific formulas. Daedalus promised me I would be wiser with each passing day, and he was right. I am now brilliant under his tutelage.

It is with this brilliance that I know why Hermes does not want to have a wedding anniversary. I can see the Fates holding the scissors, ready to clip the thread of life that is our relationship. Even at our distance, with my back to him, I can smell another woman's perfume mixing with far too much wine.

I pour the second cup. "And why is that?" I ask, hating the way my voice breaks. "Aphrodite is very excited about the party, and-"

"I love you so much, Saffron, but we can't have this party. We cannot celebrate our marriage."

The third cup is left unfilled. When the pitcher's glass

touches the kitchen counter, its clink is loud in the too-quiet space. I steady myself as the weight of his words sag over my shoulders and threaten to bring me to my knees. His statement is unfinished, littered with secrets he is about to unfold.

"If you love me so much," I whisper, but in the silence, it comes out as a bellow. "Then why aren't I enough?"

A tear rolls down my cheek, slides off my chin, and drops into the unfilled cup.

He doesn't respond for a long time. The tear streak has dried on my cheek, and the tick, tick, tick of a nearby clock counts away the moments we remain married.

"I am going to only ask you this one time, Hermes."

I curl my fingers into the counter, threatening to break the marble as my knuckles turn white. Gods, I do not want to hear the answer to my question. I've avoided this conversation for weeks, months, or years. I'm not entirely sure how long I've questioned his fidelity, how long I've evaded this question from entering the room, but I refuse to run from it now.

"And remember," I say, my bottom lip wobbling. "You promised to never lie to me again. That was the deal when we got back together almost nine decades ago. That was in our wedding vows. I want your honesty or nothing at all."

The faraway clock ticks twenty times. I counted each one with bated breaths, and then he responds. "Ask your question."

"I can smell a woman's perfume on you right now. I think it's Aphrodite's. You also reek of red wine, one of her personal favorites. The last time I saw you, almost two weeks ago, you had a bite mark on your collarbone. When you don't smell like Aphrodite, you talk only about Hecate."

"Ask your question, Saffron," he repeats, voice breaking like glass.

"You avoid being home, and several times, when you've said you were on Mt. Olympus or running errands, I find out you're in the Underworld. Spending your days with your former lover, Hecate, who everybody knows separated from her husband decades ago." I clear my throat and push down the anguish clawing its way to the surface. "I'm no longer allowed in the Underworld, yet you spend almost every waking minute there. Even when you tell me you are on Mt. Olympus or on Earth, it is a lie. You are never in bed with me anymore, and I cannot remember the last time we were intimate."

I do not ask aloud, but I lament over the question.

"I love you so much," Hermes says.

While my back is turned to him, I hear his footsteps nearing me. His hands move like a ghost's touch against my waist, and he pulls me into his embrace. This is the closest he and I have been in weeks or months. Gods, maybe even years.

He presses a kiss against the top of my head, his mouth lingering on the spot. "Please, just cancel the party. I do not want to say anything more."

"I'm so tired," I admit. "And I cannot deal with the world's problems and my marital ones, too. Tell me what you're hiding from me. Please, tell me what I need to hear because it's all too much and I'm so tired."

He kisses the top of my head again, and his hands squeeze my waist. I want to push him away and pull him closer at the same time. Another tear rolls down my cheek, then another and another. We stand in our kitchen, in the silence, while I wait for his truth and he scrounges up an answer.

Finally, he says. "Either cancel the party or ask your question."

Canceling the party means Hart and Apollo won't come together, and canceling the party means I am still drowning in his secrets. I shake my head, refusing to cancel the ball celebrating our marriage of ruins; instead, I ask what I have feared the answer to for years.

"If all I said does not equal up to you cheating, then what are you hiding from me, Hermes? Because I'm sinking in the weight of your lies. You promised me honesty, and right now, I need that. If you are not cheating on me, then what are you hiding from me?"

With his chin against the top of my head, when a sob leaves his lips, it rains on me. His hands tremble at my waist. He desperately holds me. I put my hands over his, trying to pry his fingers off when he does not answer my question. Hermes holds on. He fights to keep his hands on me for as long as possible.

I push him away, and as he staggers backwards, he lets out one guttural word. "Yes."

"Yes, what?" I ask, turning to face him.

His face is blotchy with tears, his eyes bloodshot with sorrow. He is almost six and a half feet tall, yet his body is slouched as sobs weaken him. Hermes won't look at me, his eyes on the floor, but I can see him so clearly. A god riddling with guilt and sadness, knowing he is about to lose me forever.

"Yes, what?"

Don't say it, don't say it, don't say it.

"I'm cheating on you."

He said it.

A piece of my heart shatters at his words. I fall to the floor, no longer able to hold up my legs. I sit beneath the one illuminating light in the kitchen. Its spotlight on me and my anguish. My tears start small, a few trailing down in silent defeat, but then I am sobbing. A groan, or a scream, I'm not sure which, erupts from my mouth. I am a downpour of tears and broken promises.

He falls, too, with hands desperately reaching out for me. I let him hold me, to wrap me in a hug for the last time. He causes my pain, but I need him as my friend as I process this form of suffering. My head lays against his chest, and I cry through every morsel of my body. He presses kisses on the top of my head, murmuring the same four words over and over again.

"I love you, Saffron. Gods, I love you, Saffron. I love you, Saffron."

During this level of grief, I do not grasp time. Faintly, I hear the tick, tick, tick of that clock, but I cannot process anything as the tears slowly ebb away and I am left trembling in my husband's arms. He is one of the last people I have left in this world.

Now, I am losing him, too.

"I will stay at my parent's castle as we go through our divorce proceedings. That will give you enough time to get another house."

My words are numb, so numb.

"No, Saffron, I am going to stay in the Underworld. You keep this house." He kisses the top of my head, but I flinch at his touch.

Realizing this, Hermes pulls away. He sits on the floor across from me, his back against the island.

"Why?" I ask. "Why would you stay in the Underworld instead of me?"

His answer comes out quickly, yet lethally. "Because it's Hecate, and she lives in the Underworld."

My body is spent with tears, exhausted beyond reprieve, so I can barely react to the name. I shouldn't be surprised he returned to his former lover, Hecate. She is beautiful, unburdened by death. She isn't ruined like me. Tattered after too many slashes to my heart. It's reasonable he went back to a goddess of regality and charm, rather than staying with the goddess of sorrow and disappointment.

She won my husband, but I am the daughter of the king and queen of the Underworld. I lost the fight for my marriage, but does she deserve victory over the Underworld, too? I am the proclaimed princess of the realm of the dead, but because Hermes loved another outside of wedlock, I am ostracized? The Underworld is the first place where I found love and acceptance. Now, I am supposed to lose my second home on top of everything else?

Rage comes in swift, brutal stabs.

"So, what?" I ask. "I'm not able to go to the Underworld. Is that why Thanatos and Hypnos won't let me in? Is that why my parents stand with Cerberus at the gate every time I try to go down? Because of you and Hecate? Is your adulterous ways the reason I haven't seen Diam, Zig, and Hattie in months?"

There isn't anything he can say that will make this situation better. His hands twitch like they want to reach out for me, to touch me, but he stops himself.

"Yes, that's why you aren't allowed in the Underworld. Everybody knows."

"The Underworld is my family home!" I outcry.

"It isn't right now."

"So, my parents are choosing you and Hecate over me?" My rage hides the sharpness of betrayal and the wave of sorrow that comes with it. "I'm their daughter."

He hesitates for one moment, an inner battle in his mind, then he says. "Not biologically."

My feelings of inadequacy because I am not biologically Hades's and Persephone's roars back with claws and fangs. It is one of my greatest insecurities, not being my parents' true child. This fear of not being worthy as Hades's and Persephone's child worsened when my own biological father wished for my death when I was human. For decades, they have had to remind me that I am their daughter. That they love me unconditionally.

And now Hermes tells me they will always see me how I see myself.

Not enough.

"Get out of my house," I sneer, yet the sound is breathless as I push through the pain. His face crumbles, realizing his words went too far, but he's still here. He isn't leaving, and I cannot stand to look at him. "Get out of my house!" I scream.

I do not realize I have my hands in the air until it's too late. My power curls around his bones, and I hurdle him across the room. His body flies out of the kitchen, through the hall, and slams into the front door. The magnitude of his weight, and the speed I threw him, causes the front door to collapse upon impact.

Argus has a sword against Hermes's neck in an instant, his face contorted in rage. "What did you do to her?"

I walk towards them, my legs shaky as I take in the

scene I caused. For once, the protestors at the gate are silent. They watch my unraveling and see the monster I am beneath the Savior façade. Hermes is still on the floor, lying on top of the door, but his eyes are only on me.

"I'm sorry," he says.

"You broke one of the last parts of my heart that was still pure. I will get over you, Hermes, but that day is not today. Get out."

In a blink, Hermes is gone. His winged sandals whisk him away at lightning speed. He leaves behind a broken door, Argus, and me. My many-eyed friend takes a step towards me, but I shake my head.

"I'm tired," I say weakly, but he understands.

"If you need me, I'll be out here. I'm not leaving," he says the last part with conviction.

No matter what, he has no plans of leaving my side. He is not just talking about tonight, but he means every single day until the end of our lives. I showed a monstrous part of me, one that frightens me, but he doesn't hate me for the darker side thrashing inside. He will always remain loyal until his final breath. While everyone else fades to the background, he stays nearby. A friend I never expected, but immortally appreciate.

"Good night, friend," I say, voice cracking as more tears build up.

"Good night, friend," he says in return.

But I do not go to sleep because there, I will find Hermes's untouched side of the bed. I'll see fragments of him littered across the room like memorabilia of a lost life. With the weight of Hart's drawing in my pocket, I return to the kitchen, ready to curl on the floor for the night.

TWENTY-TWO

HERMES

The moment I arrive in the Underworld, tears blurring my vision and heart unspeakably sore, Hades and Persephone are waiting for me at the gates. Cerberus sits in between them, two heads nibbling on the same bone while the middle one stares at me. The king and queen of the Underworld share the same pained expression, but they hide their sadness better than I.

"Is the party canceled?" Hades asks.

"Will she stay away from the Underworld?" Persephone inquires.

Flashes of tonight eviscerate me. For as long as I exist, I will never get the image of Saffron's face crumbling with sadness out of my head. I ruined our marriage through carefully woven lies created by her parents and me. We saved her from Styx, but we destroyed a part of her we will never get back.

"It's done, but was it worth it?" I whisper, already knowing the answer.

"It was worth it," another, more feminine voice says.

Hecate materializes in a plume of dark green smoke, wearing an array of red rubies across her neck and arms. The color matches the lipstick darkening her plump lips and the stiletto heels that make her almost as tall as me. She's a creature derived from the Underworld in a tight, leather dress that has a slit up both thighs. Her blue eyes are rimmed with kohl, the ends sharp like daggers.

"I told you that the best way to save her from Styx is by ending your marriage." Hecate curls a hand around my shoulder, squeezing affectionately before letting go. "Trust me, your decision saved her."

Together, we stride through the Underworld. Many immortals live in the Underworld or visit enough in their occupations. So, for any god or goddess who glances in our direction, we play our roles well. They will see me flaunting my mistress across the Underworld. They will realize it is a union accepted by Hades and Persephone, who walk behind us.

And I pray to any god who will listen that this lie will be enough to save Saffron's life.

TWENTY-THREE

HART SOMMERS

Fourteen Years Ago

"Can you tell me a story about love?"

I sat on my father's lap, barely twelve years old. His arms were wrapped tightly around me. I almost couldn't breathe, but I didn't want him to stop. I wanted to feel his hugs more than anything.

"Sure, my special Hart." He kissed the top of my short, brown hair. "Do you want to hear the love story between Lady Saffron and Lord Hermes? It is my favorite."

"Of course you found a way to tell a story about Lady Saffron," my mother playfully said. My brother's head laid on the pillow that rested on her lap, and as she combed her fingers through his locks, she joked. "You are a man obsessed."

"Well, it is the greatest of all love stories," insisted my father, but my mother only laughed him off with a flippant wave of her free hand.

"And what about our love story, darling?" She teased.

I watched my dad's mouth grow into the largest smile imaginable. "I meant theirs was the second greatest love story after ours."

"Mhm," Mom responded, unimpressed. "Why don't you tell the story of Lady Psyche and Lord Eros instead? They have a wonderful romance."

He glanced down at me, and in a mocked whisper, he asked. "Is your mother ill today?"

I giggled. "No, Dad."

"Did you check her forehead?" He continued.

Mom laughed from her seat across the living room. "If you weren't holding our daughter, I'd chuck a pillow at your head."

"You're distracting me from my story," Dad joked. He squeezed my shoulders and said. "Lady Saffron and Lord Hermes have the greatest love story, other than your mother's and mine. Lord Eros and Lady Psyche cannot compare, and do you know why?"

I shook my head.

Dad answered his own question. "Their love story differs from any other in history because it is flawed."

"What does flawed mean?" I asked, too young to process such a big word.

"It means it was not perfect," Mom answered, still brushing through Suraj's hair.

"Why do you like their love story if it isn't perfect?" I asked Dad, confused.

"It reminds me that even gods make mistakes on the path towards what they think is right. Lord Hermes thought he was making the right decisions in his life. To steal Lady Saffron from Lord Ares's mansion. To make her marry him so he could become an Olympian, as King Zeus promised. Every lie Lord Hermes spun, he thought he needed to because it would help them both.

The beauty in their relationship is that truth won. She made him see his tricks weren't needed, and through honesty, the greatest love story began."

Mom cleared her throat.

"Second greatest love story," Dad amended.

"So, he just told the truth, and that was it? They fell in love?" I asked.

"Not quite," Mom answered. "They saved each other's lives a few times, too. She saved him when Lady Circe turned him into a dog in the Battle of the Labyrinth."

"And you see, my special Hart," Dad continued where Mom left off. "Lord Hermes tried to save Lady Saffron every minute throughout their life. He stole her from Lord Ares's mansion before he could kill her. He refused to join Kronos's side when captured by him and his army in the arenas, and he was tortured every day until she saved him. Time and time again, he sacrificed himself for her. Protecting her before she knew how to protect herself."

"Boring," my brother cooed upon my mother's lap, and while Dad pouted, Mom ruffled Suraj's hair.

"So to be in love, you have to tell the truth and save their life. That's it?" I pondered aloud because I did not understand how they loved one another. "That doesn't sound like enough."

My mom's laugh filled the living room, rich like honey. "When you fall in love, Hartika, you will realize how big honesty and bravery can be in a relationship."

"When I meet my husband," I said that night, surrounded by my family and an open fireplace, with the utmost certainty of my future. "There will be more than just honesty and bravery. We will love each other more than anybody else in any room."

"The gods love each other very much," Dad insisted.

Yet, I shook my head.

"But you never said they loved each other. You just said they worked well together. That's not love." I glanced at my parents, who stared at me like I was older than twelve, but infinite in age, and I asked. "Does the other story have love? Lord Eros's and Psyche's."

"Let's see if it meets your requirements," Mom teased and begun a new story.

One with genuine love, not a forced one.

TWENTY-FOUR

HART SOMMERS

Pushing the front doors to my apartment complex open, I sprint out of the building of familiarity and dash forward. I have no clear destination in my mind, but my feet move in accord to something more powerful than me. I run across the newly cut grass, not caring to catch a cab or go back inside my apartment for the car keys. As the fog hangs over my vision, distorting my current reality, I let it guide me towards a different future.

To Apollo.

The further from the apartment I get, the heavier the fog becomes. I can process that a road is in front of me and I am weaving through trees, lampposts, and barking dogs, but I am no longer in the present. My vision dashes to the future, to images that have not yet happened, but I am certain will one day.

I set out on a diverging path. A beautiful one with a golden-haired god. In an array of multi-colors, I no longer push down my powers. For so long, I have feared being different. I have talked about wanting grand adventures away from my little apartment and my mediocre relationship, but there is still hesitation.

Deep down, I've always known I am not completely normal. I see the world in the present, past, and future. They appear to me like paint strokes, all bleeding in a myriad of colors and textures. Some are abstract paintings, less decipherable, but the vague idea is identifiable. Others are portraits, telling me of a specific person or god's journey. The most important are vivid. They detail every part of the piece, even the most minute part, like the pollen on top of a wayward flower and the engraving on a passerby's cufflink. This ability has always been within me, a skill that a rare few have, but I've hidden it like an unappealing trait.

For so long, I thought standing out was a crime; therefore, my abilities were abhorrent. I blame my visions for all the terrible occurrences in my life. The death of my family. My fear of leaving Lowell and the safety of our apartment.

Now, as I rush away from the safety of my apartment and move towards a scary, yet exhilarating future, my powers burst from behind my eyes. With only him on my mind, I see the next few months in a burst of technicolor excellence.

My first mile, running through neighborhoods and busy streets, I am in Apollo's mansion. Sitting on a wooden bench with Apollo a few feet away. He paints me like I am his greatest muse. There is a twinkle in his sharp, blue eyes as one word leaves his lips.

"Mine."

The second mile, as I leap over a fallen tree branch, Apollo is inexplicably close to me. His nose brushes against mine. His lips are a breath away, teasingly close, but still too far. When I run to him, I see our future. It is as I run this second mile; I feel his lips against mine as if we are really kissing. Like he isn't faraway, but nestled against me.

The third mile, I hear him say he loves me for the first time.

The fourth mile, we dance together under white chandeliers, my dress swishing behind us. He is the epitome of the sun, and we glide together across a dance floor. Our hands never separate. Anguish weighs down my face, but I still cannot stop smiling as I experience a glimpse of forever with him.

Mile five is the first time we are intimate, our bodies rolling together in a room dazzled in his artwork.

Mile six and seven are precious moments he and I have not yet experienced. Stories we share with one another. Promises we whisper moments before falling asleep in each other's arms. Kisses stolen at the most improper times, but I love them all the same.

I love him all the same. His life consumes me with each vision I have. It has barely been a day since we met, and yet I already know the beginning and middle of our love story. I know the passion that follows, as if I have already experienced it.

By mile eight, I'm standing in front of a mansion that I know is his, although I have never been here before. I should be out of breath, but I'm not. Pushing back my sweaty, slick hair, I press the red button on the side of the closed gated entrance to his house.

I'm not sure he will let me inside, but if my visions are true, then he will. Apollo, just like me, sees the future behind his eyes and he knows what awaits us. Still, I fear I ran here for nothing. I fear he wants the safety of not trying, just like I almost did with Lowell before Aphrodite came over.

There is a buzz from the intercom above the button, and the gated doors swing open.

He invites me inside.

I shouldn't seem so eager. That I should walk, not run, but my legs do not listen to my rationality. Eagerly, my feet push against the ground. I rush towards the gilded mansion that is four times the size of my entire apartment complex. I weave through the narrow, uphill driveway.

My eyes burst with visions of every kiss we share over the next years. Some kisses are filled with tears, others raw and passionate, but none of them are safe. None of the kisses I see in Apollo and my future are tame, timid, or unsure.

Each kiss tells me that safety with Lowell is nothing compared to the inferno awaiting me with Apollo.

I arrive at the front door, but before I knock, I see it's already left ajar. The fog dissipates behind my eyes, forcing me to be only in the present. I open the door the rest of the way. Three steps are all I take inside the mansion before I find him.

Directly across from the front door, there's a long hallway filled with golden framed paintings. Then, there's a fork in the hallway, separating the house in three directions. On the left looks like a music room.

There's a lyre mantled on top of a fireplace, a piano on the left corner of the room, and an organ on the right. Several guitars and violins are strewn across the maroon walls. Painted lyrics weave in between the instruments, telling stories the same way paintings do.

On the right side is the dining room. A long table with white linen draped on top. It can seat up to forty people, yet it's empty. Devoid of any company. The atmosphere is sophisticated, but it holds none of the sentimentality of the other room. This one is for guests, but the place of music is just for Apollo.

Straight ahead is a staircase, gilded leaf accents adorn the railings. Sitting on the third step from the bottom is him. I burst with a wide grin, taking another three steps. That's the moment I realize we are not alone.

Another goddess is in the room, leaning against the leaf-shaped railing with tears brandishing her brown cheeks. She is a goddess with dark hair twirling in streaks of blue and teal. I instantly recognize the crying deity as Iris, the goddess of rainbows. In her hand, she holds a piece of parchment paper with a hole in the middle. Her body shakes as tears rack through her.

While Apollo is not crying, his devastation is clear. His hands are stuck in his blonde curls, face drawn in worry. He knows I am here, but he focuses on the item in Iris's hand and doesn't look up. Does not sport the same confident smile I've seen a thousand times in my drawings.

"What happened?" I ask.

Iris startles in surprise. She just now realizes I am here. When she looks at me, there is no recognition. Why would there be? I've never met this goddess before, yet here I am, a witness to her sorrow. She doesn't respond, but the tremble in her hand worsens to where she drops the note.

The Fates play a role in every aspect of our lives, and today is no exception. The moment the note falls to the floor, a sudden gust of wind blows it towards me. There are no windows open, but the wind is so strong that the note falls right into my extended hands.

Three words are hurriedly scribbled on this piece of parchment.

Captured. Calypso. Nymphs.

"Who wrote this?" I ask.

Nobody responds, but Iris talks to Apollo as if I am not in the room. "A few huntresses are going to Saffron's house and Mt. Olympus to talk to Zeus," she hiccups through her words, crying the whole time. "We will make a plan to get her back."

I want to know who. Curiosity gnaws at me, but I am an outsider. While I see a future with Apollo and have witnessed our greatest moments like they've already happened, I am still a stranger. I have only met him today, been a meager part of his life, and I do not deserve to know everything. Gods, I do not deserve to know anything.

"I should go," I whisper, and when I turn around, I'm certain nobody heard me.

"Don't."

The one word stops me. It comes from a voice so broken, my heart aches at the sound. Slowly, I turn around. He does not stand or move towards me, but his stare paralyzes me to the spot. I'm halfway down the hallway from him, but I can see the anguish so clearly on his face.

"Please don't go," he repeats.

Iris looks between the two of us, confused at first, but then an unrecognizable emotion takes over. Her pink eyes brighten, becoming the shade of peaches, before she nods her head like she is having an internal conversation with herself.

"I'm going to see if Sika needs help to get Saffron here," Iris says.

Then, she's gone, disappearing in a rainbow arch.

For the first time, I am alone with Apollo, but it feels like the hundredth time. I once thought he was a figment of my overactive imagination. But how could I have been so dense? He is more than a wayward thought. More than a lonely girl's aimless drawings. He is a god who tilts the sun in his direction, so he is forever bathed in light.

I take a step towards him, and he stands from the staircase. We inch closer. Step by step, I gravitate towards him until we are in the hallway directly in front of the entrance to the music room.

"Who wrote that letter?" I ask, the parchment rubbing against the tips of my fingers.

"My sister, Artemis." His voice is barely above a whisper. "She was looking for a group of missing nymphs, and instead, got captured by the abductors."

Apollo raises a hand, and he roams my face with an eagerness to touch me again, like he had at Olympus Industries. He hesitates. Before he lowers his hand, I wrap my hand around his wrist, pulling him closer. His palm cups the side of my cheek. I watch his face the entire time, witnessing the moment his eyes glaze over and experience the same visions I had on my way here to him.

There is no reasonable explanation for this moment. I cannot tell anybody how I know that if he touches me, then he will see my visions for himself. I cannot explain how I know that this will only work with him, and only if I want him to see the future I've witnessed. Magic is inexplainable at times, but right now, I invite him into my scattered mind.

I let him see our future first kiss, first dance, and the first time we realize we are each other's infinity.

I see the moment he comes back to me, when the fog leaves his eyes and he realizes exactly who I am to him. "Hart," he breathes my name.

"Apollo," I breathe with the same intensity. "I'm sorry about your sister."

"How are you real?" He asks. He ignores my statement as he looks at me and examines every inch. Seeing me like a falsity that'll disappear if he doesn't ingrain every bit of me into memory. "I need you to be real and not some trick. I need what I saw in those visions to be real."

My words hold no value compared to what he says. The aching desperation in his voice cleaves at my heart, and I can only find the strength to nod. To confirm without words but a thousand feelings that I am real. The visions are real, and we will be together.

He takes another step towards me. Our chests brush together. His forehead leans down until it presses against mine. His spearmint breath kisses my cheeks and mouth, teasing what will come next. He places his free hand on my hip, but he doesn't lower himself further. We stay like this, suspended in time and each other's arms.

But I see the moment his eyes find my engagement ring.

His Adam's apple bobs painfully. "What's his name?" He asks.

I, too, swallow hard. "Lowell, but he's more of a friend than a fiancé. We should've broken up years ago."

"I see."

Apollo doesn't pull away, but he doesn't come nearer, either. His gaze dances between the engagement ring, my hip he is holding, and then my eyes that he drowns himself in. Time is limitless, yet I'm aware he is silent for a long time as he processes my relationship status and everything we are destined to become.

Then, he says. "I've lived eons μέλι. I have witnessed tragedy and beauty, yet never peace. Once, I told somebody that it was unachievable. An impossibility. But then I met you and realized that peace is not a moment in time. Peace is a person in one's life, and Hartika Sommers, you are that one person in my life. If you want your human fiancé, then I understand. I will let you live a human life, as long as I can be your friend and get glimpses of peace within your company."

He has more to say, but I interrupt him. "But what if I do not want him?"

The words are there, spoken but not spoken: what if I want you?

His thumb grazes my skin, electrifying it with each subtle movement. "Then," he says slowly, with the smallest, yet most hopeful grin. "I will make it my mission to make those premonitions a reality. While that engagement ring is nice, if you do not want him, then I will make it my mission to replace that ring with my own. If you are not afraid of the truth, of what we can be, then stay tonight with me. I have to meet with some gods regarding Artemis's capture, but I would love it if you stayed and made this terrible day end on a good note. After they're gone, I'll even make you a cup of tea."

"I do like tea."

His smile grows devious, and he pulls my body flush against his. Those lips, ones I've drawn and fantasized about for years, lean into me. They brush against me in the most teasing kiss. "Have a cup of tea with me and let me get to know my future wife. The future mother of my children. There is nothing else in this world I want tonight more than that."

I cannot stop the smile growing over my lips. "Just a cup of tea?"

"A cup of tea and a promise," he amends.

"What's the promise?"

"That with every fiber of my being, I will make it my mission to strip you bare of everything you're wearing right now, especially that engagement ring."

My lungs give out. I can no longer breathe. I wrap my arms around him and let him lift me. The note falls from my grasp, but I do not care. My legs wrap around his torso and intense electricity threatens to consume me. He is my future, and at this moment, I need him to be my present, too.

Pulling away, I say. "I would love to stay for a cup of tea."

Then his lips crash against mine, and I try to enjoy the moment. But now that I have embraced the powers I have, fog slams into me. It jolts me to the future.

I'm kissing Apollo, but I see Saffron behind my eyes, walking down into the Underworld. A dress of crimson red accentuates her large, voluptuous figure, but the gown's train resembles human blood smearing across the ground. Styx rises as Saffron reaches the river's dock. She is paler than the moon, with harsh features and eyes as black as her river and soul. Vaguely, I see a figure running to Saffron, trying to stop her from reaching Styx, but Styx ruefully smiles in my direction.

It's like she can see me watching the future. Seeing how my decision to save Lowell's life has led Saffron here, right into Styx's clawed grasp. The smile is without mirth. It's devoid of anything that can resemble humanity. The wraith-thin goddess of hatred opens her cracked lips and says three words to me, the sound like rippling water and crying souls intermingling.

"Thank you, oracle."

TWENTY-FIVE

SAFFRON

Sika, Phobos, Deimos, Dýnami, and two unfamiliar huntresses storm into my home. They expect a regal goddess; instead, they find me sitting cross-legged on the kitchen floor. A bowl of strawberries rests on my lap. I haven't left this spot since Hermes's absence. An hour or two has passed since he returned to his new home in the Underworld alongside Hecate, and I'm on my third bowl of strawberries.

Phobos and Deimos glance warily at one another, speaking about me without words. Dýnami's dark eyes glance at the strawberries, then my red-stained lips, and she is silent for the first time since I've met her. The two unfamiliar huntresses see a ruined symbol of hope, sitting in a wallow of sorrow. I do not mirror the savior the world cries out to; in this moment, I am simply a heartbroken woman not knowing how to pick up the pieces of herself.

Sika smirks at me. "Looks like you need some girl talk." She spins her body around, back now facing me, and she says to the others in the room. "Go outside and keep Argus company."

"You keep forgetting we are in charge of this group," Deimos says, referring to his brother and him.

"You keep forgetting that each time you say that, it sounds less believable," Sika retorts. "Now, get out of the house."

"Artemis put us in charge," Phobos insists.

Dýnami, who stands behind them, barks out a laugh. "For gods' sake, let's just listen to her and go outside."

"Thanks, baby," Sika says.

Dýnami winks back.

Phobos and Deimos incoherently grumble the entire time, but they listen. Eventually, my house is emptied except for Sika. Her hair bounces as she plops herself on the ground next to me, sitting cross-legged and bumping knees.

"You have a twenty-roomed mansion," Sika says as she reaches into the bowl of strawberries and steals two. "And you chose to sit on the kitchen floor." She pops the fruit in her mouth and mumbles. "Odd choice, concubine."

The old title she used as my nickname all those years ago.

It reminds me too painfully of the past. It's been almost ninety years since she and I met in the basement of Hermes's former house. I shattered one of her bones before I understood the gravity of my powers. She was the first person to tell me to embrace who I was and to stop living in my fear.

Neither she nor I have aged over the decades. We both appear around twenty years old, but while our faces have remained youthful, other aspects have changed. Her round, protruding eyes are bloodshot. Her typically infallible demeanor is absent. The radiant confidence she blinds the world with is dimmed.

"You've been crying," I say.

She grabs another strawberry, placing it to her lips as she murmurs. "You've been crying, too. Want to trade stories?"

Hermes's face flashes behind my eyes. His words of betrayal burn my ears. Yet, the thought of bringing my truth back to the surface sounds excruciating. Like the conversation between Hermes and me is real, and that is not a fate I want to embrace yet.

"You first," I say.

Sika tries to hide it, but she flinches ever so slightly. She relives the reason behind her sadness, but instead of spilling her story, she bites into the fruit. Prolonging her reality from materializing through her words. She reaches for another strawberry, then hesitates.

She blows out the loudest sigh. "Artemis and Lamb are gone."

"Gone?" I ask. "What do you mean, gone?"

Sika's hand reaches for a tuft of her curly hair, twirling the strands as her eyes follow the movement. It's an anxious tick, her hair twirling. When she moves that little piece of hair, it's always reminiscent. She touches her hair and remembers Artemis or Lamb. She looks at her hair and hates that it reminds her of two people she cannot find. Strands are plucked from her scalp, falling from her fingers.

"Artemis put us huntresses in different groups to better look for the nymphs," Sika says. "I was put with Phobos and Deimos, but Lamb stayed with Artemis and a few new huntresses. Artemis thought she found one nymph and tried to catch her. Lamb ran after her and they fell right into a trap."

I reach and gently grab her hand as she threatens to pull out a piece of her hair. Tears immediately stream down Sika's cheeks as I stop her from tearing it from her scalp. As I pull her hand away, I keep mine within hers. We web our fingers together.

"I hate not being in control," she says. Admits this fault in herself through a raw throat.

I try not to, but my eyes wander to the wedding ring on my left hand. "Me too."

Sika is silent for a while, and I do not prompt her to continue. Time lapses as Sika reorients herself. When the tears subside and her breathing regulates, she continues.

"Artemis sent a note to the other huntresses before the portal closed. She found the nymphs but got captured with them on Calypso's Island."

Calypso is a nymph, daughter of the titan Atlas, who lives on an island by herself. The island, Ogygia, is impossible to find unless she wants you to know the whereabouts. The last time she allowed anybody to find her island was a thousand years ago, when Odysseus was traveling home from the Trojan War. Now, she is back, stealing nymphs for a reason I cannot fathom.

But now I have a name.

I have a location.

For the first time in months, I know where to start.

"We will find them," I say, even if I am not completely certain. Sika needs a thread of optimism, but by her sudden stiffness, I can tell I am a terrible liar.

"Who finds Calypso's Island and lives to tell the tale?" Sika asks, her voice breaking with every passing word.

"Odysseus did."

Sika does not listen to reason. Her hand trembles in mine, itching to find a piece of her hair and rip it from her scalp. To cause herself pain in a fruitless endeavor to control something in her life.

"They're my family. I cannot lose them."

Shrugging the bowl of strawberries off my lap, I pull Sika and myself to a standing position. I tried optimism, but she doesn't need false hope. She needs solutions. An answer to the question that's terrorizing her mind.

"Grab the others," I tell her. "I have a plan."

Sika furiously wipes away her tears. She takes a few seconds to regulate herself and forces a convincing smirk on her face. She hides the honest sadness and replaces it with her unwavering confidence, so the other huntresses do not feel as defeated as her. Then, she leaves me in the kitchen and goes outside to gather the others.

I take two steps out of my kitchen when an archway of rainbows emerges. Iris, too, shows the signs of an emotionally depleted day. She lowers her head in a slow bow, whispering. "Did Sika tell you?"

I nod my head. "I need you to grab Jamila from her apartment and bring me Athena. Tell them it's urgent, alright?"

"Of course."

As quickly as she enters, she is gone.

TWENTY-SIX

SAFFRON

Sika comes back inside with everybody else, excluding Argus, who insists on staying on guard. We file into my dining hall. Nobody, not even Dýnami, tries to fill the space with jovial remarks. War is on our horizon, and that grave realization has silenced us all. We each take a seat, leaving three chairs empty for Iris, Athena, and Jamila.

I look at the two huntresses I do not recognize. "What are your names?"

Before they can answer, Dýnami does. "They're Laconia and Xiomara, but don't worry about remembering their names. They're pretty forgettable."

"You know what isn't forgettable?" Either Laconia or Xiomara sneers. I don't know which one. "My foot shoving itself so far up your-"

A blinding array of colors interrupts the huntress, reminding everybody why we are gathered together. Iris stands beside Jamila, who is still wearing her pajamas and a purple sleeping bonnet. Athena materializes near them. Although it is three in the morning, she is dressed for the day and all its macabre. But, beside them is Apollo, holding the note Artemis left behind.

"What time is it?" Jamila groggily asks.

A miniature rainbow manifests on the table in front of an empty chair, and when the colors dissipate, a cup of steaming coffee sits invitingly. "As promised," Iris says to Jamila, motioning towards the drink.

Jamila groans, then stumbles her way towards the empty chair next to Sika. The entire room hears Jamila loudly moan as she takes her first sip, following shortly behind the ear-splitting grin that awakens her. Despite the horrific day, Jamila Pyro knows exactly how to make a room light up with one smile.

"Morning, little sister," Athena says to me.

"I need a favor," I respond.

She raises a bleached eyebrow, intrigued. "What do you need at three in the morning?"

"I need you to go down to Elysium and talk to Odysseus. See if your favored hero will tell you anything about how we can find Calypso's island."

"Why do you need to know where Ogygia is?" Athena asks.

When I remain silent, she glances across the dining room. Those apathetic gray eyes assess everything and everybody in the room. She examines the huntresses without Artemis by their side. She nods a silent hello to Dýnami and Sika. Dýnami, Athena's favored huntress, does not make a witty retort or ask for a food delicacy. She only nods back.

Athena frowns. "I've heard about the missing nymphs.

Does Calypso play a part in their disappearance? And possibly another goddess's disappearance?"

Sika reaches for her hair, index finger twirling a strand.

"Yes," I say. "She took Artemis, too, so anything you can do to help will be appreciated."

"I'll talk to him at once."

Athena turns around, ready to transform into an owl and take flight towards the Underworld, but she pauses. She faces me once more. She has this uncanny ability to see through me when nobody else can. Suddenly, my wedding ring burns under her intense observation. I want to throw it across the room and scream out the truth. Only to her.

I place my right hand on top of my left, hiding the ring from view, and she frowns. Knowing the words I never say aloud. We are not friends, and while we are sisters, we are not close. Our interactions are rare and brief, but she understands.

Somehow, she always understands me.

"Thank you," I say. I'm not entirely sure what I am thanking her for, but she does.

"Anything else you need me to do while I'm in the Underworld?"

She asks a question within a question, discovering the truth from two words. She understands why I didn't ask Hermes, Hades, or Persephone to ask Odysseus. I search her out in the middle of the night, although we haven't spoken in years. Athena sees a hidden wedding ring and knows where Hermes's loyalty deviated. She is asking me if I want her to approach him when she's down there.

I shake my head, hoping my gratitude shows as I say. "No, you do not need to do anything else while down in the Underworld."

Athena nods her head. "Hopefully, I'll have answers soon. Until then, little sister."

Feathers erupt from her body. Instead of an almost six-feet tall goddess, a white and gray owl soars through the dining room and out the front door towards the Underworld.

Next, I focus my attention on Jamila, who has both hands wrapped around her coffee mug. She takes timid sips.

"Jamila, I'm sorry for waking you up, but I have a few requests for you."

"Alright," she says optimistically. "What can I help with?"

"I need a meeting with Asopus in the morning, preferably as soon as I enter the building. Call him as soon as we are done talking and tell him I know where his daughters are located. Say nothing more when he gets enraged. I want to be the brunt of it, not you."

"Alright, what else?"

I continue. "Then I need you to contact Amphitrite. Tell her I need her and Poseidon in my office tomorrow. Clarify that I need her husband sober. Tell her it's important that he doesn't have his morning vodka with a splash of orange juice. Even if he lies and says it's good for his stomach and whatever other ridiculousness he spews. I need him sober."

Jamila giggles. "I can try."

"One more thing. I don't want you living on your own right now. I'd like for you to temporarily move back in here."

She lowers her coffee mug onto the table with a soft *tap*. Four months ago, on her nineteenth birthday, Jamila informed Hermes and me that she wanted to move out. She found a cute little apartment in the busy city, but she comes home once a week for dinner. Now, I'm stealing away her little slice of independence.

Her smile falls. "Is it because of the protestors outside?" She asks.

Bloodied bluebells flash through my mind, and I brush them away. "Not completely. While they could become dangerous, they're not my main concern. There's no way Calypso works alone."

The already quiet room loses its breath. I am saying the words everybody is thinking. The first to vocalize the fear we all feel creeping nearer. A war is coming, but it is nothing like the one we fought against Kronos. We saw that war straight ahead, but whoever is pulling the strings in this imminent fight, we do not see. The mastermind has a knife raised, but the tip of the blade is nearing our back instead of our heart. Calypso is the first glimpse of the harrowing truth arriving on our doorstep.

All eyes are on me, but I focus solely on Jamila as I continue. "I have a feeling whomever she works for is also responsible for the Nosoi causing diseases in South America. And for the deaths of those mothers and children. On the slight chance the person responsible for all these deaths is doing so to get back at me, I want you where I can see you."

I do not say the elaborated truth. It's true I want Jamila where I can see her, but there's more. She's the only person left in this world that makes me want to get up in the morning. I have little desire to have more children. She is it. The only daughter I want to have. If I lose her because of a monster's meticulous games, then I lose myself, too. The last fragment of my humanity that is left after the ruins of death and heartbreak.

But in a crowd of many, I do not make myself vulnerable. I do not tell Jamila how much I love her. Do not declare that she is my daughter through love. I do not divulge the truth that I will destroy the world if anybody hurts my last line to Hattie. Instead, I keep my face stoic, never letting my voice fluctuate with emotion, and watch as Jamila solemnly nods her head.

"Can Argus drive me to my apartment so I can pick up a few things?" She asks, her voice displaying every bit of her dejection.

I nod my head as she briskly scurries out of the room.

Finally, I level my gaze on Sika. "Athena should tell us information soon. As we wait, I'd like for this group to join-"

I pause, his name on the tip of my tongue. I haven't seen him in eighty-eight years. Haven't spoken his name aloud since Hattie was alive. Yet, here I am, opening and closing my mouth with no words coming to the surface. How can he still affect me like this after so many years? The smallest jolt of electricity moves up my body, raising the hair on my arms.

I should be able to say his name with ease, it's only two syllables, four letters, yet my throat dries.

"Our father," Phobos finishes my sentence, unintentionally granting me a reprieve from saying his name. "You want us to join Ares and the huntresses he's been riding with?"

I nod my head. "Yes. Continue looking along the coastline in case Artemis or Lamb can escape and swim to shore, but do not separate again. Whoever this is used your separation to take Artemis and Lamb, so let's not give them a second chance to take more of you. Once Athena has answers, she will join you on the hunt for as long as she can. Hopefully, she will have a centralized location and we can bring them all back home in the next few days."

"And if she doesn't?" Iris asks.

Her eyes shift colors, displaying her emotions. The pink tint of her irises shifts to the darkest shade of blue. Sadness envelopes the goddess of rainbows, far surpassing the fear one should have for platonic friends. Iris takes a step forward, her colorful hair darkening to the same shade of blue, and she implores.

"What will the next step be if Athena doesn't have an answer?" she asks.

"That's why I am meeting with Poseidon and Amphitrite tomorrow. I'll tell them specifically what we are looking for in the water. If Athena doesn't get an answer from Odysseus, that is helpful. Maybe Poseidon and Amphitrite will."

"And if they don't? What then?"

Truthfully, I do not know what I'll do if Athena cannot get an answer from Odysseus and Poseidon provides no help. If none of these plans work, I do not have another idea at my disposal. Throughout the past two and a half months, every sudden catastrophe does not have a simple solution. Discovering Calypso's part in the nymphs' disappearance has been my only breakthrough. If nobody knows how to find Ogygia, then I do not know what we will do.

"Then I sail with you across all the seven seas of this world. I personally will not stop until we find them."

Iris doesn't respond; instead, she disappears into a rainbow made only out of shades of blue. With her, she takes all the huntresses, Phobos, and Deimos. When the rainbow leaves, taking the others with them, only Apollo remains. He still stands in the archway between rooms, holding the parchment paper.

"I'm sorry about your sister."

He gifts me a barely there smile. "You'll find her, but knowing Artemis, I wouldn't be too surprised if she doesn't need saving. We'll be throwing a search party together when she casually walks into the room and asks for ambrosia like she was never taken."

"Hm," I hum.

Apollo takes a step forward. "You know, Saffron, it's not a sign of weakness to smile or laugh."

"I know."

"Then why has it been years since I've witnessed either?" He walks further into the room. "I once told you that your smile is the sight of poetry, and yet you let it disappear from the world. It's a true travesty, ómorfo aínigma, to let such a wonderful sight fall to rubble."

"Ómorfo aínigma," I whisper the nickname Apollo has always had for me. I let out a huff, the closest sound to a laugh I've had in years. "Beautiful enigma."

"It took you almost three years to understand what the nickname meant," Apollo muses, his smile growing.

"You never gave me a hint, and every time I asked Hermes, he would laugh. Daedalus wouldn't tell me during our tutor lessons, either."

"But you figured it out by yourself." Apollo takes the seat directly next to me, his free hand extending towards me. I take it in mine. "You always figure it out, one way or another."

His thumb slides across my knuckles, moving to outline

my veins showing beneath my pale skin. "You smell like perfume," I whisper to him.

"Honey and vanilla, I think."

He sounds so proud of something as trivial as perfume, and I know instantly it belongs to Hart. "I'm happy for you."

"When you turned me down all those years ago," Apollo begins. "I was convinced you were my soulmate, but do you remember what you told me?"

My mind drifts to the past, when he took me to a beach for the very first time. He proclaimed his love for me. It would've been so simple to say yes to him, to fall in love with him as time went on, but I rejected him. Apollo stood before me and gave me his heart. I returned it until somebody worthy could covet it.

"I told you that one day you'd realize I am always meant to be your friend."

He holds up my hand, pressing a kiss to my knuckles. "Thank you for forcing me to wait for her."

For the first time in years, one corner of my lip tilts upwards. It isn't quite a smile, but it is close enough.

"I would do anything for you, Po."

His grin widens at my nickname for him. "And I would do anything for you, ómorfo aínigma."

In a blinding light, he disappears, returning to his home where I am certain Hart Sommers waits for him. He is gone, along with Argus and Jamila. I am alone. Left with an arrow-pierced note that Apollo leaves behind. It is only Artemis's scribbled handwriting on a parchment piece of paper and me.

The silence screaming in my ears.

TWENTY-SEVEN

HART SOMMERS

J ust as Apollo pours me a cup of tea, grabbing himself a teacup, he is whisked away in an archway of rainbows. Ceramic cups shatter on the ground into a dozen pieces. The gold-engraved white shards scatter across the tiled kitchen floor. I expect him to return before the last piece is picked off the floor, but I'm wrong. Minutes pass with no array of colors sending him back.

It's late.

Fatigue weighs heavily on my tired bones. Rationally, I know I should find my way back to my little apartment, but I do not listen to the anxiousness. Instead, I stand up and leave the empty teacup on the table.

I wander through Apollo's mansion.

There is no clear destination in my mind; rather, I let my feet guide me throughout the many rooms. I walk up the staircase, meander past closed doors without the desire to open them. Until I reach the fifth door on the right side of the expansive hallway. There's nothing unique about this door. It's not a different color. There's not a unique door-knob garnering my attention. It is as ordinary as the other rooms I ignored, yet I stop in front of it.

My hand reaches to open. The lingering caress of fog brushes against my senses, wordlessly telling me I need to enter. I need to see what awaits me on the other side. The door clicks open upon my command, and I swing the door wide. I step into my version of Elysium.

"Holy Gods."

There is artwork everywhere.

Bust sculptures of every notable deity sit in three lines across a white table, on the farthest left wall. Black vases adorned in copper dry on suspended hooks across the ceiling. There are easels filled with half-finished paintings detailing important moments of his life. Finished paintings scatter every square inch of this thousand-square foot room. Each design is meticulously created by Apollo. Every painting is detailed to perfection.

The pale blue room is a stage for Apollo's talent, which no human or god can outmatch.

My feet move of their own accord as I attempt to take in everything this room offers. I move towards the finished paintings first. Across the walls, his life story is told through a paintbrush.

He tells the tale of his mother, Leto, holding two godly children. One in each arm. Her pale skin is highlighted by rosy pink cheeks. She has the same golden locks as Apollo, but the glow of her smile is signature to only her. It overtakes her entire face, and it illuminates her narrowed, brown eyes. She cradles her two children, and I know without ever meeting Leto that this is the greatest moment of her life. The pinnacle of her happiness.

The next painting is just him and his mother, but he is an infant this time. A playful smile remains on her lips, as she holds a bow just out of Apollo's desperate reach. I can hear his mother's laughter in the scene. In almost every painting detailing Apollo's childhood, his mother always appears happy. The portion of the wall to the left of the door is dedicated to his family, particularly his mother and twin sister. Although, there is one painting of a mischievously young Hermes unhappily gifting Apollo a lyre.

The other side of the door tells the story of Apollo's failed romances.

"I shouldn't look," I murmur to myself.

Yet, my eyes do not listen to my words. They drink in every single painting taking over the wall, reading the name of his lover written beneath in perfect calligraphy.

There's Cassandra, with a mane of curly red locks. She rests her hand on her fist, staring up at him as he speaks with unabashed adoration. She is one of many who stare at Apollo with such fascination. Mouth parted in awe and face aglow.

"Stop looking at them."

But I ignore my words again and continue to gawk at his past, with an unfamiliar mixture of jealousy and curiosity.

There's Hyacinth, an attractive man with hair as dark as mine and eyes of the deepest green. Apollo holds him tightly, a dimple on his cheek as he smirks down at the much shorter Hyacinth. There's great, all-consuming love between them. Yet, in the next painting of Hyacinth, he's running towards the Underworld, leaving Apollo's life forever.

All these romances have a devastating end told in neighboring art pieces. Apollo and a long-haired, dark-skinned woman named Marpessa are kissing. In the next, she's reaching for another man. Apollo stands near them, watching a human woman choose a mortal over him.

There's another of a woman named Gaillardia. In one picture, they are gardening together, and the next she's dead in his arms. He's sobbing for her, holding her bloody corpse around a circle of women armed with bows and arrows. In scratchy, rushed writing, the same two words scribble the canvas. *Six years*. All I can see are him, Gaillardia, and the armored women I think are huntresses.

The last painting portrayed on the wall, nearest the corner, has Saffron's name written at the bottom.

In the first art piece, Saffron and Apollo are dancing at a ball together. She wears a light purple gown that further enhances her large physique in the greatest ways. The train of the dress flows behind them as Apollo twirls her around the center of the dance floor, his gaze never leaving her. Saffron is human in this image, but she is still unequivocally radiant. She has the largest grin on her face, which sharpens her high-risen cheekbones. Apollo stares down at her. Enamored, like she is the sun that he orbits around.

There is no way to stop the pang of jealousy when I see their hands clasped together, him guiding her through their dance. Hastily, I look at the next image, seeing how his heart broke by the goddess of humanity.

"Saffron made every god within the vicinity fall in love with her when she first entered the arena as a naïve demigod."

The female's voice comes so suddenly, I feel my skin jump off my bones. I turn around suddenly without seeing the second painting, and Khione is standing there. Her dark skin starkly contrasts her white, braided hair and fur coat. Even her eyeliner is white, the ends sharp as a blade.

"What do you want?" I snap.

Khione ignores me. "I never understood the gods' fascination with her. Their immediate love that held no restraint. She was like a forest fire, consuming them all. From low-level gods like Priapus to Olympians like Apollo. They all burned themselves in their pursuit of her." She stands beside me, her speed quicker than I expect. I glower at her as she stares up at the painting of Saffron and Apollo. "But they look cute together, I suppose."

"What do you want?" I repeat, my tone snappier than before.

"I half expected to find you with your fiancée after his near-death experience, celebrating the beauty of human life in each other's arms. Yet, here you are in Apollo's mansion, snooping through his art room with hearts in your eyes."

Before her hand can clutch my chin, I grab her wrist. The goddess smirks in feigned amusement, but disdain festers beneath the surface. A crack in her icy demeanor.

"Are you choosing to disobey Lady Styx this early? You signed an oath, and an oath with Lady Styx is unwavering."

"I know what I signed," I growl back at her, pushing her touch away. "She will have Saffron as we promised."

"Good," Khione purrs the word. "On the day you previously agreed to bring Saffron to the Underworld, there will be a party at Dionysus's house. I was told you were extended an invitation. She will be there and that's where you will take her."

"How do you expect me to kidnap the single most powerful immortal in the world?"

"That's not my concern, little oracle." As quickly and quietly as she came, Khione vanishes in a puff of dark green smoke.

I agreed to save Lowell's life for guiding Saffron to Styx, but I know more now. My earlier premonition returns. Saffron is walking towards Styx and her river. The latter grins and thanks me for my services. Only danger surrounds Styx, and instead of steering away from the havoc she ensues, I aid her in her destruction.

I run out of the house before Apollo can get home.

TWENTY-EIGHT

LAMB

When the sun bids the island goodnight, the nymphs curl their bodies within their cage. They fold their hands together to create a suitable pillow and rest beneath the twinkling stars. They almost appear peaceful within their captivity, wearing wistful smiles in their sleep. Upon further assessment, the truth lays bare.

Once beautiful satin, pastel gowns are tattered and dirty. The polish fades on their chipped fingernails and shows the grim underneath. Physical wounds heal almost instantaneously on deities' flesh. Yet, on a few nymphs, dried ichor remains on their knuckles from punching the cage's impenetrable bars. Their fists failures are the reason golden blood stains the soles of their feet. Their attempt to kick their way to freedom ends the same way as their fists.

The serene appearances of the nymphs hide the masked truth.

They are caged warriors fighting for freedom.

A thunderous *slam* pulls my attention towards Artemis. Fist after bloodied fist lands on her cage, but the bars do not tremble with fright. They do not waver. No matter how hard she punches or how swift her aim is, the bar that should weaken with Artemis's force remains intact. The cages are magic-blessed, and she cannot destroy magic with brute strength.

She rears back her elbow. Her gilded blood glinting off her knuckles.

I say. "It will not work. The nymphs already tried to punch and kick their way out."

"What?" she asks.

"Look at them."

It takes a few seconds, but Artemis realizes the dried blood on their feet and knuckles. The moment understanding dawns on her, she crumbles onto the floor. She hikes her knees up against her chest. Her previous look of determination falls as defeat rises to the surface.

"You can say you're right." Artemis says. Her words are muffled as she lays her mouth on top of her knees. "You knew this was a trap, and I didn't listen. We're here because of me. Because you were right, and I was wrong."

I lean my head against the cell bars and say. "I think you're mistaking me for another huntress. Maybe Sika, who would make a joke right now that she's always right. She'd declare herself the queen of rightness, with that toothy grin of hers on full display."

Artemis lifts her head, attention fully geared to me. I am the sole witness to her frown lessening, ever so slightly. On this empty island devoid of freedom, I choose to distract myself with an achievable goal. By the end of the night, I will make Artemis smile. Make her forget, for even a second, that she is not a prisoner in another god's game.

"Or," I continue, making sure my voice is as playful as possible. "Maybe you think I'm Dýnami? She would let out a laugh that sounds like a combination of a hyena and a bear, and then she would ask what her prize was."

At that, Artemis huffs, and it almost resembles a laugh. "She would request Rocky Road ice cream."

"With extra fudge."

"And peanuts on top."

"Sugar covered peanuts," I amend. "Dýnami would never eat plain peanuts."

"True," Artemis closes her eyes as she hums. "Silly me."

"I curse the day Athena introduced her to Rocky Road ice cream. It's become an addiction."

I know what Artemis sees when she closes her eyes; it's the other huntresses.

Sika has a long arm wrapped around Dýnami, who guffaws at a joke while oblivious to a piece of squirrel meat stuck between her two front teeth. Akita is rolling her eyes, always unamused by Dýnami's antics. Shikari knowingly makes more comments that will continue Dýnami's ceaseless laughter. Hound argues with Vee over some pointless historical factoid nobody else cares about. Somewhere in the distance, Artemis and I watch with amusement. When Artemis doesn't see the surrounding island, she pretends she is back in the woods with the other huntresses.

I know she sees this because I see it too. Every time I blink, I let myself forget I am here. A millisecond of reprieve before I am reminded of where I am and who stole my freedom.

"What would Frigate do?" Artemis asks, eyes still shut.

"If I was Frigate, I'd make some snippy comment like *'of course I'm right.'*" I say the last bit in my best rendition of Frigate's monotone, yet nasally, voice.

"*'The chances of me being wrong about a trap so obvious would be next-to-nothing.'*" Artemis retorts. Her interpretation of Frigate is almost identical to the stoic huntress.

"And Akita would tilt her nose so far up towards the sky with pride, you could count every individual nose hair."

I complete my goal.

Artemis chuckles. A grin blooms over her face. I, too, laugh. It's a wondrous thing, laughter, because it can erupt like a flame even in the darkest shadows.

"But instead of them, I'm with Lamb." Artemis says, as her laughter ebbs away into the darkness. "Who doesn't gloat about being right, but she makes sure I do not stew in my guilt. I'm with my longest riding huntress, who focuses on making me smile before anything else." She pauses for a moment, then opens her eyes, looks at me, and divulges. "You're a good friend, Lamb. There's nobody else I would want to accompany me in my shame than you."

"It's because I'm your best friend."

"Let's not go that far," Artemis teases.

"I didn't accompany you in your shame," I say.

There's a pause on her end, then she asks. "What is this other than shame?"

"Hope. I'm accompanying you in your hope. You wish to save the huntresses, even as the expanse of yourself. It's not shameful to risk your life for another's."

She closes her eyes. "Good night, Lamb."

"Good night," I whisper back.

Sleep takes its time claiming Artemis, but once her light

snores reach my ears, I wait alone for her to arrive. The silent stars are my only company as I stave sleep and search the beach for her entrance. I am uncertain she will come, but all magic has an expiration date, and eventually, she will need to charm the cages again. She might not show until tomorrow, or the next day, but soon Hecate will be on this island to reveal herself as a traitor, and I will be awake waiting.

Hecate will not think to look into my cage and check if I am awake. Because, in her eyes, I am not here on this island with the others. I am the oldest huntress, but I am not who deities remember. I am not bold like Sika. Boisterous, like Dýnami. Unflinchingly blunt like Frigate. Or dangerously prideful like Akita. Except for Athena, Apollo, Artemis, Hermes, and Saffron, the remaining gods treat me as they do the wind. I am present in the room, like a soft gust; I am not consequential enough to acknowledge.

There is no discernible trait of mine that intrigues the gods. I am not the tallest or the shortest huntress. The skinniest or fattest. Dumbest or the wisest. I am not the prettiest or the ugliest. Therefore, I am forgotten.

Many centuries ago, there was a time when this truth hurt me. Wounding my pride, as I stood between Raven and Willow's beauty, but then I realized the weapon my invisibility wields. My uninspiring mediocrity is a useful blade nobody sees coming into a battle of fists.

That includes the witch goddess, who emerges from a plume of dark green smoke.

Hecate walks across the sandy plains like she's done this a thousand times before. Her bare feet move towards the cages, magic whirling on her fingertips. The train of her black lace gown dutifully follows her. She is radiant, the way only a goddess can be, and goddesses as gorgeous as her forget about huntresses as average as me.

I smile at the fact.

Silently, I observe Hecate as she extends her magic to one of the nymph's cages, soft incantations escaping her lips. She spells each cage one at a time, starting with Sinope, then moving to the rest of the nymphs. Last, she glides to Artemis and me. Green, the color of moss, captures Artemis's cage.

Hecate begins her spell.

When she is two sentences into the incantation, I speak. "After Raven, I have often wondered what drives betrayal. To twist a mind from friend to enemy."

I hate saying Raven's name; the sound is bitter on my tongue. Raven was the first person to betray me, who let me trust and love her like a sister only to murder my best friend. I took Raven's life the same day she murdered Willow. Justice swiftly served, but hatred for her still cleaves at my chest. My rage for Raven is a tornado of flames, threatening to burn me to ash.

Yet, her name has a purpose tonight.

Hecate halts mid-sentence, her magic dissolving. Slowly, she turns her body to face me. Against the obsidian sky, with only the moon giving light, I barely make out her eyes. Wide, doe shaped eyes consume most of Hecate's face, the color the brightest, eeriest shade of blue, and they narrow with disgust. She glowers at me the way I look at a pestering fly. A slight annoyance, but nothing of true consequence.

"I should have checked your heartbeat to see if you were sleeping. It's a mistake I will not make twice."

"It only takes one crack to make a palace crumble."

Hecate takes a step towards me, her train swooshing across the sand. She assesses me more critically now. Takes in my elongated face, jutted jaw, and determined glare. There is more acknowledgement than ever before. She has known me for close to six hundred years, seeing me from infanthood until now, but today is the first time she has truly seen me.

"She warned Calypso and me not to underestimate you, yet your name is Lamb. Easy prey for any predator. A perfect name for a human you are meant to underestimate. To forget about."

I want to know who is the *she* Hecate refers to, curiosity snapping its fangs nearer. I will not get a direct answer. Just as freedom is currently an unachievable goal, so is the mysterious female's identity. I focus on what I can accomplish through this conversation with Hecate, an attainable goal that will lead me towards escape.

"Not all names are as accurate as Narcissus or Echo," I coo.

"No, I suppose not," Hecate hums.

Her last words display her boredom with our conversation. She is quick to dismiss, so I reel her back in. Force her attention to stay fixated on me, the huntress she continuously underestimates.

"You didn't answer my question," I blurt out.

"Am I required to always answer a human's questions?"

I ignore her question, reiterating mine instead. "What drives betrayal? What made you stand here on this beach, turning your back on Hades and Persephone?"

"That isn't one question. It's two. Did Artemis not teach her huntresses how to count?"

"I know there was a time when Raven was truly loyal to

Artemis, when there was love in her heart for Willow and me. For hundreds of years, I leaned my trust onto Raven, and she did not fail me. Yet, with one swift arrow to the heart, she showed how quick betrayal can come and steal away your faith in friends or family. She rode beside Artemis and me for centuries and turned on us, but you have been with Hades and Persephone for eons. How could loyalty sour so fast?"

My words are a part of her truth she does not wish to uncover. Hecate storms towards my cage, sharp nails curling around the top bars. She spits an incantation around me. Curses me to suffer in captivity, binding the bars to become ten times stronger than a god. Then, without my question finding its answer, Hecate disappears in a gust of smoke.

"Another crack to your palace walls, Hecate," I whisper.

My goal was never to find out why Hecate is betraying Hades and Persephone. No, I stayed awake tonight with the sole purpose of distracting Hecate long enough that she would forget to charm Artemis's cage. At least, not charm it all the way. As the other cages burn a bright green, stewing in Hecate's newest incantation, Artemis's bars burn a dim shade.

By tomorrow morning, Artemis should be able to escape.

And with that knowledge, I finally go to sleep.

TWENTY-NINE

HART SOMMERS

All too quickly, the morning arrives. My alarm clock blares at the same agonizing time as it has for the past six years. It is set for two hours before Lowell wakes up, so I can have a full face of makeup on, and ready his breakfast. For six years, I have lived like a complacent housewife, with no future for myself.

The irony is not lost on me.

I once had no future, and now I embrace seeing the future. In one day, my reality has tipped on its axis. Instead of rushing to the vanity mirror, ready to make my face another art piece, I brush my teeth. I wash the sleep from my eyes and leave the bathroom. I place my hair in a simple, off-the-shoulder braid, pull on a white tube top with a pair of paint-stained overalls. A closet full of spring dresses stares at me, quizzically wondering why I am settling for ten-year-old overalls, but I walk out of the bedroom without shame.

In fact, beneath the weight of fear, I inwardly grin at who I am allowing myself to become.

Lowell is still asleep, and I do not bother saying goodbye as I slip on my favorite worn-down sandals and leave the apartment. It isn't until I open the apartment doors that I question aloud. "Where am I going?"

Technically, I still have a job unfinished at Olympus Industries, but do I want to go there? I can spend the day at a coffee shop instead. Or I can meander around the town after years of allowing myself to hide. Do I wish to fully embrace this new world opening its doors for me?

A sleek, black car sits in the parking spot nearest me. One window is rolled down and a gorgeous face peeks out. Dangling from her manicured hands, are bags stained with grease. "Before you change your mind about getting in the car with me, I bought breakfast."

"Depends," I say to Aphrodite. "Are there hash browns in there?"

The goddess of love responds. "Enough hash browns to feed an army." Her ever-changing eyes are warm, but they speak more than her words.

Leave these safe, lightless apartment walls and explore what you deserve.

How can it only be last night that Aphrodite said those words to me? Yesterday lasted centuries, an endless terrain of catastrophes and self-discoveries, but today is a new day. Today, I can decide if I prefer the safety of naivety, or if I want to get inside the car with Aphrodite. If I will explore what I deserve, yet fear.

I get into the car.

Throughout the ride, Aphrodite and I eat breakfast sandwiches and hash browns, and she talks to me. While the goddess rambles about her escapades across the eons, she surprises me by asking about my interests, too. She inquires about my past relationships, frowning when I admit I've only dated Lowell. Her questions about me are random, always appearing in the middle of one of her rambles about an ex-lover, and they vary in seriousness.

"After Zeus threw me down on the ground, what's your favorite color, Harty?"

"Yellow," I answer.

Later on, she says. "Anchises was a tender lover, always peppering kisses alongside my neck as he," she pauses. "Who would you consider your best friend?"

The answer makes me pause.

In high school, I had three great friends who all shared my love for art. I love to paint and sketch, but each friend had a different passion in the art field. One loved the history behind art, analyzing old sculptures and paintings rather than creating them. Another friend was a sculptress, creating animals with great accuracy. The last friend painted like me, but she focused on landscapes rather than people. We were inseparable in high school, but Lowell always tagged along. My friends jokingly called him my tail because he was always swinging behind me, delighting in my presence.

When high school ended, all of them traveled the world to pursue their passion. I stayed with Lowell. Even when his interest in me faded romantically, I clung to him. It's been eight years since I graduated high school, and while I remember my friends' names, I cannot remember where they live now or who is in their lives. We faded apart, and I became Lowell's tail, limply following behind his successes.

"I guess Lowell," I answer. "He's all I have in this world."

Aphrodite's form centralizes on one body, the same dark-skinned beauty she wore last night in my apartment. She clasps a manicured hand on top of mine, the rose-gold bracelet attached to her middle finger cold against my skin.

Aphrodite squeezes my hand, then whispers. "Do you want to hear the time Ares and I were caught frolicking by my husband?"

This is how the entire car ride goes. She tells me about Ares, Adonis, Anchises, Zeus, Hermes, and a myriad of other men and women. Then, sporadically, asks me questions that range from personal to quirky.

"Bloom was one of my favorite female lovers. She had this trick with her tongue. And what is your favorite food?"

I have an entire mouthful of two hash brown patties. My cheeks are swollen like a chipmunk when I answer her. "Anything that comes from a potato and is deep fried."

Point being, the two hash brown patties in my mouth.

When Aphrodite's driver pulls to the front of the building, Aphrodite turns to me. Her face is forever shifting from one gorgeous face to the next. "When we go inside, I must ask you a favor."

The fifth hash brown patty slides down my throat like a razor blade. Many are fooled by her gorgeous appearance and inclination for inappropriate conversation. They believe a pretty face equates to a lowered level of intelligence. I see the truth behind Aphrodite's façade. She is brilliant, just like the other immortals, yet she unveils more secrets than anybody would ever know.

Did she discover my deal with Styx? Or does she know about my ability to see to the future? Suddenly, all the food in my stomach weighs down on my body like an anchor. I fidget and struggle to breathe.

"You look far too human when you fidget with the rusty necklace hanging around your neck. When you meet Hera today and draw her, I need you to stop playing with that little trinket. Hera can sniff out weakness like a bloodhound, and you are too adorable to be eaten up by such a viper."

Both their gazes wander to the feather-shaped necklace. Affectionately, I graze my finger across the rusted seam.

"It was a gift from my father," I admit. The smile on my face is bittersweet with the memory of him. "He had one just like it, and because I loved it, he got me an identical copy on my tenth birthday. I haven't taken it off since."

Aphrodite doesn't immediately respond until I feel the warm touch of her hand. She runs her index finger across the gold feather dangling from its chain, and upon her touch, little pink dots of magic rain down. The rust dissipates, and the gold sparkles, like it had the first day my dad put it around my neck.

"I thought I was going to have to stop wearing it." Still not believing the sight, I pick up the gold feather, running my fingers alongside each ridge as if the rust will return in minutes. "It's been turning my chest green recently."

More pink dots fall from Aphrodite's fingertips, and without looking down, I know she absolved my tanned skin of the green lines spattering my chest. "When did he die?" Aphrodite asks.

The day returns to my mind like a series of polaroid shots. My canvas at school. Me, running towards the principal's office. The sound of steel crashing against steel.

Mouth open in screams I can no longer hear. A crumpled body destroyed by a devastating accident.

I blink away the memories; instead, I grab the car door and open it. "We shouldn't keep Queen Hera waiting for me."

Aphrodite, ever observant, doesn't pry. "Let's go see the wicked queen herself."

She loops her arm around mine, walking side-by-side with me as we enter Olympus Industries. No matter how often her form shifts, she is always monumentally taller than I am. I try to drift into her shadow, to slink my arm out of hers, but Aphrodite smiles down at me. She pretends she is oblivious to my discomfort, keeping me in her spotlight.

"I've been waiting so long to have a platonic friend here on earth," Aphrodite says, squeezing my arm. "We must shop for dresses together for the ball. You are attending, right?" She lets out a hearty breath. As she presses the elevator button, she says. "Of course you are going. What a ridiculous question."

"Yes, I'm going."

So I can complete my bargain with Styx, somehow kidnap Saffron, and dump her into the Underworld. Most likely, I am going to the ball to die a terrible death, where I lose every bone in my body.

"Then how about this Thursday? I pick you up and we shop together. I'll pay for the gowns if you buy us dinner afterwards." Aphrodite and I walk into the elevator, and she presses level three. "Hera and Zeus's offices are on the third floor. We often joke that Saffron placed them as far away from her skyscraper office as possible. To distance herself from the dad she hates and the step-mother she hates more."

Aphrodite laughs like I am in on the gods' jokes, but when we enter the third level, nobody is there except a blonde receptionist. She has a short bob hairstyle, an upturned nose, and a perpetual frown. When she sees Aphrodite and me, her frown, if possible, worsens.

"What do you want, Aphrodite?"

"And good morning to you too, Hebe. We have a meeting with Hera this morning, yet I do not see her in her office?"

The office in question is surrounded by glass windows, letting everybody see inside. The furniture is all white, including the open laptop on the office desk. Queen Hera is nowhere in sight.

Hebe, goddess of youth, snips. "Hera insisted on visiting Saffron. She will be down shortly. You can wait in her office."

"And be delighted with your presence a little while longer? I think not." Aphrodite uses our looped arms to turn me completely around, so I face the elevator doors again. "Let's go join in on the fun in Saffron's office."

The moment the elevator doors open on Saffron's level, chaos erupts. Jamila, Saffron's receptionist, is visibly shaking and leaning against her desk. Hera's face is reddened with rage, hands curled into tight fists. Saffron stands across from Hera, completely ignoring the queen as she centralizes on a male god with calm fury.

The male god is pushed against the wall, Saffron's magic suspending him ten feet in the air. His black buzz-cut grazes the ceiling, but that is not the most concerning part of this image. It's his bones, pressing against his skin. They are ready to rupture the flesh and fly towards Saffron. His mouth is open in a silent scream, his teeth wiggling and threatening to break free.

Saffron hasn't noticed Aphrodite and me, and she takes a step towards the male god. She holds two fingers in the air. That's all she needs in order to control this god's bones. Her index finger curls downward, ever so slightly, and the god's left pinky bone juts out of his skin. The bone is still attached to his finger, not flying across the room towards its master, but it's enough damage to bring the god pain. A small stream of ichor careens down the male's digit, and his scream is no longer silent.

He wails and nods his head. "Never again, I promise!"

"Good," is her too-calm response.

She drops him.

The god crumples onto the floor. His body trembles with a mixture of pain and fear. His pinky heals in seconds, but Saffron doesn't inflict her magic on him to kill him. No, she is an instrument of terror.

Now, I understand why I agreed to Khione and Nemesis's proposal. I know why I saved Lowell's life to betray Saffron. All my life, I heard grand stories about the savior of humanity. The goddess of mercy, who was nothing like all the other gods who let humans suffer for five hundred years. My father loved Lady Saffron, the goddess of bones, but he loved who she used to be.

I see who she is now.

A monster.

THIRTY

SAFFRON

Argus waits for Jamila and me outside the front door to start the day anew. To forget about the chaotic mess that was yesterday and begin a fresh start. I want to, but from the moment he opens the doors for us, hateful screams from the protestors echo across my expansive front yard. A crease forms between Jamila's bushy eyebrows.

"Is this why you brought me back home?" she asks.

There are many reasons she is back at home with me, and angry humans are the smallest droplets in the storm nearing us. I want her close when the lightning strikes, the thunder booms, and the downpour truly begins. Secrets await every corridor, and while I have not uncovered them all, I am certain I want my foster daughter close to me when terror assails.

Argus answers, so I do not have to explain. "Partly. They're growing in numbers every day, and you are a little human."

Jamila snorts at the last statement. "You act as if you are still guarding my six-year-old self."

A few of his eyes assess Jamila, gliding up her stature. "You do not look much taller than your six-year-old self."

She laughs, slapping his arm. "Rude!"

The left side of Argus's mouth tilts upwards, displaying one of his famously rare smiles. "You're no taller than a man's kneecap, and we need you close to us so they do not mistake you for a garden gnome and step on you."

Still chuckling, Jamila interjects. "I'm five foot three."

"Exactly."

She stomps down the steps, feigning annoyance when both Argus and I see through the façade. There's a skip in her step, one painfully youthful and exuberant. It's the only sunlight in the darkness. Her unwavering optimism.

"I have missed her around the house," Argus admits, standing shoulder-to-arm with me.

He's almost two feet taller than I am at a staggering seven-foot-one, but he doesn't bend down to be at eye-level with me. Two of the eyes on his shoulder watch me as Jamila enters the car. When Argus was first sent down from Mt. Olympus by Zeus to protect me, I was unnerved by his many eyes. Now, almost eighty years later, the sight of Argus is comforting.

"I have too," I say. We walk a few steps, then I add. "You never left last night."

He appears as stoic and steady as always, but he wears the same clothes as the night before. Many of his eyes are open, bloodshot yet alert, but a dozen eyes around his elbows and knees are closed. Part of him slumbers while the rest of his body remains alert. Ready for today's level of chaos.

"I heard you crying in your room last night," he says a matter-of-factly. "I wanted to stay here in case you needed me."

My mouth opens to find words. To utter a proclamation of gratitude, because his actions last night are not indicative of a guard simply doing his duty. Zeus always fears I will come for his throne. Worries I will usurp him, like he did to his father, and his father did before him. I am perpetually monitored, no matter how many times I tell Zeus I do not wish to be queen.

Before I was forced to accept Argus as my guard, Phobos and Deimos would take turns monitoring me, under Zeus's strict orders that I must be watched. Phobos and Deimos would never complain, but the moment I entered my house, they would leave. Not even the sound of my cries would get Phobos or Deimos to return. But Argus is more than a guard. Somewhere throughout the years, between late night dinners together and conversations to and from work, we became friends.

Possibly one of the few friends I have left in this world.

"If you want to talk about him, then you know where to find me."

Argus walks down the steps, and after a few seconds, I follow him. He opens the back door for me, closing it after I slide onto the leather seats beside Jamila. Then he drives towards the mayhem. Behind the golden gates separating my estate from the rest of society, protestors stand, scream, and wave their posters. Their posters condemn me, naming me their monster, rather than the savior the rest of the world monikers me.

"They have almost doubled since last night," Jamila mumbles to herself.

"There was another murder," Argus says.

Argus drives to the gates, but reaches into his passenger seat, picks up a manila folder, and extends it towards Jamila and me. I take the folder from his hands. I open the contents, only to find another murder scene. Jamila gasps and averts her gaze. She looked away a second after seeing the macabre, but I know the image will remain burned in Jamila's memories. This crime scene will always remind her of the world's never-ending cruelty.

This female victim is pregnant and no older than twenty. One hand rests on her swollen belly, the other outstretched for the dead little boy a few feet away. The murderer ransacking my town has always killed a mother with her child, but this is the first who also about to give birth.

Even worse, the murderer has elevated their fashion of killing. They always write my name on the wall in the victims' blood, but this is the first crime scene involving bones. My sigil. Three bones are ripped out of the woman's skin. Her collarbone, right ulna, and one phalange sit in a curved formation. The image cruelly resembles a red, bloodied smile.

I close the manila folder, unable to look any longer. "How long ago?"

"The detective dropped off the folder around four this morning. Said the time of death was around ten at night," Argus answers.

"Jamila, when we arrive at the office, please call the detective and tell him I would like to meet today."

Jamila nods her head but doesn't speak.

I open my mouth, an apology preparing to leave my lips, but the protestors' screams mute any other sound.

Argus has opened the gates, and while none of the protestors pass the opening to bombard my house, they rush towards the car. Furious fists punch the window, causing Jamila to squeal. Blood-stained bluebell flowers land on the windshield. While all the humans bellow their rage from outside the car, I can make out Gareth French's voice most clearly.

"All heroes turn into villains sooner or later."

Argus slowly drives through them, and the protestors let us part. No one runs after my car to continue their assault. They wait at the golden gates for when I return, so their few minutes of anger can unleash at my home. The place I should find safest, yet dread most of all.

Jamila's hands shake on her lap, and for a moment, I wonder if I have made the right decisions for her. When Jamila's mother suddenly left, I pondered how Jamila's life would be if I sent her to live with another relative. I adopted her. Made her my daughter.

Did I curse her by raising her?

It is a question I let terrorize me the rest of the car ride.

My dazed disorientation guides me out of the car and into the elevator. I enter my office without really processing my surroundings because I am plagued with guilt-filled questions.

Did I curse Hattie's great-great granddaughter by raising her as my child? I want to do what is right for both Jamila and Hattie, but did I lead Jamila into danger through my actions? If I didn't become her guardian, she could have had a mundane life. She would not have to see horrific crime scenes. She wouldn't flinch in car rides because people are throwing bloodied flowers at her; instead, she would get to enjoy her independence in her apartment.

Did I curse her by raising her?

A scream, piercing and fearful, rips me away from my hazy thoughts. Standing in my office, I prematurely realize Jamila and I are not alone. Asopus and Hera are here, waiting for the meeting I requested in the middle of the night. We are late because of the protestors, but that does not excuse the sight unfurling in front of me.

Hera stands with her arms crossed, a sour expression scrunching up her dark-painted lips. She is not my primary focus because it is not her who screams. It is Jamila. Asopus's hand strikes her cheek, and blinding rage envelopes me. He misses his daughters, but he does not exact his anger on the two goddesses in the room. No, he attacks my daughter as retribution for failing to find his.

I raise only two fingers in the air, but it is enough. Asopus flies across the room, his back smacking against the wall so hard the foundation cracks. His skull takes the brunt of the pain, staining my wall with his ichor. When he hit Jamila, anger encompassed his face, but now there is only fear in my presence. I am the goddess with the power to kill him and, for a blinding moment, all I want is to rip all the bones out of his body and destroy him.

After I killed Epiales, I swore to never be a murderer again. I have only killed one person since that day, but Asopus dangles a malicious temptation in front of me. He makes me seethe with murderous intent. I take a step towards him.

I can feel every inch of his body trembling in fright as I hold possession of his bones. He cannot move from his place on the wall. Killing him now can be as easy as curling these two fingers I hold in the air, and he is aware of the magnitude of my powers.

"Are you alright?" I ask Jamila, who holds her cheek with one hand.

The redness is a stark contrast against her brown skin, the signs of bruising already beginning. Her hand can only cover a small portion of the handprint across her face, caused by a god who knows his strength is one hundred times hers.

Jamila nods her head, but tears are in her eyes. Her sunshine is dimmed in the overwhelming darkness of my life, and I glower at Asopus with a visible desire to steal all his bones from his body. Each step I take, I taunt his death, pulling his bones little-by-little towards me. Asopus bites down on his bottom lip, stopping his screams from desecrating the air.

"You chose the only human in the room to strike," I say the fact with an eerie calmness to my voice that counteracts the absolute rage overtaking me. "Are you truly that weak that she is the only one you will attack?"

He drops his bottom lip from his teeth. Ichor dribbles down his chin, and he stammers. "I am sorry. My anger got to me. I'm so sorry. Don't kill me."

I take another step, his bones pressing against his skin and threatening to rupture. I have no intention of killing him, but for the crime of fearing his lesser, I will make sure today is the most frightening of his existence. By the time he leaves my office, I will ensure he never wishes to lay a hand on another female or human again. If I must be the monster in his eyes, then so be it.

"You are a guest in my office. It is an extension of my home, considering how often I am here, and I invited you here to aid your search. You are my guest here, and you repay that hospitality by slapping my daughter across the face."

"I'm sorry!" he screams.

I raise my fingers, guiding him as far up the wall as possible. His hair grazes the ceiling, and I tighten my hold on the bones around his neck, so the feeling resembles a noose. Asopus whimpers, and I stand directly below him.

"We are both aware that the greatest crime in our world is to harm another when you are a guest in their home. If you needed a reminder of that rule, then go visit Tantalus in the Fields of Punishment. Zeus would agree I have every right to rip out all the bones from your body and scatter the remains in the deepest pits of Tartarus."

"I'm sorry." He repeats over and over again. "I won't harm another again. Upon Styx's river, I swear it."

"Tell me you will never harm another human, least of all Jamila."

He cries, snot rolling down his face alongside the tears.

Faintly, I hear an elevator ding, but I only focus on Asopus. The god who physically harmed an innocent human woman because of ill-placed rage. I might be more forgiving if it was me he slapped, the real goddess he blames for his daughters' continual disappearance. But no, Jamila trembles where she stands because of him.

When I take the last step towards him, I beckon his teeth to wiggle in his gums. I threaten the execution I have every right to deliver. He wants to scream. It's clear on his face, but he doesn't. Asopus knows, just like I do, that he committed a grievous act against me. I invited him to my office to tell him news about his daughters and provide all my help to save them, and he hurts one of the few people I truly love.

My index finger curls downward, ever so slightly, and the god's left pinky bone juts out of his skin. The bone is still attached to his finger, not flying across the room towards its master, but it's enough damage to cause the god pain. A small stream of ichor careens down the male's digit, and his scream is no longer silent.

He wails and nods his head. "Never again, I promise!"

"Good," I say when everything is not good. The bruise still grows on Jamila's face, her fear of my world worsening with each passing day, and the question from earlier returns with fervor.

Did I curse her by raising her?

I lower my fingers, and Asopus collapses onto the floor. He trembles on the ground, but when his eyes level with mine, they brim with disbelief. Gods are not merciful creatures; we do not grant life when death is an option. Asopus expected his execution, and so did Hera, by the shocked expression on her face. Zeus would have thrown him into Tartarus until he disappeared from the world's memory. They expect the same ruthlessness from me, his prized daughter.

But I favor redemption over obliteration.

"Oh gods, what did Asopus do?" A familiar, overtly feminine voice asks.

Aphrodite stands beside Hart right outside the elevator doors. While the former wears amusement on her many faces, Hart shows her disbelief and disgust for my actions. Her emotions paint her face with the same clarity as words on parchment. Hart takes a retreating step, but she isn't able to move further back because Aphrodite has her arm looped with her.

"Is my portrait scheduled for today?" Hera asks, almost bored.

There is a long, tense silence. Everybody expects Hart to respond to Hera. Yet, she looks at the golden blood staining my wall and floor and says nothing. Her proximity weighs down the folded drawing she made the day before, which remains in my jacket pocket. With her near, it feels as if Epiales is here and joining the conversation. A hidden apparition only I am aware of.

"Yes, and we must hurry because Zeus will be here in a few hours for his portrait. We all know how little patience the king has." Aphrodite laughs at the joke she made, but nobody joins in.

"You are on your own for this meeting, Asopus," Hera says to the male god, who rises from his sitting position. The queen of Olympus spares me a parting glance, flippantly adding. "Try not to kill any gods while I am away, god-killer."

That cursed nickname sounds acidic against her voice. She loathes my existence because I am the most powerful of Zeus's children, and she is not my mother. Hera believes the title of Zeus's true heir should fall to a legitimate child, not the product of a human woman she murdered. I hold little hatred for Hera, although she stole my biological mother from me and repeatedly tried to end my life. However, Hera's glare burns decades' worth of fury, and I doubt it will dampen throughout the eons.

Hera leaves with Hart and Aphrodite, the room silent until the elevator door clicks shut.

My eyes find Jamila's immediately. "Apollo should be at the office today. Go find him to heal you and then take the rest of the week off. Argus will drive you home."

Jamila, still not speaking, nods her head and shuffles out of the office without looking at Asopus or me.

"My daughters?"

Asopus's voice wobbles with unbridled fear, both of me and for his daughters. I motion my head towards my desk, and we walk together. He takes his usual seat, and I lean back in my chair, letting the silence linger a little longer than necessary. I let his heartbeat slow, his fear of me lessen with each passing second, and then I deliver the news about his daughters.

"We found their location."

"Where are they?" Asopus says, his voice rushed and desperate. "When are we getting them? I can leave right now, and my remaining daughters can join us."

"Asopus," my voice takes a delicate tone. Immediately, his excitement deflates because, like me, this compassionate tone is no longer common. It is present solely because of the ominous answer to his question. "They are on Calypso's Island, along with Artemis and one of her huntresses."

"Calypso's Island," he exhales his defeat. "Nobody knows where it's located."

"I know, but after you leave here, I will meet with Poseidon and Amphitrite. They will start scouring the oceans for the island. Following that, Athena will come to my office with any news she's gathered from Odysseus in Elysium Fields. Then, my last attempt will be a meeting with Zeus after his portrait is done. He was the one who cursed Calypso into exile on that island, so if neither Poseidon, Amphitrite, or Odysseus know the location, then Zeus is our best bet."

Asopus leans back in his seat, stewing over the information I provided. We are immortal, destined to be ageless, but the news brings wrinkles to the corners of his eyes where he used to smile alongside his kin. Gray slides across his dark tresses. Youthfulness transforming into mournfully depleted hope. The same god who lives in his anger and resentment is gone. Replacing him is a god already defeated.

"Thank you for the update," he says as he stands to his feet.

"If you'd like to come back tomorrow at this time, I can provide you with any information I glean from the others."

He nods his head and walks to the door. Asopus takes a single step out, one hand still around the side of the door, and turns around to face me. Only a few minutes ago, I held him up by his bones against the wall and threatened to murder him. My mercy shifted his perception of me. Before, he held hatred; now, he revers me as a god. Not his equal, but above him, the way the Olympians are superior to the lesser immortals.

"I am sorry for everything. You did not deserve my anger, and neither did your human. I swear to the River Styx that if you need help, I will always come to your aid. From today until my dying breath."

With that, Asopus leaves.

THIRTY-ONE

LAMB

There is no escape from the morning sunlight bouncing off the smoldering sand beneath my curled up body. The heat scorches my arms, scattering redness across my exposed skin, and leaving blisters from the sun's wrath. Apollo and I are friends, yet in this moment, I believe him and his sun to be my enemy.

Blearily, I open my eyes, accepting today and the agony it entails. I take several seconds to acclimate to my surroundings, to blink away the fatigue and pain until Artemis's form comes into view. She sits up, knees pressing against her chest and arms. She glances between my cage and my quickly burning skin.

"I always said you were too pale," she says as a morning greeting.

"When we get out of here, I will try to change that."

She smiles, but the expression shows her mirthless defeat. We have ridden together across centuries, and I have never witnessed her submit to terrible circumstances before. Not when we fought the Echidna, or when rumblings of Kronos's return echoed through the woods. Artemis has always been a victor, but now on an unmapped island with magic restricting us, Artemis accepts her new role as a prisoner.

I refuse to let her surrender her strength.

"Have you seen Calypso or Hecate?" I ask, recalling the previous night.

She shakes her head. "While you were sleeping, I asked the nymphs about them. They said they never physically see Hecate, but Calypso visits once a week. Most of the time, she brings food."

I might get food once a week. I swallow a newfound lump in my throat, the dryness on my tongue more noticeable than ever. *And water?* I want to ask. *Will I get water, or will Calypso let me dehydrate?* I do not say it aloud, though.

With one goal in mind, I stammer. "Then you have to go now."

Her brows crinkle together with concern. "The cage is magic restricted, you know this. Has all the sun burned away your memory?"

I whisper, just in case Calypso is in hearing range. "Hecate was here last night while the rest of you slept. She didn't finish charming your cage. I do not think she will make the same mistake twice, so now is your only chance."

Realization quickly dawns on Artemis.

"What did you do?"

"You can open those bars and swim to Poseidon. You can escape and bring back help." A hopeful, delirious smile consumes my face. "But I'd be quick. There's still some magic on those bars, and they won't be easy to bend."

"But not impossible," Artemis murmurs.

I repeat. "But not impossible."

"You sneaky genius." Artemis huffs out a laugh. Just as quickly as her joy appears, it leaves. "You can't swim all the way to Poseidon's castle with me. You wouldn't survive the trip."

"I know," I say. "And Hecate charmed my cell last night. I have to stay, but you have to go."

"But," she says, never finishing the sentence aloud.

I know her question all the same.

But what if you die?

"Then, the last act I did in this world was save my goddess from harm. That is an honorable way to go."

I glance up at the sky, where the sun sits unbothered by any clouds. The sunrise is long gone now, but I stare upwards and think of Willow all the same. If I must leave this world, then I get to return to my dearest friend. That fact does not dissuade me like it once did.

"But," Artemis says again, the word more broken this time than the last. She cannot finish the sentence aloud. Once again, I understand her.

But I cannot lose you too.

"I would hurry, Lady Artemis. You have an island to escape."

A few tense seconds of silence pass, where Artemis struggles with her decision. Then she wraps two hands around the bars and begins to pull them apart. She bites down on her bottom lip, stifling the scream edging her tongue. The remaining magic singes the skin off her hands, but she persists. That defeated expression on Artemis's face is gone; instead, she holds a look of stubborn determination I have witnessed hundreds of times before.

The bars creak as they open to her command,

expanding until there is a goddess-shaped hole. Artemis slips through. I let out a sigh of relief as Artemis's body falls into the sand. Golden handprints stain the ground, but when Artemis rises to her feet, the wounds on her palms are gone. Yet, that determination persists.

"I will come back for you," Artemis says, as if she can control the other goddess's wrath when she realizes my trickery.

"And I'll be waiting." I force my voice to hold none of my doubt. If she thinks I expect death, she will not leave me. So, I smile at her, and I pretend I am infallible.

Artemis runs across the sand, and several nymphs gasp in disbelief. A few of them scream. "Take me, too!" before the others shush them.

We all rejoice when Artemis's feet land in the ocean. I say a silent goodbye as she dips her head in the water and swims towards freedom. I should be fearful of my life once Hecate returns and realizes why Artemis can escape, but I cannot muster any feeling but elation. Prideful joy courses through me, causing my heart to beat twice its typical speed.

It also makes me oblivious.

Until the first nymph screams.

I swivel my head back at the nymph, ready to tell her to be quiet. I realize too late she is not screaming with joy at the prospect of being rescued. The nymph continues to bellow and point toward the water, and I realize with utter dread that she is yelling in fear.

The ocean, water as clear as glass, erupts in green magic.

Hecate's powers create a gated border a mere fifteen feet

away from the shore. It envelopes the perimeter of the island, and Artemis is trapped in its clutches. I try to stand, to push my cage to run towards her, but I cannot. I am forced to sit and watch as magic ensnares her in a barb of electricity. She seizes under the magic's hold, violently thrashing until her body floats to the top of the water, face down.

Screams splinter the sand beneath my feet, and it takes a minute to realize the sound is coming from my lips. I agonize in a state of guilt and astonishment as Artemis continues to lie in the water, not healing as quickly as she normally does. My hands burn like a thousand scorching suns as I wrap them around the bars, trying to pull them apart so I can reach Artemis.

I can smell the flesh burning off my palms. It lands in singed ruins on the ground between my feet. But I cannot stop. I led her down the path of fruitless escape. Now, I must watch as she lays unconscious in the water contaminated with Hecate's magic. My bellows of rage, fear, and guilt continue until my throat is so raw, I cannot emit another sound.

Hecate emerges in a tornado of green mist.

She stands regally, heeled shoes digging into the sand, as she nonchalantly glances at Artemis's body. "Hm," she merely says. "It works."

"You godless witch," I snarl, but the sound is barely human as my throat scratches and bleeds from overuse and dehydration.

That wicked magic curls around my wrists, pulling them from my bars and healing the scarred ruins. The entire time, her large, doe-shaped eyes assess me. For a second, she sees me for my strength, but then she blinks and the expression is gone. Replacing it is the same indifference I associate with Hecate.

"You would have died from those wounds," Hecate says, referring to my palms. "Aren't you going to thank me?"

"I am going to be the reason you die," I snap back.

"That's a cute thought, huntress, but a futile one." Hecate strolls towards Artemis's cage, one red-painted nail trailing the top bar. "You distracted me last night to help Artemis escape. A valiant effort, but you are trying to play a game against gods when you still bleed red. Don't you realize how pointless this fight is? It will be one you never win."

"Say that to the Echidna."

"The Echidna, who Saffron had to permanently end? No matter how many times you tried, you failed." Hecate asks. As her finger trails Artemis's cage, the bars rearrange themselves back to their former position. All the work Artemis and I made disappears with a twitch of her finger. "Like I said, you made a valiant effort, but you are no hero, Lamb, with no last name. You are only a human who fights with bows and arrows against gods who fight with magic and eons' worth of strength."

Hecate snaps her fingers. In one second, Artemis's unconscious body materializes back in her cage, and the witch goddess is gone again.

THIRTY-TWO

HART SOMMERS

Upon her first arrival at Olympus Industries, Lady Demeter decided the backyard must become a garden of her creation. Similar to the office inside, each portion of the garden is dedicated to a particular god or goddess. In a labyrinthine swirl of hedges and vines, there are over one hundred quadrants dedicated to immortals of varying superiority.

Queen Hera has a section blossoming with regality. Lilies burst from every corner, various pinks and whites bloom closest to the entrance. Purple and blue tipped flowers accentuate the back wall. They embellish the silver throne nestled between two caged peacocks, squawking with glee upon their master's arrival. A purple runner starts underneath the feet of her throne and ends at the entrance of a hedge archway.

I walk through in amazement. Her section is farthest from the building, nearly two miles from inside, but the journey is worth the beautiful landscape.

Saffron's portrait took place in her office for time efficiency, but Hera wants the glamor of her earthly garden in the artwork. As I look around the elegant sophistication, I cannot say I blame the queen of the gods. Also, as my eyes trail around the expansive landscape, I wonder which garden is designated for Apollo. Will the hedges erupt with laurels, Daphne's, and hyacinths? Or, are the vines rimmed gold in honor of the sun he claims?

I brush away the thoughts because I should not have them. One of his greatest friends is Saffron, and I am on the other side of a brewing war. To save my only family, I am betraying Saffron, and therefore betraying Apollo. My mind wanders to him, miniscule details like his breakfast or his outfit today, but I do not deserve those thoughts. Not when he will soon hate me for every decision I have made to save Lowell. A man I do not love like a fiancé, but will damn myself to save.

"We will start the stencil today, then I will return in three weeks for the second round." Queen Hera decides as she sits upon her throne, pulling me from my reverie.

"Sounds good," I say, but she does not respond. She raises her button chin and waits for me to begin. With no small talk between us, I outline the queen of the gods.

Hera glimmers in opulence.

A golden diadem sits atop her head. Her dark locks are half up in a braid that interweaves with the diadem. The bottom portion of her hair flows like a dark river in effortless waves down her shoulders, resting against her exposed collarbone. Its color, one shade lighter than black, is a stark contrast to her alabaster complexion.

The lipstick she wears is severe against her pale complexion. It is a dark plum shade across her thin, yet pronounced, cupid's bow lips. My pencil focuses on this feature, the sharp angles, and pronounced dip of her upper mouth. They're puckered and tight, her face as stiff as her rigid form. The severity of her expression highlights her sharp, angular cheekbones, and cat-like eyes. However, the forced look of regality darkens her nearly pitch-black eyes. Weighs down her naturally beautiful appearance until all I see staring back at me is a defeated woman. A mirror shattered beyond repair.

My hand slides down the canvas, creating the long slope of her bare neck, when she interjects. "You are quite pretty." There is a beat of pause before she adds. "For a human, anyway."

I open my mouth to respond; the words *thank you* on the tip of my tongue.

"Except for that bump on your nose," she adds.

I close my mouth.

We return to the silence, where she sits still as a statue, with one hand on one peacock's head. I outline the top hem of her gown, which is the same shade as her lipstick. There are no sleeves, the heart-shaped bodice tight against her upper torso, then flowing around her waist. The train is long, slipping past her shoes and creating a puddle of purple around the foot of the throne.

"Your appearance reminds me of a woman from my past," Hera says. "Io was her name."

My hand freezes over the canvas, the name transforming the room from warmth to frigidness. Io is a famous former lover of Zeus's. Hera is responsible for Io turning into a cow, and her former comments about my appearance become clearer. I remind her of a woman her husband cheated on her with, and Zeus is the next god I will be drawing.

I swallow, hard. "Would you like to stop the portrait's first session early?"

"You are darker skinned than Io, but everything else is almost identical." Hera continues, ignoring my statement. "The round eyes, big lips, cute build." Hera scoffs. "It's like she was remade for him."

Him.

Zeus.

Apollo flashes in my mind. Every drawing I've created of his image morphing into moments we've shared in person. Rushed stencils of his narrow chin and dimpled smile interweave with the sound of his laugh. His eyes twinkle the brightest shade of blue. My reality distorts itself because of him.

"I promise to you, your husband is the last person I am thinking about right now."

"I am almost tempted to believe you, but when you have lived as many eons as I have with a man who destroys your trust, all words become fickle. You may be honest with me right now, but as I stare at your pretty, human face, I see thousands of women Zeus has bedded that you remind me of. Thousands of mortals I have destroyed because they destroyed another part of me."

My hand glides across the canvas, focusing back to her narrowed eyes and darkening them further. I change her shoulders, too. Instead of making them taunt and uptight the way all previous depictions of Hera show. I display the truth. Her shoulders sag beneath the weight of a million dreadful stories that begin with her marriage to Zeus and end with his betrayal. She is not a kind goddess, but she is not wholly evil, either.

I stop creating her portrait with the image of a rigid queen; instead, I draw the truth. I draw a goddess, who is chained to an anchored marriage without love because of her title as goddess of matrimony. Before, I showed the infallible side of Queen Hera, but now I draw her like the weight of her sadness has sunk her to the bottom of the ocean. She is trying not to drown. Trying to reach a hand of trust forward. A hand Zeus never grasps.

A faraway clock tower in the middle of the garden maze blares the chime of noon, and I drop my stencil. This will take weeks, if not months, to complete, but I think it's my greatest art piece yet.

"Thank you for your stories and your time," I tell her.

Her smile appears, then falls in the same millisecond. "Until our next session."

"Until then."

Queen Hera grabs the chains of both of her peacocks, and the three of them walk out of the garden.

They leave me where I stand, cleaning up my station, and I spend these moments alone in peace. Birds sway in the sky above the garden, sporadically landing throughout the expansive labyrinth. Bees swarm around their favorite flowers, plucking pollen uninterrupted. The sun is particularly bright today. I let its rays slide across my cheeks and down the slope of my neck. I carry my box of drawing supplies in one hand, the sketch of Hera in the other, and juggle my easel under my armpit.

Zeus's sketch begins an hour from now, and if I am quick, I can pick up food from the hot dog, stand down the block and be back in time. My mind is on food, what I'll get from the stand, when I turn the corner out of Hera's garden segment.

And I see him.

Apollo stands directly across from me, no further than two feet away, with a bag of food in one hand and a lopsided grin on his face. "Aphrodite told me where you'd be," he says as a form of greeting. Then, he lifts the bag of food so I can see. "I love this deli a few blocks away, so I thought I would grab us some. My portion of the garden is not too far, and it's closest to Zeus's, so you won't miss your next appointment."

I drop the easel from under my armpit.

Apollo quickly takes a step forward. "I'm sorry. I should've asked you if you needed help. Here I am just rambling, while you are dropping stuff."

He lets out a laugh, but when he takes another step forward, I jump back. His body leans halfway down, ready to grab the fallen easel, when he notices my movement away from him. Slowly, he rises to a full standing position. My easel is now in his hand.

"I'm sorry about not returning to my house until late. It's just a lot has happened, but I will make it up to you." Apollo's smile is gone. "Is everything alright?"

His voice drips with concern, but I cannot speak.

I see him, and I see the future in front of my eyes. While I have not come to terms with who I am, the powers of foresight I'm just now realizing I've always had, I know I see a vision of our love. Our destiny is to be soulmates, which creates two perfect daughters.

Yet, I still made that agreement with Styx to bring Saffron to her on the night of the ball.

Saffron may not be the same goddess my father raved

about when I was a child, but Apollo is more than I ever imagined. I always heard stories about the charming sun god, who has powers of healing and prophecies, yet has failed in every attempt at love. I never expected my heart to skip a beat in his presence. Never imagined I would stare at Apollo and want nothing more than to be in his embrace. To kiss those lopsided lips. To leave the safe cage with Lowell that I purposely imprisoned myself in.

And I ruined everything.

Maybe not right now, but I will ruin this because of the deal I made to save Lowell's life and side with Styx. There is no way to go back on a deal with Styx. It is her oath or Horkos's punishment. Both dangerous games with treacherous outcomes.

"Hart," Apollo sighs my name with waning hope, taking a step forward.

I take one back.

"I'm sorry, but I have to go."

"Why?" He asks. "Is it really because I had to leave when you came over? Because if I must make it up to you every day for the next decade, I will. I'm sorry."

Again, Apollo tries to take a step forward, but I see Khione's cruel smile.

Hear Nemesis's wicked laugh.

I cannot respond to him; instead, I run. I forget about my easel in his clutches, or the way out of the maze, and I run in the opposite direction. That wicked laugh and cruel smile infiltrate my thoughts, clouding every pleasant vision I have of Apollo and me until it's cinder beneath my feet. My box of supplies clatters with each hurried movement. The sound is so loud I do not realize another walks through the maze.

Not until I collide with them.

My butt harshly hits the ground, and I let out a groan. The sketch of Hera is intact, but it slides across the hall at the man's feet. My box of supplies, however, opens and all my pencils scatter across the grass. Nervously, before I pick up my belongings, I look over my shoulder to see if Apollo is there. He's not.

My heart stabs with regret, one I cannot take back.

"So, you're the artist I've heard so much about," says the incredibly deep voice of the god I ran into.

"Yup."

I crawl along the ground, picking up stray drawing pencils and paintbrushes. I barely pay him any mind as I shuffle everything back into my supply box, closing the latch once more. It is only when his large, veiny hand comes into view.

His forearm is incredibly tan, but all the hair is stark white. The further I ascend, the larger the muscles in his body become. One arm alone is the size of my waist, and his neck is twice the normal width. A thick, white-and-gray beard covers most of his jawline. The tip of the facial hair lands in the middle of his partially exposed chest.

Yet, his face is as tan as his forearm, and a gasp escapes my lips when I recognize Apollo's sharp, blue eyes on this older face. He is no man at all. King Zeus holds his hand out for me, to help me to my feet, and his smile has the same crookedness as Apollo's.

I take King Zeus's hand, letting him help me up. The moment our palms touch, the fog I familiarize with my visions overtakes me. Phantom hands turn my head, forcing me to see flashes of my future with Zeus. One not told through love, but through friendship.

War burns in my eyes, but through both red and gold blood, Zeus and I become amiable. We sit together, cross-legged, in front of a roaring fireplace as I lay out an archway of sketches for him. We drink the amber liquid together, our glasses clinking in muted solidarity. In one shot of our destiny, Zeus cries on my shoulder, and I wrap my arms around him. There is nothing sensual in these visions. Only two unlikely friends coming together, as a war unlike any before ravages our worlds.

The moment I stand, I rip my hand out of his. The vision dissipates. I expect him to understand the friendship awaiting us, but he still gives me that flirtatious, lopsided smirk. While Apollo sees my visions through our joined hands, Zeus does not. He stands in front of me, oblivious to our inevitable comradery. Instead, his eyes move down the expanse of my body. A predator appreciative of the novel prey he wishes to hunt.

"Quit looking at me like that."

"Like what?" He says, playing innocent.

Rolling my eyes and extending my hand for the sketch, I say. "I need to reschedule our portrait. Tomorrow maybe?"

He laughs. It is a bellowing sound which echoes across the garden and makes the clouds in the sky amusedly jostle with him. "I am a king of gods, and you wish to reschedule with me?" The laughter grows until it comes to a startling halt. "And why should I agree with this?"

"Because your wife said so," I lie.

But it is a believable lie.

Zeus's smile falls faster than one of his lightning bolts, and he passes Hera's sketch back to me. His gaze no longer fervidly observes my body. He looks around the hedges like

Hera will materialize at any second, a scold ready on her lips solely because he flirted with me.

"I will see you sometime this week, your majesty," I say curtly.

Not waiting for his response, I run out of the maze.

THIRTY-THREE

SAFFRON

The rest of the day is spent in my office. I sit across from either a human or a god and try to solve all the problems my world has quickly accumulated. Although I explicitly asked Amphitrite to ensure Poseidon is sober for our meeting, my uncle does not walk into my office.

He stumbles.

A lot.

"God-killer," he slurs with a sloppy smile. "It's been too long since you have visited me." He collapses onto the couch against the left wall of my office, arms sprawling across the furniture. "Do I need to pick a new favorite niece?"

"I'm sure Athena is available for such an esteemed job."

He groans. "That owl-faced monstrosity couldn't handle being my favorite." In a swirl of water, a goblet of white wine manifests in Poseidon's left hand. He takes a few hearty gulps, as Amphitrite rolls her eyes and takes the seat nearest me. He lets out an obnoxious burp that rattles all the glasses in my office. "Now, why did you call me in so early? It should be a sin to wake up at this unjust hour."

"It's ten in the morning."

"A true travesty," Poseidon declares. He tips back his head, chugging more alcohol.

Throughout my office, my décor is made from animal bones. A fact Poseidon frequently forgets. I motion my index finger towards Poseidon, and a second later, a bone shaped like a knife flies across the room and shatters his wine goblet.

"I told you to come sober. It's serious."

Another circlet of water emerges in Poseidon's open palm. When the water dissipates, another glass goblet filled with alcohol appears. His grin is equally mischievous and drunken. "I can do this all day, god-killer."

"I tried hiding all the booze," Amphitrite says from her seat. "But it's hard to tell a powerful god not to drink, when he can manifest his own brewery with a twirl of his finger."

"A brewery," Poseidon dreamily says. "That would be great in the basement."

"Just how big is your basement?" I ask.

He fills his mouth with alcohol, not answering.

"Why did you ask us here, Saffron?" Amphitrite asks.

I tell her about the nymphs, Artemis, and Calypso's Island. It's a relatively short story, but by the end, Poseidon is on his third goblet of wine. I shatter this glass with another piece of bone décor, earning a pout from my childish uncle.

"What do you want us to do about it?" Poseidon asks, bored.

"You are the god of the seas, and Calypso has them captive on an island."

"What's your point?"

I glare at Poseidon. "You control all bodies of water and have the power to find the smallest fish on any spot of the seas. Calypso is on an island somewhere on the seven seas."

I wait for a moment of clarity to hit my uncle, but the moment never comes. He tilts his head to the side, twirling his beard with one hand as the other nurses a new goblet. "I fail to see your point," he says.

Amphitrite groans.

I destroy another one of his drinks.

The wine covers his torso, and he pouts. "It's sticky."

"Poseidon, can you please focus?" I ask with unbridled annoyance.

"I am listening," he insists, but he can barely keep his eyes open. "You saw a dolphin on Calypso's Island that you like, but I am not sure how that involves me."

Both Amphitrite and I share a glance.

"Darling," Amphitrite says, her voice mirroring a mother with a temperamental child. "Where did dolphins come into the story?"

His eyes lower shut as he grows more comfortable on my couch. A small smile lines his lips. "I like the dolphin noises you make when we are having-"

"Stop talking," I snap.

"Okay," he responds.

In seconds, his snores fill my office.

Amphitrite stands up from her chair. "I'll pick him up after his nap, but until then I will return to my palace and send our children searching the waters for Calypso's Island."

"Thank you," I respond.

She shakes her head, red hair bouncing off her shoulders with the movement. "Do not thank me because I fear we will find the same thing we have every time my children, husband, and I have searched for Calypso's Island. Absolutely nothing."

Amphitrite leaves in a swirl of water, abandoning her man-child, who hugs his arm like a pillow.

Athena walks into my office an hour later, and before she says anything to me, she glares at Poseidon on my couch. "Why is this imbecile here?"

"I tried to ask him for help to find Calypso's Island, but he got too drunk and passed out."

Athena dismisses Poseidon's slumbering body, striding towards the seat directly across my desk instead. Yet, she does not sit. She looms over the chair, hands curling into the top groove. Sharp nails sink into the fabric.

"Odysseus was not much help." She states the words with stoic calmness. "He confessed too many eons have passed since he entered Calypso's Island, and his memory fails him." Athena scoffs. "I favored this hero, and he cannot remember a simple geographical location. It is humiliating."

"Poor you," I dryly add.

She knows I am being sarcastic, a skill that took Hattie many years to teach, but Athena does not care. "Poor me indeed," Athena retorts with the same dry, unamused tone. "Is there anything else you need, little sister?"

To scream, is the immediate thought in my head.

"No, I'm fine. Thank you." My lie comes too easily, and Athena's eyes narrow.

"Lying is not your forte," she responds.

Yet, she does not pry.

Athena and I are complete opposites, but there is a string always tethering our thoughts together. She sees the sorrow beneath the façade, and she knows I do not want to speak about the thoughts burning through my mind. Athena simply announces her knowledge that I am lying, and she leaves without another word.

In the hour between Athena and the detective, I pull out Hart's folded drawing once more. A future never told is spun on this canvas. Epiales and I together, creating havoc just as Kronos desired. Is this image the possibilities of an alternate reality? Is this what would have happened if I chose Kronos and the titans instead of Zeus and the Olympians?

I run a finger across Epiales's curly, black mane before folding the image in half again, hiding it in my pocket.

Three knocks rap on my door.

"May I come inside?" asks a curt voice.

I allow it, and in one long stride, the human detective enters my office. He is a pale, stout man with a dark, patchy beard, and eyes that are in a perpetual squint. The expression is continual annoyance or poor visibility. Throughout the years we have worked together, I have failed to discover which reason is to blame.

"Goddess." His voice always comes out as a hoarse growl; sometimes, I wonder if he is part bear. "I must ask you-"

Interrupting, I say. "I have been informed there was another murder last night." He opens his mouth, but before he can respond, I continue. "And in the efforts of trying to frame me, the murderer has led me straight to their identity."

His jaw lowers in disbelief, but he does not move closer to me. Despite news that can end the tyranny of murders, this detective does not trust me enough to move to one of the seats in my office. He remains by the door.

"What?" He asks, unable to hide his shock.

I lean back in my seat, arms crossed over my chest. I give the notion that I am relaxed, but in actuality, excitement hums through my veins. It is a foreign, yet pleasant feeling. Today, one problem vanishes, a boulder removed from the weight I carry on my shoulders.

"I am going to let you in on a secret about my abilities, something only a few gods are aware of. I can see the life bones have lived."

The skin between his bushy eyebrows crinkle together. "What does that mean?" He asks.

"When I hold a bone, I can see its lifespan. Typically, by touching a bone, I see one person and their existence, but this murderer pulled bones out of the victim's body. They touched those bones, therefore becoming interwoven into the bones' stories."

Understanding lights his sullen skin. "You can see who has been killing these women and children, all because of the bones."

I nod my head. "As long as you bring me a bone from the crime scene. Yes, I can."

Savior.

The moniker has trailed behind me for almost a century. I never thought myself deserving of the title, and that feeling of inadequacy has worsened in recent years. Yet, today, there's a stream of light. I can save future families from a brutal loss. I can be a glimpse of the savior the humans call me.

The realization almost brings a smile to my lips. The bubbling sense of happiness reaches my heart. My lip twitches, the corners twisting upwards, but all too quickly, the light vanishes. Darkness reacquaints itself. The jar remains fallen, its contents emptied on the floor.

"How do I know I can trust your word?" The detective asks.

For a blinding moment, rage seizes me. Red overtakes my vision, mingled with disbelief. I saved the world, died to ensure every human could become free. Now, when all who I saved are dead and only their ancestors thrive, the human side of me is forgotten. An obviously staged murder scene absolves me of my title of hero. I am only a god to humans now, capable of killing simply because I can. Fury seeps through me, churning like poison.

I take a long breath, forcing away the rage. It is difficult to push down the emotions bursting at the seams, but I manage. I ignore all my feelings about his question until, slowly, I can speak.

"Was it your parents or grandparents who were slaves in the old days?" I ask.

He tenses but answers. "My grandparents. They were ten and twelve when slavery was abolished."

"Hm."

I could tell him that his grandparents could not have married if not for me. They could not have had children together without a death sentence. He would not have been born if not for me, but I do not. My question reminds him of who I am with no further elaboration. I uncross my hands and place them both on top of my desk. He stays ramrod straight beside the door, but I near him from my position at my desk.

"There is nothing I can say that will sway your opinion of me. Trust is not given through convincing words and poetic speeches. This trust you want to have can only be earned. My word is all I have in this world, but it is your choice whether you choose to trust it. Bring a bone, don't bring a bone, that is your decision. One I cannot force, regardless of my opinion on the matter, but I will be at my office until seven tonight. You have until then to choose if you trust me to save humans' lives, or if you think I am no better than frivolous gods drinking nectar on Mt. Olympus."

He opens his mouth, then closes it, and opens once more.

Yet, there are no words.

My sigh is deafening. "You may go now."

He slams the door, and I grab the folded piece of paper from my pocket, opening it once more.

THIRTY-FOUR

HERMES

Each morning, Styx waits for me at the edge of her water with her elbows perched on the riverbank. Her inexplicably dark eyes always brim with delight. I refuse to speak to her, but that damned smirk on her face tells me I am falling right into her trap. She never says the words aloud, but I can hear them all the same in my head. All the sacrifices I make, and the heartache I cause my wife, aids the wicked immortal in her nefarious plans.

I just don't know how.

Slowly, she spirals me into madness without ever opening her mouth.

"Where is Hecate?" I ask Hades, storming into his throne room early afternoon.

He sits on his throne, surrounded by the three appointed judges of the dead. Former King Minos of Crete nods at me, but I ignore him. My hands twitch, and every time I blink, I see Styx behind my eyes. When I am not tormented by her face, my mind brings me back to that cage Kronos kept me in all those years ago. I hear Typhon's laugh as he tortures me day after day. Styx hasn't laid a hand on me, hasn't uttered a word in days, but she awakens all the terrible memories of the last war.

"I do not know," Hades answers.

He doesn't raise his voice or clip his words with anger, but still I flinch.

"Are you alright, Lord Hermes?" Another judge, Rhadamanthus, asks.

"Fine," I snap. Then I ask Hades. "Where are Thanatos and Hypnos, then?"

Hades doesn't immediately reply. Instead, he observes me, noting the wrinkled clothes I wear from the night before. He sees the way my hands shake. Notices how my eyes burn because I refuse to blink and see the past and future. Hades leans forward in his throne, elbows resting on his knees, and his face slackens with sympathy.

In the distant background, Kronos's three ticking watches echo in my ears. They accompany the river's currents and Typhon's booming laugh.

"Why don't you come sit down? I'll get you some nectar and ambrosia." Hades moves to stand, but I shake my head too fast.

"No, I do not need food. I need to find Hypnos and Thanatos."

"Why?" Hades asks, his voice still holding traces of sympathy. "If this is about Saffron and last night-"

For a blinding moment, the sounds polluting my thoughts dissipate. Instead of Typhon, Kronos, and Styx tormenting my mind, I close my eyes and I see my wife. Her brilliant smile, those kissable dimples, and her delicate hands. Then, just like everything else in my life, the vision shifts. She is not here in my mind, jubilant and in love with me. No, she stares at me with tears streaming down her face as I lie to her about an affair with Hecate.

"I will not see my wife," I interrupt him before he can finish the sentence. My eyes remain closed, cursing myself with the sight of Saffron as her face wrinkles with betrayal and heartache. "Where are they, Hades?"

"Can gods go mad?"

The question is the smallest whisper, barely a sound at all, but I hear him. The third judge of the Underworld, Aeacus, has his mouth near Minos's ear. He meant for only Minos to hear his question, but Hades stiffens. Rhadamanthus scoots back his chair, distancing himself from the others.

I rush towards Aeacus. Kronos's ticking watches are louder, and every time I blink, Styx's cold eyes are waiting for me. They drive me towards Aeacus, and while I feel my fists moving, the skin splitting and healing in the same breath, I do not know what I am doing. Not fully.

"Enough!"

A powerful force propels me away from Aeacus, and my back slams into the wall closest to the throne room's exit. I'm quick on my feet, glaring at Hades, who stands in between the judges and me. He does not hold weapons because he does not need to. Hades will always be stronger than me. In this rare moment, I am grateful that I am not the more powerful immortal.

Aeacus's face is unrecognizable. Mere mush. He isn't moving, and his body is too limp. A pool of red blood circles around Aeacus and the two other judges.

"It is a good thing he is already dead, but I doubt he thought he would die twice. Much less in the safety of my home." Hades's voice is the definition of power. It radiates off him, each word projecting like a command. "Hermes," he says. "When was the last time you slept?"

"Gods do not need to sleep."

"All minds need rest," Hades insists. "When was the last time?"

I do not answer immediately, and Hades seems to understand. He looks back at his judges, where Minos and Rhadamanthus huddle around Aeacus's still dead body.

"He will wake up in the next few hours. In the meantime, you both may go."

Both men shuffle out of the room. They walk around me, worrying about their own life if they get too close. I cannot say I blame them. I stay perfectly still as they exit the throne room, but once the door closes, my legs lose their virility. My body collapses to the floor as the noises in my head grow too loud.

War drums near, unless I can stop Saffron from coming down to the Underworld. Kronos conceited face blurs with Styx's each time I blink, both of them thirsting for my agony like nectar. Each morning, when I see Styx, I feel like all my efforts are for naught. That I cannot stop the war from taking the last of my sanity.

A warm hand lands on mine. I flinch from the touch, but it returns tighter this time. Two hands, one below and one above, capture me. Holding my trembling hands until they are still. My arms continue to twitch, and the laughter of the past still pierces my ears, but the pressure helps.

"Dearest friend," Hades says. "When was the last time you stopped moving?"

"December thirtieth." The words come out cracked and depleted, but once the dam breaks, all my truths spill out. "That was the last night before I heard Styx's prophecy from the oracle emerging from the River Lethe. Since then, everything in my head has been too loud. I thought I overcame my captivity on Mt. Olympus when Kronos kidnapped me. I thought I was strong enough to forget the past. But when I heard that prophecy and the imminent war it brings, all those terrible memories returned."

Hades says nothing, does not provide comfort with words, but he squeezes my hands tighter. We sit on his throne room floor as I hear Typhon, Kronos, Styx, Circe, and all the villains of past and present tormenting me within my mind. Aeacus's words are there now, too, asking a question which now plagues me.

Can gods go mad?

"I used to try to sleep. When I would go home, I would try, but the nightmares waited. Sometimes, I think Epiales lives in my head, promising to brandish me in his powers of anguish when I try to sleep. It is my punishment for loving Saffron, for winning her when he did not."

"You are not cursed, Hermes."

"Then why am I plagued with the past? It is long gone. Eight decades have passed, but I still fear dreaming of that cage. Flinch when I hear a clock. Dread the river's every movement because Styx wants another war when I scarcely survived the last one."

The throne room creaks open, and we both whip our heads around to see the intruder. Persephone stands in the doorway in a long, flowing lilac dress. Confusion is written on her brow. Her arrival makes me jump. I pull my hand out of Hades's and stand up, dusting off the invisible debris from my pants.

"Where are Hypnos and Thanatos?" I ask Hades, who still sits on the ground, staring up at me.

"They are in-"

"Why?" Hades asks, interrupting Persephone.

"The Nosoi," I answer. "I am going to kill them all, and I want them as reinforcement."

"You know they will only return the next day. It is a daily fight with no winning outcome, but." Hades stands up to his feet. "I will join you on your hunt in South America for the Nosoi," he offers. "It is an impossible task, but I will join you, and I will bring along Thanatos, Hypnos, and members of the undead army."

There is a clause to his terms.

"But?" I ask.

"But you need to bathe and rest. Lay down and sleep, and when you wake, we will go."

"I have duties. Zeus wants me to-"

He interrupts me. "Sleep, Hermes, then we will stop the Nosoi."

It isn't a request, and I bow my head. I lie to him with silence acquiescence, then hurry out of the throne room before he can send Hypnos to put me to sleep. I move through the quiet, black halls paved with gold-trimmed rugs and adorned with black-framed portraits. Saffron's face is regal in most of the paintings, sitting nestled in between Hades and Persephone. The rarest diamond, smiling at the artist as he matches her likeness to perfection.

The best painting of her amongst the walls is nearest to my room in the Underworld. Cursing me with its proximity. I stare at a floor length portrait of her. It was made when she was human, living here as the Underworld's princess.

Her dark hair cascades down her shoulders in curly ringlets. A black tiara sits on her head. She will forever be the most glorious sight I will ever behold, and I chose to lose her to stop a war from ensuing.

"I'm sorry," I whisper to the smiling portrait of my wife. "One day, I hope you will understand."

I slip through my room, kicking off my winged sandals and sliding into bed. My back is too stiff on the mattress, while my eyes focus on the white paneled ceiling and the glimmering chandelier in the middle. Fatigue claims me, but my eyes never close.

The whole day, I stay in this bed, never sleeping but always suffering endless nightmares.

THIRTY-FIVE

SAFFRON

Two hours later, the detective brings me the bone.

An hour after that, Gareth French stews in the chair directly across from my desk, the bone sitting in between us. Argus stands at the door, arms crossed over his chest. Every one of his eyes focuses on Gareth. The tension in this room is thicker than fog, leaving the atmosphere toxic and nearly unbreathable.

"Thank you for meeting with me, Gareth."

"Didn't have a choice, goddess," is his gruff response.

Gareth French is exceptionally tall, around six and a half feet, with prominent muscles indicative of a labor-intensive job. He wears his work uniform, the construction company's logo on the left pocket of his shirt. He has a short, well-trimmed beard that gives off the appearance that he is older than twenty-five. However, his dark brown complexion is still round with youthfulness.

Yet, it is his eyes that garner my attention the most.

He is ordinarily mundane, except for those eyes. They

burn an amber shade, like a ball of fire lives inside of him. Ready to incinerate everybody in his proximity. They stew with a hunger that surpasses food or sexual desire. He starves for vengeance, a rare and deadly type I have only seen twice before now.

One was China, the human slave in Hermes's old mansion, who was teaching me how to read. When she told the story about how she lost her soulmate, Falcon, and their unborn child, her eyes burned with the same brewing hatred for the world. A starving desire to destroy all the people she blamed for their deaths, even if their demise meant hers as well.

The second person was Epiales. When he spoke about Zeus, and the punishment he suffered in order to save his nephew, Morpheus. Epiales transformed that day. His gorgeous face twisted into a grotesque, gnawing need for revenge. He changed because of his hatred against the godly king, who condemned him to be forgotten, and the other gods who did nothing to stop him.

This is a hunger for death. Vengeful people will die to achieve this feat. His hatred for me extends past himself, making a thread between him and I that cannot be severed. I can proclaim my innocence and present him the real murderer, but that thread will hold true. It is a hatred that cannot be sedated because months have left him festering, worsening into a creation beyond simple hatred.

For as long as he lives, he will want my demise. Even at the cost of his own life. It is a dangerous journey he is making, wishing to be my enemy. I have no ill will for Gareth French, will never fear a human when I am a goddess, but I know he will try to kill me and fail. I only hope that my words will save his sanity because I will not suffer because of his revenge. It is a poison only he will drink.

"I will not waste our time with small talk," I say. "You believe I killed your family, and I brought you here because I want to prove to you I did not."

Gareth reaches a hand into his pocket and pulls something out. Argus takes a defensive step forward, but I hold my hand in the air, stopping him. Gareth French cannot hurt me, he doesn't have the capability, so I watch his next actions. Wait to see if his mind is too far damaged with months of grief and misdirected blame.

He slams a photograph on my table. My desk shakes under the weight. Without touching the picture, I glance down.

Both the mother and her toddler daughter have dark brown skin and grins that consume their faces. It is an identical smile, with dimples on both cheeks, that has a contagious effect. Their daughter appears no more than three years old. Her little arms wrap around her mom's neck, squeezing as they laugh at whoever holds the camera. Happiness radiates off the photo, but I know what awaits these two females. Their terrible fate is written on the enraged grief on Gareth French's face.

"On New Year's Day, I celebrated another happy year with my wife and daughter. I kissed my little one on the forehead as I put her to bed, and I held my wife close as I fell asleep. I never knew it would be the last night I would tell them I loved them. Even when my mind went to the darkest places, I never imagined I would walk into my home, the day after the new year, and find them mutilated."

He says the last word like a knife pierces his stomach.

It twists as he continues to speak. "You were once the goddess I prayed to the most. The one I revered. But now, I know the truth. You were supposed to be our savior, but you are worse than all the rest. I prayed to you on the night of the new year, and the next day, I find my family dead with your name sprawled in their blood. I thought you were my savior, but you are just a villain playing the role of a good guy in front of flashing cameras."

Beside the photograph is the latest victim's bone, cleansed of blood and waiting patiently to prove my innocence. I reach forward, grabbing the bone, but my movement is too fast because Gareth flinches. I pause because he thinks I am going to kill him. He is so sure I am his family's murderer that he thinks I must kill him to cover my tracks.

Slowly, I drag the bone towards me. "What are your wife's and daughter's names?"

"Why?" He growls.

"I need to tell Hades and Persephone names if I want somebody moved to Elysium Fields, and I would like to put your wife and daughter in the field of heroes. I want them to have a fragment of the photograph's happiness in the afterlife, but I need their names in order to do this."

It hurts to say my parents' names because of Hermes. His comment about our relationship is too raw of a wound, but I push back my emotions. Bury them deep in a casket at the bottom of my heart. Right now, I must focus on Gareth French and the murders of countless women and children. I cannot afford to be sad.

He hesitates for the longest time, then answers. "Griselda and Trinity French."

My eyes drift to Argus. "Will you send a message to my parents with the request, please?"

"I do not want to leave you alone with him," Argus answers.

I almost smile.

Almost.

"Your chivalry holds no bars, dear friend, but I think I will be okay."

Argus often forgets I am stronger than him because his protectiveness of me is so potent. He hesitates, many eyes focused on Gareth, but eventually he nods his head and leaves the room. The door slowly, and cautiously, closes behind him.

"Why did you kill them?" Gareth asks the moment we are alone.

His voice holds both rage and confusion, but not doubt. He still believes I am his family's killer, the worst of my kind. I ignore how much this hurts.

"I have not killed a human in many, many years. It is your choice to believe my words or not, but if you will place your hand on this bone, I can show you my innocence. It is the newest victim's bone," I'm quick to say. "I can project what I see from the bone's life to you, so you can see who is really to blame."

"How can I believe you?" he asks. "You have the power to shift my image, to see what you want me to see."

"I am not a goddess of spells and magic. Even my powers have limitations. I can only show you what the bones wish to reveal, but it is your choice if you want to see the truth or not."

He reaches out a hand, but hovers over the bone. He doesn't touch it, not immediately. Instead, he asks. "What if this changes nothing?"

"I hope that won't be the case," I admit.

"But if it is?"

"There's only one way to find out."

Gareth's hand is twice the size of mine, engulfing the bone and me, but soon the image of his hand is gone and replaced with the past. We are in a small, dimly lit apartment. The living room light flickers every few seconds. Its bulb nearly expired, but the murder scene is still visible.

The young one, no older than four, already lays dead and bloodied on the floor. His mother scrambles on the ground, her sobs indistinguishable and terror-stricken. She looks between her baby, then back at the murderer, whose face both Gareth and I can clearly see.

It is Nemesis, the personification of resentment.

She strides towards the mother, a curved knife drenched in red blood. The smile on her face is cruel, devoid of any morality. She doesn't immediately kill the mother; instead, she plays with her prey. Slashes her arms and legs, pulling out bones as the mother screams for help. Begs for mercy that will never find her.

Finally, her throat is slit, her body crumbling beside her child's.

Gareth's hand wretches free, and I drop the bone. We are back in my office, but it is not the same. The screams of the mother still reverberate in our ears, no matter how silent this room is.

He clears his throat. "Who was that?"

"Nemesis," my voice is shaky. "The goddess Nemesis is the murderer."

Not me, is the unspoken line.

"At the end of the week, I would like to invite you to a ball in honor of my marriage to Hermes."

I take a deep breath. The words I utter are a mockery of

the love Hermes and I used to share. As I say the words, I see him standing beside Hecate, both tall and regal immortals. Gareth doesn't notice my hands clenching and unclenching. He is too focused on the images he saw to pay attention to the whirlwind of agony wrecking my thoughts.

"Why?" he asks.

"Because Nemesis will be there." His eyes jolt up to mine. "I think it is only fair that someone who lost loved ones because of her is there to help me execute her for her crimes."

I pull an invitation out of the top drawer of my desk, sliding it towards him. He takes it, and without another word, hurries out of my office. The door slams shut, and I shakily stand. I wait a few minutes, so I do not see Gareth again, but as the sun sets, I leave my office. Argus meets me on the ground floor, keys already in his hand.

"Am I returning you to your home?" Argus asks.

I shake my head. "No, we have one more place to go."

He opens the door for me as we exit Olympus Industries. "Where to?"

"Hart's apartment."

THIRTY-SIX

HART SOMMERS

Dozily, I stumble into my apartment. My feet trudge through the familiarity without truly processing my movements. I open the freezer, grabbing an ice tray to make myself a glass of water when a groan, one derived from pain, creaks like a faulty floorboard.

I still, one ice cube in my hand, hovering over the empty cup. My eyes dance to the clock above the kitchen sink, seeing it is three in the afternoon. Lowell should not be home for another two hours. I drop the ice cube in my cup, along with two others. As I fill my cup with sink water, the groan returns.

Turning my head, I look back at my living room adjacent to the kitchen. "Who is there?" I ask.

I wait for a figure to emerge from the emptiness, for invisibility to wane away and reveal an immortal face. The moment never comes. The groans cease, but my unnerved state doesn't wane. I lean against the kitchen sink, taking slow sips of my water as I look around my small apartment. From where I stand, I can see the entire living room and the short hallway where the bathroom, my bedroom, and Lowell's bedroom are located.

Another groan, the weakest one yet, emits from the hallway. It is more of a croak, a dying proclamation from a voice that is losing its ability to function. I reach forward, trading my glass of water for a spatula. I wrap both hands around my weapon, taking hesitant steps towards the hallway.

"Lowell?" I ask, hoping to the gods it is him and not a creature waiting to drag me down to the Underworld.

Each step I take is measured, a calculated move laced with caution. My spatula is raised high in the air, ready to strike if anything jumps towards me with malicious intent. I peek inside the room closest to me first, which is mine. Cautiously, I use my elbow to open the door further. Already, a scream erupts from my lips as I jump into the room.

I spin around, spatula swinging through the air without aim or true intent. Yet, nothing is there. My room is exactly how I left it, with an unmade bed and a side table spilling with half-finished drawings. I glance at the ground beneath my bed, wandering if I should peek underneath to make sure a monster doesn't wait for me to fall asleep tonight.

"You are going mad," I mutter to myself. "There are no such things as boogie monsters."

Still, just to be safe, I look under my bed. My hands tremble the entire time, but sure enough, there is nothing there. No boogie monster with nine-inch claws waits for me, licking lips with a hunger for human flesh.

I leave my room, venturing to the bathroom next. This

time, I kick the door open, screaming as I rush towards the shower curtain, rip open the material, and throw my spatula. The moment my spatula leaves my hands, I process the surrounding scene, and I immediately regret my decision.

Lowell lays naked in the shower, body trembling. He doesn't have the strength to block my assault. The spatula bounces off his forehead, and he lets out the tiniest, most devastated whimper.

"Holy gods," I gasp.

The spatula lays in the tub alongside him, and a piece of his skin falls with it. Clumps of flesh fill the tub, and instead of water, little streams of crimson blood trail into the drain. His own body is betraying him. He tries to stop the carnage by wrapping his hands around his biceps and holding pieces together. His attempts are temporary solutions; I know once he removes his hand, the skin will fall around him.

His eyes are bloodshot and swollen with tears. He cannot speak. He just stares at me, begging me for help. I collapse onto my knees outside the tub, and I reach for him. Before I can touch him, he flinches. Fear in the pain contact can cause. I freeze. His mouth trembles, but he can no longer let out a sound.

I just saw him last night, scared but unscathed, and now he is in ruination.

"What is happening to you?" I ask, unable to stop the disgust in my voice.

His once beautiful face, unscathed by any of the world's strife, stares up at me with grotesque desperation. His nose is nothing but muscle, cartilage, bone, and blood now; the skin is completely bare. His forehead is slowly peeling in stripes, and his lips are black like soot.

He removes one hand from his arm, and the skin flutters down into the tub like a snowflake in winter. Bile rises in my throat, and nausea churns my stomach. He lifts his index finger, shaking as he points at an item behind me. Holding his finger exerts too much energy, and it limply falls back into the tub. More skin flutters off.

"What is it?" I ask as I spin my head around.

A note is carved into the back of the bathroom door.

And it is addressed to me.

Oracle, it says. The word is harshly clawed into the wood by what I think is a knife. **The Nosoi have been plaguing South America for months; now, it is their turn to plague him. On Friday, he will breathe his last breath unless the Savior is brought in front of the River. Remember who you are loyal to.**

Then, at the very bottom, two words are written with perfect precision.

Queen Styx.

"H."

Skin around Lowell's chin slips as he speaks. The nickname he's called me since we were children now sounds achingly morose. This one letter causes him to wince in pain, and I walk back to him. Falling on the ground beside the tub, I reach forward. I do not touch him, but I let my hand trail an inch away from his face. Two tears fall down his cheeks. Even this makes him groan with discomfort.

"I'm here," I whisper.

"I," he croaks.

A fit of coughs wreck through him.

"Don't try to talk," I tell him.

He shakes his head. "I am." Another round of coughs

shakes his body. Skin drops off him in steady clumps. "Sorry," he finishes.

I know what he is apologizing for, and it has nothing to do with his ailment. We were once best friends, and before that, we romantically loved each other. Yet, when those affectionate feelings disappeared, neither of us admitted the words aloud. Instead, he cheated, and I became a shell of who I once was.

He is saying he is sorry for no longer loving me the way he used to. Lowell apologizes for cheating on me. For continuing our charade of a put-together relationship. Tears continue to stream down his cheeks because he blames himself for our predicament. Maybe, if he wasn't cheating, he wouldn't have begun affairs with nefarious-minded goddesses who had ulterior motives.

"I'm sorry, too."

I am sorry I didn't admit the truth before today, that Lowell is a friend instead of a significant other. Maybe if I didn't fear my honesty, Lowell and I would've broken up. He wouldn't have cheated, which leads him to two manipulative goddesses, who use him to get to me. Perhaps, if I confronted him for his adulterous ways, this fate could have been avoided.

But maybe life was always meant to take this dreadful turn. One, where I must become a traitor, and Styx must meet Saffron at the blackened river.

I wrap my hands around the rim of the tub, the closest I can get to touching him, and I ask. "Do you remember the night you proposed?"

He groans as he nods his head.

"That's when I knew. Think of how many years we could have been happy if I had just said no on that bridge."

Lowell places his hand on the rim of the tub, too. It is a few inches away from him and mottled in scars and blood. But this gesture is his way of saying, *me too*.

"You are the greatest friend, though."

His pinky reaches out for me, the tip a breath away from mine, and he says, *you too*.

THIRTY-SEVEN

SAFFRON

Argus leads me to Hart's door. It is the only apartment with a doormat in the front, but it does nothing to dissuade the grungy truth of this place. The door mat does not hide the door's chipped paint or mask the dreadful, moldy smell. It is as useless as a strip of duct tape on a crumbling building. Completely useless.

I knock three times on the door. We wait a minute, but there is still no response. Again, I knock three times. Once again, there is no answer.

"Do you hear that?" he asks.

At the same moment, a whimper escapes from underneath the door and hits my ears.

It is a sound of devastation, with a feminine lilt that must be Hart. I lift my knee up. With one swift kick, the door falls to the ground. We bulldoze through the tiny apartment. Its size is the equivalent of my kitchen. We follow the whimpers to a white, slightly ajar door. I do not know what I expect to find. Argus and I enter a bathroom too small for four occupants.

In front of me is the last sight I expected.

A tall, lanky man lays indisposed in a bathtub, but there is no water covering his body. I see every mutilated part of him. His bloodied mouth. Skin covering the tub's floor, while his body is rebelling against him. Without the skin on top, his muscle tendon peeks through the excessive blood. I witness the devastating effects of the Nosoi birds in a country free of the diseased creatures.

"I can explain," Hart says. Her words are rushed, and her fear of me is suffocatingly clear.

"Go get Apollo, Paean, or Asclepius," I say to Argus without turning to face him.

"Not Apollo," Hart says. At the mention of her fated soulmate, she sounds more terrified than before. My eyes wander to where her hand is, just an inch away from the man in the tub.

I clench my jaw. "See if Asclepius or Paean can be pulled from the infirmaries in South America."

Argus leaves without a word, and as he retreats, we are silent. Hart's frightened eyes widen. I can hear the heavy thumps of her heart wildly beating and smell the burning flesh slipping from the male human's body. I have a thousand questions. They begin with the Nosoi-infected man. Continues to her involvement with Apollo, and they end with the drawing she made of Epiales that still sits in my pocket.

But I wait until the door closes behind Argus.

The moment the door clicks shut, the sound echoing in this tiny space; I speak. "Explain. Now."

THIRTY-EIGHT

HART SOMMERS

There is a second of hesitation, where I ponder my decisions and whether I should tell Saffron the truth. As if Styx is in the room, standing beside her scratchy name on my door, I feel her stare as she bends me to her will. The contract dangles in my periphery, reminding me I made a deal to betray Saffron.

To betray Apollo.

It is the thought of him that stops my hesitation. I made a deal to give Saffron to Styx, but I never swore to deceive Apollo. I never agreed to hide the deal I made with Styx from Saffron, only that I would bring her to the Underworld the night of the ball. While I made the wrong decision agreeing to help Styx, I can tell Saffron why I made these dire choices. I can atone to Apollo without losing him completely.

In a tornado of white mist, Saffron lays wet rags on Lowell's breaking body. He winces each time the damp fabric touches his skin, but then he sighs like a fragment of his pain ebbs away. It is then, as she heals my dearest friend, that I begin my story.

I tell her everything while she assists Lowell, delicately placing rags on every part of his body. She gives him ginger care, as if he is not a stranger to her, but an extension of herself. I saw her interaction with the river god in her office and quickly condemned her as a monster, but seeing her now with Lowell, I realize the gravity of my mistakes.

I begin my story with the drawings of Apollo I've been making for years, but I glaze over Lowell's affairs. He won't look at me as I tell her about the two women I knew he was cheating on me with, who I later found out were Khione and Nemesis. Saffron glances between us, catching onto the emotions behind my explanation.

Understanding darkens her features. "You were falling in love with a man you thought was fictional. Meanwhile, your fiancé was in bed with goddesses, yet neither of you suspected the unordinary situation you were in?"

Lowell winces as he shakes his head.

"I just thought I was over imaginative," I say.

"Continue, please."

I obey. I tell her everything about my phone call with Adonis, my car ride with Argus, and meeting Apollo for the first time in Olympus Industries' lobby. My voice wavers as I admit the future I saw when I touched his hand, but when I look at Lowell, he has a tiny smile on his lips. There is no shred of jealousy on his face; instead, that smile shows his happiness for me.

I cannot smile back. "But I ruined it with him because when I came home, Khione and Nemesis made me choose Lowell's life or-"

I pause, meeting Saffron's eyes.

"Or?" she asks.

"Yours."

It is not me who responds, but Lowell croaks out the one word. He flinches in pain, and red blood bubbles on the white towel around his throat. Saffron waves her hand and another rag materializes on top of the bloodied one.

"You are too weak to talk right now," Saffron says softly, almost lovingly, to Lowell. Then her eyes wander back to me. "Please explain."

I tell her every detail about our conversation, then all my interactions since. Finally, I point to the door, where Styx's warning is carved into the wood. Throughout the entire explanation, Saffron intently listens. She nods her head throughout, but she never interjects. She waits until I am finished with my story.

Then she stands and walks to the door with the message. Her arms are crossed as she peruses it once, twice, and then at least a dozen more times. I follow her until we are shoulder-to-shoulder, standing in the shadows of Styx's cruel words.

"So, Styx finally wants to call in her favor." Then, ever so quietly, she says. "That's why I haven't been allowed in the Underworld."

A tear slides down her cheek, but she wipes it away as quickly as it comes.

"What favor?" I ask.

Staring at the door the whole time, Saffron says. "When I was a human, on the day Kronos started the third war, I was in the Underworld. I was surrounded by enemies and my best friend, Hattie." Her voice cracks at the last few words. Another tear slips, and she wipes it away as quickly as the last one. "My best friend was in danger. It was stupid and rash, but I tackled one enemy and threw us both into the River Styx. I didn't know how to swim, and I knew how bad Styx was, but I only thought about Hattie and how badly she needed my help."

At her friend's name, Hattie, another tear falls.

She doesn't wipe this one away.

My father told me every story he had ever learned about Saffron. All her monumental fights, courageous sacrifices, and romances. Yet, Saffron tells me about a tale from when she was a human desperate to save a friend. It is a story I have never heard before. It is one of the missing puzzle pieces to the mystery surrounding Saffron, Styx, and this looming war.

"I would have died in that river if Styx didn't save me, but she is not benevolent, and her help had a price. I had to agree to one favor, which I could not ask questions about or deny. Now, it looks like she has come to collect what she won all those years ago." She runs her tongue along her mouth, jaw ticked as a third, fourth, and fifth tear slide down her cheeks. "And I think Hermes knew this."

"Hermes?" I ask, puzzled.

What does her husband have to do with any of this?

She turns to me suddenly, but instead of answering my question, she says. "I understand why you made the deal because, just like me, you wanted to save your friend. I know how friends hold your heart. You made the best decision you could for Lowell, but it is time to let me take over."

Lowell sleeps in the tub, face covered in rags but tense with pain. Even in his slumber, he cannot avoid the agony of the Nosoi disease.

"Take over how?" I ask.

"The night of the ball, I will go to the Underworld by

myself. I will make sure Styx knows you are the reason I am there, and it will absolve you of your oath, but you are forbidden from joining me."

"Forbidden, why?"

"I forgot how often humans ask questions," she says. "You will go to the ball with Apollo, and you will distract him as best as you can while I leave and go to the Underworld. Lowell's life is my obligation now, not yours."

Apollo doesn't need to be distracted. He has been oblivious to all of this, which means she is lying to me. Giving me a job with zero importance or purpose so I will stop my line of questioning. Yet, I persist.

"Why are you lying to me? Why shouldn't I go to the Underworld with you? This is my fault."

She shakes her head. "No, it isn't your fault. It is mine because almost ninety years ago, I made a deal with a goddess I knew better than to trust, and I foolishly believed I never had to atone for that mistake. Styx will come for me, to call in that favor, and if I must go to her, I would like to save a life or two along the way."

A life or two.

Saffron pulls a folded piece of paper from her jacket pocket, extending it towards me. I know what is in her hand, but I take the drawn paper. I open it, and just as I suspected, it is the drawing I created of her and the mysterious man around a ringlet of death. The sight of her hands raised, decorated in bloodied bones, sends a shiver down my spine.

"Do you know who the god in the drawing is with me?" she asks.

I take in his dark, curly locks and the tattoos covering her pale flesh, and I do not have an answer. He is a lean immortal, with muscles subtly hidden beneath his clothing, but strength radiates off him. He bears no weapon, but at six feet tall with the power of an ancient god, he is the blade in this war.

I shake my head. "I have never seen him in my life."

"That is because he is dead." I jolt my eyes up to her, but she stares at the drawing, like she cannot look away. "You drew Epiales, the god of nightmares, who I killed almost ninety years ago. All pictures of him were burned after his death. You should not know his face, but you drew him in perfect detail. And this scene you created has not happened yet. A future that should not exist for a god who is dead."

This isn't like drawing Apollo before I have met him. This is something different. Something morose. I drop the paper from my hand, but Saffron catches it. She holds the drawing in both hands, staring down at Epiales's image. Heartache manifests her features, twisting her mouth into the deepest frown.

"No normal human being can create art how you do." Her words are a whisper, but they scream in my ears.

"I don't understand," I admit, but it is only a partial lie.

The familiar fog returns over my eyes, dusting away the present and showing me the future. A future where I am surrounded by gods and a room full of my artwork, which details a war not yet fought. A life not yet told. I see both the future and the present. Presently, Saffron takes a step towards me in my living room, but I also see her in the future.

She stands on a battlefield of her own creation, horrifically manifesting a river through towns with the citizens' blood. Their screams span miles. They almost mute Saffron's desperate sobs. Almost. But I can hear her. The devastation in her voice as she begs her body to fight against Styx's powers. To stop killing the humans she loves.

Saffron takes both my hands, the drawing sandwiched between us. "Why did you think Nemesis and Khione were having an affair with your fiancé? Out of all the single humans and gods of this world, why would two powerful goddesses choose your future husband as their concubine? While he may be an attractive young man, he is no Adonis. It is unnatural for two goddesses to happily share the same man without a morsel of jealousy. It is unnatural for two goddesses to want the same man, especially one of Lowell's low rank and only slightly above average looks. So, why? Why are they so intertwined with Lowell's life, if not for you?"

I try to pull away my hands, but Saffron holds tight.

"Why would Styx force a random human girl to sign an oath to kidnap me, the single most powerful creature in this world? The father of monsters, Typhon, ran from me in fear. Still hides from me to this day. Yet she chose you to subdue me. She has countless immortals at her disposal, who have a much better chance of capturing me, but she chooses you."

"I'm human," I say, but she interrupts.

"Her loyal goddesses choose your fiancé to bed, and it has nothing to do with him, but everything to do with you and the powers you have."

My blood runs only red, but I feel the magic emitting from the drawing nestled between our hands. Once more, I repeat. "I'm human."

"Humans do not need to remind themselves what they are. You are not joining me in the Underworld on the night of that ball because I think Styx wants you down there as much as she wants me. And because I love Apollo, I refuse to let you die because of a mistake I made when I was a naïve human girl in way over her head."

Die.

The word holds a terrifying finality that I am not prepared for. I stumble away, but with our interlocked touch, she pulls me back. My body shakes, but she keeps me still. My eyes swim with tears, but she doesn't judge me for when they fall. I let out my trepidation onto sympathetic ears.

"Why?" I ask, not saying more, but she understands. "What is wrong with me?"

Why does Styx choose me to torment? Why does Styx want me to bring Saffron down to the Underworld? Khione and Nemesis are loyal servants to her, and they would die trying to bring Saffron down to the river. There are other ways Saffron can go to the Underworld and uphold her favor, but I am the one Styx pursues. I am the one Khione and Nemesis has stalked for months. Maybe years.

"Oracles went extinct before I was born, but it looks like nothing ever truly dies in our world."

"What is an oracle?"

Oracles were not a topic we learned about in school, and they are not in any book I have ever read. The word is as unfamiliar to me as a foreign language, but Saffron looks at me with wonderment.

"Are they evil?" I ask.

"Not in the slightest," she responds.

"They couldn't come," says an extremely gruff voice. We both whip our heads around, and Argus stands in the doorway with a brown suitcase in his hand. "But Paean gave me medicine that will lessen the pain."

"Thank you, Argus," Saffron says. She pulls her hands out of mine. "May you help them both get to my house? They will live with us for the foreseeable future."

"Will you not be joining us?" he asks.

"I have an errand that I must run alone first."

"But-" I say.

She stops me. "We will talk more later, but if Styx wants you, then I refuse to let her have you." Saffron says to Argus. "Protect her with your life, dear friend."

"Anything for you."

Saffron storms out of the apartment, stepping over the broken door laying on the floor, and I look at Argus. He frowns at me, unamused by his newest task.

"I'll grab the boy," he grunts.

THIRTY-NINE

SAFFRON

It has been too long since I have been in the Underworld.

After Hattie died, I used to visit nearly every single day. I couldn't cope in a world without her in it, so the Underworld became more of a home than Earth. I spent countless days with Hattie, Zig, and Diam, laughing with them in the second most beautiful place in the world beside Mt. Olympus. Hattie and Diam live in Elysium Fields, the grandiose haven in the Underworld.

Then, one day, when I tried to come down for dinner, my parents and Cerberus stopped me at the gate. They told me Hattie, Zig, and Diam didn't want me to visit anymore.

"You are living in the past," my mother said. "They want you to live in the present."

Now that I realize the truth, I remember it was the first week of January when my parents turned me away. Before this new year, I was a princess in the land of the dead. I was loved by them all and never steered away. Then something shifted.

Someone shifted.

The moment I saw Styx's name scrawled on Hart's bathroom door, everything became clear. Styx wants me in the Underworld to grant the favor she asked of me almost a century ago, and everybody knew except me. Hermes and my parents learned about Styx's plans, and instead of telling me the truth, they pushed me away.

Instead of trusting my strength, they let me believe the worst of them. All so they can protect me from Styx. I do not need protecting. I need the unwavering love of those around me. They choose to lie to me. Sheltering me from strife through omissions after promising truthfulness. Hermes is willingly seen as an adulterous leech. Prefers, I see Hades and Persephone as fickle, absentee parents. Because they fear Styx more than they value my happiness. More than they trust my actions.

I walk towards the black gates separating the Underworld from the land of the living. Cerberus stands at the gate. One head shows his excitement with a tongue flopping out of his mouth, but the other two wear hesitance on large, furry faces. Two large, unsynchronized barks begin, and I know he is alerting somebody of my presence.

Hades?

Persephone?

Hermes?

"I love you," I say to Cerberus as I walk towards him. "But I am getting through these gates with, or without, your approval."

I raise my hand in the air, and I stop him from moving. He is under my control as if strings connect my fingers to his bones. Cerberus lets out a tiny whimper as I walk past. I place an apologetic kiss on the top of his head.

The Underworld is dimly lit, without a sun or a moon to tell the time. There is only an expansive cave, adorned with lantern lighting. Two parts illuminate the brightest, and that is the castle miles away and the ferry boat Zig controls. I walk towards the river's edge, each step more frigid than the one before it.

Zig is at the end of the river opposite me, smiling as he comforts the newly deceased sitting and whimpering in his ferry. He shuffles recently deceased humans onto Asphodel Meadows, waving at the befuddled souls as they saunter into their eternal homes. I have missed that crooked grin, with one front tooth slightly longer than the other. It is a sight I never get the privilege to see anymore. When Zig turns around and sees me at the front of the river, his smile immediately dissipates.

Normally, one of my longest friends would rush to embrace me in a hug, but today is different. Fear transforms my once jubilant friend. Both hands wrap around his skiff. Hurriedly, he pushes through the river. His smile is replaced with a horror-struck gasp.

"Get away from the river!" He screams.

I do not move. Instead, I wait for Zig to rush through the river, desperation clear in his hurried movements, until he jumps off the ferry and runs towards me. Every other time I have met him on this dock, Zig has pulled me in his arms for the world's biggest hug, but today is not an ordinary day. His hands grab my biceps, fingers digging into the flesh. His terror-stricken eyes assess me like I will combust in flames any second.

"What are you doing down here?" he asks, breathless and afraid.

I know why he does not want me down in the Underworld. Just like my parents and Hermes, Zig has lied to me, too. Shielded me from the truth because he does not believe I can save myself from Styx. I hide the betrayal rushing through my body in gusts of fiery pain.

"The Underworld was once my home. Why can't I be down here?"

Zig's hands tremble against my arms. "It's not safe for you here, milady."

We both stare at each other, yet our periphery is on the river. Our primary focus is on Styx's home. She can emerge at any second. Claim the favor I promised her many years ago. There is nothing Zig can do if she collects, and he knows this, too.

"I am the only immortal who can never die. There is no place that isn't safe for me anymore."

Zig shakes his head, and sandy hair falls over his forehead. "Not everywhere is safe. Especially not here." He whispers as he talks, afraid of who could be listening. "Do you remember what I promised you when I first met you all of those years ago?"

I remember the first time I met Zig all too well. We were both humans chosen by Ares to be his slaves. Zig, with his charming smile and overwhelming optimism. He helped me, as much as a human against a god could. He gave me fresh clothes, glamorized a better world, and swore to always protect me.

"I remember."

"Say it, milady."

"You promised I would live for as long as you did. That you would always keep me safe."

"I want to keep that promise," he says. "So, get out of the Underworld. This is a battleground you will be a casualty of if you stay. Run, with no plans of looking back."

I have loved, and mourned, him throughout our years together. Cherished his friendship with great fervor. Other than Hattie, Zig has been my closest friend in life. I want to ease his fear. I want to listen to him and turn on my heels. Run from a war I inadvertently started, when I was a child drowning in the River Styx. But I cannot. While I am here with Zig, my mind goes back to Hart crying. I see the mutilated body of her friend, dying from a disease Styx brings into the world.

"You're dead, Zig." I hide my agony at the words, but they ring with honesty. "Your promise to me was fulfilled when your heart stopped beating."

Beside us, the blackened river ripples with activity. The previously damp atmosphere turns to ice, and the dead aimlessly roaming through the waters moan in agony. Zig's nails are deep in my flesh, puncturing the skin as true terror manifests on his long, angular face. He uses his grip to pull me away, but I do not move an inch. I stare at the bubbles rising to the top, waiting to see the goddess who readies herself for a war.

But before I see her, I hear him.

"No!"

Hermes's voice is more fearful than any I have ever heard.

A blur of a god zips through the Underworld, his body moving too fast to distinguish. My husband pulls my attention away from everything else. Before I can push him away, he grabs me underneath my armpits and hoists me through the air. Zig's hands are ripped away. Hermes flies me out of the Underworld before a single strand of Styx's impossibly black hair breaks the surface of the water.

He swiftly pulls me out of the Underworld, and in only a blink of an eye, he drops me into our bedroom. His chest heaves, but not from exhaustion. He travels the world at warp speed, journeying between continents within minutes every single day. Hermes rests a hand on the bedframe and exhales fearful, haggard breaths.

For a moment, I forget the lies and take a step towards him. He has been my greatest love for decades. When Hattie, Zig, and Diam died, Hermes became my best friend, too. He has always been more than just my husband, and as fear sinks its talons into him, I want to be near him.

He cannot speak because his breathing is too rough, and his heart is beating too fast. I place my hand on top of his, squeezing, but then he pulls me into a tight embrace. His arms tremble, but his grip is firm on my body. I wrap my arms around the back of his neck, like I always used to throughout our marriage.

With him this close, his shattered sighs brush against my ear. He is a god who can heal himself from all physical wounds, but he is unscathed right now and still suffering. I squeeze him tight, his body flush against mine. For minutes or hours, I'm not sure which. I hold him until his breathing calms, his arms stop trembling, and he can exhale a few words.

"Are you alright?" he asks.

Without thinking, I press a kiss to his cheek. There is instant regret with the action because he is lying to me. I do not know if he is really having an affair with Hecate, or if it is one of his many tricks in his pursuit to keep me away from Styx. As soon as my lips leave his skin, I untangle myself from his embrace.

I take a step back, but his hand stays on my waist, keeping me close. "Not yet." He nudges me closer to him. "Just a few more minutes, please."

I did not come down to the Underworld tonight to see Styx. I left Hart so I could see Hermes and give him one more chance at honesty. He has known about Styx this whole time, and he has been tricking me, like I am another one of his clever pranks. My heart has been a game he shreds to keep me away from Styx, but he is also my husband. Tonight, my hand reaches out for him, giving him one last chance to be honest with me before he falls from my grasp.

Before we divorce.

I step into his arms again, and the feel of his lean body is so familiar to me. We have been distant with each other for years, maybe decades, but his touch still reminds me of home. There is the tiniest spark when my arms circle around his narrow waist. The scent of sandalwood and lavender, which is uniquely him, encircles me. I lay my head against his chest, breathing in his smell for possibly the last time.

"Do you remember the day of our wedding?"

"Yes," he says. "I remember that day like it was yesterday."

We married on a warm June Sunday, ordained by an annoyed Hera, and surrounded by all our family and friends. The ceremony was beautiful, but more than that, it was a day of unadulterated honesty. We confessed to each other our greatest worries about marrying one another, and we both made a sacred promise.

I swore that my conversations with him would never cease. He feared he would make a mistake, and I would never speak to him again. Like when he betrayed my love for a chance to become an Olympian, and I didn't talk to him until after I saved him from Circe. Hermes always wanted to know that no mistake would be too great. That we would stop talking to one another again. I ensured him that day that I would never stop being his friend.

In return, he swore to never deceive me again. He may be the god of trickery, but as his wife, I am supposed to be the exception to his abilities. I told him I could not be in a marriage of lies, that no matter how much the truth scares him, he must tell me. Hermes promised me honesty, but eighty-five years later, I hold him and wait for him to tell me the truth.

I press a kiss where my head lies, right in the center of his chest where his heart rapidly beats. "I have some questions for you."

"Okay." The word wavers on his tongue.

"Are you really cheating on me with Hecate?"

I never thought I would find myself here in our bedroom, asking about Hermes's fidelity. He has been loyal to me throughout our years together, and I never questioned his love. Even now, I do not believe he chooses Hecate over me. I believe it is a carefully orchestrated fib created so I would cancel the ball and avoid the Underworld.

Here is his lifeline. A chance to admit he is lying and tell me the truth about Styx. I stare into those vibrant green eyes, and I wait for him to give me what I need most. Just as he swore on our wedding day, I beg him now to divulge the truth. I want him to admit that he is not an adulterer, but he is a god who lies when he is scared.

He is silent for so long that if I didn't have my arms around him, I would think he isn't here. I place one of my hands on his cheek, my thumb grazing his clean-shaven face. I never look away from his eyes, and I never stop the internal chant begging for his honesty. There are many things I can forgive, but not his lies.

"Hermes," I say his name like broken glass. "Is that the reason you do not want me to go to the Underworld? Because you chose Hecate over me? Because you want to live in the Underworld with her, rather than on Earth with me?"

There's a moment of clarity on his face.

He has an idea that I know the truth. Hermes searches my face, trying to find the answers to his own questions. Both of his hands move up the expanse of my body, fingers dancing across the slope of my neck, before he captures both of my cheeks. Tears are fresh in his vision, swimming with truths waiting to be spilled, but instead, he kisses me.

He tastes like a part of me, and I cling to him. Our lips brush against one another with feverish passion, tongues joining and bodies colliding. I snake my hand underneath his shirt, feeling the warmth of his body. My fingers sink to the waistband of his pants, pulling down the material.

I undo the button holding his pants up, and he sharply pulls away. His hands leave my body. His lips are still red with my kiss. Hermes rummages a hand through his shaggy locks, breathing heavily and refusing to meet my eyes.

"I love-" he stops himself.

I step towards him. "Hermes, please..."

Don't lie.

Don't make me lose you, too.

"I choose her," Hermes says.

A part of my soul wilts with three small words.

"So," I say. "There is nothing else going on. You're just cheating on me?"

"Yes."

I do not mistake how wobbly his voice is and the terrible execution of his lies. But it is a lie all the same. He shatters the promise he made to me on our wedding day. He tries to trick me like he had when I was a human girl, who was too unbelievably infatuated with him. I am not the same girl who didn't know how to read, who giggled at everything, and who believed every word that left his deceitful mouth.

I learn from my mistakes, and I refuse to be a part of his lies anymore. Even if he believes his words are meant to protect me, he should know better. I deserve honesty more than a shield in a battle he doesn't want me to know about.

I walk towards the vanity on the far right of my bedroom. Grabbing the parchment scroll on my desk, I turn to face him. My hand holds out the papers, and my voice is impossibly apathetic, as I say. "Then sign the divorce papers."

He pales. "Saffron, I don't-"

"Don't what?" I ask harshly. "You said you chose Hecate over me, and here is your chance to have her." I stroll towards him, my hand still holding out the divorce papers. "My part is already signed, so the moment you fill out your portion, it will be sent immediately to Hera. Our marriage will be over."

I went to Hera shortly after her session with Hart earlier

today. Hera called me every despicable name in the book after I asked her for the divorce papers. After nearly two hours of her hateful spews, Hera created this divorce settlement. I get the house, but Hermes gets anything else he wants.

"If you are telling the truth and you are cheating on me with Hecate, then I do not want this farce of a marriage any longer."

This is his one last chance to be honest. To salvage the ruins of this relationship.

A tear slips from Hermes's eye. "But I love you."

"People who love each other do not cheat. People who love each other do not lie." I slam the divorce paper against his chest, my eyes locking with his. "Either tell me you are not with her or sign the damn papers."

I manifest a pen, and he takes it.

The life string of our relationship severs as he signs his name on the dotted line, then drops the papers like they burn his flesh. Before the settlement can reach the ground, they disappear in a plume of smoke. Lightning strikes right outside my window, the sudden change of weather indicative of the failed marriage standing in this bedroom.

"You promised me you would never lie to me again, but all you know how to do is hide the truth. Now get out of my house."

Hermes bows his head, then he is gone.

FORTY

HART SOMMERS

rgus shows me to my guest room. It is on the third floor in the east wing, nestled in the labyrinthine mansion. Mercifully, a bathroom is adjoined to my bedroom, so I do not have to suffer wandering the halls for a toilet because Argus doesn't speak a word to me. He drops off my suitcase full of clothing beside the door, and he leaves before I can offer a word of appreciation or a question.

For a few hours, I attempt to sleep. I lay my back on the most comfortable mattress, staring up at the gold-and-red tiled ceiling. Despite the perfect bed, I cannot bring myself to slip into the void of unconsciousness. There is something else I must do, even if my fatigued body screams for rest. Fog slips and slides across my vision, obscuring my confusion and leading me out of the bedroom and towards another room.

I could not independently find the kitchen, yet I maneuver through this expansive house as if I have been here a thousand times before. My hands roam where they wish, finding a gold doorknob and twisting it until the door swings open. An equally tired Saffron sits on the floor. She is cross-legged, with her back resting against the footboard of her bed. She stares at an unopened Monopoly box, frown worsening with every passing second that she's alone with her thoughts.

"Are you alright?" I ask.

She does not appear shocked by my presence, and she does not look up at me. Her finger traces the Monopoly box as a hoarse, unauthentic laugh escapes her lips.

"That is always a dumb question to ask because it is always answered with a lie." Saffron's laugh dies, and after a few tense moments of silence, she asks. "Why are you in my room?"

"I don't know," I admit.

Saffron nods, saying nothing else. I should turn around and attempt to find my guest room, but I do not. Instead, I sit across from her and the Monopoly game, and I open the box. She watches as I assemble the game, chooses the shoe piece for herself, and winces when I pick up the hat piece. Slowly, I lower the piece back into the pile and pick up the thimble instead.

The first few turns are in complete silence. We only talk when we purchase spaces. I realize Saffron does not want me to leave, but she also does not want to talk about what is troubling her.

"What is an oracle?" I ask her after purchasing North Carolina Avenue. "You didn't have time to explain earlier, and I never learned about them in school."

"You never learned about them because they have been extinct for almost two thousand years." Saffron drops her dice, then lets out a quiet curse when she lands on one of my properties. She pays me, then says. "Admittedly, I might not be the best god to explain their existence, since I am the only one who is too young to know one."

"You know one now," I say.

Her dark eyes meet mine. "Yes, I know one now."

She passes me the dice, and I accept. "Can you explain what you know about oracles?"

"I only know what my storyteller has told me." She does not explain who her storyteller is, and I do not ask. Instead, we play this game and Saffron tells me the story of oracles. "They are humans with the ability to see the future. In ancient times, they were favored by Apollo, and the most powerful became part of the Delphi. The rarest could see thousands of years into the future and could live twice as long as a typical human. Nobles from all around the world came to see the Oracles of the Delphi and discover their fates. It is there that the noble warrior Achilles learned of his fate. And that's when Theseus's father, King Aegeus of Athens, discovered how he could have a son to carry his legacy."

She speaks of the pleasant times of the oracles, but I want the devastation. I need to hear the travesty that awaited my kind, and what could await me if I am not careful.

"What happened to them?"

Saffron moves her shoe five paces forward and asks. "Are you sure that you want to know?"

"Yes," I say with zero hesitation. "I need to know."

"About two thousand years ago, the world saw the decline in oracles. They were becoming a rarity as the new world was beginning, and there were only twelve powerful enough to be a part of the Delphi. About half of them were over a hundred years old and near their deaths. While they were smaller in numbers, they were still undoubtedly powerful, until one night there was a terrible fire. All twelve Oracles died and the power for humans to foresee the future died with them. Apollo doesn't enjoy talking about it, but those deaths wrecked him. He was the one who could not save them in time. All he found were their charred remains among the debris."

"How did the fire start?" I ask, and as the question enters the air, fog returns to my vision and I am no longer in the room with Saffron.

Instead of the future, I am in the past. I sit inside of a circle beside twelve other women, all varying in age, weight, and ethnicities. They all hold hands, and all of them are staring at me. The fire already builds around the columns, holding the building upright. None of the oracles try to run and evade their fate; instead, they stare at me with the smallest smiles.

"Nobody knows what happened that night," Saffron says. Yet, her voice is faint amidst the roars of the fire, and the unrelinquished screams of the oracles' imminent deaths. "Some say candles tipped over."

There are no candles in this room, except for a single one on my lap.

"Others say a nobleman or low-level god was angered by an oracle's premonition," Saffron says.

Simultaneously, all the oracles shake their head, denouncing Saffron's words.

"Last, there are rumors that one oracle started it because she no longer wanted her powers."

Again, the oracles shake their heads.

"Then what happened?" I ask the surrounding oracles.

Smoke enters the room, coating the ground until I cannot see my own feet. The oracles cough, but none of the smoke enters my lungs. I am journeying through their experience, suffering only by proxy. Saffron is talking, but her voice becomes noiseless like the wind. It is the oracles I hear, their voices on endless echo as the flames rise and their deaths loom over the ceiling.

The eldest, with stark white hair and deep brown skin, speaks first. "On the eighty-eight night of the eighty-eighth year, when crimson shifts to gold, a prophecy will unfold."

Another oracle, with wheat-blonde hair who holds the eldest one's right hand, speaks next. "From the ashes of time, eight figures will rise."

"Eight, the sacred number of immortality, seals the destiny of a seer and a savior, a heart and a hammer, a singer and a seeker, and a hero and a huntress." As the smoke becomes too thick, I can barely make out this oracle's face. Her skin tone is like mine, a shade of light brown with reddish undertones, but the rest of her image is too mottled by the inferno.

To her right, a different oracle speaks. "A river of black will cease to exist, unless the one with sight sees through the mist."

"A world of hatred and oaths will prevail, unless the oracle can see the truth and derail." An older oracle says, her voice raspy from overuse and a long lifespan.

Another oracle says. "The ultimate fate is decided when the heart twice fails, and from the savior, a terrible scream will wail. The sound will echo forevermore, and from the scream spawns a war."

Consuming fire reaches the oracles' gowns, igniting

them all, but they do not bellow. Instead, a new oracle says. "Hatred and Sight, oh how they will fight."

Another says. "The winner is untold, but one thing is known."

"Whichever side has the hammer which swings," says one.

"The hero who knows he must bleed," says the next oracle.

"The muse who no longer sings," says an oracle with her entire face melting in front of my eyes.

"The seer, who sees the future with great speed," another dying oracle says.

"The huntress who clips the monster's life strings, the heart whose life will cede, the savior with death she brings, the seeker with life he leads, will be gifted the role of eternal queens or kings."

It is the oracle with the same skin tone as me who says the last few lines. The rest of the oracles are dead around her, transforming into ash and disappearing with the wind. Only this oracle is unscathed, even as the fire laps at her ankles and ignites her white tunic. She strides towards me, and as the candle in my hands extinguishes, this oracle's fire illuminates the room. She lowers herself in front of me, taking my hands and burning the flesh of my palms. There is no pain, only knowledge that this fire will take me too unless I listen to her words.

She smiles at me, and the sight is almost identical to my mother's in every way. Except her eyes. She has the same brown eyes rimmed with gold as me. Thousands of years have transpired between our lineage, but her appearance is too similar to my mother and mine. She is our ancestor, paving the way to my birthright as another oracle.

"The world will crumble like Pompeii," she says. "But the seeker will guide fallen friends away. To safety, the seeker will find the ashes he will revive. The world will be unlike any other and will eternally thrive."

Through the wisps of fire, the female's face switches back and forth between the mysterious oracle and my mother. Their voices mold together, until I am not sure who is speaking to me. Who is from the past and who lives on in my memory.

"Unless the hatred wins, then the seeker and the seer, the hero and the hammer, will surely die."

The smoke engulfs the oracle in front of me, turning her into ash before my eyes. I open my mouth to scream, but before the sound can pierce my ears, I am gone from the Delphi and sit in front of Saffron again. She is oblivious to the past I have relived as she moves her shoe piece six paces forward, passing go, and collecting money as she continues to talk.

"They were told to be the most powerful of humans that did not have any relation to the gods, and they were loved by all," Saffron says. "Unfortunately, I know little else."

"That's okay," I say, because I know far too much now.

I know I am the descendant of an oracle of the Delphi, who passed her gift from mother to daughter across centuries. My mom gave me this gift, even if she did not know she had it, and now it is my destiny to claim.

I know why Styx wants me to deliver Saffron because the prophecy the oracles told me is about Styx. She will reign over the world for all eternity unless I can stop her. Styx wants me in the Underworld with Saffron so she can kill me. She equally wants to capture the savior and stop me from finding the seeker, the hammer, the hero, the huntress, the heart, and the singer.

I am more than just an oracle.

I am Styx's ruination.

Saffron passes me the dice, but the two items drop from my trembling hands. She glances at the fallen dice, then back at me, and she thinks she understands why I am terrified. She does not know what I have just witnessed, and the power which is rapidly growing within me. Saffron thinks I am scared because I am the first oracle in two thousand years. In actuality, I am scared because I have just realized I will save the world from Styx or die along with humanity's freedom.

"When I discovered who I was, the prophesied daughter of Zeus and Metis, I knew that this discovery came with danger." Saffron says, her tone sympathetic. "I was something new, and a new creation comes with a thousand prophecies and a million enemies. Power comes at a price, one I hope you will never have to suffer through."

I pick up the dice, knowing all the danger that awaits me as I fight against one of the most powerful immortals in existence. For the rest of the night, Saffron and I do not sleep. We play rounds of Monopoly until the sun rises.

FORTY-ONE

HART SOMMERS

When I was sixteen years old, I had my first premonition. I did not know that I was an oracle or what abilities I was manifesting. I was only a kid who drew a terrible image she hoped wouldn't come true.

It happened in art class on my brother Suraj's fourteenth birthday. I was surrounded by my friends, laughing and making small talk as we made our interpretation of a perfect vacation. They teased me for my choice. Telling me traveling to the destination was the worst part of any vacation. I continued my drawing regardless of their opinion.

My family vacations were always on the beach, and each time we drove together, I discovered undiluted peace. Lyric-less, acoustic guitar flowed out of the car radio and my mother sang along. My father would become a percussionist, his fingers mimicking sticks as the steering wheel became the drum set. Suraj hummed softly in the background, the perfect accompaniment to our mother's gentle soprano.

I would always look out the window and take in the ever-changing scenery, as my family became a slightly off-kilter band.

My favorite musical group.

I outlined my dad's tan car, adding the dent on the bumper after I ran over the mailbox my first time driving. When I was shading the dent, fog obscured my vision. Now, I know that the fog is magic seeping through me, diverting my sight to the future rather than the present. But for the first time, I panicked.

My heart sped up, beating hard enough to break a rib, and my body convulsed. I vaguely felt my body falling off my work bench, clattering on the ground as my friends screamed for the teacher to help. Then, there was no awareness of my surroundings. My friends' voices dissipated, along with the teacher's rough touch on my shoulders as she tried to wake me; there was only the dreadful future.

Mom and Dad pulled Suraj out of school for a lunch date in honor of his birthday. It was a yearly tradition they had for both of us. Suraj laughed in the car, the sound greater than any music, as my father drummed his fingers along the steering wheel. Suraj made jokes with my father, who chuckled in response, but Mom did not take part in their joy.

She stared at me with a sad resolution. "You won't have time to stop it," she said.

Confused, I asked. "Stop what?"

I glanced at the clock on the radio, and it was blinking 12:45 back at me. It was an hour into the future, right after my parents picked Suraj up from school. My mother smiled at me, but there was no warmth in the expression. Only a vast pool of sorrow drew from my mother's lips, curving that smile that haunted me for years after their death.

"One day, you will know how to save," she said as my father

screamed in the background and slammed on his brakes. "One day you will love. Through that love, you will save."

"You're not making any sense."

A massive semi-truck slipped out of their lane in the opposite direction and headed towards my dad's car. My dad threw his arm over Suraj's chest, who sat in the passenger seat, but he could not stop the semi-truck. My mother stared at me when the semi-truck going seventy miles per hour on the highway slammed into the car.

She never looked away as the glass exploded around them.

The car flipped seven times down a steep hill to their right. Suraj's screams were replaced with the sound of him gurgling on his own blood. My mother's eyes stayed focused on me as my father lay dead in the driver's seat. His head rested on the steering wheel he often drummed, but his eyes were unfocused and unblinking. Suraj fought to live, but eventually the gurgling sounds ended, and he joined our father in the Underworld.

Mother died last, never looking away from me.

When I came out of the vision, I looked at my artwork first. Not the teacher who hysterically called the nurse. Or my friends, who crowded around me and asked a thousand questions at the same time. I stared at the artwork, where the car's radio clock beeps 12:45 as it lays at the bottom of a hill. Destroyed beyond recognition.

I ran out of the classroom as fast as I could with the artwork in my hand, and I went to the principal's office. Once there, I told him they needed to call my parents and tell them to stop driving. The clock taunted me as it grew closer to the time of their death. I didn't understand my powers then, but I knew I was correct. I knew they were going to die if my principal didn't call them and warn them.

He didn't believe me.

I was hysterical, crying to him and his secretary, but they just dismissed my words as a panic attack and morbid creativity. They told me I could wait in the nurse's office until I calmed down. At one o'clock that afternoon, my principal came to the nurse's bed and sat on the corner of the bed I laid on. He was white as a ghost, with guilt swimming in his eyes that showed the first sign of cataracts. He loudly gulped, and he admitted I was right.

My entire family died that day, exactly how the painting depicted.

For a decade, I feared my abilities. It was one reason I turned down a job position in the art field. Why I stayed in an unhappy relationship with Lowell, and why I did not complain about the prison that I willingly put myself in. I blamed myself for not stopping their deaths, and I blamed these powers of premonition I never wanted to have. For the last ten years, I have purposely sabotaged my life because I felt guilty for their deaths. Deaths I saw an hour early but still could not prevent.

But as I drive with Saffron and Jamila to Olympus Industries, and we stop in front of the doors where Apollo waits for me, I understand what my mother said. She knew I would blame myself for their deaths. That I would shun myself from the rest of the world with that guilt trailing after me. She might have even known about Apollo and how I would push him away because I wanted to leave him before he left me for my mistakes.

Apollo stands in the doorway. He nervously bites down on his bottom lip, and I finally understand my mother's words during that vision. I closed the door on my powers, only allowing them to open when I dreamed of Apollo's face. I usually can only see visions a few hours or days into the future, unless I am around him. When Apollo's near, I can see the future in vast arrays of color. I can see years forward and centuries back in time.

Because he is my soulmate, and I am done closing the door on myself and my powers. I am the damn oracle, the first to be acknowledged in centuries, and I will be with Apollo. It is my destiny to play a part in Styx's war, and I will defeat her with Apollo by my side.

The moment Argus stops the car, I jump out and run towards Apollo. He expected me to run like I did yesterday, or to question the future we saw because I have only known him for a few days. But this isn't a romance that started only a few days ago. It has been etched in our history since the day I was born. Each time my foot hits the ground on my journey towards him, I see another bit of our future.

Us together in a tub filled with bubbles, laughing as we plan our wedding. A smear of pink paint crossing his cheek as I fling a paintbrush at him with a joyous grin on my face. His arms tighten around me as his eyes lower to the wedding ring I wear on my finger. His kiss, warm like the sun, as it peppers my neck, collarbone, and chin. The declarations of love we make, tears we cry, and fights we forgive each other for.

I see it all as I leap into him, wrap my arms around the back of his neck, and slam my lips against his. I know he saw the visions I had on my way to him because he kisses me with the same fervor. There is no hesitation as his mouth claims mine, tongue sliding across my bottom lip and demanding access. He does not question how quickly I have switched from running from him and running to him; he simply accepts me. Every jagged and insecure piece of me.

One hand is around my waist, holding me against him, while the other combs through my curly hair. He tugs on the strands as a moan escapes my lips and enters his. Electricity vibrates everywhere. Scouring from the top of my head, nestling beside the butterflies in my stomach, and reaching the tips of my toes. Apollo consumes me, and I happily let him as our future plays like a movie in both our heads. Every pleasant moment told through blushed cheeks, stolen kisses, and wondrous touches.

I pull away from him, smiling as his teeth drag my bottom lip until I am too far away for him to hold on. My smile never fades as I take another step away and see that we are no longer at Olympus Industries. Instead, we are in his art room, where my eyes instantly move towards the wall filled with his former loves.

"It's gone."

Instead, the only painting remaining on the wall is from the first day we met. My hands are splayed across his chest and my eyes are wide with disbelief. He stares down at me with wonderment. I am the answer to every hope he's had across the centuries.

"I saw a can of spilled paint, and I knew you came in here last time." He takes a step towards me, watching me as I stare at the painting that tells our first story together. "I thought this room meant I lost you, and that made me realize my past is inconsequential. I had only known you for one day, and the thought of losing you because I clung to my past nearly destroyed me. The moment I realized I needed you more than I needed a reminder of my heartbreak, I took them down and started a new painting."

He takes my hands, pulling them up to his mouth as he places a tender kiss on each knuckle.

"This will be a wall filled with our stories, my destined third love and I."

Apollo leans towards me again, lips dusting mine, and I let his words echo in my head. *My destined third love and I.* These are the words I let sing in my head, replacing my mother's placid voice or my brother's. I hear Apollo's proclamation in my ears as I take off his clothes, one article at a time.

As we lay down on the floor together, molding together and becoming officially one another's, I smile at the words.

My destined third love and I.

FORTY-TWO

HART SOMMERS

We lay together in each other's arms in his art room. In the far-right corner, I see a glimpse of a new art piece drying on an easel. She is the most radiant goddess, with round, high-risen cheekbones and dark eyes which warn you of the power she holds. There isn't a pang of jealousy like the last time I saw a drawing of Saffron in Apollo's room, not as he lays kisses on my bare shoulder.

"What is the drawing for?"

"The one of Saffron and Hermes?" he asks, not looking away from me. Never ending his line of kisses on my body.

"Yeah."

"It was from the first time I saw them together at one of Dionysus's galas. It is going to be their anniversary present. The was the first time I saw them, and realized how much they loved one another. They danced together for hours, and not once did her smile falter. Not until he stopped dancing with her."

"She has a really pretty smile."

"And rare now, too." There is a sadness in his voice, his eyes now roaming over the drawing. "I have seen that smile less and less, but it is still there somewhere behind the morbidity of her life."

"What happened between the two of you?"

I turn my body so we are staring at each other, and he holds out his hands. "Do you want me to tell you, or do you want to see it yourself?"

Hesitantly, I place my hands on top of his.

He intertwines our fingers. "Close your eyes, μέλι, and once they are closed, I want you to picture Saffron and me."

I obey. My eyes flutter closed, and I think of the two of them together. Their story of friendship and unrequited love emerges spurts of color, like an empty canvas ruined with many layers of spilled paint. I cannot distinguish any of these stories, which run and mottle together. I can make out a rare smile, or an unfamiliar, female laugh, but there are no clear images.

"We were on a beach in the story you want to find, so picture us on a beach. Feel the sand beneath your toes, the sun blaring down on your skin..."

"The smell of salt water," I say as the sense invades my nostrils.

The unneeded images fall from the canvas within my mind, and only two remain. They move like a motion picture, side-by-side. In the video on the left, they are not on a beach but nestled close together in a dim room. There is no warmth in this room, with sharp corners, no furniture, and no sunlight. If I had to guess, I would assume they are in a basement.

They both sit cross-legged, knees almost touching, when

314

Apollo smiles at Saffron and says. "Sunshine doesn't have a smell, at least not technically. But I correlate sunshine with the smell of a beach."

"I've never been to a beach before," Saffron says. "Epiales told me about beaches when he was teaching me about islands, but that's it. I've always been curious about them, though."

This is not the same Saffron I know. The past and present Saffron share the same blinding beauty, but there is no harshness in her dark eyes in this video. She brims with youthful joy, eyes smiling alongside her widening lips. For the first time, I notice dimples on her cheeks, but it is not just her jovial demeanor that has changed throughout the years.

She sounds different, too. Here, beside Apollo, Saffron has an excited lilt. She is a constant bubble of elation. Present Saffron's voice is as sharp as a blade, unforgiving and brutal. She sounds ready to strike a man down.

"When the war is over, I'll take you to a beach. You will get to experience just how annoying sand can be, but how wondrous it is to listen to the sound of the waves gently crash onto the shore."

The video on the left crackles and fades, and the second video begins. The image on the right takes place on a beach, and Apollo's hair is much shorter this time. Some time has passed between the two scenes, either a few months or years, but Saffron still appears joyful. She lets out a giggle as her bare feet slide into the sand, nestling in between her toes.

"You weren't kidding about the sand," she says with amusement. "It is weird."

Apollo's eyes level on her smile. Focusing on her lips. Again, I should be jealous, but I am not. I am here in Apollo's arms, destined to be his soulmate from today until my last day, and

Saffron is not. I do not hold a flame of jealousy for the past that I cannot control.

"Come on," Apollo takes her hand and leads her deeper into the beach. "Let's get you by the water."

For hours, the two laugh together, splashing each other with water and making jokes at the other's expense. It isn't until sunset that they sit down, hips touching, in the sand. Saffron lays her head on Apollo's shoulder, a smile still on her face.

"It is a shame we didn't find a crab. Hattie said I would love them. She said they're furry and sweet."

Apollo laughs at her. "Right, furry and sweet. That is how one would describe crabs."

Saffron wrinkles her brows. "Is that sarcasm again?" *His grin widens, and she humphs.* "One day, I will get Hattie back."

The beach grows quiet, and in this silence, Apollo's thoughts come alive. "You never answered my question that night in the Labyrinth."

Confused, she asks. "What question?"

"What would you do without Hermes?"

She thinks about the question for a moment, trying to remember the conversation, then says. "He survived the war. I do not have to think about losing him now. Now that he is alive, he will live forever, which means we will be together forever."

Her naivety is apparent, even through the vision. She does not realize the longing expression on Apollo's face, the way his eyes roam over her lips with delirious desire. Her head stays on his shoulder, not understanding how close they are and how tempting that makes her. She obliviously believes she and Hermes are going to be together forever, solely because they cannot die.

Not because there are other options.

"ómorfo aínigma," Apollo says, these two undecipherable words in Greek. "Please answer the question."

"Are you ever going to tell me what that nickname means?" Saffron cheerily asks. "Nobody else will tell me, not even Daedalus, during our tutoring sessions."

"I'll make a deal with you. Answer my question, then I will answer yours."

"Okay." She ponders his words, giving a tense silence to the empty beach, then says. "I could live without Hermes. That doesn't mean I don't love him, I do, but I could survive without him in my life. It would hurt, but he isn't my entire world. Just a small, but meaningful, part of it."

"I love you," the words come out of Apollo almost by mistake.

Her eyes widen, finally looking at Apollo. "What?"

"I," he stops. "I love you, Saffron. And I know it is terrible to say because you're dating Hermes, and you are still mourning Epi-"

Saffron flinches. "Don't say his name." Pain crosses her features as she adds. "Please."

"You're still mourning him, but I needed you to know that I love you. That Hermes isn't your only option."

"I know he is not my only option," she says. "But.."

He cups her chin, tilting it so their lips are a breath apart. "But, what?"

She roams his face, searching for a part of him she could envision herself with, but ultimately frowns. "But you're not an option, Apollo."

"Why not?" he asks, desperate for her to change her mind. "I love you, ómorfo aínigma. My beautiful enigma. You have made me think of nothing else but you. Made me delirious just to see one more smile, hear one more laugh. Why am I not an option when you plague my thoughts?"

"Because I do not deserve you."

His hand wavers on her chin. "You're wrong."

"No, I'm not." Her voice takes on a somber, sympathetic tone as she reaches forward and cups his face with her hand. They are inexplicably close right now, noses touching and lips an inch away. Her thumb drags across his cheek, taking in his features with appreciation but not love. "You are one of the greatest males I have met in my life, and you deserve the greatest love story ever told. I will not be that for you. I think I could be happy with you, but it would not be love. It would be a friendship, one we would pretend was more until that game of pretend ended us."

She leans forward, and they share the smallest kiss. It is not derived from passion or love. Rather, the kiss tells him the truth he needs to hear. It is a taste of goodbye. A farewell to his hopes of becoming more to Saffron. When she pulls away, she drops her hand from his cheek, and he does the same for her chin.

"Did you feel any sparks?" she asks.

He hates his answer, so he is quiet for a while. "No," he winces. "I didn't."

"When you meet either him or her, they will give you the greatest sparks. It will feel like your skin is burning off, but you still want a little more of that pain."

"Like you and Hermes?" Apollo asks.

"Yes," she whispers.

He doesn't notice, but I do. She is lying. She knows the touch of a soulmate, but she knows it is not Hermes. I know because when Apollo says Hermes's name, her smile slightly falters. She glowed when she spoke about the spark of love, but Hermes's name dimmed her. I am oblivious to Saffron and Hermes's love story, but I know she feels that electricity with another.

Not Hermes.

The image fades, and Apollo holds my chin like he held Saffron's on that beach. Except, there is electricity. The feel of his skin turns mine to molten lava, lighting up my body in the most pleasant form of pain. He feels it too. I know he does, because of the radiant way he stares at me like two pieces of the sun live in the gold within his blue eyes.

"I love Saffron. There's no denying that. There will always be a part of me that loves her, just like I loved Hyacinth, Daphne, Gaillardia and the others of my long past. But they hold nothing on you, μέλι. With your perfect honey-colored eyes and the way you make me feel like there is nobody in this world but us."

He presses his lips to mine, and as he pulls away, he stays close enough so I can taste and feel his words.

"Saffron and the others were what I wanted before I knew what a soulmate was. Before your grandparents were even born. She reminded me I had somebody waiting for me who would make me feel more than she ever could. She told me I would have a love unparalleled to anything else, and you're that person. You're the soulmate I've waited eons to find, and your Lowell and my Saffron mean nothing compared to us. My destined third love and I."

Before another word can escape his lips, I wrap my arms around the back of his neck, and I accept him and nobody else.

Even as Styx's laugh taints my thoughts, telling me the great storm is nearer than I think.

FORTY-THREE

SAFFRON

I am in my office with Jamila, spending a few moments enjoying lunch, when an archway of rainbows materializes.

The first person I see is Iris, iridescent in every shade of pink and red, and beside her is one of Artemis's huntresses. She's the freckled-face one, whose appearance reminds me of Panda. Roxie, I think her name is. Roxie's arms are tied with rope, as well as her ankles, and a fresh cut alongside her cheek drips with blood every few seconds.

But when I see the god, whose back is to me, he steals away all my attention.

"Don't make me," Ares snaps the end of a sentence I didn't hear the beginning of, then he freezes. He looks around my office, then slowly turns until he faces me. His body is tense, and his hands curl into meaty fists. "Afternoon," he says.

Afternoon.

I have tried to talk to him every week for the past eighty-eight years. He has avoided me. Each time I am on Mt. Olympus, I search for him, trying to finish the story left untold when I was human, but I never find him. He is always gone when I look for him. In the beginning, when I was still naïve, I thought it was a coincidence we never saw one another.

But I know better now.

Ares has been avoiding me since the night I turned into a goddess, and he didn't want to come see me today, either.

I lower my gyro, and without looking away from Ares, I tell Jamila. "Go eat your lunch at your desk, please. And make sure nobody else comes inside."

"Okay."

She shuffles out of the room, taking her lunch with her. The moment the door slams shut behind her, I tear my gaze away from Ares. "Why is one of Artemis's huntresses tied up?"

Roxie's body shakes as she sobs, knees quaking beneath her.

Iris motions to Ares. "Ask him," she says. "He was the one who found out Roxie betrayed Artemis."

I do not want to look at him again. When I see him, I rewind back in time to the night I nearly killed him and the nights he nearly killed me. His eyes are midnight blue as they clash against my brown ones, and his presence reminds me of everything we haven't finished discussing. Pages that still have not been turned.

We are suspended in time, staring at each other from across the room with no words spoken, until Iris snaps at Ares. "What is wrong with you?"

Clearing my throat, I ask. "How are you certain she's a traitor?"

He focuses his attention on Roxie, refusing to meet my gaze again. "I have ridden with Artemis and her huntresses on-and-off for eons. They're loyal to her and the oath they swear. None of them have tried to seduce me, and all the huntresses I've flirted with have threatened to cut off a piece of my body if I continued talking to them. Most huntresses won't even look at me, but this one." He points to Roxie, who flinches at the motion. "Tried to-" he clears his throat, audibly uncomfortable as he adds. "Is too handsy to be a loyal huntress."

The burn of my magic singes the tips of my fingers. It is the only warning I have before my magic reaches for Roxie, slamming her to her knees. She lets out a cry of pain, but with my magic, I control her jaw bones and slam them back together. Now, she can only whimper.

"That's not all," Iris says. She reaches for Roxie, grabs a fistful of her strawberry blonde hair, and pulls her neck backwards until the smallest mark catches my attention. Roxie is Artemis's newest huntress. She did not live during the time of human enslavement and should not have a scarification mark, but a mark taints the skin behind her ear.

"What is that a mark of?" My question takes a deathly tone.

Immediately, the sobs and whimpers halt. Roxie cannot move, not as I hold reign over her bones, but she glowers at me with hatred. Foolishly, I have been comparing Roxie to Panda because of their similar physical features, but she is not anything like my dear friend. Instead, Roxie reminds me too much of Glasswing. She wears the same manic, unblinking expression Glasswing wore in the Underworld before I threw her into the River Styx.

I release Roxie's jaw, letting her talk, and fury spews from her thin lips. "A river in honor of the only true queen of this world."

She doesn't say her name, but she does not need to because I know she is referring to Styx. The goddess with whom I foolishly offered a favor to. My parents and Daedalus warned me about Styx and the evil she could unleash on the world. I was told to avoid Styx, and instead I made a deal with her that has come back to haunt me decades later.

"Who else is working with her?" I ask Roxie, but she does not supply me with my answer.

"It took some time, but she gave me a list," Ares says. "She wouldn't tell me all of them, and she refused to tell me the names of the other huntresses working with Styx."

"But some are better than none. Thank you."

He walks hesitantly towards me, removing a rolled-up piece of paper from his jacket pocket. He extends it towards me, and when I accept, our fingers graze one another. Fire and electricity and something more erupts from the touch. We both quickly pull away.

Our eyes meet again. "No problem," he says just as softly.

I try to ignore him, but that is like trying to forget about lightning when a storm strikes. Or the rainbow after the rain subsides. Still, I turn away and face Roxie. Her face morphs with Glasswing's, reminding me again that anybody can be deceived. Even if I gave her a chance to be saved from her certain death, she would still choose the blade; she would still choose Styx as her queen.

"What has Styx promised you?" I ask her.

I half expect her not to answer. She looks deranged with unblinking eyes and a feral grin, but she explains. "Queen Styx told me about a prophecy given to her by one of the late Oracles of the Delphi. She told me queendom was her prophesied right, and all who join her side will become immortals. I will be more than a huntress. I can become a goddess. Who doesn't want to live forever? To bleed gold and have power at their fingertips?"

I didn't, but I do not say those words aloud.

"You can kill me right now, like you've killed countless before me," Roxie continues. "Because when Styx rules over this world, she will bring me back to life and make me immortal. It will be you," she glares at Iris. Then, she looks at Ares. "And you who will die and stay dead."

Neither Ares nor Iris seem concerned. I do not tend to judge people's strengths based on their appearance, but Roxie is one of the tiniest humans. She barely reaches five feet tall, and both of her arms are the size of one of mine. Although she has ridden with Artemis, she has garnered no muscle mass from the rigorous training. She is weak, both in the mind that easily bends and in her malnourished body.

"Put her in the Fields of Punishment," I tell Iris. "Tell Hades to give her the most gruesome punishment of them all. I want Sisyphus and Ixion to weep with gratitude when they see her torment, and I want her to have a perfect view of the River Styx. Let her watch as Styx does nothing to save her."

The mania on Roxie's face falls, and she is a frightened human once again. I paralyze her jaw again, silencing any further words, and then both she and Iris are gone. Only

Ares remains in my office, standing only a few feet away from me.

"I tried to see you."

He nods his head. "I know."

"I.-"

But I stop.

There are a thousand things I want to say right now. A million words rush through my head, begging to be released. There was once a time I thought he would answer all my inquiries, confirm every theory I had in my head. Especially after we defeated Kronos together, and he began a story he never finished. Ares bows his head, refusing to look at me again, and I accept the questions that will never be answered.

"Thank you," I say instead. "For bringing Roxie here and giving me a list of the names."

He nods his head. "I'm going to go tell Zeus now."

His voice is stiff, his heels already moving backwards towards the office door. Far from me. He spins around, briskly leaving my office, but a bit of who I was before re-surges when his hand touches the doorknob.

"I tried to see you before my wedding." I want to pull back the words, but instead of retreating, I elaborate. "Phobos and Deimos stopped me right in front of your door, but I knew you were inside your house. I came to see you before my wedding, but you had your sons turn me away. You're always turning me away when I try to find you."

His hand tightens on the doorknob. "And now you're celebrating your eighty-fifth anniversary. Congratulations." Ares turns back once more and gifts me with the saddest smile. "You deserve more than the world. I hope he gives you that."

He opens the door and leaves.

The sparks of electricity on my skin do not lessen until hours later.

FORTY-FOUR

LAMB

Three suns have risen and fallen. Three moons have made their appearance since I have been captive in this cage on Ogygia. The sun has been especially cruel, battering down on my flesh until it blisters and peels off my body. After three days of suffering, the pain has gone numb, and I fear that most of all. Pain means your body is still fighting, and now I feel nothing.

There has been no water, no food, and no shelter. I bathe underneath the sweltering heat, lips cracking and begging for nourishment of any kind, but salvation never comes. Today, my eyes remain shut, unable to open as fatigue unlike any before heavies my body.

"Lamb," Artemis says. Her voice displays her urgency. "Stay awake."

This is the worst part about my slow, agonizing death. Artemis must watch, unable to save me from the fate I have been handed. Each day, she pulls at her cell bars, trying to open them and get to me. Yet, each day, her attempts do not work. Instead, the stench of her burned flesh intermingles with mine. The smell makes the nymphs gag, but Artemis continues to pull and rip at the bars to no avail.

I am surprised Thanatos has not taken my soul yet. My dry tongue begs for water I will never receive, and a part of me wants to accept death. To have Hermes take my soul to the Underworld and reunite me with Willow and all my fallen friends. Maybe, if I die here, Hermes will find Ogygia and save the others. Perhaps my death will have a purpose.

"Lamb," Artemis says again. "Open your eyes." There is a pause, and then a broken, "please."

I cannot.

I have always sworn to listen to Artemis, to be her devote follower, but today I cannot obey. Dreariness seizes my body, stealing away any strength. I open my mouth, begging for anything, but there is nothing.

No water.

No food.

No hope.

"Lamb!"

She screams my name this time, desperation clear and overwhelming. My body floats between the conscious world and something much darker, and I cannot find my footing on either side. Artemis tugs me to her land of the living, her bellows begging for another moment with me. Another conversation about nothing and everything. Another sunset with apples and fond memories of Willow.

"You're right," Artemis says, attempting to lure me back to the land of the living. "I do like Iris, and that scares me because the last woman I loved died. But then again, you are always right. I cannot think of a time when I won an argument against you. Open your eyes, and I promise I will tell Iris how I feel about her. I will run right up to her, and I will kiss her. I will stop being afraid, but I cannot do that without you. Out of all my huntresses, there is none I need as much as I need you. Your guidance. Your optimism. Gods, your friendship. I need you more than I need anybody else. So please, my closest friend, open your eyes."

Artemis's screams grow louder, and I know she is trying to pull apart her bars again. To help me. Pain and desperation explode from Artemis, and I want to console her. To tell her everything is going to be alright, but I cannot open my eyes. I cannot speak.

Yet, behind my closed eyes, I can see.

Willow stands at the end of a narrow hallway, right in front of a door partially opened. Behind the door is a burst of white light illuminating down the rest of the hallway. I know this is death, the pathway to the Underworld, but there is no fear. I see Willow, and I am happy.

She looks exactly how I remember. Her braided locks are up in a messy bun, and she wears the same outfit she had on when she died. The leggings are cleaned of her blood, the shirt unblemished. A smile warms her heart-shaped face.

I take a step towards her. "Hi."

"I always told you that you should be careful what you wished for. You wanted to be more tan, and now look at you."

We both glance at my red, blistering flesh. I take another step towards her, nearer to the Underworld and its bright, welcoming door. "I never stopped the sunrise and apples." Another step. "Never stopped the stories about you."

Faintly, I can hear Artemis. She screams. "Wake up! Stay with me!"

But I focus on Willow and take another step. "Once a week, Artemis and I have an inspirational monologue of the day with the other huntresses. One of the newer ones, Vee, really enjoys them. We keep the memories of the past alive."

"Reaper would be happy to hear her inspirational monologues have outlived her," Willow says. "Her and I often spend time together in Elysium Fields."

Another step. "And Copperhead?" I ask.

Copperhead died with Willow in Poseidon's mansion, killed by traitorous huntresses working with Kronos. We all mourned their deaths for years, praying for their safe passage every morning and night. I walk down the long hallway, hoping to see them all again. To hug Copperhead. Laugh with Reaper. Have an apple and a story time with Willow.

"She is good," Willow says. I take another step, but Willow shakes her head. "You do not get to come any closer."

"Why not?"

Artemis's yells grow louder, no longer a whisper but an echo in this hallway. Willow follows the sound, her expression morphing into love as she hears Artemis's voice for the first time in decades. I try to step towards Willow, but an invisible wall separates us.

"No, no, no, no," I chant. "I do not want to live in suffering anymore. I want to be with you again."

"Your story does not end on Ogygia," Willow says. "It will end on a battlefield surrounded by our sisters in arms.

You do not die of dehydration, but you die saving the lives of the huntresses you love most."

"But what if I want to die now?" I push on the wall, screaming when it does not budge. "What if I am done fighting and I want to go with you? I miss you so much."

"I miss you too," Willow says. "And sooner than you think, we will be reunited, but not yet. Right now, you are meant to survive. You are meant to fight for our goddess and our sisters."

"Please!" Artemis screams in the back of my mind, louder than ever. "Don't leave me too!"

Willow's smile is soft, but it is a goodbye. "Until we meet again."

Willow goes behind the door, and she closes it behind her. I scream until my throat is raw, begging Willow to come back, but she doesn't. In the blacked-out room of my unconsciousness, water drips from the ceiling onto my face. It starts off slowly, a few patters here and there, but then a torrential downpour washes over me.

I open my eyes.

Clouds cover the sun and rain showers down on me. I open my mouth, enjoying the first droplets of water in three days. Artemis sobs in her cage while I drink the rainwater, bathe in its coldness as the pain of my blisters returns. But pain means I survive. I absorb the pain and the water, but as my battered body has its reprieve, I wonder if I want this mercy.

Or if I hoped I died.

FORTY-FIVE

HERMES

Every day for the past week, a group of immortals from the Underworld and I travel to South America to kill the Nosoi. From the moment the sun rises, I ready myself for battle. My role as messenger of the gods is untended, as my primary focus is defeating the Nosoi.

Stopping Styx.

Achilles, Atalanta, Thanatos and Hypnos are beside me each time, while Persephone and Hades take turns joining us in the fight. When Hades accompanies us, he brings an army of the dead, with rusted swords and an inability to die. Yet, no matter how many gods we bring to the battle-field, there are twice as many Nosoi birds the next morning. Whoever wields the power of the Nosoi remains a mystery, causing us to fight an uphill battle with no victory in sight.

Hecate is assisting us for the first time today. I clasp on my winged sandals as she stands beside me, lacing together knee-high, black heeled boots. Her legs are endless in the boots, matching a pair of leggings the same hue.

"Heels aren't the best shoes to wear during a fight," I say.

"Who knows? You might be more successful if I let you borrow some of my pumps." She smirks at me as she ties the top knot.

I cannot muster the same amusement at my failings. "One day, the immortal creating the Nosoi will show themselves." But I do not believe my lie, so I switch topics. "You promise the ball isn't happening?"

Tomorrow, the ball Aphrodite and Dionysus plan to host in Saffron and my honor will not happen. Hecate has assured me every day since I signed the divorce papers that my efforts worked and the ball is axed. Saffron will be safe at our home or within Olympus Industries, rather than at a ball surrounded by Styx's allies. They cannot get to her as easily now since the ball is canceled.

Even though my closest friend continues to tell me it worked, and the ball is over, there is a kernel of doubt growing inside me. I push down the fear as Hecate says, "I promise, it is canceled."

I force the words to sound real in my head. "Then, let's go."

Thanatos, Hypnos, Hades, Achilles, and Atalanta wait outside my bedroom door as Hecate and I exit. Thanatos holds his scythe tightly in his grasp, while his twin brother spins two daggers tipped in sleeping potions. Hades rests his helmet of invisibility underneath his armpit, an all-black sword points at the ground. Achilles and Atalanta, the two decomposed corpses in our group, are dressed in armor identical to the days when they were alive.

Hecate's magic whirls around us all, encapsulating us in her green mist. Before I am whisked away from the Underworld, my gaze wanders to the same spot it has every day since that cursed prophecy existed. I look at the River Styx, and Styx stares back. We are over two thousand feet away from each other, but I can still see the pride on her face, like she has already won.

I hate her.

It is the thought that drives me when Hecate lands us in the first South American country, Venezuela. Black and gray decomposing birds fly overhead, swooping down towards fleeing humans. There are three times the number of birds today than yesterday, but Hades raises one hand in the air and the ground crackles under his command. Bony hands pull themselves out of the ground. They creep their way towards the battleground even as flesh drips off their body like honey.

I push down the defeat already clamoring through me, and I let out a terrible battle scream. Caduceus materializes in my hand, and I take flight. I rush towards the birds, swinging Caduceus. My staff smacks into skulls, deteriorating the bone with one hit. They fall like raindrops, crashing on the ground they've tainted with their presence. I continue to swing my weapon. I destroy dozens when thousands, maybe millions, fill the dying country.

It takes hours, as millions poison the air, but soon the ground is littered in their cindered remains.

Next, Hecate transports us to Colombia. Millions of Nosoi spread their diseases across the failing lands, and millions of Nosoi die by our blades and magic. Then, we're off to Ecuador, Peru, and then Bolivia. We kill Nosoi by the hundreds of millions in Paraguay, Chile, Argentina, and Uruguay. The sun sets by the time we finish destroying the Nosoi in Brazil, and in the nighttime, we decimate the diseased birds in French Guiana and Cayenne.

Our bodies are sore and our weapons are drenched in black blood when we end the last Nosoi in Guyana. Hades takes off his helmet, appearing beside me as I stand with the doctor in the town with the highest casualty rate. Eighty-seven percent of humans have fallen and died in this little town in Guyana, and the doctor in front of me shows the first signs of his own ailment. Brown lesions curve his jaw, hidden slightly behind a patchy beard.

"Thank you," the man says with a bow. He doesn't lift his head, but I can hear the dreadful hope in his voice as he asks. "Again tomorrow?"

"We will be back tomorrow," I say.

The doctor's tears drip onto the ground. "Thank you."

We fill the infirmary tent, where Asclepius hurriedly works, with medicine of his own creation. Asclepius is the god of medicine, known for creating healing tonics of rapidly outstanding success. Yet, it barely lessens the pain of the incurable disease, but it is something. Asclepius, god of medicines and son of Apollo, barely spares us a glance as he rushes from patient to patient, sweat dribbling down the sides of his face. But I can see the truth in this room.

If the Nosoi do not go away for good, this entire town will be dead by the end of the week.

"Are you ready?" Hecate asks, half her body inside the tent. "I'm going to transport the rest of us out of here."

"I'm going to help Asclepius for a while," I say. "You all can go."

Hecate wants to say more, but she doesn't. She nods her head, wishes me a good night, and leaves with everybody else. I stay with Asclepius, applying ointments to the disease riddled bodies. Holding hands and accepting prayers from the dying who want a god's blessing before leaving this world. I wrap gauze around the arms and legs of patients whose skin is decomposing while their heart still beat.

Until the first sign of sunrise, I am here.

On my flight home to the Underworld, I stop at my old house with Saffron. I fly beside our bedroom window, where Saffron sleeps in our bed alone. She does not know that today's destiny could be the start of a war that will destroy this world. She slumbers, looking as beautiful as ever, without knowing that a prophecy promises her endless pain.

"I'm sorry," I whisper to the bedroom window, knowing Saffron cannot hear my words but needing to say them, anyway.

I fly to the Underworld, where I clean myself, eat breakfast, and begin again.

FORTY-SIX

HART SOMMERS

T he night of the ball is here.

A day when a war between Styx and the gods begins, where victory is uncertain, but Saffron's sacrifice is unavoidable. Aphrodite and I get ready together, her joyous laughter contradictory to my growing dread. She makes jokes and tells stories of her sordid past, and I force out laughter as the pit in my stomach worsens.

Aphrodite dons a flower headband. My long hair is curled, with a braid encircling the left side of my head. A golden chain interweaves with the braid. The colors match the gold, feather necklace I never take off. Now that the rust is gone because of Aphrodite's magic, the necklace gleams from the sunlight peeking through the windows. It looks just as it had when my father first gifted it to me.

Our dresses, which we picked out together two days before, are gorgeous garments. Hers is a strapless, pale pink, tulle gown that has a corset top. Mine is floor length, made of silk, and is burnt orange. It is a sleeveless garment, with thin straps and a slit that ascends my left leg. The gowns are exquisite, but beauty does not negate the gnashed truth awaiting tonight.

There are three knocks on the door, then two women stroll inside.

The first goddess is Saffron, who wears a blood red gown accented in gold embroidery. She is the only one whose gown has sleeves that expose her shoulders and drape down the length of her arms like a cape. The golden embroidery cinches her waist, giving her voluptuous figure an hourglass appeal. Her lips are painted red, hair a combination of curls and braids. She is radiant. A queen without a crown.

But it's the same gown I saw in my vision.

The one she wears when she walks down to the Underworld.

To Styx.

The second goddess is Iris. Her hair is in a beehive-shaped bun, the brown of her hair intermingling with streaks of magenta and periwinkle pink. Her gown is pastel and displays every color of the rainbows she manifests. The strapless dress is corseted in the front and adorned with flowers. The bottom half expands and stops right before her ankles. Glittery makeup lines her dark skin, starting at the curve of her forehead down to the length of her jawline.

Iris rushes towards Aphrodite first, clasping each other's hands and cooing over the others' appearances. Saffron walks towards me. I moved into Apollo's house right after we cemented our relationship, but Lowell stayed with Saffron. In the past week, I have visited him three times, but after his nose started to wither, I couldn't look at him without a sharp pain of guilt.

"He's alright." She answers the question before I ask. "Argus is staying with him tonight, making sure nothing happens to him."

"And so Argus does not stop you," I say.

For the first time, I witness Saffron's smile in person. It is tinier than the ones I witnessed when I took Apollo's hands and saw their past, but it's present. The corner of her red lips tips upwards and she smirks.

"I'm glad the Fates gave Apollo a wise soulmate. Gods knows he needs a partner with common sense."

"Thank you," I say.

For she is the reason I get a future with Apollo. Saffron is right. If I join her in the Underworld like I originally intended, I will die. If she didn't know the truth and went to Styx without me, then today would have been the last day of my life.

Lowell's life, too.

The smile on her face wavers. "If you feel something is amiss tonight, or have any bad feeling, find Apollo or Iris. She will stay by your side whenever Apollo isn't there, but do not stay unattended." Saffron goes into the pocket I didn't know was in her dress, and she pulls out a rolled-up piece of paper. "Here is the list of everybody to avoid at the ball. If they so much as look at you, tell Iris and she will take you away."

I take the paper, unroll it, and see a list of thirty gods and goddesses. There are some names I expected on this list, like Khione and Nemesis, but there are dozens more I did not expect. Two of the Muses, Erato and Urania, are scribbled on this piece of paper. Priapus, a low-level fertility god, is there; Peitho, the female personification of persuasion, is too.

"Holy gods," I gasp, taking in all the names of those who are ready to start a war against Zeus and the Olympians.

"Keep that list well hidden. Iris has seen it, but nobody else," Saffron says.

"Because even you do not know who you can trust?" I ask.

She doesn't answer. "Do you have a pocket in that dress?" Stiffly, I nod. "Good, put it there and don't show anybody until you must. Okay?"

"I got it," I whisper.

"Why do you two look so depressed over there?" Aphrodite asks. "Today is a celebration!"

Saffron glares at Aphrodite, any semblance of a smile gone. "Let's just go," she says.

Aphrodite ignores Saffron's annoyance, grabs Iris, and leaves the bedroom in a rush. Saffron and I follow, moving down the staircase and out the door, where Apollo waits with a golden chariot.

He compliments my outfit with a crème suit and an orange tie. His curly blonde hair is pushed back, one curl left untamed and hanging over his forehead. The moment he sees me, a widespread grin encompasses his face. He stares at me like this moment is the greatest of his life. My heart skips a beat, for nobody is as perfect as Apollo.

"There aren't enough words to describe how beautiful you look, μέλι."

He helps me into the chariot, sitting me nearest the door, and once everybody is inside, we soar into the sky toward Dionysus's mansion. Aphrodite laughs and Apollo kisses my hand, both oblivious, while the rest of the chariot expects a war.

FORTY-SEVEN

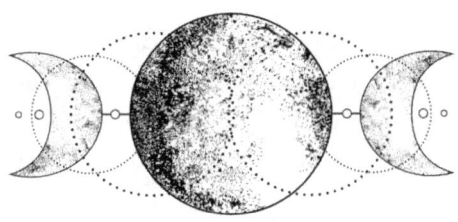

HECATE

I have both dreaded and anticipated today. On the eighty-eighth day of the eighty-eighth year since Saffron became a goddess, all my deceit will be revealed. I must emerge from the shadows of my treachery and blatantly betray every immortal I have called friends for millennia. If only they had allowed me to be happy and in love, then I would not have to harm them.

But alas, Styx is my only way to Mastiff.

So, today, my friends must fall.

I easily convince both Hades and Persephone to join in the massacre of the Nosoi. They do not know I am the one coming back each sunrise and manifesting more Nosoi than the day before. They let me fight beside them, killing the same birds I create to weaken the gods. To drive Saffron towards self-defeat.

We are in Brazil when the sun sets, and the ball is about to begin. I destroyed every invitation belonging to an immortal in the Underworld and blocked Iris's messages.

My friends save the humans in South America, oblivious to the carnage awaiting their loved ones at Dionysus's mansion tonight. They believe they are saving lives when they are aiding Styx and me in our journey towards her eternal reign.

My magic slices off the head of a bird nearing Hermes's face, its beak an inch away from cutting his cheek, but then I lower my hands. I murmur an incantation, silently apologizing as my magic grows like fog across the ground. Only Hermes is flying in the air; the rest of our friends are on the dirt ground.

Persephone stops first, spinning around to face me with confusion crinkling her dark, narrow brows. "What is this?" she asks without accusation in her voice. Even as the mist grows, sliding up her legs and around her torso, she does not believe I am betraying her. She trusts me so much that even when Thanatos and Hypnos cough next to her, she doesn't assume the worst. Instead, she repeats. "What is this? A way to stop the Nosoi?"

Persephone knows better, but she has the warmest heart. Hypnos falls to his knees first, hands wrapping around his throat as he tries to fight my magic and fails. He collapses on the ground, unable to wake. Only then does Persephone push aside her disbelief and finally sees me for who I am. Hades rips off his helmet, coughing and wheezing. But he does not stop. He sees his wife in danger, and despite the magic pulling him under, he stumbles towards Persephone and me.

Thanatos has fallen, and with Hades's powers depleting, the undead crumble into a pile of bones. Achilles and Atalanta last the longest amongst the dead, striding towards me with swords raised, but before they can reach me, they dissolve, too. Back to the Underworld, where their king and queen will not join them.

"What is the meaning of this?" Hades asks, voice ragged as the mist rises, covering most of their faces.

"I did not wish for her to be my last resort," I say. My voice breaks, but not because of my mist. The tiniest prick of regret hits me when Persephone stumbles into Hades, and they both tumble onto the ground together. His arms are wrapped around his wife's, unsuccessfully shielding her from the fog. "But you wouldn't let me bring him back to life."

"Who?" he asks.

But Persephone's face falls with realization. "The human slave," she says. She has more to say, but a round of raucous coughs seizes her words.

I blame the tears building up in my eyes on my magic, which constricts my vision. Both Hades and Persephone are hazy figures. "He was my soulmate, and you wouldn't let me have him back." I hiccup and add. "She will let me have him back. She will let me turn him into a god."

They never respond. Both Hades and Persephone fall into the deep sleep my magic lulled them into. If devastation didn't wrack my body, I would find ironic humor because I put the god of sleep, Hypnos, into a magic-induced slumber. Fought him with his own powers.

Hermes cannot see what is happening below because of the mist, so when I take it away, I transport the unconscious bodies into the infirmary tent. They will not awaken, and neither will the humans and doctors who fell to my magic hours ago. There is only Hermes and me now.

Unlike Persephone, Hermes trusts no one anymore. It was so easy to convince him to avoid his wife because of his mistrust. It is how I could get him to go along with the façade that he and I were having an affair, which led to his divorce. Now, as he lands on the ground, his suspicious stare wanders from the empty battlefield, the dead soldiers' bones, and then me.

He takes two seconds. That's it. Two seconds to stop seeing me as a dear friend and former love. Two seconds for him to realize I am the one who has viciously betrayed him.

"Why?" he rasps out, the sound harsh and decimated.

I move towards him. "I warned you she was not your soulmate. Your destined third love, but you did not listen to me."

My heeled boots pierce the wet ground with each step, another stab to the back of my former friends. Hermes glowers at me but doesn't retreat. He stands firmly on the ground, even when I am chest-to-chest with him. He flinches, but doesn't smack my hand away as I reach for him. Sink my red-tipped fingernails into his chin.

I force him to follow the movement of my lips as I say. "You are not her heart, and so you were destined to break. The divorce was inevitable. I only quickened its pace."

"I thought you were my friend." He spits his words across my face. "I loved you and trusted you."

"And I will always love you," I say honestly. "But I love Mastiff more. I tried to warn you on Mt. Olympus all those years ago. I tried to give you hints of my deceit so it would hurt less when the day came."

Realization dawns on him fast and true. "The story about your soulmate."

I nod my head. "If you can believe me, I am sorry. Hurting you was one of the last things I wanted to do. It has been the part I dreaded most."

Before he can respond, I press my lips against his for one last time. I flick my tongue against his bottom, forcing his mouth open just enough to let the sleeping magic enter. He freezes for a second, unsure how to respond, but then he pushes me. Hard.

I stumble back a few feet, one strand of hair falling from my high-risen bun. By the time I move that piece of hair out of my face, Hermes collapses on the ground.

"If it is any consolation," I say to my friend's unconscious body, believing he cannot hear me. "Today is the last day I infect the world with the Nosoi. Styx only wanted to incite Saffron's fear and make her feel like there was no other option but her. The Nosoi were only one out of the three instruments Styx used against Saffron. It was just a lucky coincidence that the Nosoi also kept you away from Saffron."

The worst is over, and as my former friends slumber in Brazil, I transport myself across the world to Ares. He sits around a campfire with his sons, Phobos and Deimos, and a group of huntresses. They pass around a canteen while Deimos tells a story about a goat, a ghost, and a farmer. It has one rambunctious huntress laughing so hard water comes out of her nose.

Then Ares sees me, and his smile vanishes.

All their happiness dissipates.

The older huntresses, who wear scarification marks of the past, glower at me. They see me as a monster, instantly untrustworthy, and I hate to admit it, but they are accurate in their assumption. I am the worst one here. Newer huntresses look between the others and me with confusion, not fully recognizing who I am. They know I am a goddess, but not why my presence sours the surrounding air.

The scattered traitors in their midst pointedly ignore my presence. Those huntresses, who gave me the coordinates to find their camp, sit amongst their sister in arms. Patiently waiting for an order to strike. They look anywhere than where I stand, fearing looking at me will tell the others of their treachery.

"Ares," I say. "I need to talk to you in private."

Ares has never liked me. Terrible recognizes terrible, and his apprehension of me has only grown since our captivity together under Kronos. Just as I learned a secret about him in those cages, he started the learn the truth about me, too.

Hesitantly, he says. "Why do I need to do that? My sons and the huntresses are great company. It would be a shame to leave them and be stuck alone with you."

"It's Saffron," I say.

Normally, the quick-witted god of war is blind when it comes to Saffron. His mistrust of me dissipates. He believes he hides his affections for her well, but I was there with him on Mt. Olympus when we were all tortured by Kronos. I saw the way he flinched each time Saffron's name was uttered. The way he glowered at Hermes with barely contained jealousy, which the latter was oblivious to.

Ares loves Saffron in a blinding, all-consuming fashion, and it is his greatest weakness. Perhaps that is why I haven't seen him around her recently. He knows she is his Achilles' heel, and when you are the god of war, having a known weakness is death on the battlefield.

"What about her?" he asks, but worry is evident in his voice.

"We need to go to her. She needs you."

The lie is terrible and barely planned out. One of the

few huntresses I know by name, Sika, crosses her arms over her chest and raises an eyebrow. She is skeptical of my lie, but it does not matter if she follows my words. I only care about Ares, who stands to his feet and brushes the dirt off his pants.

He says to Phobos. "Continue the story. I should be back soon."

Before he can move towards me, Sika says. "Ares, wait."

"What?" he asks, spinning around.

Sika glowers at me, not at him. "I can come with you."

I cannot wait until I can kill them all, starting with this huntress and the blonde one on Ogygia. Placing my hands behind my back, they cannot see the way my hands curl into fists. I betted on Ares's blind devotion to Saffron, but I never considered the huntresses. I should know better than to underestimate them after the stunt the blonde one, Lamb, pulled on the island. Yet, here I am, underestimating another one.

"Hurry, Ares," I say, trying to make my voice sound urgent. "We have to be quick. She needs you *now*."

Ares never responds to Sika but rushes towards me. She stands, watching with apprehension as he furthers himself from her and nears me. It is difficult to hide my satisfaction as I stare at the resilient huntress. He grabs my arm, and the glare I give the huntress tells the words I cannot speak aloud. *I win this round.*

As I transport us away, Sika has an arrow placed on her bow. She is ready to strike me down. Ares and I are gone before the arrowhead can touch my skin.

Before Saffron, Ares would have known this is a trap, but he hears her name and sprints to her without examining his surroundings. Unlike Sika, he does not realize his imminent danger until we are in the basement of my home on Earth, and he is locked in a cage wrapped in my magic. The same poison I gave the others floods Ares's cell. Fills his nostrils and has him staggering to the floor.

"You bi-"

Before he can finish the insult, he is unconscious.

Waiting to be used for further instruction.

But my night is not over. I spin my hand above my head, and I materialize a sheer, floor-length silver gown. I accessorize with diamond earrings and two bracelets on one wrist. My makeup is complete with red-painted lips, and I transport myself to my final act of treachery for the night.

I arrive at Dionysus's mansion.

FORTY-EIGHT

SAFFRON

When gods live forever, the boredom of a never-ending existence is momentarily replaced with gossip. Hundreds of immortals frolic across the dance floor, or sip on a glass of wine, but all of them are looking at me. They see me walking down the long staircase with Iris instead of Hermes. By the growing smirk on Hera's face, one she attempts to hide behind a flute of champagne, the whispers have already begun. Whispers she started when the divorce papers returned to her.

"Why is everybody staring at us?" Iris asks. I do not respond, but she does not stop. When we reach the last step, she asks. "Where is Hermes?"

"It doesn't matter," I say the grandest lie. He may no longer be my husband, but Hermes will forever matter, even if the thought of seeing him right now makes me physically ill. "Keep an eye on Hart all night. If you even think one traitor is coming towards her-"

"Don't worry about me," Iris says. A waiter flutters by with a tray of red wine. She plucks up two glasses, passes one to me, and clinks the drinks together. "I will protect her with my life. Just get Artemis back home."

I do not know what has transpired between Artemis and Iris, but it's something powerful. I know Iris's desperation to get Artemis back from Ogygia outweighs her rationality. She does not question why I need her to monitor Hart, why Hermes is not here at our anniversary ball, or how I will get Artemis back by the end of the night. Her need for Artemis's safety makes her the perfect goddess to help me because she will never question my motives until it is too late.

She will not realize I am gone until I am already under Styx's claws.

Apollo and Hart follow shortly behind us down the staircase, but they are not paying attention to us. Nervousness and excitement are whirling together in her widening eyes as she takes in the surrounding scene. As she always does when she is nervous, Hart twiddles with the gold-feather dangling around her neck. Apollo looks only at her, watching her face with a widening grin of his own. I have never seen a male as happy as Apollo is right now, and the sight pulls at a piece of my heart.

But like all beautiful sights, time ruins them.

Out of my periphery, Zeus's hulking frame comes into view. Beside him is Hera, in a plum, floor-length gown and a diadem more extravagant than usual. It is almost a foot tall and gives the appearance that Hera is taller than her petite five-foot one frame. Zeus's outfit clashes with hers as he sports a white suit with bright orange accessories. If their unhappy union is not clear in the way they distance from each other while saddled side-by-side, then their outfits display the truth.

"You might want to get closer to them," I say to Iris, nodding my head toward Apollo and Hart. They move towards the dance floor. He spins her body close to his. "And away from Zeus and Hera."

Iris glances at Hera, her primary boss, and quickly leaves before they get too close. I wish I can run away, too. Escape the unavoidable conversation from the biological father, who wishes I died as a human, and the step-mother, who continues to beg for my death.

"You look lovely today," Zeus says.

"Thanks."

Hera clicks at the root of her mouth. "Why are we having this get-together when you returned your signed divorce papers to me the day before?" She takes in the extravagance intended to be in honor of my eighty-fifth marriage anniversary with Hermes. Disapprovingly, Hera adds. "Why must we celebrate failure?"

"What would be preferred, Hera? To stay in a marriage that is lethal to us both, or to end it and find true happiness?"

I am not talking about Hermes and me. My questions are a jab to her marriage to Zeus. A miserable union in every way. Hera frowns, but not with the same level of anger that I typically expect from her. Humiliation fuels the downturn of her lips.

"Why must you two always argue?" Zeus asks, exasperated.

I ignore him and say to Hera. "I believe I made the right choice, given my circumstances. One day, I hope you will find the courage to admit divorce isn't failure, but freedom."

Her face reddens with fury, and if I look close enough, embarrassment. "You believe just because you are-"

"What are we talking about here?" An amused voice interjects, arm wrapping around my shoulders. Dionysus smiles down at me, dimples more apparent than ever. "I hope it is about how smoking hot you look in this dress because, my gods, you are stunning. Red is beguiling on you."

"No," Hera snaps. "We were talking about how much of a disappointment-"

"You caught me. I don't actually care." Dionysus takes a step back and extends a hand to me. "Please, you gorgeous vixen, make my day and dance with me."

"If you'll excuse me." I do not spare Hera or Zeus a second glance as I take Dionysus's hand and move towards the dance floor. "Thank you," I say.

"Ariadne is the one who made sure I came to your aid. She said that if I did not help you, she would only let me have three lovers instead of six. How can I be the god of orgies if I only have three lovers?"

He spins me on the dance floor, and when I am brought back to his chest, I cannot help but laugh. "You two have the oddest marriage."

His grin is blinding. "Why, thank you."

As we dance, I observe the room, waiting for two particular attendees to arrive. Nemesis is the first of the two, wearing a black gown and her hair up in a braided crown. She momentarily glances at me, but when she finds my eyes already on her, she quickly looks away. My eyes follow her as she descends the stairs and across the room to the bar.

The farthest spot from where I dance with Dionysus.

"Would you do a favor for me? One without questions?" I ask Dio.

"Now, I'm intrigued. Tell me what this favor with no questions involves. Does it involve you, me, and a closet?" Dionysus leans in and teases. "Because I have had several fantasies about such an event."

"I was thinking of you, the closet, and Nemesis."

"Nemesis." He ponders the thought and says. "I could dabble a second time with Nemesis. Do you have a particular closet in mind? The closet nearest is next to the bathroom on the second floor. It has a treasure chest with lots of fun-"

"That one works. Just don't finish your sentence." I pull away from our dance. "She is at the bar in a black dress. And thank you again."

"For you, I would do almost anything." Dionysus pulls my hands up to his lips, kissing both on the knuckles, and ventures towards Nemesis.

Almost as soon as Dionysus leaves my side, another god asks for a dance. Each time one song ends, another god takes over, prancing the subject of the ball around the dance floor. Yet, my eyes never wander to them. I focus on Dionysus and Nemesis instead. They drink together, laugh together, and then head up the staircase hand-in-hand towards the second floor closet as instructed.

"Where is Hermes?" the god I am currently dancing with, Aristaeus, asks.

"Can't tell you," I answer.

Aristaeus laughs like I told a joke, spinning me out and

back into his arms. He is a proficient dancer, but the entire time, I remember Hermes and my first dance within the gazebo at his old home. That was one of my favorite days in existence, and now every time I move to music, I think of that night. The feel of Hermes's body against mine, the nervousness radiating off both of us as we experienced a type of love we never knew before.

Now, that dance is a reminder that Hermes and I are no longer Hermes and me. He is continuing his string of lies, perhaps with Hecate by his side. Meanwhile, I am living a dreadful existence, where I trust nobody. Not even the god who promised me honesty and love forever.

A hulking figure in tattered jeans and an over-worn shirt stands at the top of the staircase. He takes my attention away from Aristaeus. Without waiting until the song is over, I pull myself away from Aristaeus and march towards Gareth French. He looks dreadfully out of place in a ball of sophistication and formal attire. Although I sent him a suit in his size, he has chosen to stand before me in his everyday attire.

"Where is she?" Gareth asks, not caring about introductions and formal conversation. I lead him towards the same closet Dionysus brought Nemesis to fifteen minutes prior. "Is she in there?" he asks, pointing to the closed door where the sounds of her and Dionysus's seep out.

"Yes."

He kicks down the door. Dionysus lets out a terrible scream, plucks up his shirt and throws it over his body. "If you wanted to watch, you could have asked nicely," Dionysus says. "My poor door."

Nemesis pulls down her dress, then looks between

Gareth and me with confusion at first, then with terrible realization. "The oracle was right."

"Get out, Dio," I say.

"Getting out." He shuffles passed Gareth and me, careful to step over the door, then he looks back and asks. "Who should I bill the broken door to?" Nobody answers. "Got it. I'll just go."

Soon, the only sound in the closet are Nemesis's heavy breaths. She crumbles onto her knees, hands clasped together. She stares up at me like I am the only goddess in the room. One she must pray to for salvation. But salvation is long lost for her.

"What do you wish for her fate to be?" I ask him.

There is still hesitation on his face. He is still uncertain I am not his family's murderer, even after I gave him proof. It is difficult to dissuade your first belief. No matter how evidence lines up against another. He clenches and unclenches his fists, silent as Nemesis weeps.

"She stabbed my wife eighty-seven times," Gareth says. His voice is inexplicably low and guttural with grief. "My daughter had twenty-seven knife wounds. I want one hundred and fifteen bones, the same amount as the marks she left on my family. On my world."

"The oracle was right. The oracle was right."

Nemesis says the words repeatedly. Sometimes, they come out in yelps, other times they are muffled murmurs. She never explains her sentence, and I do not care to ask. She does not stop saying that one sentence until I lift my hands and rip the first bone from her body. Then all she does is scream. None of the guests can hear her over the loud music and raucous laughter. Even if they could hear her, there would be no mercy.

One by one, I rip out bone after bone.

Gareth whispers the numbers as I go.

"Fifty-seven, fifty-eight."

I once swore I would not kill again. Not after my heart shattered after my last murder. I promised myself I would not become like the other gods, flippantly killing without a second thought or a morsel of remorse. I swore I would be better than them, but my magic is designed to kill. Nemesis's gold blood splatters across the room, painting my face and blending into my gown. I try to find a part of myself that feels bad about my actions.

I cannot find them.

The last of my naivety dead.

"One hundred and fourteen," he says.

Nemesis isn't alive anymore. She lays in a heap of muscles and blood, but I still take her skull. It is the last bone I rip from her body, placing it between Gareth and my feet.

"Your family is avenged," I say without looking away from Nemesis's bloody skull. He, too, stares down at the proof of her death. "They live a peaceful afterlife in Elysium Fields. When your eventual day comes, you will join them in the tranquility."

"And her?" he asks. "Will she be there?"

I shake my head. "Nemesis will never experience peace with this death. A death delivered by me is voidness. No Underworld. No Elysium Fields."

He does not thank me, but he picks up the skull and walks towards the exit.

"And Gareth?" I say. He turns around. "No more protestors at my gates."

"No more protestors unless I find out you lied," he says.

Then he is gone.

I stay in this closet a little while longer, taking in the catastrophe I created. In the past, I mourned every life I had taken, but now there is a gaping emptiness settling in my stomach. I do not bother wiping the blood off my face as I step out of the closet. A few workers see me and respond with apprehension. They glance at the ichor painting my pale flesh, but I ignore them and move to the railing.

For possibly the last time, I look down at the dance floor. I wordlessly say goodbye to everybody in my life as they unwittingly enjoy the last night before an unspeakable war begins.

Psyche and Eros waltz together, but her head rests against his chest and she lets him guide every movement. Their love is clear, even from where I stand. Zeus and Hera are on the dance floor as well, but their dance isn't a proclamation of love, like Eros and Psyche. Instead, they scream at one another every time Zeus's eyes curiously wander towards another person.

Poseidon and Amphitrite are drunk, stumbling over each other's feet as they attempt to dance. Poseidon accidentally throws her across the room when trying to pick her up mid-dance. She stumbles to her feet a few seconds later with a widespread grin on her face.

From here, I can read her lips as she says. "Do that again."

Hephaestus and Aphrodite glide around the room, only hindered slightly by his limp. Her figure changes with each spin of their bodies, while her pale pink dress stays the same. Hephaestus stares at his wife with wonderment, while her gaze meanders with the same perusal as Zeus's. I even see her wink at a female server.

Last, I see Apollo and Hart. He holds her face with both of his hands, and he leans down to press a kiss on her lips. The truest love cherished beneath the chandelier lights. With them as my last image, I use my powers to transport myself away from the ball.

In a tornado of powdered bones, I leave and venture towards the Underworld.

Towards Styx.

FORTY-NINE

HART SOMMERS

I have lain witness to Apollo and Saffron's magnanimous houses, which span acres. Rich with artwork and excellence. I have seen the brilliance of Olympus Industries. Witnessed both the illustrious sophistication of its offices and the glorious garden waiting to be awed in the background. Within this short time in the gods' orbit, I have experienced the greatest sights, but Dionysus's house is my favorite of all.

The front yard spans two miles before reaching the marble steps of the mansion. Freshly cut grass twined with pine trees is the first thing I see as we pass through the white gates. A story is told within his front yard of debauchery, excitement, and love.

Statues weave through the yard, varying from laughing, marbled people with open mouth and grapes dangling above. Others show the story of how Dionysus met his wife, Ariadne. Plucking her from an island and making her his wife. A story of heartbreak is told, too, though I do not understand its origins. Two statues of men, hands pulling apart as one bids farewell, nears the entrance. It's clear by the carved tear that the man who leaves never returns home. The man who does not return is wrapped in vines, except for where his hand reaches out for the other.

Apollo may be the god of the arts, but Dionysus uses statues to tell his own tales, and I think it is beautiful.

The chariot stops right in front of the fifty steps leading to the house's double doors. Dionysus's house is the same marble color as the steps and the statues, but ivy and grape vines scour the columns holding up the front porch. They slither across the steps, decorating the plain home with dark shades of green.

Wine fountains are on either side of the staircase in both red and white. Halfway up the staircase, Apollo leans over, cups his hands, and scoops up a handful of white wine. The others continue ascending to the ball, but I stay with Apollo. He turns his body and extends his hands towards me.

"It will be the greatest wine you've ever tasted."

I lean forward, drinking the wine from his hands, and the bitter sweetness soothes my tongue. He is right; I have tasted no wine quite like this. It is both sweet yet bitter. Soft yet poignant. A moan escapes from my lips as I drink the wine, and when it falls from Apollo's opening hands, he reaches for me and presses his mouth against mine.

It is a chaste kiss, but when he pulls away, he hums. "The greatest wine I have ever tasted."

When we reach the top of the staircase, two men in crisp tuxedos grab hold of the serpent-shaped doorknobs and invite us inside. They bow at us as we walk, as if I am the equivalent of a god, because I have my arm around an Olympian. I nod my head back at the two men.

"Welcome," a woman says upon our entry. She holds out a tray of white wine. "Would you like a glass?" she asks.

Another woman to our left says. "Or would you prefer red wine?"

The women wear the same crisp tuxedos as the men, both bowing just as the doormen had. Apollo plucks two glasses of white wine for us, giving me one before guiding me to the top of the staircase overlooking the ballroom. While I have never been to Mount Olympus, I doubt there is another sight as superlative as this.

The ballroom has the same alabaster sheen as the exterior of the house. A dozen diamond chandeliers hang from the ceiling, sparkling light upon the dance floor. The nine muses are on platforms suspended in the air, their gowns glittering like another chandelier in the sky. The room is all white apart from the guests, who dress in all shades of color. Even the rug runner on the staircase is cream colored, and I fear walking on it will dirty it.

We move down the staircase together, arms looped, and I cannot take my eyes away from the beauty of this moment. I am finally here, at the pinnacle of perfection, and yet I only feel dread.

Darkness, so ominous and dreary, weighs upon my chest, and I cannot free myself. I try to dismiss the darkness, to free myself from its heavy hold, but every attempt is futile. It ensnares me, promising I will never be free from the terror that will occur. I will suffer tonight, the onyx fog in my head warns.

I hear him say. "Hart."

I tilt my head towards him, seeing the sunlight in all its

splendor. I lean in close to him, my shoulder resting against his chest, and I revel in his scent of sunshine and honey. He guides me down the last steps, then onto the dance floor. Instead of observing my surroundings, I look up towards the gorgeousness of his face, designed just for my eyes, and realize I am in love. A love that is so otherworldly. Too quick yet just right.

I have loved many people, like my family and Lowell, but they differ from this sensation of electrifying every part of my body. Their love didn't transcend me into an entirely alternative universe, not like this. Those blue eyes, which are as clear as the sky on a perfect Sunday morning, twinkle with the same ardent affection as I have for him.

"Are you just going to stare at me all night, μέλι, or would you like to dance with me?"

There's a prick at the back of my neck, a jolt of shock that only comes when somebody is watching me. We are one of the first couples on the dance floor, and I am unfamiliar to most immortals in this room. I am a spectacle to a few curious gods, but I know most who stare at me are working with Styx. Without looking up, I know a few Muses are observing Apollo and me from their place ten feet in the air. Some with curiosity, but most with an explicit order to make sure I die tonight.

"Let's dance," I say.

Time seems to disappear when he and I are on the dance floor. The motions between us are dripped in lust, passion, love, and everything in between. My feet burn in agony because of these heels, but I do not want to stop. I never want this moment to fade.

"I should have known." Apollo spins me towards him,

bodies joining and the scent of sunlight wrapping around me.

"Should have known what?"

He slows us down to a stop and grabs my face with both of his hands. "That you are exactly what the Fates spun for me from the moment I saw you in that adorable sundress. I have never witnessed something as peaceful as you."

"What?" I ask. The wording is so odd it pulls me back.

"Saffron once asked me if I had ever known peace, and I told her in all my eons alive, it was an impossibility. It simply did not exist, but I was so wrong. You, in this moment, are every bit of serenity rolled into one person. You are my peace and my salvation."

He pulls his lips into mine, and I am gifted with the same level of peace he speaks about. The world's issues fizzle away, and I am resplendent in his touch. The feel of his mouth against mine, our bodies pressed together. I know I will never find a moment as perfect as this one.

For minutes, hours, or days, we continue to dance. He introduces me to a few goddesses, like Amphitrite and Athena, but mainly keeps me to himself until Dionysus arrives. His hands are covered in gold blood, and he nervously says. "Po, I'm going to need you for some clean-up help."

"Clean-up help?" Apollo looks at Dionysus's bloodied hands, then up at Dionysus. "I thought Ares wasn't coming, so why is there so much blood?"

"Clean-up help, now." Dionysus grabs Apollo's hand, then says to me as he runs away with him. "Nice to meet you, human girl!"

Apollo shoots me an apologetic look, but he does not stop Dionysus from pulling him away. I watch Dionysus drag Apollo up the flight of stairs when Iris stands next to me.

"Want to get a drink?" she asks.

We are on our second glass of wine when the first inkling of danger arises. The nine muses sing in perfect harmony, so when two abruptly stop singing, the tune shifts.

Two Muses, Urania and Erato, take an advancing step away from their sisters. The two traitorous goddesses stand on the edge of their elevated platform. They tip their feet forward until they fall off the platform and towards the ground. Both flip in the air, and when they land with a cacophonous crash, they hold twin swords in their hands.

"All hail Queen Styx," they say.

Zeus steps forward, face reddening. "What is the meaning of this?"

"We need to go," Iris says. She wraps a hand around my arm, ready to transport us away, but she is stopped by a gust of green smoke.

The magic explodes in the center of the room. Gods in the nearest vicinity, like Eros and Psyche, are thrown across the room to make room for this omnipotent power. Iris tries to transport us away, but the magic stops us. We're trapped in a room full of enemies wishing me dead. The magic seeps through the entire ballroom. It slams the exit doors shut, boards up the windows, and materializes over a dozen weapons for various traitors in the room.

Priapus receives a double-bladed axe.

Khione gets an ice laden spear.

Peitho holds a newly manifested set of throwing knives.

Kratos wields a sword almost as large as my body.

"Hecate," Iris snarls with hatred lacing her tongue just

as a war breaks out in the middle of the dance floor. "She's working with Styx."

"What does that mean for us?"

"It means," Iris says with clenched teeth. "That this is going to be a bigger war than we thought."

FIFTY

HART SOMMERS

Hecate, the goddess of witchcraft and necromancy, is a figure of statuesque beauty and lethal devastation. She stands in an emerald cloud of her own creation, assessing the crowd of partygoers with an air of superiority. Like she can destroy us all with a snap of her fingers, even Zeus, who manifests twin lightning bolts in both his hands.

"What is the meaning of this, Hecate?" he asks.

"This is the beginning of your end."

He throws both lightning bolts, one right after the other, but as the bolt nears her, she manifests two green shields. Zeus's weapons bounce off her magic, slamming against the crown and shattering the alabaster floor. As he creates more, throwing one right after the other at her, she deflects them all while her eyes are roaming the crowd.

Iris grabs my hand. "Stay down," she says and pulls me forward. We crawl to the back of the bar, hiding alongside the two human bartenders. "She's here for you."

"How are you certain?" I ask.

"I'm not, but all the best strategists play on the side of paranoia. Until I hear her scream out her intentions for someone else, in my eyes, you are her target."

In a miniature rainbow of every shade of red, Iris materializes a six-foot-long staff. She is careful to turn the staff sideways, so the top does not alert Hecate of our hiding spot, but her weapon surprises me. Her affinity is a rainbow, which I have always associated with peace and happiness. The light after a storm.

But there is nothing calm about the rage curling her lips into a predatory scowl. No, she sits crouched on the ground beside me, but her body is tense, anticipatory of the battle polluting the festivities.

I cannot see anything from where I hide, but I hear the truth in all its grotesque glory. Lightning bolts catapult through the air, screams ricochet off the walls, and bodies fall onto the ground in great defeat. Swords meet swords, the cacophonous clink of steel echoing in a room of sorrow and death. Glass shatters. Chandeliers crash. Gods scream.

Iris slams a hand against my mouth, stifling any sound as a shadowy figure nears the bar, but she cannot curb the sounds of the frightened bartenders. One gasps, and the enemy is no longer a shadow. One muse, with her dress ripped short for easier fighting purposes, spins her dual swords with dark eyes focusing on where I hide.

Iris is right, they are here for me.

And she refuses to let them have me. Iris jumps to her feet, staff already swinging through the air towards the Muse's skull. Narrowly, the Muse tilts her head back; the staff hitting the air where her chin was a moment before.

She falls back into a crouching, fighting stance, dual swords still spinning, but her attention shifts to Iris.

The Muse smirks. "Just give me the Oracle and we don't have to do this."

"But you forget, Erato." Iris moves into a fighting stance, staff in a half-spun position. "I have been wanting to beat you to a bloody pulp for eons."

The Muse, Erato, screams as she rushes towards Iris, and Iris charges back. Both swords smash into the center of Iris's staff, which she holds at both ends. Their faces are an inch apart, snarling at one another with thousands of years' worth of discontentment. Iris jumps into the air, using the momentum to lift both her legs, and kicks herself off Erato's chest.

Erato soars across the room, body crumbling on top of a circular table. Iris lands on her feet, hair spinning through the air as she turns to face me. "Go to the back corner of the bar and make yourself invisible."

One bartender, a heavyset man, says. "Hide behind me."

Erato is standing up, brushing the table's wooden shards off her body as I crawl into the farthest corner. The bartender uses his larger height and build and sits in front of me. He still whimpers, appearing too frightened to move, but he shows a glimpse of bravery amid fear.

They rush towards each other, Iris pushing the fight further away from the bar while remaining close enough to run to my side if another danger arises. Swords swipe through the air faster than I have time to process, but Iris's staff matches Erato's speed each time. They are battling for more than just their lives or victory in this fight, but they duel with me as the prize. One craves my blood on the floor, while the other pushes her body to its limit so I can live another day.

My life is essential in a war, but I am nothing more than a damsel waiting for her rainbow-clad knight to save her. I hate sitting behind another shield, frighteningly waiting for others to fight the battle I will lead. That is the prophecy. The oracle against hatred. Me against Styx.

With the bartender pressing his back against the opening I hide behind, my vision is limited. Almost no light filters into this spot, so blindly, I move my hands around the ground. I search for a weapon of any sort, hoping for a wine opener but pricking my finger against a sharp, broken bottle instead. More gingerly this time, I drag my fingers up the length of the bottle until I find the neck, wrapping my hand tight around it.

A few minutes later, and a handful of cuts stinging on my arms and wrists, and I have a second broken wine bottle in my hand.

From where I hide, I can see a corner of the fight. Iris's rainbow-tinted staff is a bright spot in the darkening ball-room, and I easily find her spinning her staff above her head. She jumps away from Erato's sword as she thrusts it towards her stomach, but in Erato's distorted need for bloodshed, she ignores Iris's staff.

The top of the staff, with a partially pointed tip, slams into the top of Erato's head. Ichor splatters across the battleground, staining Iris and turning Erato's black hair gold. She stumbles a few feet, drops one of her dual swords. In the two seconds before the wound heals where she feels unimaginable pain, Iris strikes.

With a scream I can hear from my hiding spot, Iris swings her staff through the air. She clocks the side of

Erato's face. Her eyeball pops, not completely leaving the socket, but it holds on with sheer force. Before Erato can process the pain, Iris brings her staff down, then upwards until it heaves into the bottom of her opponent's chin.

Teeth fly with gold, but even after Erato collapses to the floor, Iris does not end her assault. I'm quickly learning that Iris's eyes and hair change color with her emotions. As she hits Erato again and again with her staff, her magenta streaks of hair and light pink eyes turn the darkest shade of gold. They match the color of Erato's massive blood loss as Iris hits and hits and hits.

When Erato's face is unrecognizable, her wounds so severe that not even a goddess can instantaneously heal, does Iris stop.

"Holy gods, I'm in love," the bartender hiding me says so quietly, I almost didn't hear his confession.

Her bronze skin is covered in Erato's blood, and with her now-golden eyes sparkling, she ensures I never underestimate her again. She should be the goddess of foxes, unsuspecting creatures until danger arises. Only then do they show the carnivorous bite of their canines.

But there is always someone larger, and hers comes barreling towards her with a double-edged axe raised.

"Behind you!" I yell.

Iris swings around just in time, her staff catching Priapus's blade. He moves faster than Erato, and as soon as their weapons clang together, Priapus slams his head forward. His forehead smashes into Iris's nose, causing her to stumble first.

I nudge the bartender hiding me. He looks down. "What?" he whispers.

"Here," I say, passing him one of the broken bottles. "Just in case."

His Adam's apple bobs, the fear re-settling. "Why are they trying to kill you?" he asks.

As soon as he takes the bottle, he wisely looks back at the fight. Once again, he pretends I am not here. Like he is not risking his life by protecting me. The other bartender, an older female, already ran away from us. He, however, stays. Risks his life for mine.

"I can see the future."

"Do you see how this ends?" he asks.

Quieter than I would like, I admit. "It doesn't work like that."

A breathy laugh, one that has no inch of humor inside it, leaves his lips. "I was hoping you would at least lie and tell me I will see my family again."

I wince. "Sorry."

"Only joking."

No, he isn't.

Iris wipes her nose, a heavy stream of ichor coating the back of her head. She spits at Priapus. "That wasn't very nice."

"Never said I was a nice guy."

They circle each other, neither one making another strike. Priapus is the suspected winner, both bigger and faster than Iris, but the latter does not seem convinced she will lose. She assesses her opponent with a level of concentration someone who knows they will lose doesn't display. Her nose is already healed, but the dried blood remains caked on her nose, lips, and chin.

"Why did you join her?" Iris asks.

The question confuses me. From the way she and Erato

fought, it was personal. It was a relationship that has been cemented over the eons, hardened into a weapon they both wielded in their fight. Iris doesn't have that same visceral reaction to Priapus. They look at each other more than strangers. It is friends-turned-enemies. Iris didn't ask Erato about her motivations, but she asks the god she hardly knows.

Why?

Priapus stops circling Iris. They stand perfectly still in a ballroom of jostling, fighting bodies. He answers. "I am nothing but a fertility god, barely remembered by the humans who are supposed to worship the gods. Worship me!" He screams the last two words. "I am a god, and they are weaklings. Meant to fear me. Meant to pray to me, just like they pray to gods like Zeus and Poseidon."

"You are better than Zeus and Poseidon," she says. "I've always known that about you. Your strength has always burned bright."

He grins at Iris, his sense of fight gone as his ego is stroked. "Exactly!" He yells. "I am worthy of a crown. Why should I live my eternity like this? So easily forgotten when I deserve a spot among the Olympians."

"What is she doing?"

I do not realize I ask my question aloud until the bartender answers. "She's being the goddess of my dreams. She is distracting him."

"Distracting him for what?"

He does not need to answer. Priapus is so preoccupied with his conversation with Iris that he stops paying attention to his surroundings. He continues to gloat about himself as Hera, the queen of the gods, creeps up from behind him. Raising the dagger in her hand.

"You know, I proposed to Saffron before Hermes," Priapus says. "That ungrateful brat turned me down, even after I showed her-"

Before he can finish his sentence, Hera stabs him in the back. He opens his mouth, ready to let out a scream, but then the craziest thing happens. He disappears. One second, Priapus stands in between Hera and Iris, but the next, he ceases to exist.

"The Dagger of Chains," I gasp.

Hera wipes the remnants of ichor across her already ruined gown.

"You have the Dagger of Chains?" Iris asks Hera, as bewildered as I am, that the dagger still exists.

The dagger is the invention of Daedalus, when he was a human, and Kronos. Daedalus, a brilliant inventor of Ancient Greece, started the creation of the Dagger of Chains to imprison gods. He wanted to tilt the power in the humans' direction, but he never found the last component to activate its powers.

Kronos did, and he imprisoned almost every god within that dagger.

His only mistake was not putting everybody within the dagger when he had the chance. Greed consumed Kronos, and instead of captivity, he demanded death from Saffron. As history has already told, Saffron decided Kronos deserved to die instead. The gods were freed from the Dagger of Chains, and then the textbooks end. They never told me how the gods were freed and what happened afterwards to this infamous dagger.

Clearly, Iris did not know the fate of the dagger, either.

Hera only shrugs. "What?" she asks. "I am the queen of the gods. Of course, I am the one who kept it."

Iris has more questions. It's clear on her face, but she suppresses them. Instead, she says. "Guard the opening of the bar, and don't let anybody get past."

Hera rears back, disgusted at Iris's words. "You are my messenger. My inferior. Who are you to-"

Iris runs to me, ignoring Hera's words. Despite her anger, Hera listens. With the Dagger of Chains tightly clutched in her hand, she stands in the opening and waits for more traitors to rush towards her. To fall under the dagger's vast powers.

Iris crouches down to the floor in front of the bartender. "Thank you," she says to him.

"I love you," he blurts out.

"How sweet, but I like women," Iris says, then asks me. "Do you have any ideas on how to break through Hecate's magic and get you out of here?"

"What?"

"Don't what me, you heard me."

"I don't get why you're asking me. I'm just a human."

"No," Iris says firmly. "You're not. You can see the future, which means you know the best outcome. I need you to tell me what to do next. They can't have you."

To anybody that might get past Hera, it appears like Iris is having a tense conversation with a scared bartender. I am so well hidden that Iris can barely make out my figure, her attention darting between my mouth, my forehead, and my shoulder.

"I don't know how to use my powers. Not really."

Iris tries not to show her impatience, but it seeps through the air like a pungent stench. "How have you tapped into your abilities before?" she asks.

"I need some help!" Hera yells.

Erato is awake again, fighting Hera alongside the other Muse, Urania. All it takes is one slash of the knife to imprison Urania or Erato, but Hera's fighting is sloppy compared to Iris's. She blindly swings the dagger back-and-forth, but this only momentarily stops the Muses. A third god, with ice-blonde hair and snake bite piercings, jumps on top of the bar with a sword gripped in both of his hands.

Iris joins him on the bar. She expertly kicks his feet out from under him and slams her spear into his neck. The Muses inch closer to Hera, and time is waning.

"Do you have a piece of paper and something to write with?" I ask.

A heavily used writing pad slides behind me, followed by a ballpoint pen.

And I draw, begging the Fates that this works.

FIFTY-ONE

HART SOMMERS

top shaking, I curse to myself, to little avail.

Each smooth line is an unidentifiable zig-zag across the writing pad. Beneath the roars of battle, I cannot focus on a single image. I am drawing without a target, attempting to make circles and creating scribbles instead. The back of the bartender's neck drips with sweat, his fear mounting higher and higher, and soon it'll be too high to come down from.

I have never considered myself a brave person. When others run from trouble, I join them. The Fates are cruelly gifting me the role of the heroic oracle when I am a coward. So, I think of this nameless bartender. My hands move across the worn-down paper, already indented with his scratchy penmanship. I stare at the back of his head, never looking down at what I create.

I force myself to think of him, this bartender with more courage today than I have had in my entire life. It is the real reason I made that deal with Styx. I love Lowell, who is part of my family, but the truth is I am a coward. I couldn't say the word *no* in front of two goddesses, but he could have. A sword lodges in the middle of the mirror behind the bar. Shards of glass fly everywhere, but he doesn't move. A piece slices across his cheek, but he doesn't flinch.

He continues to hide me, continues to risk his life, and for that, I focus on him. I use his strength, his courage, and it guides my hand. Slowly, as green magic and gold blood fall from the ceiling like raindrops, a familiar fog overtakes my vision. My hand quickens its pace on the writing pad, breaking the flimsy, cheap paper, but it doesn't matter.

I see it all.

Every doomed battle plan plays in my mind. There are ones where we are victorious, but the bartender dies. Another where I die, with Apollo holding me and begging for me to live. Then, finally, I see a way for us all to live. I witness our victory. When the fog dissipates, my magic of foresight gives me our tool for survival. I look down at the writing pad. Nothing on the page makes sense, not the harsh slashes or the random circles at the corners. It doesn't matter.

I tap on his shoulder.

"You got a way out of here?" he asks.

"Switch spots with me."

"What?" The bartender whips his head around. "You are supposed to hide."

"Gregory," I say his name. The one he never gave me. He does not wear a name tag, and there is not a wayward ID on the ground. I know his name with only my abilities guiding the answer. First, shock widens his eyes, but then there is understanding. "You are going home tonight with blessings from the gods, as long as you switch spots with me."

Gregory is almost six and a half feet tall. He takes a considerable amount of time, twisting and wincing, but he eventually squeezes into the cove. Now, it is me who sits in front of him, barely blocking his hiding spot. It does not matter if I truly cover him because he is not the primary target. None of these gods care about another human, especially when the oracle sits in front of him with only a broken bottle as a weapon.

"When you see a god rushing down this aisle, use that broken bottle and slice his heel. It is all you have to do," I say as I stand up to my feet.

"Okay," he says in the quietest voice, almost completely drowned out by the screams of the battleground.

"Iris!"

"What?!"

Scars litter her biceps, healing and re-forming like a brutal dance. The god fighting Iris has her barely balancing on the bar top, the soles of her feet dangling off the edge, but she doesn't stop. She never takes her focus off her opponent, but I cannot say the same for him. The god turns his almost-white eyes on me, interest alive, and runs his tongue over his snake bites.

This one second is all Iris needs to defeat him. With his predatory stare on me, ready to leap on me and abandon Iris, she swings her staff. It smashes into his kneecaps, breaking them instantaneously. He lets out a scream as he collapses, then falls off the bar, body splaying on the dance floor.

"We only have a few seconds before he gets back up. What is the plan?" Iris asks.

"Don't let Apollo save me."

Her eyebrows crunch together. "That's not very specific."

"You'll understand."

I jump onto the bar and stand beside her, but she is not my focus. I stare up at the ceiling instead, where Hecate remains on her cloud of green smoke. Khione stands on another cloud, but hers is made entirely out of ice. Hecate and Khione are a formidable duo, their movements synchronized as they assault Zeus and Poseidon.

Hecate turns her smoke into whips, which continuously slice open their skin. She tries to wrap the whip around Zeus's neck, but he catches the weapon, curling it around his hand. When he pulls on the rope to knock Hecate off her cloud, the whip dissipates. He stumbles, then lurches another lightning bolt at Hecate. One of the throwing ice knives Khione created stabs him in the stomach.

Poseidon is beside his brother, but he is completely inebriated. He continues to manifest water bullets, but his aim is atrocious. I'm not sure if he is trying to aim for Hecate or Khione, but his bullets knock down every single chandelier. He is one of the most powerful gods at the ball, but he is causing just as much harm to our allies as the enemies.

Nobody else can help Zeus, except me.

"Hecate!"

The largest, bluest eyes meet mine across the battlefield, and she grins. She says something to Khione that I cannot hear from our distance, but then she is flying towards me. I jump off the bar, running towards her. I continuously remind myself of my vision, that I will not die as I run towards the most powerful witch goddess, but fear has a funny way of ignoring rationality. It exists to twist conscious thoughts, causing them to convulse and shrivel away.

I force myself to pretend I am not Hartika Sommers. As I run towards Hecate, I am Saffron, the goddess of bones with the power to kill every god in this room. While leaping over broken pieces of chandeliers and dead humans, I force myself to pretend I am Zeus, king of the gods with the power of the sky at my behest. I am Hades, ruler of the Underworld with the dead at my beckoning. I am every hero in every story I have ever read.

Atalanta, Achilles, Perseus, Theseus, and Jason pump through my veins like they are here with me right now. Like they are joining me in my fight against a formidable opponent. It is their sword I wield, not a broken wine bottle. With the heroes of the past in my head, this is my thousandth battle rather than my first. I convince myself that my thoughts are real as Hecate lurches down, grabs my throat in her hand, and hoists me off the floor.

As I fly in the air, and Hecate's focus is on distancing me from gods who can save me, I lock eyes with Zeus. I have known since I first met him, he would save me three times in my life. Tonight is the first time the King of the Skies protects me. With one nod, we complete a conversation that began three days prior.

Then, I face the witch goddess.

I force myself to pretend, until it is real, that she does not frighten me. She brings me up to the highest point of the ballroom. Our heads graze the spot where the biggest chandelier once dangled. Her red-blood painted lips curl into the largest grin.

"Finally, we meet," she says with eerie delight in her tone.

She tries to frighten me; I deliver her fear in return.

"When Styx dies, it will be with my hands around her throat."

I have not seen that future, unsure if my words are truth or fiction, but as I say them, they feel real. Like I have been given a glimpse into a small piece of a future that doesn't want to fully divulge. I must look certain, though, because Hecate's armor cracks. For only a millisecond, she forgets about everyone else in the room. She hears my words, detailing Styx's death, and Hecate regrets her decision.

It is only one millisecond, but it is enough.

Zeus does not throw a lightning bolt, but it is a javelin that splits the air and lodges in the back of Hecate's skull. The spearhead pokes out of her left eye, a mere centimeter away from my cheek. I am unscathed, while Hecate's eyes roll to the back of her head. She will not be unconscious long, but we do not need an eternity.

Only a few minutes to escape.

All her power dissipates. The doors unlock, the windows open, but worse of all, the cloud keeping us fifteen feet in the air dissipates. Suddenly, I am falling, body flipping through the air without a safe landing. Zeus runs toward me, but none of the immortals with wings are in attendance. My only hope is the nearest god, who stumbles while standing upright.

"Catch her!" Zeus yells to Poseidon.

"Catch who?" he asks.

Finally, his eyes move towards the ceiling. He creates a wave underneath his feet, bringing himself five feet into the air to catch me before I plummet to my death, but he can't keep the waves intact. As soon as I land in his arms, he loses his grip on his powers. The waves evaporate, and Poseidon crashes onto the ground on his back, his arms still tight around me.

Poseidon groans. "I'm too drunk for this."

FIFTY-TWO

SAFFRON

When I was human, I often found fascination in small, trivial wonders.

Like the taste of strawberries. The first time my toes sunk into the sand, and the first time I wrote an entire paragraph without a spelling error. When I won my first game of Monopoly without Hermes letting me win, and the warm hug of a loved one. Or my first sip of champagne on my twentieth birthday, followed by crying when I thought the champagne bubbles were going to burn off my tongue. Then, the relief when I discovered the bubbles would not cause me harm. Otherwise inconsequential, miniscule details in my life brought me unmeasurable joy.

But over the years, those small moments drifted away. I learned about this world and discovered the melancholy devastation of death.

There isn't a particular day when the sparkle dimmed because the descent towards depression became so gradual. The darkness overrides the light too subtly to notice until I couldn't find my way out. I no longer see the beauty behind the taste of strawberries, even when it burst across my tongue. There is no relief behind the bubble of champagne, or fearlessness when I see a shark's fine poking from the top of the ocean. Victories in a game of Monopoly do not hold the same ebullience, and hugs have become rarer with each passing day.

Horror and dread are the only emotions I expect.

It is all I have known for decades. Horror in the way murder can still be grotesquely executed in a life unburdened by slavery. Dread when another sunrise comes and the sense of peace I have longed for never arrives. Horror in every heinous act I am sworn to solve as the world's Savior. Dread when every terror cannot be easily remedied through determination and power.

I am younger than the other gods, yet my happiness withers away with the eternity I am shackled to. There are days when I reach out to the woman of my past, who I used to be and loved. I try to claim her, be her again. She is shown only through my reflection, agelessly youthful and wearing the same half braided up-do from the past. Wearing the same high-risen, chubby cheeks and red or purple gowns. Yet, there is no warmth in the smile I force. No glint in my eyes that once crinkled with continuous amusement.

I believe the human side of my soul left when my friends died, and only the rigid goddess remains. They were two sides of me, intertwined and beating within my heart, but one died. The lighthearted extension of myself, which everyone around me preferred. Only the darkened soul is left behind. Hermes liked the human side of me best. Hades and Persephone, too. They preferred that girl, mourning her death as they cast aside what remains.

Yet, as I walk down the steps towards the Underworld, my red train dragging the dirt behind me, I pull my lucky Monopoly dollar bill out of my bra. I hold on to the flimsy piece of paper in remembrance of who I once was. Of the part of me that will forever love the shaggy-haired god who gave me this and has a proclivity towards stealing the items he loves most.

I slide my thumb up and down the Monopoly dollar bill, the same one that I've cherished since the first time I played Monopoly with Hermes. The very first dollar bill I hid when I thought it was real currency. It is my solace. I caress the worn-down paper as I reach the gates and crouch down to pet one of Cerberus's heads.

I scratch behind one of his ears just as he likes. A second head licks the side of my face, tail wagging. The third nose nudges against my free hand, and I pet this head, too. My fingers find their way through his soft, dark fur. I bask in their company a little while longer. Avoiding my fate for just a few minutes.

"You are such a good boy." Then I hold all his bones under my control, freezing him to the spot. "I'm so sorry," I say to him. His six eyes widen with betrayal, but he cannot let out the whimper or lower his once swaying tails. "I'm so sorry," I say again.

I open the black gates to the Underworld and walk past my favorite three-headed dog. The black gates sit upon a hill, and a trail leads from the top down to the River Styx's dock. It is paved by black asphalt, but I drag the dirt from outside the gate with me as my three-foot train flows behind, carrying in the grime from the outside.

The streak of dirt serves as my footprints, marking my arrival. A few roaming ghosts glance in my direction, but none of them stop. They continue their endless trek across the Underworld. None of the dead care as I willingly lead myself into complete destruction.

It takes Zig a moment to notice my arrival. He sits cross-legged on the dock, his skiff resting on top of his lap as he looks out at the dark, expansive Underworld. He must find beauty in the darkness because he stares at the rolling hills, many rivers, and Victorian style castle with a content smile. Until he glances over and finds me nearing his dock.

Then, there is only terror.

He scrambles to his feet, not caring when his skiff falls into the river. Zig rushes towards me, tripping in accelerated desperation. "You need to leave!"

"I can't."

He reaches me, hands on each of my shoulders. Before he can try to push me, I paralyze all the bones in his arms and hands. The rest of his body shakes as he tries to move his arms, but after a few seconds, his face crumbles with defeat.

"Please let me protect you," he says.

"She can't," another voice says. "We made a deal."

A whip of black river shoots out of the bank and slams into Zig's chest. His hands are ripped from my body, and he soars across the Underworld. He collapses onto the floor, headfirst into a rock, and doesn't get back up. A bubble of red blood spills from the back of his head, staining the rock, and I rush towards my friend. I fall to my knees beside him, pressing my hand against the back of his head to ease the pressure.

"You forget he cannot die," says the same eerily

392

monotone voice. "He still heals as slowly as humans, but you forget where we are. Who he now is."

Half of Styx's body breaks through the river, looking exactly how I remember her eighty-eight years ago. Still nightmarishly pale, with wet, black hair sticking to her narrow face. Ancientness and regality intertwining to create her, an instrument of beautiful destruction. She does not glance at Zig, whose blood continues to slip through my fingertips and create a pool in between my feet.

This is the goddess who has been crumbling the world I fought to rebuild.

She is responsible for the Nosoi killing a majority of citizens in all South American countries. It is her orders that started Nemesis's murderous spree across my city against defenseless mothers and children. She orchestrated the abduction of Artemis, Lamb, and the nymphs. She has ensured that every second of my days is spent in vain, stripping away the remnants of my amity until only chaos lays in the wake. I tighten my grip on the fake Monopoly dollar before stuffing the material back into my bra and standing up to my feet.

With one last look at Zig, whose chest still rises and falls, I move towards Styx, who wades through the river and rests her elbows on the dock. Dark eyes always examining me. Gleaming with every move I make towards her. There isn't a prideful smile upon lips, or a sign of victory on her face. She doesn't think she has won yet, even as I present myself to her like a wrapped present with a bow on top.

And that terrifies me.

She sees the future paved in her direction, but she doesn't rush towards the finish line. Styx patiently expects every move. Plotting every counterstrike should one of her meticulously orchestrated plans go off-kilter. She is too wise, an opponent I never wished to face. Yet, here I stand on the outer edge of the dock, overlooking her and her river. Facing the worst immortal who only holds hatred and deviousness in her heart.

"Before I take another step, I want you to swear to me that Lowell Ablack will be healed from his wounds, and the Nosoi will be gone."

"I hold the power, yet you pretend otherwise. It seems the years have not diminished your naivety, young one."

I force my face to remain stoic, to not show the way my skin crawls when her old nickname for me resurfaces. Young one is what she called me the first time I met her, deep within the river and scarcely surviving her frigid company. She has existed longer than the Olympians; to her, I am the tiniest blimp in her history. A young, feeble-minded presence she can easily bend.

"Come closer," Styx says. "My next words will not reach others' ears."

Every sentence is phrased like a command, leaving no room for negotiation or reconsideration. She makes me want to listen to her, like a string of coiling around my body. She tugs me forward. Guides me exactly where she wants me.

I do not move.

"The Nosoi-" I begin

"When I have you, the Nosoi disappear. The disease the birds inflicted will vanish. The nymphs will return to their everyday lives. Artemis will reunite with her huntresses. The murders in your city will end."

"Swear that to me."

She ignores me, knowing she has all the power, and I am only a pretender.

"You should have arrived sooner than today," Styx says. "Think of all the lives you would have saved. All the days Asopus would not have wept over his daughters. Such a shame you did not uphold your name as savior fast enough."

I cannot stop myself from flinching at the last sentence. Blades hurt, but words inflict lingering agony. Styx knows the worst pain to inflict on me, and that is the barbed truth she forces down my throat. She is right. I have known about her plans for me for several days, but I hesitated. Instead of coming here as soon as I knew the truth, I spent my last days with Jamila. I continued making plans I would never see the end to, and I avoided Styx longer than I should have.

As she commands, I move towards her.

"Swear to me that what you say is true," I say.

She does not, for Styx sees herself as a queen, and queens do not obey others' orders. Her words could be lies, but they can be truthful, too. My fate ends on this dock either way. I walk until my heeled feet are an inch in front of her chipped, bloodied fingers.

"Where is the Oracle?" Styx asks, voice still monotone, but her eyes narrow into thin slits.

"You won't be seeing Hart. She upheld her deal with you. You only asked that she deliver me to the Underworld, and she has. She did not need to be present for the end of her deal to be fulfilled."

She doesn't vocalize her disappointment, but it is there. Festering underneath her stoic expression, darkening her already black eyes. Her already destroyed, chipped nails dig into the wooden dock, dragging until the ground is stained with thin, uneven streaks of her golden blood. This is how she handles her own failures, through self-inflicted pain. The wounds heal quickly, but the blood dries on her flesh, serving as a reminder she does not have Hart.

"The Savior is enough," she says the obvious lie, but it isn't for me. She says it to herself, to remind herself that she did not completely fail. "A Savior who promised eternal loyalty to me, which means she cannot kill me or those who follow me."

"I killed Nemesis just fine."

Just then, Styx smirks. It is the tiniest expression, barely considered a smile, and utterly devoid of elation. The sight can ignite nightmares, fuel screams of terror. "Next time you see one of my loyal servants, try to kill again. I assure you, with our oath now spoken once more, it will not happen again." She extends one of those bloodied, chipped hands, and she says. "Take my hand. You have a favor to deliver to me. One you may not question or deny."

She speaks back the oath I promised many years ago, and I have no choice. My body obeys her commands before my brain can process my actions. My hand intertwines with hers, and it is colder than ice. It feels like death has seized my body, chilling my veins and stopping my heart. This moment is the closest I will come to dying, and I want to scream until my vocal chords rip and my lungs shred to pieces. I refrain myself.

Instead, I look over at the Fields of Punishment.

Just as I requested, Roxie is in perfect view of the River Styx. Birds that look mysteriously similar to Nosoi peck at her flesh. They tear apart every bit of her, and she can only watch with tears in her eyes as Styx ignores her suffering. Utter devastation wrecks her mutilated face because she knows Styx will never come save her. She will forever be punished for the crimes she committed in Styx's name. There will be no reprieve, despite what Styx promised her.

The river I associate with the Underworld lifts into the air, and Styx and I rise with the swirling black liquid. The water wraps itself around our bodies, forming like snakes around my arms, legs, waist, and neck. It suffocates me, squeezing out my ability to scream. My eyes burn as the water splashes against me, momentarily stealing my sight, but I feel the zip of pain slicing through me as my body travels through realms.

As I am pulled from the Underworld.

FIFTY-THREE

HART SOMMERS

One blink and one flash of lightning dissolves the ballroom from my vision.

The glass-scattered alabaster floor at Dionysus's mansion is gone. Now, my feet are beneath plumes of white clouds. Wine fountains are gone. In their place are columns twenty feet high. The previous feel of pleasant debauchery disappears. Now, there is only the weight of godliness, and it is suffocating.

Holy gods, I'm on Mt. Olympus.

A large, circular table sits in the middle of the ceiling-less room. Ten of the chairs are identical in style and size, but on either end of the table there are two stone thrones. One has a diadem hanging off the edge and a peacock feather on the right armchair. The considerably larger throne has a seven-foot-tall lightning bolt leaning against its side.

The largest throne has Zeus sitting upon it as he stares at me with equal amounts of anger, confusion, and gratitude. Hera strolls towards her throne. She sets the bloodied Dagger of Chains on the table in front of her before pushing back her dress's train and sitting down. She acts as if she has not fought a battle and does not wear others' blood on her face like makeup. Regal as ever, the queen crosses one leg over the other and patiently waits for the other Olympians to take their seat.

Dionysus is quick to scramble to his seat while Poseidon stumbles forward. Athena rolls her eyes in admonishment at her uncle as she takes her spot closest to her father, Zeus. Poseidon, in turn, sticks his tongue out at Athena, mumbling "owl face" at her as he finally sits. Demeter and Apollo are the last two Olympians who attended the ball. Demeter takes her seat, but Apollo doesn't.

He moves towards me, taking my face in both of his hands and tilting it up. "I'm so sorry," he says.

"Why are you apologizing? I'm the one who-"

He interrupts me with a pulverizing kiss. I can taste the sweat from the battle and the wine from the pleasanter moments of the night. I wrap my arms around him and cherish his kiss before all my lies destroy the time we've had together.

Zeus clears his throat once, twice, then loudly yells. "Sit down, Apollo!"

He pulls away, only to kiss me once more and repeat. "I'm so sorry."

"No, I'm the one who-"

Again, I'm interrupted. As soon as Iris appears, a rainbow transports Apollo. He is no longer beside me, but sitting at his spot at the Olympian table. Iris stands where Apollo did, the only other occupant present who is not an

Olympian. She loops an arm with me, her hair and eyes now a calm blue.

"Where is everyone else from the party?" I whisper-ask.

"The moment Hecate became conscious, she took the other traitors and left. I transported the human workers home, which is why I'm late to the meeting."

"Artist," says a deep, commanding voice that can only belong to a king.

"Her name is Hart," Apollo says, visibly unamused with his father.

"Three days ago, you told me to throw the javelin." Zeus leans forward in his throne, elbows nestling on the armchair. I'm not sure if he is waiting for me to sprout wings or slit my wrist to show a stream of gold blood, but when neither happens, he asks. "How did you know I needed to throw that javelin?"

Three days ago, when our portrait session was rescheduled, I told him three words at the very end of our session. *Throw the javelin.* I didn't know why I needed to say those words, but now I do. My eyes dart to Apollo, and I hope he can see with my eyes how apologetic I am for all the lies I am about to reveal.

I open my mouth.

"She is the first Oracle of the Delphi in two thousand years."

The words are not mine.

Apollo said it.

He stands now, palms splayed on the stone table, as he tells me how much he has known. "We are all aware of the burning of the Delphi," he says.

I do.

That is where I saw the circle of oracles, all holding

hands and accepting their flaming deaths. It is where a woman, who I am certain is an ancestor on my mother's side, told me the prophecy that promises Styx's queendom unless I can alter her plans. The fire felt real, dancing across my skin with a sinful promise to burn me, too.

Apollo continues. "But two days before the fire, my most powerful oracle, Aashritha, came to me. She had just gone down to the Underworld to deliver a prophecy for Styx upon the goddess's request, and the prophecy frightened Aashritha. It told of Styx's rise to power unless an oracle could find a hammer, a heart, a singer, a seeker, a hero, a huntress, and a savior. She said that once she left, she knew she doomed the world by giving Styx that prophecy. She knew she was going to die before the next full moon and made me promise to aid the oracle that will stop Styx. An oracle, Aashritha believed, would be from her bloodline."

Aashritha's face burns bright in my mind. Her calmness as the flames licked at her flesh, and her soft-tempered words I instantaneously knew as truth. Although thousands of years have transcended between us, I see the similarities in her appearance and my mother's. I see the same honey-colored eyes on her as I see in myself every morning.

"I requested a meeting with you, Father," Apollo says. "And told you it was urgent. The same night I came to tell you about Aashritha's worries, the burning of the Delphi happened. The only proof of the prophecy dying in a pyre. You didn't believe the prophecy because Aashritha fell into the River Styx and could not speak her truth. You didn't want a war with Styx when it could have been fought, but I refused to forget about that prophecy."

"I would have never ignored a threat to my crown," Zeus says.

Apollo sharply turns to Hera, who refuses to look up from the table. "You remember, though."

She says nothing, but that speaks everything.

"Pretend you forgot all you want, Father, but I know the truth."

Apollo pauses as he tells the story. Although it has been two thousand years, he grieves the loss of the oracles. Specifically, Aashritha. His hands curl upon the stone table, veins popping out of his forearm, as anger and sorrow intermingle.

"It is common for an oracle as strong as Aashritha to have a lineage full of oracles. She had a sister, Devasree, who had seven children. For over a thousand years, I watched her lineage grow. It became a full-time job, lingering over Aashritha's descendants. I waited for any sign of foresight, but just like the rest of the world, the ability to become an oracle disappeared with the deaths of those in the Delphi. I never stopped watching over that family. Until Kronos and the titans were released from Tartarus. The strife of war had overridden everything else."

The entire room listens with rapt interest. Not even Poseidon, who can barely hold his head up, makes a contriving comment to change the focal point. Everybody waits for Apollo's next words, realizing the link between the Delphi and me.

"I always thought Styx played a part in releasing Kronos and the titans, but I knew nobody would believe me. Label me as a conspiracist. Admittedly, through the years of human enslavement, I forgot all about the prophecy. Forgot about Aashritha's warning and the promise I made to her to protect her descendants because one of them would be the first oracle. Even after Saffron defeated Kronos, I continued to forget. Until a beautiful human stumbled into me at Olympus Industries and showed me a future with her as my wife. With a single touch, she reminded me about Aashritha and that prophecy." His smile is weak as he says to me. "If it is any consolation, I was going to tell you everything tomorrow. I just wanted one last night with you and peace before it all came crashing down."

It is why he apologized, because just like me, he hid my truth. We had different reasons for our secrets, but it was the same secret only in variations. He knows the origin, but not the most recent revelations, while I am the opposite. We both kept the truth of my abilities secret until this moment. But how can I blame him for the same crime I committed?

The laugh that escapes me is one free of the burdens of lies. "I was going to tell you about my abilities tomorrow."

That cursed smile grows over his lips, the one I quickly and maddeningly fell in love with. "Gods, I really want to kiss you right now."

"You both make me want to retch," Poseidon groans.

"No, that's the liters of alcohol you guzzled down like an ape," Athena retorts.

"You are a disease. Go away and infect Styx's army. That's a surefire way to get rid of them." Poseidon lays his head on the table, oblivious to the *certain* finger Athena lifts in his direction.

"Shut-up, both of you," Hera snaps. "You are insufferable creatures."

"There's more," I say in a tone so quiet I hope nobody hears me.

I'm not so lucky.

"What else?" Apollo asks.

My hand is fast around my necklace as I jumble through my story. I begin with my arrival at Olympus Industries. I talk about finding Khione and Nemesis in my home with weapons on Lowell, and the deal I made to save his life. They are not the worst parts of this story, however. It is Saffron's involvement that I hate the most. I rub the tip of my thumb across my feather pendant repeatedly, trying to elicit strength from my father's gift. My words are rushed as I explain Saffron finding Lowell and me after he was infected by the Nosoi.

I end with the ball, when Saffron left to meet with Styx in the Underworld in order to save Lowell's life and uphold my bargain.

Zeus is up in an instant. All the stories proclaim Saffron as Hades and Persephone's adopted child, who Zeus cast aside. His expression now proves the history textbooks are partially wrong. Twin lightning bolts materialize in his hands. On his face is a feral desperation only a parent has for their child. His eyes burn as bright as his lightning bolts, his muscular body trembling with equal amounts of fear and rage.

"Where is my daughter?"

He is ready to strike me dead. Iris takes a step in front of my body, ready to shield me if Zeus's anger drives his following actions, but he won't harm me. His arm is raised, ready to smite me down, but his grip on the lightning bolt shakes. Just as I am certain we will become friends of war, I know anger is an act. A barrier hiding the guilt and fear of not believing the prophecy. The same prophecy that will cost his youngest daughter's life.

"Ogygia," says a male voice.

We all turn to Dionysus. He looks so out of place

amongst the more regal gods, wearing a silk shirt exposing most of his bare chest. He looks the youngest too. As he struggles with his own part in Saffron's capture, he appears almost child-like. A kid amongst elders, ready to be scolded for his mistakes.

Dionysus clears his throat, trying to put together his jumbled thoughts. "She asked me for a no-questions-asked favor tonight."

"Which was?" Hera asks the question her husband is too emotional to say.

"To seduce Nemesis in a closet. It wasn't an unpleasant task, so I had no problems with it. Didn't think to wonder about it until she kicked down the door while we were inside and told me to leave." He rummages his hand through his disheveled blonde locks and says. "When I was walking out, she whispered one word to me. Again, I thought nothing of it. I should have, but I didn't. I went about my night, drinking and forgetting about it all, until I found Nemesis's bloody remains in the closet."

"What did she say?" Hera asks, as Zeus still cannot find his words.

"Ogygia. She whispered the word Ogygia in my ear."

Calypso's Island.

The one place in the world destined to be unfound.

FIFTY-FOUR

SAFFRON

My shoes land on the sandy ground, the grainy material slipping under the platform of my heels and brushing against the arches of my feet. The Underworld's icy temperature is instantly replaced with sweltering heat. Even in the nighttime, when the stars and moon twinkle down at us from their place in the sky, sweat immediately builds on the back of my neck.

Hesitantly, I open my eyes.

Dozens of cages litter the island. All the nymphs, who have gone missing in the past three and a half months, sit as prisoners. They still wear the tattered gowns they were kidnapped in. Their faces are sullen with hopelessness until they see me. Their joyously cacophonous screams fill the once quiet beach. They thank me for finding them without realizing the danger of standing beside me.

Beneath the yells, a voice croaks out. "Help her."

Artemis has two hands wrapped around a cell bar. Dark green magic, instantly recognizable as Hecate's, ignites the bars. They burn Artemis's palms, but she doesn't let go. She shakes the cage with unbridled desperation.

"Help her," she says again.

I turn my gaze to my right, and I see who needs my help most of all.

Lamb is not a goddess, who can easily heal from the sunburns and live without food or water. She lays curled in a ball on the floor. Her arms are covered in blisters. There is not a piece of her uncharred. Lamb's arms cover her face as much as possible, but I can make out the dark red tip of her long nose peeking out.

Ignoring Styx, I rush to Lamb, collapsing onto my knees in front of her cage. I wrap my hands around her cell bars and I pull them apart as Hecate's magic burns away my skin. I bite my bottom lip to suppress a scream as I create a hole in Lamb's cage large enough to grab her and pull her out. Artemis's sobs of relief join the nymphs' orchestra of cheers.

I rip the three-foot train of my gown into two strips, then materialize water and dump the contents on the chiffon fabric. I wrap the material around Lamb's exposed arms, and she erupts in a bellowing scream. Suddenly, she is awake, and pain scrunches her long face. I cover both her arms, then tear another part of my dress to cover her face until only her eyes show.

"Your strength is admirable," Styx says. "Each cage was specifically spelled so the strength of ten gods could not pry those bars apart. You made the act appear easy. Like breaking a matchstick in half."

The palms of my hands are already healed, yet Lamb whimpers beneath me. I think of water and food, letting the items materialize in front of me. Laying Lamb's head on my lap, I tilt her head back and say. "Open your mouth."

She obeys, and I let trickles of water slide down her throat. Unless she can leave this island and get help from a god, she will die. Even now, as I slowly give her bite-size pieces of bread and provide her with water, she is barely reacting. Barely alive.

"You said you would let them go."

I whirl back to glower at Styx, and I catch the first inkling of emotion on her face. She does not look at me. Her eyes narrow on Lamb. Anger and disappointment clash in her snarl. She expected Lamb to be dead before I arrived, but Lamb survived the terrible odds thrown at her. She lives, much to Styx's displeasure.

And now she must uphold our deal.

Most immortals underestimate the huntress, or do not care about their existence. Why does Styx glare at Lamb like she is her unraveling? Why does Styx care that Lamb is surviving the island?

Her left index finger picks at her jagged thumbnail, the only sign she gives when a plan goes off-kilter. "We are waiting until my second-in-command comes."

The minutes tick by at an agonizingly slow pace. Styx picks, picks, picks at her already ruined fingernails, withering them away until they are bloody stumps on her fingers. Artemis weeps in her cage, never taking her eyes off Lamb as I slowly feed her water and bread. Lamb whimpers, but she never speaks. Every bite she takes and gulp she swallows takes every morsel of strength from her body.

In the black of night, it is easy to see the gust of green smoke materialize beside Styx. When Hecate materializes with a black bag swung over her shoulder and a silver gown splattered in gold blood, pure fury seizes me. She drops the black bag to the ground, sand sweeping up around the heavy weight, but she does not look at me. Refuses to meet my heated glare.

She and I have never gotten along, not since my days as her prisoner growing up in the human cells. Even in the rare moments when she showed kindness to me, I couldn't bring myself to like her. When she allowed me to see Epiales in a dreamworld of her creation and privately say goodbye, my disdain for her did not waver. The feeling festered, but never grew, until Hermes said he was having an affair with her. The hatred I felt as a child for Hecate returned, burning like an inferno in my heart.

Yet, I never imagined her as a traitor.

I never thought that her arrival would make me wonder if Hermes is working with Styx, too.

"Let them go," I snarl at Hecate. "You disgusting, feral traitor."

Hecate turns to Styx, waiting for her leader's orders. At that, Styx stops picking at her fingernails and says. "Send the nymphs back to their rivers."

Hecate snaps and a green ball materializes in each of the nymphs' cages. The nymphs are trapped inside, while the bubbles rise and carry them out of Ogygia. Smoke covers the entire bubble, obscuring the nymphs' views, so they cannot report the island's location. Ensuring nobody finds me.

This is my destiny.

Ogygia and me.

"I want you to return Artemis and her huntress back to their group," I say again. "You got me here like you wanted. You do not need them."

Styx looks at Hecate. They have a conversation through their stare. Hidden words I cannot hear.

"Take them away," Styx finally says.

Hecate bows. "Of course, your highness."

She snaps her fingers again, and Lamb dissolves from my lap. Turns into mist and leaves alongside Artemis. The cages disappear with them, until I am truly alone with Hecate, Styx, and the black bag the former is opening.

One by one, Hecate pulls out a piece of bone. A tibia. Scapula. Sternum. Spine. She goes as slowly as possible, placing each bone side-by-side, and the magic sings to me. It says the same two words in a deep, male voice I thought I would never hear again.

My queen.

My queen.

My queen.

Quickly, tears cascade down my cheeks, dripping into the sand around my feet. Disbelief mingles together with raw devastation.

I return to the day I murdered him. Killed my storyteller so I could free humanity. He was not a perfect immortal. He was littered with flaws, but they were flaws I loved because they were a part of him. I loved Epiales, and I had to kill him.

Now, his bones are laid out in front of me. There is no ability to appear strong in front of my enemies as I see Epiales's bones. Hear his voice chanting his nickname for me. My sobs are not meek or well-hidden. They are loud and heart-wrenching. Snot and tears mangle my face, destroying my makeup and resolve.

"Why?" I finally ask when Hecate places his skull in front of the rest. "Why are you doing this to me?"

"We are granting you a favor," Styx says. "Call it a trade amongst friends."

"*We are not friends*," I snarl.

"You are my obedient and loyal servant," Styx says.

Styx moves towards me, careful not to touch any of Epiales's bones. Every advancing step she makes feels like centipedes finding their way underneath my skin. Crawling around in my bloodstream. Nibbling on me from the inside out. She does not lower herself to my level. Instead, she holds an air of superiority by standing over me. Her feet are right in front of my knees, towering over me as I sit on the ground.

"I would like to call in my favor," she says.

I know the favor. The moment I hear Epiales's bones singing to me, a part of his soul calling to me once again, I understand why I am here on Ogygia. I do not understand why this is the favor Styx wants from me, but I know what she is about to ask.

Before she can, I turn to face Hecate. She takes in the fury and sorrow laying wake across my tear-stained face as I hold up my hands and demand her bones. She betrayed me and everybody I love, yet when I try to summon her death, nothing happens. Just as Styx says, now that I am reminded of my oath of eternal obedience, I cannot kill her soldiers. There is nothing in this world I want more than to see Hecate suffer. I drop my hands in defeat.

Hecate lets out a sigh of relief.

Styx's stoic face never changes. "I order you to agree to the oath you had sworn to my river. You will bring Epiales, personification of nightmares, back to life. Return him to our world, so that my prophecy may come true. Let my war begin with his resurrection."

412

My hands already rise, obeying a command I cannot refuse. "How does he start this war? He's been dead for almost a hundred years." When silence greets me, I scream. "Tell me!"

Styx raises a dark, arched brow and says without opening her mouth. *You do not have the power to command me.*

I'm stalling, I know. Hecate and Styx know, too. If this was Kronos I was fighting against, he would tell me everything. All the details of his plans, down to why I am essential to them. But Styx is not Kronos. She does not think blindly but with lethal precision. She does not spill the origins of her actions with pride like Kronos did. Styx understands the power of secrecy.

"Bring your heart back to life," she orders. "Now."

"How are you certain I can? I have never brought a soul back to life. That is *her* power, not mine."

I jerk my head in Hecate's direction. She is the goddess of necromancy, not me. Yet, it is me they ask to bring Epiales back from the dead.

"I have already tried," Hecate divulges. "I cannot bring any gods, titans, or monsters you've killed back to life because they are not truly dead. They exist in another realm entirely, and you are the only one who can bring them back to our world."

"Enough talk," Styx says. "I have waited thousands of years for this moment. I will wait no longer."

Without the emotional strength to stand, I crawl towards his remains. Styx steps aside, watching me. The soft cadence of his voice intermingles with the sand. When I place his skull in my hands, flashes of his life invade me.

I see the days of his happiness, when no tattoos

attempted to cover his many scars. I witness the day Morpheus brings a silver-haired girl to Epiales and asks him for a favor. To help them escape a world that will never let Morpheus love one of Heracles's human slaves. A day that irreversibly changes the path of Epiales's life.

I feel all the emotions he had with each encounter. The hesitation Epiales had when Morpheus begged for his help. His loyalty, which guided his decision to betray Zeus's rules. To assist his nephew and his soulmate. The pain he experienced when Zeus punished him for their crimes.

Then I feel his love burning wickedly and uncontrollably when he first met me. He loved me from the first dream we had together, and it grew like wildfire with the second, twentieth, thousandth, and all those in between. His need for revenge constantly battled his love for me, a duel within his head with no simple solution.

Last, as my magic rises through the air and molds his bones back together, I experience his last day alive.

The silent resolution he had. The adoration he had for me, which never wavered, even in those last seconds. He looked over the crowd on his day of execution and hesitated on Ares and Hermes. Internally, he asked himself which god I will choose to be with, now that he was going to die. He was on the line of execution, and in his last seconds alive, he spent the time praying to Aphrodite. Begging she would ensure my happiness with one of the two gods.

I sob as the skull leaves my hands, levitating out of my touch to rejoin the rest of his bones. The moment his skull touches the rest of his skeletal build, white magic bursts across the sky and he transforms in front of us all. First, there is muscle, blood, and tissue. Next, unblemished skin scatters across the newly formed body.

There are no more scars or tattoos.

Last, his distinct facial features slip into place. The silvery eyes and plush lips. Curly black locks. Cheekbones, sharp as knives. Thick, black eyebrows. Large, narrow nose. They all manifest, adding the finishing touches to him, and then he collapses onto the sandy ground without a scrap of clothing.

He doesn't wake, but he lives.

"Holy gods, it worked." Hecate cannot hide her disbelief.

Styx merely nods her head in approval. "We will visit soon."

I am not forced into a cage, but I am a prisoner here, just like the nymphs and Artemis. Except, unlike them, I know nobody knows how to find this island. It is unsearchable. Hecate flicks her wrist, disappearing in a circle of her magic, just as a wave of Styx's black river transports her away. They all disappear.

Except Epiales.

FIFTY-FIVE

HERMES

At first, when consciousness claims me once again and I open my bleary eyes, my spotty vision catches the sight of Saffron. She looks identical to the night I first claimed her, stealing her away from Ares's mansion before he could murder her.

She shadows over me in a blood-coated, oversized white shirt that stops at the middle of her thighs. Wearing nothing else but that old shirt with splatters of her red and gold blood, she catapults me back to the past. Reverberates me back to the night I promised myself that I would die before letting anything terrible happen to her.

Her terrified expression captures me as she reaches out a hand, begging me to take her away. Whisk her to a place where she will be safe from harm. A silent plea burns my ears, but my failure is loudest of all. It bounces off the ground like bombs, shattering my illusion until Hypnos stands over me instead of Saffron. It is his hand that tries to help me to my feet, rather than Saffron's, imploring me to accept her crying for help.

I blame the smoke and dirt for the tears blurring my sight. "I failed her," I say to nobody in particular.

Hypnos doesn't respond, but he hears me. He keeps his hand extended until I blink away the tears, take his hand, and allow him to help me to my feet. My vision distorts again for a few seconds. Hecate's sleeping tonic is not completely out of my system.

Hecate.

The name is poison in my mind. Aside from Saffron, I trusted Hecate the most. She has been at my side since the dawn of my existence. Even after our whirlwind romance imploded, we could not stay away from each other for long. We went from acquaintances, lovers, and then became the greatest friends throughout the eons. But now, all the history we have shared is tainted with her treachery. She will always remain one of my greatest loves, but she is also responsible for the worst betrayal of my existence.

I hear her words, until it feels like blood spills from my ears, dripping onto my shoulders. *"You are not her heart, and so you were destined to break. The divorce was inevitable. I only quickened its pace."*

Hecate referred to the heart from the prophecy. The Savior's heart. Like a shard of glass sliding down my throat, I whisper. "Saffron's heart."

After hearing it for the first time on New Year's Day, I have memorized every word of that cursed prophecy.

The ultimate fate is decided when the heart twice fails, and from the savior, a terrible scream will wail. The sound will echo forevermore, and from the scream, spawns a war.

If I am not her heart, the soul destined to shatter the

savior with their death struck twice, then who? Why did Hecate orchestrate every terrible fight and every blasphemous idea about adultery to break us apart? Who does Hecate believe has my wife's heart more than me, the god she chose above all others?

Suddenly, the day of our captivity on Mt. Olympus sparks in my mind. It was the day Circe turned us all into dogs, ready to die by Saffron's magic. Each of us was asked if we wanted to change our loyalties, except for Ares. The reason Ares was left a prisoner on Mt. Olympus, rather than inside the Dagger of Chains, remains a mystery to me. Even decades later, that question remains a mystery. But that is not the part of that day burning the brightest in my memories. Hecate's response to Circe before turning her into a dog makes too much sense now.

"I have plans for my future, dear daughter. Joining Kronos would make all my plans crumble into ash, and I cannot afford that."

Another memory of our time in captivity returns. It was the night she told me about her human soulmate, who her husband Aeetes killed.

"Now, he is left swimming in the River Styx, while I have to survive in a world without him. I would do anything to be with him again. No matter how terrible, I would do it."

I cannot remember the last time I saw Hecate's husband, Aeetes. I didn't think about him or his sudden disappearance until now, standing in the wake of Hecate's betrayal. And her betrayal isn't new. No, she has been on Styx's side for at least eighty-eight years. It is why she chose potential death over Kronos's side. It is why she told me the story of her soulmate. She wanted to justify her actions, knowing I was too oblivious to realize she was apologizing for future discretions.

Gods, I am a fool.

In a circle around me, there are gods and newly healed humans. The latter inspect their unscathed bodies, where skin once fell in grotesque clumps and black sores infected the once healthy tissue. Their confusion is shadowed by their unwavering relief. The Nosoi are gone, just as Hecate promised in my last seconds of consciousness, but I know the cost of their disappearance.

"They have Saffron," a grave and devastated Hades says.

He has his arm looped through Persephone's, her head resting on his shoulder. Even behind the lingering smoke of Hecate's magic, I can see Persephone's red, puffy face. The sorrow weighs heavily on her because of Saffron's safety and Hecate's betrayal. I know she is staring at me and seeing a mirror image of herself.

"It is the only reason we have woken from Hecate's magic," I say, concluding our worst fears.

Styx has won this portion of the fight, and our first defeat tells us the grave truth about the rising war. We thought we were stronger than Styx, wiser because we have the experiences of the world while she has been imprisoned in a river. We were blind, stupid fools because each time Hecate told us a plan, we followed. Believing she was on our side. When Hecate advised us all to keep Styx's prophecy a secret from Saffron by any means necessary, we agreed because Hecate was our friend. A wise and loyal goddess who has seen many battles with us.

I force her out of my head, focusing instead on Hades and Persephone. Thanatos, Atalanta, and Achilles stand behind them, faces grim and weapons lower to the ground. Their stance is as deflated as their hope.

"My life has been most fortunate," Hades says. "As the king of the Underworld, I have had the fortune of the largest kingdom. Ruling over the most populated area in the world. The greatest Grecian heroes are my most trusted guards, and the great Cerberus proudly protects my gates. I am the God of Jewels, with more money than any other immortal. Rubies, emeralds, pearls, diamonds, and all the splendors most humans would die for. It spills from my fingertips. Zeus believes he has the greatest role amongst the gods, but he is wrong. I hold the most power. Eventually, all of humanity becomes a resident in my domain. It is me who controls their fates. The Fates have fortunately shined down on me, gifting me with more power than many others."

Despite the boastfulness of his words, he is not bragging about his accolades. There is a somberness to his tone. A level of depredation worsening the wrinkles on his forehead, deepening the bags underneath his eyes. He does not cry like Persephone, but his voice displays his vulnerability. I have only ever seen Hades disarrayed like this once before. The night they had to send the infant Saffron away to the jail cells because of Athena.

"My power is endless," he says. "I could fight my brother and win, but I am powerless in the one thing I wanted most in this world. Zeus has fathered children throughout the eons, across continents both accidentally and purposefully. Poseidon, too. But no matter how desperately I beg the Fates for the same curtesy or use my powers to will it, I cannot create a child in the traditional sense."

Persephone runs her hand up and down Hades's arm,

trying to comfort him in a time of desolation, but he does not relax under his wife's touch. They move closer to me with every sentence, while the humans surrounding us listen with rapt focus.

"I know all this power came with a consequence, and I should have known a god who rules the dead could not create life. Persephone always wanted children, and when she left my realm and returned with swollen bellies, I could not blame her. She was the goddess of spring, the season which epitomizes new life, and I represent the land of death. I was fine with her having children with other men because I can give her all the jewels in the world but that. She had Melonie and Zagreus with Zeus, but I was still childless. I still searched for a child of my own."

I know the direction of this story, as do the other gods around us, but I still listen. Never deviating my attention from Hades as he moves forward, opening his shattered heart for everybody in the vicinity to witness.

"Then you and the Fates answered my plea. You gave us Saffron." A bittersweet smile slightly curls his lips, the corners hiding beneath his beard. "The moment you flew down to the Underworld with a crying baby in your arms, Persephone and I had our chance. She was biologically Zeus's, just like Persephone's other children, but he didn't know she existed. He didn't know he created the most beautiful baby in this world, and so I took her as my miracle. As if she was born from the love between Persephone and me."

"The nights I held her in my arms will always be the greatest of my immortal existence. Even after we had to send her to the prisons to save her, I would still visit. Saffron was all that I had in this world, and I went to her once a week while she slept. She was always in a cell filled with other humans, nearest a boy close to her age as she slumbered, and I counted the days until I could bring her home. To have my daughter back and never let her go."

I have never seen Hades cry. Not once in the many eons we have spent beside each other. When a sole tear slides down his face, I cannot hide my disbelief. Persephone, too, stares at that sole tear as if she has never seen her husband cry before.

"One night when I saw her in that prison, sleeping on someone's lap like a pillow, I promised her I would never lose her again. My lies are the reason my daughter is gone. I can blame Hecate for advising us in the wrong direction, telling us to lie to her, but I did not have to listen. I could have gone to Saffron, kept her close to me, but I was so blinded by my fear that I did not see the danger until it consumed me."

Several humans jump away from the circle they have created around us when a black fire ignites beneath Hades's feet. They run, tripping over their own feet with newfound terror, as the ground crackles and groans. The arid dirt splinters under the weight of Hades's fury, taking shape like a horribly spun web. Decaying hands sink their blackened nails into the ground. They pull themselves up from the depths of the Underworld. Some have knives clenched between brown-and-black teeth, while most are the blades others must wield.

At least three, maybe four million crawl from the jagged openings. Most are nothing but skeletal creatures, but there are at least a hundred thousand who have recently died. Their skin is intact in blotches, eyes straining to remain in their sockets.

The flames surround Hades and Persephone, and they enliven the bright blue of his eyes as he narrows them with murderous intent. "It is time I use the powers the Fates have gifted me to remind Styx why she hid from me in her river. Grab my granddaughter and whoever else you can, and join us in Poseidon's castle. We defeated Kronos there, and that is where I will peel the skin off that bitch's body."

The onyx fire consumes the army, leaving only the rubble and me.

EPILOGUE

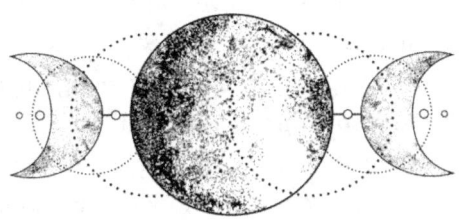

HECATE

I land upon the Atlas Mountains with Styx on my right and Calypso to my left. Both Calypso and I are six feet tall, and we tower over Styx's petite frame, but she is the one who radiates power. Green magic swirls around my arms, igniting the dark night, but Styx displays her endless power through merely existing. Every step she takes and breath she exhales turns the surrounding air frigid, shifting the happiest soul into their most feral state.

"How does it feel to be queen of the world?" Calypso asks, and I suppress an eye roll.

False flattery does not suit Calypso, and by the frown forming on Styx's lips, she disapproves as well. She turns on her heels and stares up at Calypso. Calypso is a whole head taller than Styx, yet she cowers when our leader's dark eyes narrow in displeasure. Styx takes an advancing step. Their bodies a breath apart, and Calypso shudders.

"I am a firm believer in acting on the side of pessimism," Styx says. Her voice is always monotone, both regal and devoid of emotions. "Cockiness stems from optimism, and cockiness leaves room for a lack of precision. To succeed in any endeavor, every plan must be meticulously analyzed for any potential flaw. When a person becomes prideful and elated with self-worth before winning battles, their mind wavers. If you believe you are already victorious, that means you have already lost."

Styx reaches forward, clutching the dangling gold necklace around Calypso's throat. She twirls the chain around her index finger. The necklace allows less and less airway, and eventually, Calypso must follow the direction of Styx's finger. It is so tight that the chains dig into her neck, pinching the skin. Calypso is nose-to-nose with Styx now, who continues to show no expression. Not happiness at her control, anger at Calypso's overconfidence, or horror at her actions. Styx doesn't know how to feel anything but pride.

"You insolent child," Styx says, although Calypso is thousands of years old. Compared to Styx, few are older. Most are children in her eyes, barely existing. "The moment I believe I have won the battle is when I sit on the throne on Mt. Olympus with a diadem on my head. Until then, nothing is certain. If I ever hear victory on your tongue a moment too early again, I will rip it from your pretty little mouth."

Styx releases the necklace, and Calypso stumbles backwards. She clasps her throat as it heals from Styx's touch. While Calypso cannot be strangled to death, the fear she has for Styx grows. She sees the possibility of death in Styx's company, but Calypso has nowhere else to turn. Like me, we are forced to be Styx's minions because we have no other alternative. The gods exiled Calypso eons ago, forgetting her existence, while the gods condemned me to a life without my soulmate.

For that, we have no choice but to bow to the personification of hatred.

"Wake up your father," Styx orders Calypso.

She stumbles towards the titan, who holds the world upon his shoulders within the Atlas Mountains. He is in a state of pained hibernation. While he is still alive, cursed to stand here for the rest of his existence, his mind has disassociated from the endless agony. Fallen asleep, so he does not have to feel every inch of pain that radiates throughout his elderly, yet brawn, body. Yet, even with eyes slammed shut, groans of pain escape his lips. Forever suffering because of the gods.

Calypso's momentary fear vanishes as relief washes over her. She is normally entombed on Ogygia, and with her father cursed at the Atlas Mountains. I wonder how long it has been since they have seen one another. A smile finds its way across her lips as she reaches out a hand and places it on her father's shoulder.

"Dad," she whispers. "Open your eyes, please. It's me, Calypso."

A terrible groan leaves his lips, like the act of opening his eyes is too painful, but slowly he obeys his daughter's wishes. Bloodshot blue eyes stare at Calypso, but soon they wonder to Styx and me. His face winces with confusion.

"What is going on?" he asks, voice raspy from lack of use.

Styx says. "I have a proposition for you, Lord Atlas."

Calypso cuts Styx off. "She resurrected Epiales and is restoring the fight against the gods."

"And Kronos?" Atlas asks, voice tinged with hope. "Is he back too?"

"No," Styx answers. "As much as you cared for him, he was an insolent fool. He thought his charm and strength would give him a crown, and as we both know, he was wrong in those beliefs. If he lived again, he would lead our army right back to their deaths. The Fates gave him two chances to win the war against the gods, but now it is my turn and I would like you on my side."

Calypso squeezes Atlas's shoulder and says. "We have a god that will take your place, too. You will be free from your servitude."

His appearance has withered over the eons because of the strenuous weight of the world. He appears the oldest of all the gods, wrinkled around the eyes and over the fore-head. Yet, there is brewing power within this titan. A strength that pairs well with Styx's intellect and my magic. He will be revered in our army, and he grins with the same sudden realization.

"I'm at your service, Lady Styx. Who do you have in mind for taking over my place here?"

Styx looks at me. "Get him," she orders.

I snap my fingers, and Ares manifests alongside the rest of our army. He lays unconscious in the Minotaur's arms. My green magic swirls around him. I keep him in an unconscious state until it is time for him to awaken and take Atlas's burden.

Adonis is the only human in the group, but several huntresses await our commands with the rest of Artemis's pack. Devoted gods, goddesses, and the monsters I've resurrected scour the grounds of the Atlas Mountains beside Adonis. The only creatures who are not in attendance are the ones Saffron killed, like the Echidna. While I am the goddess of necromancy, Saffron's power over bones supersedes my abilities. Yet, I have helped Styx create a plentiful army brimming with strength, intellect, and magic.

Atlas roams over the many faces of our allies, seeing the numbers we have accumulated over the years, and he understands. "How long have you been plotting your uprising?"

"It does not matter. The uprising is here, and I am allowing you to be a part of it."

The answer is thousands of years.

Since one of the last oracles of the Delphi told Styx her fate as the eternal queen of the world, Styx has patiently waited for the Savior to emerge. She has plotted every detail, set up every plan with alternatives in place if one plan faltered. She has been meticulously one-step ahead of every opponent. Hands reaching towards the ultimate prize.

Eternal queendom.

"Kronos relied too heavily on humans during his war. He forgot how fickle minded they are, how easily they will switch sides. They saw Saffron, a goddess with red blood, and they forgot all the years the gods enslaved them. They were fools who can turn the tide of any war, so the most powerful must be eliminated." Styx stands in front of Atlas, hand gripping his chin and nails digging into the flesh. He barely winces, and while I cannot see Styx's face from where I am, I know she approves of his strength. "I will make you one of my Olympians if you take a small army of monsters and destroy every huntress."

"Even the ones we are working with?" Calypso asks.

Nobody answers.

Styx told a select few about the details of the prophecy surrounding her uprising as queen. I am one of the rare few who know the truth and how vital the huntresses' deaths are to our success. One huntress is destined to defeat the greatest monsters. Whoever she is, she will aid in Styx's downfall. Instead of trying to discover which huntress holds the power, we must kill them all.

"It will be done," Atlas swears.

She pulls her nails out of his chin. Tips drip with ichor, and she turns to face me. "Replace them," she orders.

I snap my fingers, and Atlas and Ares switch spots. Before Ares can stop his fate, Atlas is freed, and the weight falls upon Ares's back. He is awake now, my magic stripped from him, and he lets out a bellowing scream. Ares stands up to his full height with the world on his back. His hands grip onto the heavens. He is statuesque in his position. The same position Atlas once had.

Atlas cracks his back several times, then his neck, before a widespread grin envelops his lips. "Finally."

"What is the meaning of this?!" Ares roars, glowering at me the entire time. "Traitor!"

"Where would the huntresses run, god of war?" Styx asks.

Ares's gaze swivels towards her, and shock overtakes his features. "You are supposed to be in the Underworld. In the river."

"The huntresses," Styx repeats.

Ares is a wise god, and he knows he does not have time to be stunned by Styx's freedom. He focuses on her question and the herculean weight upon his shoulders.

"I hope I am there when Saffron rips every bone out of your body," Ares seethes. "I'm not telling you anything."

Styx lets out a soft hum, but she doesn't press Ares for more information. She focuses back on Atlas. "The huntresses will ride with Artemis again now that I have freed her from Ogygia. Start scouring for them around the border nearest Ogygia, and I am certain you will find them."

Assuming the traitorous huntresses haven't killed them yet.

Atlas runs to the cliff side of the mountain, jumping off and rushing towards the huntresses he has been ordered to defeat. As he leaps off, every single monster but Typhon joins him. The Minotaur, Sphynx, and many others hunt the huntresses with one clear aim.

Kill them all.

Styx's dark eyes narrow on me next. "Go on the hunt for any lower-level gods and goddesses and bring them to me. We either build our army with immortals who want more out of their existence, or we imprison them so Zeus cannot use them against us. I want all the lesser gods. Bring them to me." She motions her head towards the two Muses who joined her cause, Erato and Urania. "And take them with you."

I twirl my fingers in the air, and my magic wraps around Erato, Urania, and me like emerald thread. Before my magic obscures my view, I look once more at Styx. I can envision the ghastly future awaiting us. One beginning with a dark crown on her head and ending in the world's destruction.

Then, I am gone.

Left to follow Styx's bidding.

Left to bring carnage upon the world I once loved.

GLOSSARY IN ALPHABETICAL ORDER

Achilles: Infamous hero in the Trojan War. Demi-God son of a sea nymph named Thetis.

Adonis: Human male notorious for his beauty. Lover of Aphrodite and Persephone. Slain by Ares as a boar.

Aeacus: Demi-God son of Zeus and Aegina. Once dead, he became one of the 3 judges of the Underworld.

Aeetes: Husband of Hecate & king of Colchis.

Aegeus: King of Athens. Father of Theseus.

Ambrosia: Food of the Gods.

Amphitrite: Wife of Poseidon and Queen of the Seas. One of the 50 Nereids. Daughter of Oceanus & Tethys.

Anchises: Famous Lover of Aphrodite. Father of Aphrodite's son, Aeneas.

Apollo: God of Prophecies, Music, Poetry, Art, Truth, Healing, Sun, and Light. Twin Brother of Artemis. Son of Zeus and Leto. One of the 12 Olympians.

Aphrodite: Goddess of Sexual Love and Beauty. Wife of Hephaestus. One of the 12 Olympians.

Ares: God of War and Bloodshed. Son of Zeus and Hera. One of the 12 Olympians.

Argus: Many-Eyed Giant. Slain by Hermes. Hera's guard in most stories.

Ariadne: Wife of Dionysus. Once a human princess, who helped Theseus defeat the Labyrinth. Daughter of Minos.

Aristaeus: God of Beekeeping, Honey, Shepherds, and Cheesemaking.

Artemis: Goddess of the Hunt, Wild Animals, Vegetation, Chastity, and Childbirth. Twin Sister of Apollo. Daughter of Zeus and Leto. One of the 12 Olympians.

Asclepius: God of Medicine. Son of Apollo.

Asphodel Meadows: Largest segment of the Underworld. This is where almost all the dead are placed.

Atalanta: Famous Female Hero. Member of the Argonauts.

Athena: Goddess of Wisdom, Crafts, and Battle Strategies. Favorite Daughter of Zeus. First born child between Metis and Zeus. One of the 12 Olympians.

Atlas: Titan condemned to hold the skies for eternity after the first Titanomachy War. Father of Calypso.

Asopus: God of Four Rivers. Famously known for his 20 nymph daughters.

Calypso: A nymph, who was exiled to the island Ogygia. Captured Odysseus on his way home from the Trojan War. Daughter of Atlas.

Cassandra: Almost Apollo's Lover. Tricked him into giving her power of seeing the future. Once he realized the trickery, he cursed the gift of prophecy so nobody would ever believe her prophecies. Daughter of King Priam and Queen Hecuba of Troy.

Cerberus: 3-Headed Dog of the Underworld. Child of the Echidna and Typhon. Guards the gates of the Underworld.

Circe: Witch Goddess. Daughter of Hecate and Aeetes.

Charon: Ferryman of the Underworld. In this story, he is the former Ferryman of the Underworld.

Daedalus: Creator of the Labyrinth. One of the wisest men in Greek Mythology.

Dagger of Chains: Fictional dagger created by the author. "Created" by Daedalus to imprison immortals. Inspired by the Tibetan Phurba Dagger.

Deimos: God of Terror and Dread. Twin Brother of Phobos. Son of Ares and Aphrodite.

Delphi: Delphi is a town on Mount Parnassus in the south of mainland Greece. It's the site of the 4th-century-B.C. Temple of Apollo, once home to a legendary oracle.

Demeter: Goddess of the Harvest. Daughter of Kronos and Rhea. Mother of Persephone.

Dionysus: God of Wine, Partying, Fertility, Insanity, Festivity, Orgies, and Theatre. Son of Zeus and Semele. One of the 12 Olympians after Hestia gave up her spot for him.

Echo: Famous Lover of Zeus. Hera cursed her to only speak in others' echoes.

Elysium Fields: The Underworld's version of heaven. Most gods and scholars are sent here.

Epiales: Personified Spirit (Daemon) of Nightmares. Almost completely forgotten in mythology. Brother of Hypnos and Thanatos. Son of Nyx.

Erato: Muse of Lyric, Erotic Poetry, and Hymns. One of the 9 Muses.

Eros: God of Love and Sex. Son of Ares and Aphrodite. Husband of Psyche. Has arrows that, once shot, can either turn you deliriously in love with the first person you see. Or, it will make you hate them.

Elysium Fields: The "heaven" in the Underworld. Heroes live there for eternity.

The Fates: Three weaving goddesses, who represent the inescapable destiny of humanity.

Fields of Punishment: A land in the Underworld, where the worst humans are sent to suffer for all of eternity.

Hades: God of the Underworld and Jewels. Eldest son of Kronos and Rhea. Husband of Persephone. One of the 12 Olympians.

Hebe: Goddess of Youth. Daughter of Zeus and Hera. Wife of Heracles. Cupbearer to the Gods.

Hecate: Goddess of Witchcraft and Necromancy. Wife of Aeetes.

Hephaestus: God of Blacksmithing, Metalworking, Sculptures, and Fire. Son of Hera. Husband of Aphrodite. One of the 12 Olympians.

Hera: Queen of the Olympians. Wife/Sister of Zeus. Daughter of Kronos and Rhea. Goddess of Marriage and Childbirth. Notoriously hates Zeus's children outside of wedlock.

Hermes: God of Thievery, Trade, Wealth, Luck, and Travel. Son of Zeus and Maia. Messenger of the Gods.

Hermaphroditus: God of Effeminates. Son of Hermes and Aphrodite.

Hestia: Goddess of the Hearth. Eldest daughter of Kronos and Rhea. Gave up her role as an Olympian for Dionysus.

Horkos: The Personification of Curses and Avenger of Perjury. If you disobey an oath you swore, Horkos will come for you on the 5th day of the 5th month and curse you.

Hyacinth: Famous Lover of Apollo. Killed by another god, Zephyrus, out of jealousy.

Hypnos: Personified Spirit (Daemon) of Sleep. Son of Nyx. Twin Brother of Thanatos.

Ichor: Gold Blood of the Gods.

Io: Notorious Lover of Zeus. Turned into a cow by Zeus in an effort to hide his adulterous ways from Hera.

Iris: Goddess of Rainbows. Messenger of the Gods. Specifically Works for Hera.

Ixion: Man who tried to seduce Hera. In the Fields of Punishment, eternally spinning on a wheel of fire.

Jason: Greek Hero and Leader of the Argonauts. Retriever of the Golden Fleece.

Khione: Goddess of Snow. Daughter of Boreas and Oreithyia.

Kratos: Personification of Strength. Son of Styx.

Kronos: Titan of Time. Son of Gaia and Uranus. Defeater of Uranus. Fallen Leader of the Titanomachy Wars.

Labyrinth: A maze created by Daedalus in Crete for King Minos. The Minotaur lived, and hunted, in here.

Lethe: Personification of Oblivion. Has dominion over the River Lethe, where the deceased souls go when they wish to forget their existence. Daughter of Eris.

Marpessa: Famous Lover of Apollo. Notoriously chose a human male instead of the god.

Melinoe: Goddess of Madness and Nightmares (not to be confused with Epiales, the personification of nightmares.). Daughter of Persephone and Zeus.

Metis: Titaness daughter of Oceanus and Tethys. Zeus's first wife. Mother of Athena. Second child was believed to become the most powerful immortal. Killed by Zeus.

Minos: King of Crete. Orchestrator of the Labyrinth. One of the 3 Judges of the Underworld.

Minotaur: Half-man, Half-beast. Son of Queen Pasiphae and a white bull. Slain by Theseus in the Labyrinth.

Mount Olympus: Home of the Gods. Located in the Skies.

Morpheus: God of Dreams. Son of Hypnos.

The Muses: Nine Goddesses who defend the arts. Provide entertainment for the Olympians.

Narcissus: Mortal man, who was so obsessed with his appearance that he could not pull his eyes away from the water's reflection of him.

Nectar: Drink of the Gods.

Nemean Lion: Vicious lion with impenetrable fur. Defeated by Heracles during his 12 Labors.

Nemesis: Goddess of Divine Retribution and Revenge.

Nike: Goddess of Victory.

Nosoi: Personifications Spirts of Plague, Sickness, and Disease. In this story, their form are birds, but their form is everchanging.

Odysseus: Hailed wisest hero of Greek Mythology. Famous for the Trojan War and his journey home.

Ogygia: Island where Calypso was exiled. Known as a distant island most could not find.

Oizys: Goddess of Misery, Anxiety, Grief, Depression, and Misfortune.

Olympians: The 12 major gods of the Greek Pantheon.

Olympus Industries: A fictional skyscraper building created for this story. This is where the gods meet when conducting business on Earth.

Oracle: A person (typically females) considered to provide wise, prophetic insight. Another common terminology is seer.

Paean: Physician of the Gods.

Paris's Judgement: After Eris tossed an apple labeled "to the fairest" around Hera, Aphrodite, and Athena, the women fought to see who was the fairest. They made a Trojan prince, Paris, decide who was the fairest goddess and each promised him a reward. Paris chose Aphrodite as the fairest; in return, she made a woman named Helen fall in love with him.

Peitho: Personified Goddess of Persuasion, Seduction, and Charming Speech. Daughter of Oceanus and Tethys.

Perseus: Demi-God son of Zeus and Danae. Slayer of Medusa.

Phobos: God of Fear and Panic. Twin Brother of Deimos. Son of Aphrodite and Ares.

Persephone: Queen of the Underworld. Goddess of Spring. Daughter of Zeus and Demeter. Wife of Hades.

Pompeii: Once a thriving and sophisticated Roman city, Pompeii was buried under meters of ash and pumice after the catastrophic eruption of Mount Vesuvius in 79 A.D.

Poseidon: God of the Seas. Son of Kronos and Rhea. Husband of Amphitrite. One of the 12 Olympians.

Priapus: Low-level Fertility God.

Psyche: Goddess of Soul. Wife of Eros.

Rhadamanthus: Demi-God son of Zeus and Europa. Once dead, he became one of the 3 judges of the Underworld.

Sinope: River Nymph. Daughter of Asopus.

Sisyphus: Man who tried to cheat death twice. Cursed in the Fields of Punishment to eternally push a boulder up a hill, only for it to fall to the bottom again.

Sphynx: Female Monster. Body of a lion, head and breasts of a woman, wings of an eagle, and tail of a snake. Defeated by Oedipus.

Styx: Personification of Hatred. One of the Eldest Immortals. The strongest oaths are to her river.

Titanomachy War: A 10-year war between the Titans and the Olympians.

Typhon: Father of Monsters. Greatest Monster in Greek Mythology Existence.

Urania: Muse of Astronomy. One of the 9 Muses.

Zagreus: God of Rebirth. Son of Persephone and Zeus.

Zeus: King of the Olympians. Youngest son of Rhea and Kronos. God of Lightning and the Skies. Father to most Gods and Demi-Gods.

ABOUT THE AUTHOR

Trish D.W is a woman with a lifelong dream of being a full-time author. She has dreamed of this moment since she was a little girl at recess writing scripts rather than playing on the playground. Each day, her dream becomes a clearer reality, and she is grateful to everybody who has purchased her novel.

FOLLOW TRISH D.W ON THE WEB AT:

trishdw.com

Instagram & TikTok: @authortrishdw